Lords of the Black Banner

Fractured Empire Saga Book Two

Starr Z. Davies

Character Assassin Books

First published in the United States in 2021 by Character Assassin Books an imprint of Starr Z Davies, 1328 Lynn Avenue Altoona, WI 54720 USA. Email: starr@starrzdavies.com

Cover design and typography by Katrina Designs
Book layout and design by Starr Z Davies & Atticus software
Maps, glyphs, and illustrations relating to maps by Starr Z Davies & Inkarnate software

All characters within this book are fictitious, and any resemblance to persons living or dead is purely coincidental.

Contents

Chapter One Heir of Genghis

For Kyle Fingerson

MONGOLIA 1450-1500
OIRAT UYGHUR TERRITORY
KHANGAI MOUNTAINS
ALTAI MOUNTAINS
ZAVKHAN RIVER
TIANSHAN MOUNTAINS
TURFAN
HAMI
GA

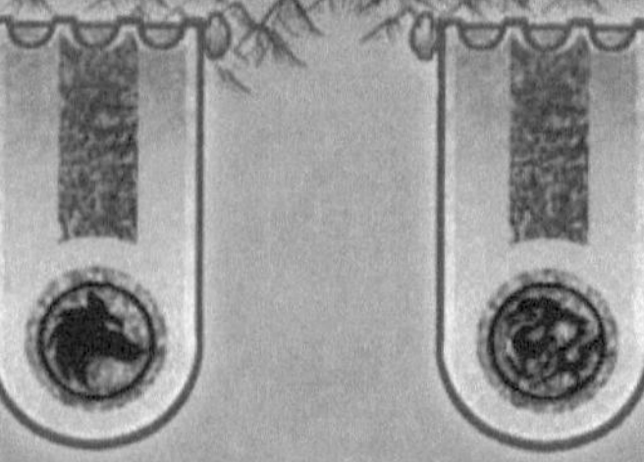

LAKE BAIKAL
KHENTII MOUNTAINS
ONON RIVER
HULUNBUIR GRASSLANDS
MT. BURKHAN KHALDUN
KHERLEN RIVER
TUUL RIVER
GREATER KHINGAN MOUNTAINS
BORJIGIN YUAN TERRITORY
MONKE BULAG
LAKE DALINUR
XILIN RIVER
KARAKORUM
LAKE BAIKAL
GOBI
DATONG
BEIJING
BAUTUO
HUAN HO RIVER
MING TERRITORY
KHARAKHTO
ORDOS
YINCHUAN
YULIN
YELLOW RIVER
IDOR
WUZHONG
XIAN
ZHONGWEI

GREAT HORDE
MONGOLIA 1450-1500
OIRAT
UYGHUR

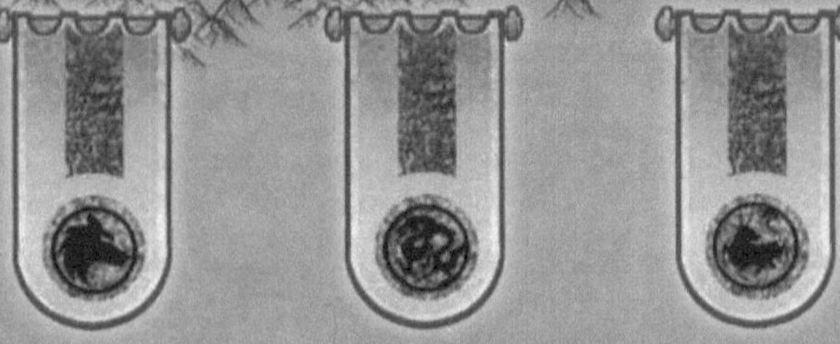

JALAIR
KHORCHIN & KHARCHIN
JURCHEN
KHORLOD
BORJIGIN
ONGUD
CHAKHAR
ORDOS
MING

Royal Lineage
Through 1464

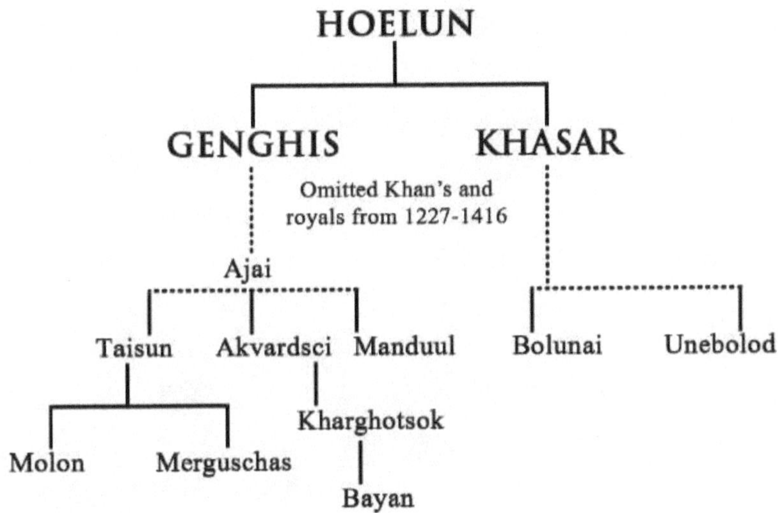

While there are certainly other royals before Ajai, for the purposes of this series, only those after him will be listed to avoid confusion. Esen is not listed on this chart because he does not descend from this royal tree.

Glossary & Pronunciation Guide

TERMS

airag (eye-rahg) – alcoholic drink made from fermented mare's milk, typically milky in color

arban (ahr-bahn) – unit of ten Mongol warriors

Bankhar (bahn-khahr) – traditional sheepherding dog of the Mongolian steppe; 24-31 inches tall at the shoulder with typically dark brown hair

Biyelgee (bey-eel-geeh) – traditional dance of celebration and community

black airag – stronger version of regular airag with a longer fermentation process, typically clear in color

boal (boh-ahl) – honey wine

boqta (bohk-tah) – column-like headdress decorated with beads and silver; the taller the boqta, the more prominent the woman wearing it

buuz (boos) – meat stuffed dumplings

deel (deal) – robe-like wrap worn by the Mongol people, traditionally made of silk, velvet, or woolen felt with ties or silver buttons and belted at the waist with a belt; lined with sheep's wool or fur in the winter

ger (grr) – round, dome-like house made of Birchwood lattice and lathes, then covered in wool felt; known in America as a yurt

gonji (goonj) – a princess

jagan (jah-gahn) – unit of 100 Mongol warriors (or 10 arban)

jinong (gee-nong) – a prince

kurultai (kuh-ruhl-tai) – a gathering of tribal lords where they elected the next Great Khan

mingghan (min-ghahn) – unit of 1000 Mongol warriors (or 10 jagan)

orlok (oor-lahk) – field commander of multiple tumens

paiza (pie-zah) – a golden medallion of safe passage, given only to high-ranking officials as a means of protection under the Great Khan *shanaavch* (shah-navsh) – headdress made of long strings of beads and bells, typically silver, coral, or turquoise

sulde (sool-duh) – a banner made of colored horse-hair, typically arranged in a circle

toortsog (toort-sogh) – hat made of silk, sometimes with fur or felt lining and a knot of colored tails or feathers at the top; typically worn by noble men

tumen (tyoo-mehn) – regiment of 10,000 Mongol warriors

uni (oo-nee) – a pole made of birch; used as a support beam for the ceiling of a ger

CHARACTERS

Alayitung (al-eye-ih-toong) – Borjigin commander; Vice Chancellor

Albeq (al-bek) – Tabun khan

Altan (ahl-than) – Lady and commander of the Jalair; Hulun's daughter

Arslan (ahr-slahn) – Mandukhai's night guard

Batu (bah-too) – Bayan's missing son

Bayan Bolkhu Mongke (bay-yahn bohl-koo mohng-kay) – Borjigin prince; last true descendant of Genghis Khan

Berkedai (buhr-ke-dahee) – Khorchin commander; Bayan's guard

Bigirsen (big-er-sehn) – Uyghur warlord; Manduul Khan's Vice Regent; orlok of the southern tumens of the Great Khan

Bolunai (boh-loo-nahee) – Khorchin khan; older brother of Unebolod; descendant of Khasar

Boke (boh-kay) – Borjigin tribe; young leader of Manduul's royal guard

Boragan (bow-ra-gahn) – Ongud Lord; son of Korgiz khan

Borogchin (boh-rohg-chin) – Borjigin princess; niece of Manduul Khan

Chenghua (jen-gwa) – Ming Emperor

Dashai (dah-shy) – man who saves Bayan in the Gobi

Degghar (dehg-ghahr) – Chakhar man; Siker's father

Enkh (enk) – Bayan's servant

Esen (eh-sehn) – Oirat Lord and leader; Borjigin Butcher

Esige (eh-seeg-hay) – Borjigin princess; niece of Manduul Khan

Genghis Khan (jehn-giss) – First Great Khan of the Mongol Nation; died 1227

Getei (jet-ehee) – Ongud soothsayer

Guden (goo-dehn) – Chakhar khan

Hulun (huh-loon) – Lord of the Jalair

Ibarai (ee-bar-eye) – Uyghur Lord/commander

Issama (ee-sah-mah) – Bigirsen's Uyghur advisor

Jaghan (jahg-han) – Jalair tribe; Togochi's wife

Jangi (jahn-jee) – Uyghur warrior; Nemeku's guard

Khasar (kah-sahr) – brother of Genghis; son of Hoelun

Khosoichi (co-soy-chi) – Borjigin shaman; serves Manduul

Khutulun (koo-too-loon) – daughter of Kaidu; warrior princess

Korgiz (koor-gihs) – Ongud khan

Mandukhai (mahn-doo-khahee) – Ongud daughter of a lord; Manduul Khan's second wife

Manduul Khan (mahn-dool) – Oirat-Borjigin ruler of Mongolia; descendent of Genghis Khan

Mingtau (ming-taoo) – Chakhar elder/commander

Molon Khan (moh-lohn) – 17-year-old Great Khan before Manduul; Manduul's nephew; killed in battle

Nahai (na-hi) – Uyghur commander; Issama's right hand man

Nergui (nair-gooee) – Mandukhai's loyal Ongud guard; murdered by Bayan

Odgerel (ode-ger-el) – Khorchin woman; Unebolod's servant

Odsar (ohd-sahr) – Unebolod's dead wife

Paisahan (pie-sah-han) – Oirat khan

Qolotai (co-lo-tie) – Issama's third wife

Samur (sah-muhr) – great-great-grandmother of Bayan

Satai (sah-tie) – Lady of the Alaguchid tribe; wife of Unige

Seguse (seg-oo-say) – Uyghur warrior; Borogchin's spy/messenger

Siker (see-kur) – daughter of Degghar; Chakhar girl; Bayan's lover

Soke (soh-kay) – Khorchin commander

Sorkhogtani (sor-kog-ta-nai) – Kublai Khan's mother

Taisun Khan (tahee-soon) – Manduul's older half-brother; killed by Esen

Tengghar (tayng-ghahr) – Khorchin lord; Bolunai's son; Unebolod's nephew

Toregene (tor-eh-jenay) – Ogedei Khan's wife; empress for five years

Torgus (tohr-gus) – Mandukhai's guard

Torudur (tor-oo-dur) – Togochi's eldest son

Tsetseg (zeht-sehg) – Esen's daughter; Bayan's mother

Togochi (toh-goh-chee) – lord and General of the Khorlod; Manduul's loyal sworn brother (no blood)

Tuya (too-yah) – Mandukhai's Ongud servant

Uingen (oo-in-jen) – Issama's first wife

Unebolod (oo-nuh-boh-lod) – lord of the Khorchin; Manduul's loyal sword brother (no blood); Orlok of the northern tumens of the Great Khan

Unige (oo-nee-kay) – Alyghuchid Lord/leader; Borjigin loyalist; a member of Manduul Khan's council

Yeke (yeh-keh) – Uyghur daughter of Bigirsen; Manduul Khan's first wife

Yungei (yoon-geh-hee) – Khorchin commander; Bayan's guard

Tribes and Locations

Bautuo (bow-to-oh) – Ming/Mongol city north of the Huang Ho River

Borjigin (bohr-eh-gin) – tribe of the Great Khan Genghis

Chakhar (shah-kahr) – tribe of the southern steppe; Siker's tribe

Datong (dah-tong) – Ming/Mongol city near the Great Wall

Gansu (gahn-soo) – corridor between the mountains and rivers leading into China

Great Horde – tribe of the far norther steppe (Russian territory); formerly the Golden Horde

Hami (hah-mee) – oasis city in the Gobi connecting the far east to the far west

Huang Ho (wang-ho) – Great Loop river, also known as the Yellow River

Hulunbuir (hoo-loon-boo-eer) – eastern Grasslands of the Khorchin & Kharchin tribes

Jalair (jah-laheer) – tribe of the northernmost steppe

Khangai (khan-gahee) – mountains west of Mongke Bulag

Karakorum (kah-rah-koh-rum) – Mongolian sacred capital city

Kherlen (curl-ehn) – river of the Mongol steppe

Kharchin (car-chin) – subtribe of the Khorchin

Khorchin (koor-chin) – tribe of Genghis Khan's younger brother Khasar; Yuan Dynasty ally

Khorlod (koor-lahd) – tribe of the eastern steppe; Togochi's tribe

Kokegota (co-keg-oh-ta) – Ming-controlled city

Mongke Bulag (mohng-kay boo-lahg) – Manduul Khan's capital in the Orkhon Valley

Oirat (ohee-raht) – collective of four major western tribes who oppose Borjigin rule; commonly called "Four Oirat"

Ongud (ahn-goot) – tribe of the southern steppe; Mandukhai's birth tribe

Orkhon Valley (ohrk-hohn) – lush river valley of the Mongol steppe

Tabun (tah-boon) – lesser tribe of the eastern steppe

Tohom (too-hom) – red, rocky cliffs at the edge of the Gobi
Turfan (tur-phahn) – city in the former Chagatai khanate
Urainkhai (oo-ree-ahng-high) – southern tribe of the steppe
Uyghur (wee-ger) – tribe of the southwestern step; formerly Chagatai
    Khanate
Xilin River (jgee-lyn) – river along the southeastern Mongolian territories
Yinchuan (yin-chwahn) – city bordering the Huang Ho River and Great
    Wall into the Ordos basin
Yulin (you-lin) – city along the Ming-Mongol border

MILITARY STRUCTURE

Arban = 10 men
Jagan = 100 men (10 arban)
Mingghan = 1000 men (10 jagan)
Tumen = 10000 men (10 mingghan)
Officer - man in command of a single jagan or arban
Commander - officer in charge of a single mingghan
General - commander in charge of a tumen
Orlok - field marshal in charge of multiple tumens; military strategist

*Did we not shed enough blood
in the name of peace and unity?
We cannot relinquish ourselves
to the enemies of the Mongol state.
If we break the rules of the great Genghis,
all doors of destruction will be opened.
High heavens, have mercy
for the fate of the wolves.*
~ Lady Mandukhai

Salted Tea and Rumors

Mandukhai sat in Dust's saddle on the hill to the east of Mongke Bulag, closed her eyes, and tilted her head back to bask in the sunlight. A warm breeze caressed her skin and ruffled her *deel* around her ankles. Three years had passed since her vision of Genghis Khan. Three years since losing the only child she had conceived, a bitter failure that still stung deep in her heart. Three years during which she had acted as a faithful wife—more than she had before her vision. Manduul was not her future—the vision made that clear enough—and that knowledge offered endless comfort. It made pleasing him much less painful. She did not know when the winds would change, but she could feel them coming as surely as the wind against her skin.

During those three years, Mandukhai's wisdom and level head had earned trust and loyalty from several officers in Manduul's camp. While Manduul was not blind to Mandukhai's part in court, he did not know how much loyalty she had acquired through his men. He would die and leave her widowed one day, as Genghis Khan had hinted in her vision. She had to be prepared to protect herself and Esige, as well as Mongke Bulag.

Today, as every day, Mandukhai rode Dust up to the hilltop and observed how Mongke Bulag had swelled in size. Domed *gers* dotted the horizon in clumps. More tribes and families joined the Great Khan as

Bayan, Vice Chancellor Issama, and Unebolod continued their mission along the Ming border.

Jalair families were among the first to join the Great Khan in Mongke Bulag, and they had assimilated so well into the encampment that Mandukhai could no longer tell where their tribe ended and the Borjigin tribe began. They, along with the Khorlod and Khorchin, who had joined the Khan in the early days of Mongke Bulag, had become part of the Borjigin in a way that the other tribes had not yet managed. The Jalair commander, Altan, continued along the borders with her *tumen* to keep away enemies of the Khan—and for the best as well; Altan had been a rough influence on Esige, giving the princess notions of battle and glory that she could never fulfill simply because she *was* a princess.

Mandukhai thought back to when she had first arrived in Mongke Bulag four years ago. It had been a fairly small capital, consisting only of the remaining Borjigin, along with a few thousand Khorchin and Khorlod loyal to Unebolod and Togochi. Now, Manduul had three more tribes under his wing in the makeshift capital. Mongke Bulag served as a hub to nearly forty thousand Mongols spread across the northern steppe.

Not all the families had come to Mongke Bulag out of loyalty to the Great Khan. A few Uyghur and Asud milled among the tribes. While Manduul maintained peace between the tribes, some tensions remained high—particularly between the Uyghur and Khorchin. Manduul had moved their sections of the capital as far from each other as he could to avoid any mishaps.

Mandukhai, too, swelled with pride to see their numbers grow. While she was uncertain what the future held for her, she knew she would need as many tribes united behind the khanship as possible to face whatever would come.

Dust bent his neck to graze on the sparse grass. Mandukhai stroked his neck and loosened her grip on the reins to lessen the resistance. Her two guards lingered nearby, close enough to protect her, but far enough to give her privacy. It had been hard to teach them such lessons when Manduul had first assigned six new guards to her protection after Nergui's murder and losing her child. The attempted assassination had put Manduul on edge, and he worried one guard would never be enough.

Mandukhai now had to walk with two men always in her shadow day and night. They had taken their role as her guards seriously, constantly crowding so near to her they felt more like a stifling suit of armor than her guards. Manduul had insisted on their endless presence, and it took her the better part of a year to train the six of them on how to afford her the space she needed without smothering her or disobeying Manduul's commands. Failure would be certain death, and such a penalty would motivate them far more than anything she could offer.

A single rider raced in her direction, making the guards stiffen in defense. Mandukhai easily identified Esige by the streaming hair rippling in the wind and the effortless way she rode her horse. The girl she once knew had transformed into a stunning young woman. At fourteen, marriage wouldn't be far off in her future, but so far, the girl had scorned every boy who had made an advance.

Esige's spirit was as fierce and wild as Mandukhai's own, and it filled Mandukhai with great pride. Marriage seemed a poor fate for a girl who could fight just as well as many of the men. But she was a princess, a niece of the Great Khan, and she would have as little choice in the matter as Mandukhai had herself—possibly less. Out of respect for Esige's uninhibited spirit, Mandukhai became just as selective about the man Esige would someday marry. None of them were good enough.

"Mother!" Esige called out with open enthusiasm as she reined her mount in hard enough to make it buck beneath her. Her face was flush with excitement and youth. *Have I lost such a flush?*

"Does your uncle know you've ridden out again?" Mandukhai asked, amused at the exhilaration on Esige's face. Whenever the girl called her "mother," it filled Mandukhai's heart to the brim. Esige was the only child she had not failed ... yet. Mandukhai had not found many to love in her life so far. But Esige certainly ranked high above the others. It had little to do with Esige's spying skills and more to do with how spirited and warm the girl was around her. The bond between them was stronger than Mandukhai had ever felt with anyone else. Esige was the only salve on Mandukhai's wounded soul.

"Who cares?" Esige grinned devilishly, controlling her labored breathing after the hard ride. "I have to prepare myself for the inevitable."

Mandukhai raised a brow sharply at her, though inside she struggled to keep her pride from overflowing. "And what inevitability would that be?"

Esige's mare danced, but the girl effortlessly reined the mount to obey. "That one day, I will face a man who challenges me, and I cannot make it easy for him. If a man cannot capture me, he cannot have me."

Despite her best efforts to keep a cool face, Mandukhai couldn't help but smirk a little at this. Capture the bride was a common practice among nobles. The bride would be placed on the mount of her choice and given a brief head start before her suitor would give chase. His job was to catch her and pull her onto his horse before they crossed the finish line. It was a way to show that the bride was worthy of her husband and that he was strong enough to be worthy of her. For Mandukhai's marriage to Manduul, this tradition had been skipped in favor of a swift union. Mandukhai knew Esige wouldn't need the head start. In fact, she felt great sympathy for the man who would have to capture the young woman.

"You know these things are not quite that simple," Mandukhai said. "It's a formality, not a necessity."

"I will not end up like my sister." Esige's demeanor shifted, and a fire burned in her dark eyes.

Mandukhai flinched. Borogchin had sent multiple messages to Mandukhai through her trusted spy, Seguse, and she continued to do her part keeping a close eye on Bigirsen. However, only twice since Bigirsen took away her from them had Borogchin returned to visit. By that time, her son Nemeku had been just old enough to ride a foal while tied to the saddle.

The good news had been that Bigirsen had enemies amongst his own men. Borogchin had seized the opportunity to make those men her spies and allies. It offered some comfort to know that those men would protect her to their final breath from outside forces and from her own husband.

"I also came to fetch you," Esige said, pulling Mandukhai from her thoughts. "The Ladies Satai and Jaghan have invited you to tea."

Mandukhai groaned inwardly. She got along quite well with Jaghan. Togochi's young wife was close to her own age, and the two often walked the capital together. Around Satai, Mandukhai felt a bit more guarded. Satai's husband, Unige, served as one of Manduul's advisors, and the older woman seemed to think this entitled her to make demands of her queen. Mandukhai wouldn't trust Satai at all if the woman didn't have outright and visible scorn for Yeke. By Satai's estimation, Yeke was a Uyghur and not worthy of being a Great Khan's wife, let alone a queen. Mandukhai would need women such as Satai on her side when the inevitable came, so she suffered through the woman's company.

"Very well." Mandukhai heaved out a sigh and turned Dust toward the camp. "You will join us."

Esige scoffed. "No insult intended, Mother, but I will not." She turned her own mount to ride beside Mandukhai. The guards trailed behind them. "Lady Satai infuriates me, and I'm afraid that one of these days I will throw a knife into her open mouth and make sure she swallows it."

"Hardly the actions of a princess," Mandukhai said tersely, though her heart wasn't in it. She couldn't fault Esige's frustrations.

"I never asked to be one."

"You would be worse off if you weren't."

This lulled Esige into silence as they approached the fields of white *gers* and turned toward the area of camp where Satai's ger rested. Were Esige not the niece of the Great Khan, she would have either been forced into a marriage arrangement already, enslaved for some unchecked insult to one of the men in camp, or dead—possibly for much the same reason.

The sun burned high in the wide blue sky. Mongke Bulag buzzed with activity as men bartered with each other to exchange goods, women pounded wool into felt or carried water or various goods from one place to the next, and children ran between *gers* with sticks and pretended to swordfight. Everyone parted for the queen as she passed, and Mandukhai inclined her head in gratitude.

Since the capital had grown, Mandukhai and Manduul had instituted designated pits for slop and excrement away from the *gers*. Disease was a serious threat with so many gathered. Ever since those pits had been moved away from the *gers*, the stench of filth had lessened and allowed a pleasant breeze to blow through Mongke Bulag without causing one to cover their nose and mouth. The air was fresher, tinged with sweat, leather, and the occasional whiff of cooked mutton.

Satai's home rested in the center of her own tribe's segment of Mongke Bulag. The exterior's white canvas walls were adorned with the blue of the Borjigin, though they were not Borjigin themselves. Satai stretched her hand to display such colors, proclaiming her family and her people as a direct extension of the Great Khan with the blue ribbons along white.

Esige shifted in her saddle. "Please don't make me do this," she hissed. She sagged in her saddle as they approached Satai's ger. "I'll do anything. I'll pound felt for a week."

Esige often shirked her responsibility to learn the art of creating felt, coming up with any excuse she could to get out of the tedious, exhausting task.

"You know as well as I do that she will expect you to be present," Mandukhai said.

Esige grimaced. "I know. But you could make some excuse for my absence."

"And why should I do such a thing?" Mandukhai teased. "If I must suffer this, you will be right beside me."

"I would rather be plunged into a frozen river."

Mandukhai shot a warning glare at Esige as they drew close enough to see Satai's serving girl standing outside the door, waiting for them. To Esige's credit, she sat up straighter and raised her chin. They arrived beside the front door and handed the reins over to the serving girl as they dismounted. Esige ducked into the *ger* behind Mandukhai.

The inside of the *ger* was brightly lit with lanterns hanging from the ceiling lathes, and the smoke hole opened to the sky. Mandukhai had been in this *ger* a hundred times before, but each time, an extra detail caught her attention. As she inclined her head to offer a polite greeting to the hostess, Mandukhai noticed the new mattress on the floor opposite the bed that doubled as a sofa. Curled up on the new mattress, Satai's two-year-old son, Alag, slumbered. Seeing the young boy so close to the age her own child would have been opened the wound on her heart. Mandukhai swallowed the lump that swelled in her throat and averted her gaze.

Satai enjoyed displaying her husband's wealth, and she often acquired new baubles to set on the alter against the northern wall or on the dish shelves beside the altar. Compared to most *gers* aside from Manduul's, Yeke's, and Mandukhai's, this one placed opulence on exhibit. Somehow, it always smelled of fresh herbs that calmed Mandukhai's nerves.

"Lady Mandukhai," Satai trilled once Mandukhai offered her formal greeting, "I'm so pleased you made it."

Mandukhai didn't believe Satai had doubted her attendance. "It would be rude of me to refuse when I had no other pressing matters to attend."

Satai's hair was drawn up off her neck and adorned with silver chains and bells that chimed with each movement. The silver highlighted the few strands of gray in her dark hair. Her husband had served under Manduul in the first year of his khanship, when they rode against the men responsible for killing the Borjigin princes before him. Satai was Unige's reward for the battle won, a woman of low noble birth whose first husband had died in the fight. Having no children with her first husband, Satai went willingly with Unige when he had claimed her. Mandukhai couldn't understand such women who would just give themselves to any man who staked a claim on them. Having been married and widowed, Satai was older than Mandukhai by at least ten years. She and Unige had only Alag, and Satai doted on the boy too much. He would become a weak warrior if Unige didn't put a stop to Satai's doting soon.

Satai had a table set near the center of the *ger*. Jaghan rose from her seat and smiled brightly at her friend as Mandukhai entered. Jaghan had a stunning smile that could light up a *ger*.

Unlike Satai, who put her wealth and power on display and expected lesser men and women to defer to her husband's superior rank, Jaghan remained humbled and grateful for all that she had. She hailed from the Jalair tribe, and within a year of arriving in Mongke Bulag had caught Togochi's attention. Mandukhai had enjoyed watching their romance blossom—even envied it. Jaghan was a young, beautiful girl of sixteen when she had married Togochi, and the celebration had been a festive event. Within a year, they had their first son, Torudur. Now Jaghan was pregnant with their second child. *Why do they get two when I could not even have one?* Mandukhai thought sadly as she noticed how large Jaghan's stomach had become.

She was happy for her friend's good fortune, but it stung as a bitter reminder of what she had lost—even after three years of searching, they still had not uncovered the man Altan who had hired that serving girl to poison her and her child. Mandukhai had given up hope years ago that they ever would find him.

"Please sit, Jaghan," Mandukhai said, feeling bad that the other woman had stood for her in the first place with her stomach as large as it was.

Jaghan breathed a sigh of relief as she sat back down. "Princess Esige," Jaghan said politely.

Esige offered a sugary-sweet smile and swept into the room with all the grace of a queen, despite being just shy of fourteen years. She didn't wait for Satai to invite her to sit before claiming her place at the table—an obvious display of her rank over this older woman—and the action drew a tight-lipped grimace from Satai that Esige no doubt enjoyed.

Once they were all seated, a serving girl poured each of them a cup of salted tea. Satai drank first, a sign that the tea was safe. Mandukhai had grown cautious since losing her child after drinking poisoned tea—a fact that everyone in the Mongol Nation seemed to know about now. Esige raised her cup and breathed in the fumes, then set the cup down without taking a drink. The action seemed curious to Mandukhai. But as she took her first drink, she instantly understood Esige's hesitation. It was strong and bitter. *Much like Satai*, Mandukhai mused.

Their hostess made small talk through the first cup of tea and engaged them in mundane conversation: rumors and gossip, all of which Satai absorbed eagerly from every source and would later pour out like water from a bucket over anyone who would listen. Mandukhai found this task both tiresome and troublesome. One day, Satai's rumors would stir up true trouble.

"I overheard a Uyghur woman talking about the return of the men who went south last year," Satai said casually. "Do you know of this, my Lady?"

Mandukhai sipped slowly to consider her answer. She knew Manduul had sent a messenger to Issama, but he had not told her to what end. The mission along the border had been Issama's plan: send Bayan, the Golden Prince, to stir up rebellion among the Ming-controlled Mongols cautiously so the Great Khan could raise the black banner, sweep in, and reclaim their land and people, further unifying the fractured empire. It was a surprisingly clever plan which Issama had orchestrated quite efficiently.

From what she had heard, so far Bayan had done well in his task. It should not have surprised her. The Golden Prince had a tongue to match his namesake and could easily pull others into his orbit, even if he did not know how to lead. She had not realized Manduul had recalled the military *tumens* of warriors he sent south, but she could never allow Satai to know he had left her out of that piece of politics. It would make her appear weak and possibly strip away some of the power and authority she had over the women in Mongke Bulag.

"It is unseemly for women to discuss such things over tea," Mandukhai said carefully.

There must have been some truth to the rumor or it wouldn't have been worth repeating, but Mandukhai did not know the extent of how many would return. She made a mental note to speak to Manduul about it later. Being surprised like this made their marriage appear weak.

"What does it matter?" Jaghan asked, as if sensing Mandukhai's dilemma. "Your husband is here already. As are ours."

"Is Une coming back?" Esige sat up straighter with the eagerness of a child on her youthful face. She adored the *orlok* much as a girl adored her father. Perhaps more. His training had never been lost on her, and before he had left on this mission, he had given Esige a new bow to strengthen her arm, then taught her how to fire from horseback in that breath of a moment when all hooves were off the ground. He had also given his dog, Kilgor, to her care. Esige had taken care of Kilgor as if it were her sacred duty.

Mandukhai scowled at Esige's reaction, but the girl only shrank back a fraction.

"Yes," Satai said. "And rumor has it the Golden Prince will remain behind."

Mandukhai breathed a small sigh of relief at that. While she did not like Bayan gathering so much power and support so far from home, she was pleased he had been sent somewhere far away from Yeke. While she had never caught the two of them in the act, she suspected they were having an affair behind Manduul's back. She also never forgot what Bayan had done to Nergui. Unebolod had uncovered the truth, that Bayan had murdered her Ongud guard. However, they did not have enough evidence to bring this truth to Manduul and convince him. Nor did they understand why Bayan did it. Instead of accusing Bayan of murder, Mandukhai held her vengeance close to her heart. One day, she would see justice done. When the time was right.

"You mustn't put too much trust in rumors, Satai," Mandukhai said as she set down her cup. "It's dangerous to spread the wrong ones."

Jaghan cocked her head to the side and studied Mandukhai.

"So, he is returning?" Satai asked.

"I'm afraid some matters of state are not mine to divulge," Mandukhai responded, pleased with her ability to evade answers without making herself appear ignorant.

"He can stay away, as far as I'm concerned," Esige said briskly into her cup.

Mandukhai slapped her, drawing a wounded expression from the girl as she rubbed her cheek. "He is your future Great Khan and your kin. Do not speak ill of your kin."

For just a moment, Mandukhai felt bad for admonishing Esige. When the two of them were alone, she allowed Esige to speak freely, but the girl needed to learn that such things were for the privacy of the ger and not to be spoken around others. Insulting the Golden Prince in front of anyone could get her into serious trouble.

Esige lifted her chin defiantly and straightened her back as Satai cast a satisfied, smug smile in her direction. Jaghan dipped her head toward her cup to lessen Esige's humiliation.

"I'm sorry, mother," Esige murmured.

After tea, Mandukhai excused herself from the others and went in search of Manduul. She could not afford to be surprised like that again. If something was happening, she needed to know about it.

Manduul had not been difficult to find. He sat atop his throne in the gathering tent, reviewing reports that had come in over the past few days. As Mandukhai entered, he lifted his gaze to hers and smiled briefly before returning to his task.

Mandukhai approached the dais and settled in her chair a step below his, waiting patiently for him to finish reading a report.

"You wait for something, wife," Manduul said, staring at the paper. "Out with it."

"Did you recall the southern *tumens*?"

Manduul sighed, and the sigh turned into a cough that shook his whole body. He didn't stop until one of the serving girls brought him a cup of *airag* to wet his throat. Mandukhai's brows drew together as she watched him hack.

"Are you well?"

"Fine." Manduul waved a hand and leaned back in his throne, gulping down breaths. "Just had some dirt caught in my throat from my walk this morning."

Mandukhai wanted to believe him, but the vision came back. The words of Genghis Khan echoing in her mind. *He is no Khan.*

"Don't look at me like I'm a wounded animal," Manduul grumbled. "I said it's nothing."

As Manduul gulped down air, she swore she heard him wheezing. A bit of dirt wouldn't cause such a reaction, would it?

"You asked about the *tumens*," he said, changing the subject. "Yes. I recalled all but enough to protect Bolkhu on his mission. I need them here."

"What is more urgent than the uprising against the Ming?" Mandukhai asked, taking his cup and setting it aside to shift closer. "You haven't told me something. What troubles you?"

Manduul scowled and waved a paper at her. "This. It's the third report within six months of the Oirat gathering together. They are up to something, and I need Issama to help."

Issama. His name sent a shiver down Mandukhai's spine. He had arrived in Mongke Bulag on Bigirsen's orders one year ago and quickly landed himself into position as the Vice Chancellor. Issama was certainly a clever man, more so than Bigirsen. Something about Issama set Mandukhai on edge. Manduul had been quick to accept the man's confidence—too quick.

Issama had established a bond of trust with Manduul and a friendship with Bayan that Mandukhai found unnerving, yet she could discern no good reason for these feelings other than her gut instincts. Issama was respectful to her—to everyone—and she had learned he was the only other person at court as intelligent as her in thinking things through. She should be grateful for his arrival. Yet she couldn't shake that discomfort.

"You fear an Oirat attack," Mandukhai surmised.

Manduul nodded bitterly. "Payback for our attacks on them."

"Attacks I warned you and Bolkhu both against."

Manduul slapped his hand against the armrest. "Now isn't a time for your self-righteous unbraiding." His voice rolled off the felt walls. "I would rather see this end without more fighting, and I need Issama to do so."

"So, he is the only one you've recalled?"

Manduul rubbed his forehead and shoved the stack of papers at her. "No. Bolkhu will continue his work. The rest are to return. He does not need them anymore. Activity along the border has increased. Bolkhu is doing as I asked."

Mandukhai gathered the papers, but her reading skills remained minimal. She couldn't understand most of what he laid in her hands, despite the lessons she had undertaken. She needed to learn how to read, and quickly.

The news that stuck in her heart was not regarding the Oirat or the border mission, but that she would see Unebolod again. Their parting had been distant, as most of their interactions with each other had been since losing their child. Perhaps he sensed a change in her. Or maybe she sensed a difference in him. Unebolod had distanced himself from her after the miscarriage, except when he shared the evidence implicating Bayan in Nergui's murder. After that, he had volunteered to lead raids, hunting parties, and scouting expeditions. So many that, in the last three years, they had hardly seen each other. At first, Mandukhai assumed Manduul suspected something and was trying to keep them apart. But when she overheard Unebolod insisting fervently on leading another expedition in Manduul's name, she knew the fault did not fall on her husband.

Unebolod avoided her.

CHAPTER TWO

From the Ashes of Former Glory

Bayan kept his head down as he followed one of Issama's scouts through the Ming-Mongol border town. According to Issama, this area of Ordos had little Ming presence. Most of the Ming border guards remained further south, closer to the mountains and their precious wall at Yulin, where food and reinforcements were plentiful. Mongols here lived in relative peace with the nearby Ming, and often sent tribute to the Ming emperor, Chenghua. It made Bayan's stomach churn with disgust that any Mongol would pay tribute to the Ming.

Though news of a new Mongol prince had spread far and wide already, few recognized Bayan so far south. To be safe, Bayan dressed down for these covert meetings so no one might connect him to being the prince. In such a place as this Ordos village, it would be easy to lose one's head to the wrong Mongolian Ming-loyalist.

The scout leading Bayan turned a corner, peering cautiously across the street before allowing Bayan to step around with him. All the houses in this small village were squat and cramped. How could true Mongols live like this?

For a year, Bayan had been slithering along these border tribes with Issama, who always seemed to have the right answer and kind words for the prince, and with Unebolod, who knew one hard truth Bayan would give anything to erase. Bayan spent that time spreading tales of the Borjigin Yuan Dynasty's return to power. Manduul had ordered him to plant the seeds of adventure, plunder, and glory for those who were bold enough to whet their appetites on Ming riches.

During his first meeting with a rather surly tribal Lord, Bayan had spoken Issama and Manduul's carefully crafted speech full of promises of former glory, but the words didn't ring true even to him. The Lord had been less than receptive to the idea of revolting against the Ming. He outright rejected the idea that anyone was coming to help them and sent Bayan, Issama, and Unebolod on their way.

Unebolod had given Bayan another of his knowing glares—a reminder that he simply waited for Bayan to make a fatal error that either would cost him his life or that Manduul could not ignore. Bayan remained unclear whether Unebolod told Mandukhai what he knew of Nergui's death; it hung between them like a balanced knife waiting to drop. Much to Bayan's relief, Manduul's patience had been seemingly without end. But under Unebolod's vigilance, Bayan could not risk failing.

The streets were all cramped and dirty, and the stink of refuse permeated the air. Stools and pots rested beside humble homes. The Mongols here had assimilated themselves into local Ming culture. Bayan wrinkled his nose in disgust. The sooner they could leave this place, the better.

Desperate to succeed, Bayan could not let that first meeting fail. He had returned to that obstinate Lord and had abandoned Manduul's carefully crafted speech. Instead, Bayan had trusted his own luck—his natural charisma. In Bayan's experience, speaking so formally often came across as fake. They could not stir up trouble along the borders if they didn't inspire passion and glory. By the end of the meeting, that Lord had listened intently.

Dozens of secret meetings had passed since then, and it emboldened more of the Mongols to prepare for a war against the Ming. But only when the time came after Bayan raised the black banner of war.

The scout guiding him through the cramped streets tonight hissed at Bayan and nodded to the connecting street. Unebolod and Issama waited back at camp for his return. They rarely accompanied him anymore. Bayan peered around the corner and spotted a squat building with a single lamp lit in a window. The construction was rough and reminiscent of Ming culture: dried mud, rough stones, and wood frames with a thatched roof. Bayan grimaced.

Bayan nodded to the scout in understanding and slipped through the shadows toward their target. He hated slinking along like this. It felt just as false as the words Manduul had given him. Why should he, the Golden Prince, hide in shadows when he could rally the surrounding tribes? Yet both Issama and Unebolod insisted he remain as inconspicuous as possible, and he had learned a hard lesson about deviating from their plans.

These clothes itch my skin, he thought bitterly as he pressed his back to the wall beside the door and knocked once, quick and soft. Bayan hated commoner wool and longed to don his silk again.

The scout edged closer to the door as it opened, putting himself between the prince and the inhabitants—no doubt out of instinct to protect the Great Khan's heir. The man who opened the door pressed the tip of his sword to the scout's neck without breaking skin. It impressed Bayan that the scout did not flinch.

"I bring Manduul Khan's messenger, as promised," the scout whispered, glancing at the street from the corner of his eye.

The older man scowled, glanced at Bayan critically, then lowered his sword and ushered them inside. Bayan didn't have to be told twice. He didn't enjoy hiding in the shadows of the street.

The inside of the home was just as cramped as the street outside. Nearly a dozen local commanders and Lords packed into the small space. A long stone stove rested along one wall, currently cold. Several men sat on the cold stovetop while others sat on benches around a small lacquer table. Tall bamboo shelves held various metal pots in the corner. A blanket hung over an opening into another room that he could only assume was the owner of this home slept. How he longed to sleep there in an actual bed. How he longed to go home! *And I can, as soon as I finish Manduul's mission*, he thought. All their eyes fell on him the moment he entered.

"He's a child," one man said, not bothering to whisper.

"I'm old enough to command a *tumen* of ten thousand," Bayan said sharply.

Several men scowled in doubt.

Bayan raised himself to his full height, which had grown significantly in the past two years. At eighteen, he stood nearly a head above most men—except Unebolod and a handful of Manduul's guards. As Bayan raised to his full height, many of these men dropped their skeptical scowls.

"How long have the Ming suppressed you?" Bayan asked without missing a beat, standing confidently before them with his chest puffed out and chin held high. "How long have they raided your people, killed your sons, abused your women? How long before you stand up to them?"

"We do not have enough men to fight back," an elder said. "And when we move goods between tribes to help stave off hunger, the Great Khan's Golden Prince raids our caravans. Thanks to this so-called prince, we are losing our goods. How does the Khan propose we fight back with nothing to fill our bellies?"

A flicker of doubt crossed Bayan's face, but he swiftly recovered. To his knowledge, none of his men were raiding any Mongol caravans—though they had stopped a Ming caravan and gave the goods to one of the Mongol tribes.

"He doesn't care, Mingtau," another man grumbled.

Bayan turned to face the accuser. "I *do* care. That's why I'm here. You've heard the rumors," Bayan said. He waited for them to consider their answer and nod. "They are true. Manduul Khan has an heir, and soon, he will raise the black banner, call on the tribes to join him, and retake our lands. Lands the Ming stole from us."

Men shifted and exchanged uncertain glances.

"I won't fight for a thief, even if he calls himself a prince," a young commander said, clenching his fists in his lap.

"The prince is no thief," Bayan snapped, unable to control his temper in this hot, humid, and cramped house. How could they doubt him? How could they dare say such things about him? Bayan caught himself holding his breath and forced himself to relax.

"But ... who else would raid our caravans?" another man asked.

"Who indeed?" Bayan retorted. His patience wore thin as the stifling air pressed against his chest. He wanted out of this place. "The prince did not raid your caravans, nor did any of his men. I can promise you that. Someone is acting against him, trying to stop him because they know if he gains your support, they have lost all power."

The scout shifted closer to Bayan's side as one man suddenly stood.

"And who would do such a thing?" the man they had called Mingtau asked.

Bayan took pleasure in watching the older man tilt his head back to look up at him. He could think of several answers to that question, but only one made the most logical sense. "The Ming Emperor."

The men broke into a flurry of protests at this. Most concerning were regarding why the raiders were Mongol bandits.

None of this was going as Bayan had expected. Aside from that first meeting, all the rest had gone smoothly. He always stirred up the right words to rally the men against the Ming. This time, the tribesmen seemed to prefer the heavy hand of the Ming emperor. Their voices rose to a crescendo, and Bayan struggled to even hear himself think over the noise. Soon, they would attract the attention of neighbors if it didn't stop.

Bayan raised his voice strong and sure above the din so that everyone could hear him clearly. "You disgrace your Mongol heritage." The words caught their attention like fire, drawing nearly a dozen scowls in his direction. Bayan knew he had to barrel forward before one of these men decided to cut off his head. "Were we not once one nation under the rule of the Khan of khans? Were these not *your* lands, instead of the Emperor's? Our former strength is falling into disrepair, and if we don't unite to restore it soon, we will be too late."

"The Ming leave us alone as long as we leave them alone," Mingtau said. "Why unbalance a balanced system?"

"They leave you alone because their old emperor was weak. The new one is young and inexperienced," Bayan replied. "But once this new young emperor has enough power, he will look to the Mongol Nation once more. He will ride to war and chase you from these lands that belong to us. And we will have fallen so far apart that no one will ride out to help."

Some men had gone red in the face, and Bayan hoped that anger was not directed at him. He moved one careful, confident step at a time around the packed room. His hands sweat clasped behind his back as he stepped close enough for any of these men to draw their swords easily and kill him. If there was one thing he had learned under Manduul's tutelage, it was that men respected power and fearlessness. Even if Bayan didn't feel fearless, he had to make them think he did.

"The Great Khan has not come to our aid in centuries," the young commander said. "What do we owe him?"

"Are you Ming or Mongol?" Bayan asked. "Because when I look around me now, I see Ming homes, Ming farming, Ming clothing." He leaned close to the young commander and swept his hand over the commander's shoulder to punctuate his point.

The commander glared at him but clamped his jaw shut.

Satisfied, Bayan turned to the older men in the group. "Some of you rode with Molon Khan. A few of you may have even ridden beside Manduul Khan when he avenged the deaths of the Borjigin princes. Are your memories so short?" He scoffed at them and resumed his casual walk around the packed room.

"The time to unite is now," he said, staring down every man as he passed. "The time to fight back for what belongs to us is coming. We will strike like a viper at the Ming court before they gather their full force against us. We will gorge ourselves on their riches and women. We will restore the Mongol Empire that once belonged to Genghis, Ogedei, and Kublai. We will no longer bow to this emperor!"

Bayan observed as some men shifted and sat straighter. Others nodded in agreement. They were on the hook. Now he just had to pull them in.

"We Mongols were not created to sit in homes and farm the land," Bayan continued. "We were born in the saddle, bow in our hand. We were reared with a thirst for adventure and a restless spirit. We grew stronger together as we plundered the world and took what was rightfully ours. Everything under the blue sky is mine. It is yours. It is *ours*!"

A few of the men voiced cheers of agreement.

Bayan stopped beside the stove and stared at the earthen door. After a moment of consideration, he placed his palm on the handle, tested the heat, then pulled it open once he was satisfied that it was cold.

"This is what they have done to us," he said, waving his hand toward the open stove piled with ash. "They have locked us into our spaces, turned us against each other, and reduced our power to ash."

He plunged his hand inside and prayed the ash wouldn't burn his hands, then seized a fistful and held it up high for everyone to see. Holding the warm ash in his fist heated his already hot skin, but he could show no sign of pain or weakness in front of these men. "But has our fire gone out?"

Gradually, each man shook his head or voiced an emphatic "no."

"Then let us unite and rekindle the ashes of our former glory." Bayan tipped his fist and let the ash drift to the floor. "Help us reduce this emperor's power to ash and extinguish *his* flame once and for all." He turned in place, meeting all the eager, angry eyes staring back at him. "Throw off the chains Emperor Chenghua has yoked you with and show his guards the true power of the Mongols!"

"And why should we listen to you, a simple messenger from the Great Khan?" Mingtau asked.

"Because," Bayan swallowed, knowing he could end up dead speaking these words if the men present decided not to heed his call. "I am Bolkhu Jinong, nephew of Manduul Khan, and your future Khan."

Unebolod had packed light when he left on this mission with Bayan and Issama. He only brought what he could strap to his horse, and he shared a ger with a few of his commanders. But Unebolod was a hard man, used to sleeping on the ground under the open sky or riding in his saddle for days. When desperation struck, he could sleep while riding. His men were much the same, all seasoned fighters ready to ride at a moment's notice or sleep in the open when necessary. They required very little.

Issama, on the other hand, had a cart packed with materials to build a ger wherever they stopped, as well as a wealth of food and other supplies he deemed necessary. Unebolod despised Issama, the Great Khan's new Vice Chancellor. He was too confident. Too certain. Too calm. Everything he did had a distinct purpose, and often Unebolod struggled to decipher what the Uyghur man was up to—which only made Unebolod mistrust him even more; a confident and calm Uyghur was as dangerous as a scorpion in the Gobi.

Issama's presence was unsettling, but Manduul had grown to trust the man in the past year. And despite how much Unebolod despised Issama, the man's tactics had been grudgingly brilliant—and at nearly eight years younger than Unebolod. He hated to give the man too much credit, but Issama knew what was going on before anyone else even caught a slight whiff of it. Unebolod respected the intelligence but hated the man.

This entire mission had been Issama's idea. Bayan had wanted to charge his men in and liberate their subjugated Mongols. But the first attempt to stir up doubt among the border tribes toward the Ming almost a year ago proved to be near catastrophic.

Bayan had ignored both Unebolod and Issama when they had advised moving with caution to avoid raising alarms. The moment the local tribe near the city of Kokegota had heard the Golden Prince had arrived, they rallied their forces and charged against the Great Khan's men, assuming it was an invasion, proving that some of the southern Mongols were more loyal to the Ming than their own Khan.

Thankfully, Unebolod and Issama's scouts had received a warning in time to prevent disaster. Once the local commander had been talked down, Issama arranged for a meeting on neutral ground. The first of dozens of such meetings.

Unebolod checked the saddle straps to ensure everything was secured. Bayan would be back from tonight's secret meeting soon, and he wouldn't be happy with the news. If Unebolod could find any satisfaction from slowly torturing Bayan, this news would drive an arrow through the boy. He almost smiled at the thought of the dumb look Bayan would surely adopt.

"What do you suppose our young Lord will say when he finds out we are leaving him?" Issama asked as he stepped up beside Unebolod, guiding his own horse.

Unebolod glanced at Issama's smug face—*why is he always so smug?*—and shrugged. "It doesn't matter what he says. When the Great Khan calls us back, we go back. The prince's word is not superior to our Khan."

Issama stroked his mount's nose and nodded. "True. Yet our prince always has an opinion about everything."

"Let us hope he is wise enough by now to hold his tongue and hold the line."

A wave of cheering voices rose like a tide washing over the two of them. Only one thing would cause such a response.

Issama smirked. "I suppose we are about to find out."

Bayan galloped toward them, stopping his chestnut mare hard enough to kick up dirt in the air. Unebolod waved it away with a scowl. *Always the showman*, Unebolod thought bitterly.

Bayan turned his mount to look over the carts and mounted men. "Are we going somewhere?"

"*We* are," Unebolod corrected, nodding toward Issama to indicate just the two of them.

Issama shot a glare in Unebolod's direction and said, "We received a message from Manduul Khan while you were away. He summons *orlok* Unebolod and I back to Mongke Bulag."

Bayan looked for just a moment like a wounded animal. "But not me?"

A flash of satisfaction surged through Unebolod. Bayan was a boy seeking his father's respect.

Unebolod shrugged. "He has his reasons, but he says we are to hurry back. You are to stay and continue this mission."

"Nothing is more important than you completing this mission," Issama agreed.

Unebolod hated when Issama agreed with him.

Bayan dismounted. "You leave now?"

"That's what 'hurry back' means," Unebolod said tersely.

Bayan shot him a treacherous glare.

Unebolod knew that, should the Khan die, Bayan would likely try to have him killed. The prince had no love for him. *Maybe Bayan doesn't care for me because I don't fall prey to his silver tongue,* Unebolod considered with amusement. Or maybe because Unebolod knew Bayan's secret.

Neither Unebolod nor Mandukhai had indicated that Unebolod had told her the truth about Bayan killing Nergui three years ago. The why of the murder remained a mystery, though.

Bayan constantly squirmed around Unebolod as if afraid Unebolod would share his knowledge with everyone should Bayan step out of line. Unebolod took great delight in seeing the pitiful whelp kowtowing for silence.

Unebolod had told Mandukhai the truth as soon as she was up to visitors after the miscarriage. She had taken the information with an air of grace and dispassion that made him wonder if she blamed Unebolod for not finding the killer of their child as well. Not that she would ever say as much, but Unebolod felt the failure all the same. Between that failure and Togochi's sharp warning when he learned the truth, a chasm had grown between himself and Mandukhai.

Issama bowed to Bayan. "I'm afraid we must leave tonight. But we leave you with five thousand of the men to command and finish your task." He held out his hand and Unebolod observed as Issama and Bayan shook like old friends. "You've done well, Bolkhu *Jinong*. I am honored to have been on this journey with you. I look forward to finishing it together."

Unebolod felt a twist of disgust. Issama ingratiated himself with both Manduul and Bayan at every opportunity, a despicable act.

Unebolod turned away from the two and mounted his mare. "Keep the scouts out riding in search of Ming patrols," he commanded. "When the emperor hears what you are up to, he will come."

Bayan grinned like a boy far too eager to see battle with no real understanding of what that would mean. "Let him come."

Issama shook his head and chuckled as he mounted his horse.

Within the hour, Unebolod and Issama left the Golden Prince in the fields of the Ordos plateau. Five thousand men followed them north to their homelands. Like most of the men ready to go back home and see their wives, Unebolod was eager to return and see Mandukhai. It had been far too long, and he missed her fiery temper and spirit. He looked forward to seeing her ... and feared their inevitable encounter.

Chapter Three

Springing Traps

MING-ORDOS TERRITORY – 1468

Five thousand mounted warriors waited on either slope overlooking the valley below, tucked back amid dawn redwood trees and gray boulders that lined the valley walls. The horses were stashed away and their muzzles wrapped to keep them silent as Bayan's men waited. He had organized a brilliant plan to discover who was stealing from the Mongols in his name. His men had loaded several carts full of food and felt, as well as two carts carrying materials to construct a ger. It was just enough to entice whoever was behind these raids. A small party of Bayan's best fighters were disguised as Mongol peasants in these humid lands, and they walked alongside carts pulled by yaks. Their swords hid in the carts or under deels to avoid raising suspicion. Fewer than one hundred of his men walked or rode mounts alongside the caravan.

According to Mingtau, one of the local Chakhar commanders, this valley saw the most raids. Bayan had sent scouts through the area, and they confirmed that something had recently happened in the valley. Suspicious that this was a trap, Bayan insisted that Mingtau and his men accompany him on the mission. He placed Mingtau's men on the opposite side of the valley, where they were at more of a disadvantage to escape should this be a trap to close Bayan and his men in—a stroke of Berkedai's genius during initial planning. His guard and best friend perpetually remained suspicious of anything that threatened Bayan's life.

Now, Bayan stroked the nose of his chestnut mare, Andayar, to keep her calm as he surveyed the valley below. A scout rushed up to him from a narrow passage behind him.

"They are coming from Xi'xia," the scout confirmed. "It's a small party. Maybe a hundred at most. We can easily crush them."

"I want some men taken alive," Bayan said. Excitement and fear pumped through his veins as he turned his gaze toward the caravan lumbering along the valley floor. "I want to know who they serve and why they are spreading these lies."

The scout nodded and turned his mount to carry out the prince's command along the lines. Bayan had already commanded Mingtau to make sure they captured as many of the men as possible for questioning. Whether the commander would listen to him had yet to be determined. Bayan remained uncertain if he could trust the man.

At a signal from Bayan, his men prepared bows and kept a careful eye on the valley. Sweat dripped down Bayan's neck, but he resisted the urge to wipe it away. This land was hot and humid. He longed to return to the cooler dry air of the north. He smiled as he thought about the women there while insects buzzed in the air. Horses to flick their tails to swat them away.

No one moved as they watched the valley where this force would appear to head off the caravan. Not for the first time, Bayan wished Altan could be there with him to fight this foe. She would fight fiercely and, when the battle was won, she would mount him and ride him just as fiercely as she had fought. Just as she had after the battle against her own Jalair tribe. Thinking of her proved to be too much of a distraction as one of the commanders along the line whispered to him that the enemy had entered the valley.

Bayan strung an arrow and took a calming breath. Women could wait. Right now, he had to find out who was stealing in his name.

With a vicious whoop and cry, the enemy surged into the valley and attacked the caravan. But his men high above were ready. They drew bows and fired, intending to injure but not kill. Thousands of arrows rained down on the valley below, and the enemy cried out in alarm and shouted for retreat. The stiff way they rode their horses appeared unnatural to Bayan, and their own arrows had not been nearly as accurate as a Mongol should have been. These Mongols didn't fight or ride like Mongols.

In a single volley from his men, nearly half of the enemy force fell from their saddles. Yet they still fought fiercely against Bayan's men.

With Berkedai among those on the ground, Bayan knew Berkedai would swiftly take control of the fight. The trap had sprung. Bayan blew a horn for his men in the hills to ride down to join their brothers. In moments, five thousand Mongols leaped into their saddles and surged down the valley walls toward their foe. On the other side of the valley, Mingtau's own five thousand warriors closed in. The rear guards on either side held a closer position to the mouth of the valley from which the enemy force invaded. They closed around the exit like a tide of bowmen crashing down a rocky shore. There was nowhere for the enemy to run.

By the time Bayan's mare reached the valley floor, the fighting had turned vicious. Even outnumbered and dismounted against such a superior force, the enemy fought with desperation toward the point of retreat, with little more than swords remaining.

"*Chuh!*" Bayan whipped Andayar with the reins to pick up her pace. She had a long, powerful stride. They crashed through the enemy together, trampling anyone not fast enough to get out of their way. All around them, their adversaries swung their swords at the legs of horses to dismount men, or at the legs of the men in saddles.

Already, Berkedai had captured and tied more than enough men for Bayan to question. He called out an order to kill the rest. Now that none needed to remain alive, the fight ended swiftly. They vastly outnumbered their enemy. In minutes, both Bayan's and Mingtau's men walked among the dead, stripping them of anything worth keeping to toss into the carts. They dragged the dead to the mouth of the valley where they had come from and left them to rot as a warning.

"A clever ruse," Mingtau said, riding his mount up beside Bayan.

Bayan considered whether he should trust this was the end, and whether Mingtau would betray him. Yet this victory would bear fruit for Mingtau's people. Striking out against the Khan's heir now would only bring vengeance down on his head.

"Not clever," Bayan said. "I'm surprised you didn't do this yourself. It was almost too easy."

Bayan dismounted and strode toward Berkedai as Berkedai tossed a bound prisoner alongside the rest against the wheel of a cart. Twenty survivors. Bayan could get the information he sought from this many.

"My Lord, these are not Mongols," Berkedai said as Bayan joined him.

Bayan frowned and crouched in front of the prisoners, examining each of them closely. "Who do you serve?" he asked one man.

The prisoner scoffed and spit in his face. Berkedai swung his sword and took the prisoner's head.

Bayan rose and stared down at each of the bound men. "I am Bolkhu Jinong. You are stealing from *my* people in *my* name. The first man to tell me whom you serve will live. The rest will die."

Three of the men began rambling over each other as the rest glared at Bayan in open defiance. It only took a moment to realize these men were not speaking in the Mongol tongue. Bayan couldn't understand a word of it, but he understood enough to identify them.

"Ming raiders?" Bayan turned to Mingtau. "Have you heard of such a thing before? Ming posing as Mongols to raid us?"

Mingtau shook his head. "As long as we remain peaceful, they leave us alone."

Peaceful. Bayan sneered. Peace with the Ming was an abomination. There could be no peace. "What are they saying?"

Mingtau fell silent, listening as the three men continued rambling, desperate to save their lives. As he waited, Bayan nodded to Berkedai. The prisoners who remained silent were executed with arrows in the neck. The sound of the arrows thumping through their necks was like a hammer against dirt, followed by blood trickling like water over river stones. Bayan averted his gaze and focused on the three who remained.

"They are local commanders of Ming forces," Mingtau said slowly. "They beg your mercy. They vow to serve you if you do not return them for the emperor to find out what they've done."

They are afraid the emperor will find out? This could only mean they had acted independently, without commands from their superior officers. Sending them back to the Ming would surely be a death sentence, but it was no less than they deserved. Bayan had no use for Ming slaves who would just as surely turn on him as serve him.

"Send them back to their emperor," Bayan commanded.

"But my Lord, the emperor will know you are here," Mingtau said, glancing at the three men as they desperately pleaded for their lives, reaching for Bayan's boots.

Bayan stepped back out of reach. He turned a fierce gaze on Mingtau. "Did you hear nothing I said before? We are here to rise against him, not cower in fear. We are Mongols."

Berkedai hauled one of the men to his feet and shoved him back in the direction they had come from. More of Bayan's men followed the command, dragging the pleading, protesting Ming soldiers beside them.

One man wrenched himself free and rushed toward Bayan, but before he could take three steps, one of Bayan's men shot an arrow through his eye. The Ming soldier dropped dead on the spot.

"See that the supplies are returned to their owners," Bayan commanded as he mounted his chestnut mare. "Berkedai, put a man you trust in charge to finish this."

"My Lord." Berkedai bowed.

Bayan rode away from the valley and back toward the camp with a handful of his guards. Now that the fight was over and the truth revealed, he could see to finding a woman to warm his bed.

Everything ached. Bayan tried his best to show no signs of weakness in front of his men, but he hadn't been raised in battle like these men. Bolunai, the Khorchin tribal khan, had attempted to harden Bayan with his fists, but it did not seem to have the desired effect. Bayan could take a punch, though he preferred not to, but he could not handle battles without his limbs aching all over. Did all men feel this and just smothered it beneath a mask of strength as he attempted to do?

At sunset, Bayan stopped beside a river near the camp to wash off. He ordered his guards to keep watch as he stripped out of his armor and clothes and dunked into the cool water. It seeped into his aching flesh like a salve. Bayan struggled to keep from sighing in relief, afraid the guards would see it as weak.

The fewer battles he had to engage in, the better. Bayan had insisted on charging in when Issama and Unebolod were with him, mostly because he felt they expected as much from him. As much as he hated sneaking around, it was much simpler and far less dangerous than charging into a fight on a saddle.

Once he had washed the blood and dirt away, Bayan stepped out and rinsed blood off his armor, then slipped on the dirty clothes. He could do nothing about them until returning to his ger. He mounted Andayar and carried on into the torchlight of camp.

A figure paced near his ger, and as he rode closer, he could tell it was a female. Had someone been sent to please him? Bayan certainly would not object. As he dismounted and commanded his guards to keep watch, she stepped into the torchlight toward him.

Bayan groaned. He feared this day would come. With the Chakhar numbers increasing near his camp, it was only a matter of time before she showed her face. Did she hold a grudge against him for killing her father?

"Siker."

"So it is true," she said as her eyes scanned him over. "You are Manduul Khan's heir?"

"Let me guess, you have changed your mind now that I'm set to be the next Great Khan," he said, tossing his reins to his servant, Enkh, to hobble Andayar's hooves beside Bayan's ger.

"No."

"Then why are you here?"

Siker inched closer. "You are in danger, Bayan."

He snorted and entered his ger. She followed without invitation.

"I was in danger the day you first found me in the desert," he said, tossing his armor aside unceremoniously and stripping off the bloodied deel unashamed of her presence. She had seen it all before, anyway. "Since birth, honestly. Nothing has changed."

"You have."

Bayan strode toward her so fiercely Siker stumbled back away from him until her back was pressed against the wall. He hesitated so close to her. Siker wasn't so plain anymore. He no longer had to squint to find her attractive, like he used to. The past four years had been kind to her. He had hoped to find a woman for the night. One found him, instead. Bayan ran his fingers along her neck, then pulled her deel loose. Siker quivered at his touch, sending a rush of arousal through his body. Even after all this time, it was easy to fall into old habits around her. He pressed a heated kiss against her neck.

Siker released a shuddering breath. "Bayan, please."

"Are you going to beg this time?" He murmured against her flesh. Some part of him knew dimly that Siker had likely married since his departure. Another part of him, the louder part of him, did not care.

"They are coming for you," Siker said.

Though he heard her words, the desire burning in him drowned their meaning out. His lips trailed along her neck as his fingers tangled in her wild hair. "Let them come."

"Bayan ..." The rest of her words trailed off as his fingers slid between her legs.

Bayan had learned a few new tricks in the past four years. He intended to share them all with her. Her protests for his life faded into moans of pleasure. In a matter of minutes, the old natural rhythm of their animalistic needs replaced all the urgency in her warning.

The men and women traveling with Bayan broke down their gers the next morning. Now that the truth about the Ming trickery had been revealed and his name cleared, Bayan intended to complete his mission along the border and share the Ming deception with everyone he could find. It was a bold move to dress as Mongols and raid caravans, especially without the consent of their emperor. Either they never expected him to arrive, or the Ming intended to sow dissent between tribes. Bayan could only hope that one of those two men who survived his attack had raced back to tell the emperor that Bayan rode along the border. He wanted to enrage the emperor, then disappear.

Without Issama advising him, Bayan could feel his wits slipping. Deciding to break camp and move had taken him the better part of the morning, as he had debated whether he should take a stand or move on. Siker had warned him again that he was in danger, but he found women often saw danger lurking in every shadow, and he waved off her concerns as he set to work taking down his ger.

As she helped him, he noticed more than once how she continually glanced furtively in every direction, as if she feared his own men would collapse around him and attack. Berkedai would never allow it. He would kill even the slightest whisperer of disloyal aspirations.

"Quit jumping at shadows," Bayan grumbled as he passed her with a bundle of lathes to load into the cart.

Siker edged close to him and lowered her voice. "Bayan, not everyone here is happy to have the Great Khan meddling in their affairs. Some of these men are content with how things were under the Ming."

Bayan heaved in the bundle and snorted. "Then I will teach them how wrong they are."

Siker grabbed his arm as he turned away, jerking him around to face her. "You have become more arrogant than ever. Listen to me. I didn't come all this way to be ignored."

Bayan smirked. "Did you feel ignored last night?"

"That is not what I'm talking about, and you know it."

Bayan's shoulder sagged. Siker never had a sense of humor. "I appreciate your concern. It's sweet. But I have everything under control. My men are monitoring the Ming. Berkedai is monitoring the men. I am monitoring Berkedai. Manduul is monitoring me. Everyone has someone to report to and someone to watch over. Let the men handle the warfare. You can handle this." Bayan handed Siker an empty *airag* churning bucket.

Her lips compressed so tightly the edges turned white before she threw it in the cart and stormed off.

As the final materials were loaded into the cart and strapped down, Bayan mounted Andayar and took in Mingtau's camp in the distance. It had grown in size as more Chakhar tribe members had joined them. Siker's family must have been among the Chakhar.

Siker appeared beside him, placing a hand on his leg as she gazed up at him. *Had* she married since he left her? It would not be the first married woman he had taken. Could any man really love her?

"You should go back to your husband," Bayan said from atop his saddle, poking for the truth. "He must be wondering where you disappeared to all night."

Siker frowned. "He died last summer."

Bayan had no response. Did she expect him to take her with him this time? His interests hadn't changed. While she was mildly more attractive than she had been four years ago, Bayan valued his freedom for as long as he could wrangle it. One day, Manduul would die and he would be married to Yeke and Mandukhai. Bayan had no interest in rushing toward that fate.

"Go north, Bayan," Siker insisted. "Return home where you will be safe."

"I'm not safe anywhere." Bayan recalled the discontent he often saw in Unebolod's sharp gaze and was certain that the moment Unebolod had a chance to kill him, he would seize it.

A horn blew to the south, then repeated all along the western watches. Bayan stiffened in the saddle and checked his bow to be sure it was handy.

"Bayan—"

"Go home, Siker." He kicked Andayar into action, riding toward Berkedai as she called after him. "What is it?" he asked Berkedai.

Horns blew along the eastern watches now as well, making Bayan's chest heave in fear.

Go north, Bayan. Siker's warning rang in his head, as he quickly realized north was the only direction they *could* go if they were to flee. *I told Mingtau not to run, so I cannot either, or he will see me as weak.* Bayan cast a longing gaze northward. He wanted to go home.

Berkedai stood in his stirrups and stared westward across the rolling plateau dotted with sparse maidenhair trees. "Ming soldiers."

Bayan's heart fell into his stomach. *Already?* He had kicked the hornet's nest, and now the swarm was upon him. Some part of Bayan had hoped to be long gone before the emperor attacked. "How did the scouts miss such a force?"

"Should we leave the Chakhar to fight the Ming off as we ride north?" Berkedai asked.

"No!" Bayan's response was too quick. He took a careful breath. "No, I told them to fight. So, we fight. Send word for the carts to move north. We will catch up to them once this is over."

Berkedai bowed in his saddle and kicked his mare into action.

Bayan did not know what else to do now but charge into battle. He sounded the horn to send word to his commanders, and the dulcet tone echoed through his ranks. In minutes, the full force of his five *ming-ghans*—each a thousand men strong—rode west. Hopefully, Mingtau had enough men himself to defend south and east.

As his *mingghans* moved at a slow trot toward the advancing Ming lines, Bayan assessed the enemy. Their forces would be equally met on the battlefield, which meant he had to pick off the edges with arrows before the Ming drew too close. At least a thousand cavalry flanked the wings of the Ming army, as well as the rear guard, bows and swords in hand. As Bayan increased the speed of his mount to a slow canter, the lines of his five *mingghan* units matched his speed without command. Ming archers covered the wings between cavalry and pikemen. Ming pikemen along the front lines lowered their pikes to pick off the Mongol mounts and break the lines. Bayan spotted their commander at the center of the mass easily enough. That would be their target.

Ming archers released a volley of arrows too soon. Most of the arrows fell pathetically to the soil, skipping across rocks and dirt. Bayan watched as a few arrows bounced uselessly off Mongol shields or armor.

At this point, Bayan knew he could not have held back his men if he wanted to. Their bloodlust had risen, and they lifted their bows as one while the lines of his *mingghans* broke into a gallop alongside him. The long line curved inward at the edges to trap the Ming forces. Nerves knotted in Bayan's stomach, but he did his best to push aside the apprehension and focus on his aim. Years of hard training had prepared him for such an encounter, and he raised his bow high, taking aim.

As he released, his line followed his lead. Thousands of arrows shot fast and powerful into the front lines of pikemen, throwing soldiers off their feet. He watched as the Ming line collapsed, only to be replaced by a fresh line. Bayan wished he had his own lancers to crash through the front lines and scatter the Ming formations. But the lancers had returned to Mongke Bulag with Unebolod.

Ming archers shot another volley of arrows, but their bows were not as powerful as the Mongol bows or armor. Most of the arrows glanced off helmets or chest plates with little damage. Only a few of Bayan's men went down with a well-placed arrow to the neck. Even as the arrows struck, the *mingghans* released another volley of their own.

For a moment, enemy arrows passed in the air, creating a hum of strings and shafts. Bayan ducked behind his shield as one arrow flew toward his head. This time, more of the Ming pikemen, archers, and footmen fell than before. The Ming commander barked an order, and the cavalry on the outer flanks spread outward and charged into the Mongol force.

In moments, the enemy army roiled in chaos, but their commanders held the lines with force, striking any who broke ranks. Mongol and Ming forces crashed together like two massive waves. Horses trampled the footmen unfortunate enough to stand in their way. Ming archers fired with enough force to knock Mongol warriors off-balance, ripping Bayan's men from their saddles.

Bayan swiftly replaced his bow with his sword. In close quarters, bows were as likely to kill his own men as they were the enemy. He hacked and slashed desperately at any man careless enough to come near. When his sword wouldn't do the trick, he kicked Andayar back so she stamped the enemy down. Mongol riders on the wings closed around the Ming force like a vice, and Bayan was certain they would defeat the enemy.

A knot of the Ming commander's guards raced toward Bayan, and he called his own men around him. But in the heat of the battle, his men were too far to reach him in time. Somehow, Bayan found himself surrounded by a sea of Ming soldiers.

Desperate, Bayan circled back, only to find himself trapped in a wall of Ming troops corralling him toward the Ming commander's guard. Shouts rang out over the clash of swords, squeals of men and horses, and thunder of hooves. Bayan could barely discern Berkedai's voice. He didn't dare take his eyes off the command guard as it fought its way toward him in a tight knot.

A horn sounded. A surge of panic rose in Bayan's chest. Something had gone horribly wrong. All across the battlefield, the Mongol lines collapsed. His *mingghans* had more men on foot than on horseback. Bayan continued swinging his sword like a cudgel through the mass of Ming troops, but he was outnumbered, and the command guard lumbered ever closer.

Bayan dared a glance to locate where the horn had sounded, only to discover a full *tumen* of ten thousand Chakhar riders galloping away. Everything seemed too slow for a moment as Bayan took in the horror of their impending defeat. More Ming troops closed in on the southern flank of his men.

Not everyone here is happy to have the Great Khan meddling in their affairs, Siker had said. Had someone betrayed him? *Some of these men are content with how things were under the Ming.* Had Mingtau betrayed him to keep the Great Khan out of the south? It would never work. If Bayan died, he knew Manduul would send everything he had against the south. Sweat coated Bayan's forehead, making his helmet slip. *But I don't want to die.*

"Bolkhu!" Berkedai's warning shout came too late.

An arrow thumped against Bayan's chest hard enough to knock him off the saddle and lodge in his armor. His back hammered against the unforgiving earth, knocking the air from his lungs.

"To the prince!" Berkedai's voice roared over the thunder of battle.

Bayan gasped for air, relieved that the armor had stopped the arrow. Before he could climb to his feet, a Ming soldier swung his sword down at Bayan's neck. He rolled aside as another blow landed on the back of his armor. He tried to stand, but something slammed into his back and sent him sprawling on the ground. Dirt coated his mouth and covered his face. Andayar reared her front legs in the air and came down on another Ming soldier. Bayan watched as the man's skull crushed under the force of the mare's hooves. Blood sprayed in his face.

A Ming horse charged toward him. Bayan rolled aside to his feet, attempting to scramble out of the way. Before the rider reached him, a thunderous thump of arrows rained down on the command guard bearing down on him. Bayan instinctively ducked, shielding his head with his arms. When he looked up a moment later, Berkedai appeared at his side on horseback, holding the reins of Bayan's mare. Without a second of hesitation, Bayan scrambled onto Andayar's back.

"Retreat with the prince!" Berkedai hollered, then signaled for arrows.

As the Mongol riders fired, the Ming commander shouted an order deep in the knot of his own guards. His sword pointed directly and unmistakably at Bayan.

"Go!" Berkedai commanded. "They are here for you. We will guard your retreat."

Retreat. Bayan loathed the idea of retreating, of allowing the emperor to think he had won. Yet in all his life, Bayan had only one instinct. To survive. He had fled assault before. This would be no different.

An *arban* of ten guards around Bayan tightened ranks, firing arrows without mercy and swinging swords when their foe came too close. As they rode away from the Ming commander and his guards, the Chakhar raced over the ridge to the south into the fray, replenishing his forces and giving Bayan a chance to escape.

Bayan blinked blood from his eyes, unsure if it was his or someone else's. As his *arban* helped him escape the fray, Bayan wondered if maybe he had made a serious mistake coming here. How could he ever hope to take on the Ming when he couldn't win this minor battle? Bayan now longed for the safety and comfort of Mongke Bulag. After all, Unebolod was only one man, and Mandukhai only a woman. He would rather take his chances with the enemy he knew.

Bayan's guards rode north with him until he crested a hilltop overlooking the raging battle below. The Ming had attacked the camp on all three sides—south, east, and west. Ming to the east had raced away, disappearing in the distance with Mongols giving chase. They had concentrated the largest portion of their forces in the south, where the Chakhar fought like devils to route them. The Ming to the south had shifted course and raced west to join with the army there. This had brought the Chakhar to the aid of Bayan's men on Ming heels.

The Ming had nearly routed the full two *tumens* of ten thousand Mongol warriors each by dividing the Mongol forces all across the battlefield—over twenty thousand Mongols in total. Yet as the Chakhar pressed the Ming forward, Bayan's *mingghans* pulled back to form a ring on the northern edge of the battlefield on Berkedai's command.

And then the carnage began.

Under the relentless pressure of the Mongol ring of warriors striking against the edges of their lines, the Ming defense finally collapsed and broke away. They retreated south with several thousand Chakhar on their heels. Bayan watched as the Ming likely sought refuge in whatever pass they had come from. In their wake, they left thousands of their own dead strewn across the battlefield.

As Bayan watched, panting and wiping his sleeve against his brow, he couldn't help but wonder who had been scouting that pass. Either the scouts were inept and should be punished, or someone had allowed the Ming to sneak upon them. *Some of these men are content with how things were under the Ming.* This insult could not go unpunished. Why had the Chakhar turned away on the battlefield before coming in at last?

Bayan wiped blood off his sword with his silk belt. He flicked drops onto the ground beside Andayar. Anger pulsed through him. Siker had tried to warn him, and he hadn't listened. He would listen now.

CHAPTER FOUR

Uneasy Truths

Mandukhai's stomach twisted in uneasy knots as she waited in the gathering tent. Scouts reported the *tumen* would return from the south today, and her inevitable meeting with Unebolod increased her anxiety. Would he want to see her? Would he want to talk to her? In the weeks and months following the loss of the child, he had grown distant. Mandukhai often blamed herself for loss.

Mandukhai shifted slightly in her seat in the gathering tent and glanced at Manduul as he waited patiently for the men to arrive. With each passing moment, her heart beat faster.

In the first few weeks after losing the child, she had turned the events leading up to the loss over in her mind repeatedly. Knowing the child was a danger to others in power, she should have been more careful. Had she been more vigilant and less consumed by her grief and anger over Nergui's murder, she may have suspected the tea was poisoned before drinking it. She would have sniffed out the bitter scent of the herb before consuming it. It was not as if Mandukhai had been unfamiliar with mugwort. She had used it to after Manduul forced himself on her to prevent conceiving his child.

The guilt over missing something so significant as mugwort and pennywort in her tea had driven her away from Unebolod, unable to face his disappointment, terrified that he would blame her and reject her. After losing her child, she just didn't have the heart to lose him.

Once she had overcome the hardest part of her guilt, Mandukhai had moved on to align what had happened with her vision of Genghis Khan.

Genghis said she would give her heart once to passion and once to compassion, and she had no longer doubted who possessed her heart in passion. But had he meant she would give her heart to Manduul as well? He had certainly become surprisingly compassionate following the miscarriage. Yet, as time passed, the resentment toward Manduul for raping her in a jealous rage that the first year of their marriage remained buried deep in her heart. She could never give her heart to him.

Mandukhai's hands sweated in her lap. She glanced at the open door to the gathering tent. How much longer would they be waiting for Unebolod and Issama to arrive?

For the next two years after the miscarriage, Unebolod had volunteered for missions in the Great Khan's name and would disappear for months at a time without so much as a goodbye. When the mission south to agitate the Mongols along the Ming border had been proposed, Unebolod had been first to volunteer his services as *orlok*. Mandukhai had wanted to beg him to stay; she had wanted to summon the courage to tell him she still loved him, that he still possessed her; yet none of these words would surface. Their final conversation before he left had been as brief and distant as every other since the miscarriage.

Mandukhai bit her lip and glanced at Togochi. He had suspected something had happened between Mandukhai and Unebolod. The extent of what Togochi knew, she remained unclear on. Perhaps all of it. Perhaps almost none of it. Togochi had said nothing to her about the affair, though. Unebolod had given her no sign that Togochi knew either.

Yeke sat in her usual place, hands folded in her lap and eyes fixed on some distant point.

Since Bayan's departure, Yeke retreated further from everyone. She was but a shadow of the woman she once had been. At times, Mandukhai had been certain she witnessed madness in Yeke's vacant expressions.

Upon hearing the *tumen* would return, Yeke had come out of her shell. Yet the moment she learned Bayan was not among the returning men, she retreated once more. This odd behavior only increased Mandukhai's suspicion that something significant had happened between Yeke and Bayan.

The crunch of boots against the hardening ground outside drew Mandukhai's attention toward the door before Unebolod or Issama entered.

Boke—head of Manduul's guard—hardly spared a glance at Issama as he stepped through first.

Issama's movements were fluid, like water over smooth rock. He even seemed to float toward the head of the room. Mandukhai only spared him a glance, immediately distracted by Unebolod as he ducked inside and marched forward. Where Issama moved like water, Unebolod marched like stone; stiff, formal, and confident that his very step could crush the earth beneath him. The two men bowed before Manduul, holding until the Khan waved for them to rise.

Mandukhai struggled not to bite her lip as her stomach twisted in knots gazing at Unebolod. It took all of her willpower to avert her gaze to avoid it lingering too long.

"I hear you had some success along the border," Manduul said.

"Indeed, my lord Khan," Issama said formally. His voice flowed like water as well, relaxed, cool, and confident. "The Golden Prince has proven himself quite capable of gathering the confidence of those who lead the southern *tumens*. Though he has gone off our agreed dialogue."

Manduul grunted and rapped his fingertips on the arm of his throne. Mandukhai recognized this as a sign of his impatience. When she had heard he had summoned these men back, she'd inquired about the reason for cutting their mission short. Manduul had stated so many were unnecessary so far south, particularly with the Oirat stirring up trouble along his own borders. He needed his men back. Something about this explanation had not settled well with her. Manduul already had enough men in Mongke Bulag to hold against the Oirat. Why did he need another *tumen*? How many thousands did he assume were necessary? Forty? Fifty?

"Bolkhu can be impulsive, but I sent him because his charisma is enchanting," Manduul admitted. "If any could succeed in this task, it is him."

Mandukhai wanted to focus on the conversation, but she could feel Unebolod's eyes on her. It made her face burn. Her gaze flicked to Unebolod, who stared at her with such cold-faced intensity it made her heart quicken. The gaze only lasted for a moment before he turned his attention back to Manduul. But it had been more than enough to rattle her. What did that gaze mean? Had he returned with a burning desire to rekindle their extinguished flame, or did he still resent her for what happened?

"My wives will arrange a feast to celebrate your safe return," Manduul said, pulling Mandukhai back to attention. He watched her expectantly.

"Of course, my lord Khan," she said, inclining her head and making the *boqta* headdress chime.

"Good." Manduul rubbed his hands together. "See to it then. I have a few more matters to discuss with these two. Togochi, see that we reward their men for their courage and loyalty."

Togochi bowed deeply before turning to march out. As he left, his gaze flicked from Mandukhai to Unebolod so quickly she was not sure if she had truly seen it.

Yeke rose from her seat like a phantom and drifted toward the door. Mandukhai followed, her back straight, avoiding the penetrating eyes of Unebolod, but in doing so she glimpsed Issama's suspicious gaze locked on Yeke until she was out of sight. What was *he* thinking about? She dismissed it for now, unable to shake Unebolod's presence from her mind.

There had been a time when Mandukhai could read Unebolod's eyes, despite his stoic expression. Perhaps it was the rift between them, or perhaps the passage of time. But she no longer knew what he thought as he looked at her. What Mandukhai did know for certain was this: His presence still struck something deep within her that stirred her desire.

Seeing Mandukhai in the gathering tent brought a rush of emotions back to the surface that Unebolod had expertly pushed behind a wall of duty. He did not have time for such emotion right now. While he had not given Togochi his word that nothing more would ever happen with Mandukhai, Togochi's warning after the miscarriage had been clear enough. As long as Manduul lived, Unebolod could not touch Mandukhai. Distance and his wall of duty were his best defenses.

Manduul had never discovered the truth of the child. That it belonged to Unebolod and not himself. Desperate for justice, Unebolod had spent months attempting in vain to track down the source of the poison. The girl, Sarnia, who had been friends with the serving girl who poisoned Mandukhai, had disappeared nearly a year ago. She has been the only link to the man, Altan, who allegedly gave the serving girl the poisoned tea. Sarnia's disappearance had raised Unebolod's suspicion, but he had been unable to track her down. Altan remained as smoke in the wind, as he had always been.

Unebolod blamed himself for the loss. He had known the child would be in danger from the moment Mandukhai had confessed she was pregnant. He had sworn to protect them. He had failed. He had failed knowing something could happen. He had failed at finding the killer, Altan.

To make up for his failure, Unebolod threw himself into every task he could find to protect the Khan's people. It was the only way he could find to make amends within himself. Duty above all else.

When Issama had proposed the plan to reignite the flame of former glory along the Ming border where their own Mongol people had been subjugated, Unebolod had eagerly heaved himself at the opportunity.

As Mandukhai left the gathering tent today with Yeke to prepare the feast, her gaze met his. Uncertainty shined in her dark eyes: uncertainty and something he could not identify. *She is even more radiant than I remember*, he thought.

Manduul excused Boke and his guards, ordering them to stand outside and close the door behind them. They bowed before stepping out, leaving only Manduul, Issama, and Unebolod. Even the servants left them alone. Unebolod could not be certain how he felt about this turn of events. What could be so urgent Manduul would dismiss even the servants, guards, and Mandukhai?

A fit of coughing overcame Manduul the moment the door closed. He hunched over, then spit a wad of phlegm into a cup. Unebolod tensed as he observed the Khan's state. Manduul drank from another cup, then sank back into his throne with a sigh.

Beside Unebolod, Issama cocked his head and watched Manduul like a hungry bird watches a worm. Issama was far too curious for Unebolod's comfort. Still, he could not help sharing some of the curiosity. Manduul appeared more run-down than he remembered. During the last year, Manduul had clearly lost some weight as well. Perhaps not enough for anyone in the capital to notice, but enough for his eyes to see after a year away.

"I have summoned you back to Mongke Bulag for several reasons," Manduul began. "First and most pressing is the activity among the Oirat. Issama, I know you have connections to the tribe. I need you to use those connections to find out what Paisahan khan is up to. I fear the Oirat khan is preparing to retaliate against either my heir or myself."

"What sort of activity, my lord Khan?" Issama asked.

"Scouts report their forces amassing along our western border, near the Khangai Mountain pass," Manduul replied, dabbing his mouth with a cloth. "I expect they will attack. You will diffuse the situation if possible, and if not, you will organize my *tumens* to protect our people."

Unebolod flinched, then shifted uneasily. "My lord Khan, if he is to organize the *tumens*, what do you need of me?" As *orlok*, it was Unebolod's job to organize the Great Khan's northern *tumens*. A task Unebolod excelled at.

Manduul winced as he shifted in the seat. His age showed more since Unebolod had last seen him. Dark rings made the pools of his almost black eyes even deeper and the corners of his mouth sagged ever so slightly.

"Time, brother."

Unebolod's brows wrinkled in confusion. Time? Organizing the field of battle, supply lines, commanding leaders of the *tumens*. These were all skills Unebolod had sharpened over the years. He was adept at battle strategy and field marshaling. But how did one marshal time?

Manduul waved a hand. "I will explain in a moment." He turned his attention back to Issama.

Unebolod bristled. He could feel the muscles in his shoulders tighten as he clenched his fists. Being dismissed in such a way when he could feel himself losing what little rank he had in the capital crawled under his skin.

"Should the Oirat attack, you will be my *orlok*, Issama. Your council has been fair and wise, and your tactics since arriving in Mongke Bulag will serve our people well in the months to come."

The air escaped Unebolod's lungs as if Manduul had punched him hard in the gut. His chest heaved with anger as he tempered his outrage. Manduul and Issama continued their conversation, but Unebolod's rage muffled his ears. First, Manduul had handed the line of succession over to Bayan—an inept and traitorous boy—after promising it to *him* years before. Now Manduul took away the command Unebolod had held since the beginning. Unebolod knew he should remain silent, but he could hold his tongue no longer. This was a grave insult.

"My lord Khan, have I done you some dishonor?" Unebolod interrupted sharply. "Have I not served you well since the beginning of your khanship? Have I not been a loyal servant to you and the Mongol empire? Why do you give my command to another?"

"Unebolod, I asked you for time," Manduul said with far more patience than Unebolod had a tolerance for at the moment.

"Time." Unebolod scoffed. "What does that even mean, Manduul? I cannot control the rising or setting of the sun or the phases of the moon. No man can control time."

Manduul's fingers rapped on the arm of the throne. "I did not ask you to control it. I ask you to give it." He heaved out a sigh that brought on another surge of coughing.

Rage pumped through Unebolod's veins. All his life, he had lived in Manduul's shadow, obeying his commands, only questioning when Manduul asked him to. He had lost his wife, two children, the khanship, his place as heir, and Mandukhai. Now he had lost the last piece of his life that gave him purpose. Manduul had no need for two *orloks*. His army was not large enough. The oath he had sworn to obey Manduul tasted like bitter, spoiled milk in his mouth.

Unebolod's muscles coiled so taut he thought they might snap. He wanted to draw his sword and strike Manduul down, but his honor would not allow it. Besides, if he killed Manduul here and now, he wouldn't make it out of the gathering tent alive. Maybe he could take Issama out before the new *orlok* could strike him down, but Boke and the rest of Manduul's guard would descend on him. He could only take one or two men before they would kill him.

Manduul spit into the cup again as he righted himself. "Brother, I have a task for you I could not trust in the hands of any other man. It is precisely because of your unwavering loyalty that I place this burden on your shoulders. And I understand it is a lot to ask."

Unebolod quivered with rage. His fingernails bit into his palms as his fists tightened. "What duty could be greater than commanding your armies?"

"When I named Bolkhu, you kneeled before him and swore the same oath you swore to me, to follow him with gers, horses, salt, and blood."

Unebolod did not bother correcting Manduul. He had given Bayan no oath of any sort. Nor would he ever.

"In exchange, I swear this oath to you now," Manduul continued. "In return for your unyielding loyalty to myself and my nephew, should either of us fall and the line of Genghis finally be extinguished, you and your heirs will inherit the khanship line. Tonight, as we feast, I will swear this in front of all of my people, so there is no question who will rule in our stead." Manduul bowed his head toward Unebolod. "I ask you for time. Can you give me this?"

Unebolod's hands fell slack at his sides as the anger dissolved in a surge of shock. Could it be this easy? As long as Bayan had no heirs, Unebolod could at last take hold of the khanship ... and the line would remain with his sons by official decree. Unebolod would only have to dispose of Bayan before he had sons. After Manduul's eventual death, Unebolod could seize everything. Only one issue with this turn of events remained. Manduul still lived, and Unebolod did not know for how long. That gave Bayan plenty of time to produce sons. And at the rate the boy spread his seed, it was a miracle he did not already have a dozen of children.

"Your will, my lord Khan," Unebolod said. His voice was steady once more.

Issama had stiffened through the exchange with his hands folded together before him inside the sleeves of his deel. Unebolod wondered if Issama had designs of his own that this news would unravel.

"Good." Manduul nodded briefly, then adopted a wistful expression, staring past both of them into some distant future. "I have spoken with my shaman frequently. Khosoichi is doing all he can to delay the inevitable, but there is no avoiding it. I am dying."

Unebolod's heart lifted, then plummeted. *Dying?* For years, Unebolod had prayed for this news, but now that Manduul spoke the words, it felt too soon. He hated him and he loved him.

"Are you certain?" Issama asked.

Manduul nodded regrettably. "This is why I summoned you back. In the spring, I will call Bolkhu back and prepare him. Khosoichi believes he can hold off the inevitable for a year or two at most. Bolkhu will need you both during the transition."

Unebolod knew he had to be careful how he chose his words from this moment on. He could say nothing that could be construed as an oath to Bayan. Yet he also needed Manduul to trust him to support Bayan.

Manduul's face shifted to a sterner expression. "Speak of this to no one else. Not even my wives. I will tell them when I can no longer hide the truth from them, but until that day comes, there is no need to worry them unnecessarily when they can do nothing about it. I also do not want to alarm my people or alert our enemies. A line of succession has been established. I just need you two to carry out my final wishes."

Unebolod still couldn't understand why Manduul would remove him from his post as *orlok*, though. He could still serve the Great Khan and the Mongol empire while acting as an heir. Manduul would not dare name Unebolod in the direct line of succession to prevent him from fighting in battle and save him from death. Such an act would dishonor Unebolod. A Mongol who could not fight was not a Mongol worth following.

"Manduul, my men will wonder why I have been demoted," Unebolod said. "What shall I tell them?"

"You misunderstand me, brother," Manduul said. He breathed in a careful breath of fresh air before speaking again. "I have just promoted you. And within the week, you will take your men back to the Khorchin to ensure their full backing when Bolkhu transitions into power. I am depending on you to maintain peace and gather more support from other Lords in the east."

"You're sending me away?" A jolt of shock rock through Unebolod. Leaving would mean he could not see Mandukhai; they would not be able to formulate their own plan. Something else also occurred to him. Unebolod once more clenched his fists so tight the nails bit into his palms.

When Manduul died, Bayan would then be married to Mandukhai. The very idea of that pretentious runt pressing himself into her filled Unebolod with rage and disgust. He could not allow it. Bayan would have to die. But how could he have the prince killed without breaking his oath or turning the tribes against him?

"This is not an exile, Unebolod," Manduul said a bit tersely. "You will gather the *tumens* under your command and support Bolkhu's right at *kurultai* when the time comes. Can you handle this? You will be his heir, as will your children, assuming he has none. You will build your own army to command as *orlok* in his name. I am giving you a great gift, brother. Take it."

"Of course, my lord Khan," Unebolod said, bowing to Manduul. "You honor me." Perhaps this would work to Unebolod's benefit. *I can go east, gather support for myself to be the next Great Khan, and see that Bayan dies in an accident so none of those men support him instead.* Unebolod's plans already began hatching in his mind. This trip would, indeed, be a gift.

Then he would return to Mandukhai as the man she deserved, with his honor intact.

"You have earned it." Manduul shifted and winced again, then reached for a cup of *airag*. "Now, go prepare for the evening's festivities. We have much to celebrate, and much to commemorate."

Both men bowed deeply to their Khan and left.

Unebolod watched Issama float toward the Uyghur section of the capital. He could have sworn he saw a triumphant smirk on the new *orlok's* face.

One week, and he would take his men and return to the Khorchin lands for the first time in four years. One week, and he would lose the chance to see Mandukhai daily; he would lose the opportunity to make amends.

Once Manduul died, though, he would rid them both of Bayan. Then he could have it all.

One week until he left Mongke Bulag.

One year until everything was his at last. The knowledge strengthened his steps.

CHAPTER FIVE

Bones of Genghis

Mandukhai worked tirelessly with the help of Esige, Yeke, Satai, and Jaghan to organize a celebration of the return of the warriors. The work had been extensive, and Mandukhai commanded the women of the tribes in a flurry of activity, much the way an *orlok* would command the field of battle.

She had put Yeke in charge of arranging the Square for the celebration. It was a task Yeke could easily complete without too much thought. Mandukhai didn't trust her to complete anything too complicated.

Nearly an hour before sunset, everything was ready. The animals were butchered and prepared, and the *airag* flowed. It was not as boisterous an event as her wedding or Bayan's name-day, but the men who returned enjoyed the company of women and regaled tales of their time in the south. Musicians played. Wrestling matches sprang up in rings all around Mongke Bulag.

Esige sat at a table nearby, surrounded by girls of less noble birth than herself. Boys punched and shoved each other in attempts to show off for the princess. Mandukhai smiled to herself as she watched two boys wrestle for Esige's attention. Although she couldn't hear what Esige said, the boredom on her face as she spoke sharply to the boys certainly was clear enough. They ceased their wrestling, limbs still tangled, and stared at her in stunned silence.

Once again, Mandukhai envied Esige. She did her best to give the girl every opportunity to become the woman she wanted to be, even if the inevitability of marriage loomed in her future. Esige would be a strong wife and leader. Her husband would need to be a perfect match for such a fierce woman.

This realization drew Mandukhai's gaze to Unebolod. He sat at another table with several of his Khorchin commanders, their heads tucked together as they ate, drank, and conversed. Mandukhai could hardly contain her curiosity. Each of them wore masks of urgency that opposed the jovial nature of the event.

Unebolod looked up, and his gaze met Mandukhai's. Though his face remained as hard as stone, Mandukhai thought she saw a hint of satisfaction in those captivating eyes, which only enhanced her interest.

"Don't you agree, Mandukhai?" Jaghan asked.

Mandukhai started. Jaghan sat beside her, leaning against Togochi for support.

Mandukhai had been so drawn into Unebolod's stare that she had completely missed the conversation. As she fumbled to recover without giving herself away, flustered that she had acted so childishly, Togochi followed her gaze and frowned with his arm around Jaghan's growing waist. His hand rested on her belly. Just seeing the two of them so happy with a child on the way made Mandukhai's heart ache. Could she never have such happiness?

While the distance between herself and Unebolod had grown over the years, Togochi had become a close friend. That Jaghan had become such a good friend of Mandukhai's also helped strengthen her friendship with Togochi. He had become something like a protective older brother to Mandukhai—sometimes annoyingly so. At times, he had even come to her to express frustration over some decision Manduul had made. Though he remained unfailingly loyal to Manduul, Togochi occasionally found himself frustrated with the Khan's behavior. That Togochi trusted Mandukhai enough to vent about Manduul meant more to her than she could ever tell him. Mandukhai also understood that Togochi knew she and Unebolod once had feelings for each other, even if he didn't know the full truth.

"She didn't hear you, my love," Togochi said flatly.

"I'm sorry." Mandukhai dipped her head in shame, setting down her cup of *boal*—honey wine.

Before Jaghan could repeat herself, Manduul rose from his seat and raised a hand. A hush fell over the crowd like ripples away from a tossed pebble. Once Manduul was satisfied he had everyone's attention, he began.

"First, I want to give thanks to Issama for his unending patience and wisdom, and for his role in aiding our Golden Prince as Bolkhu ignites our former glory along the Ming-controlled borders. Your service to your Great Khan and his heir is superior, my friend." Manduul raised his cup of *airag* toward Issama, who nodded his head humbly and raised his own cup.

Mandukhai also offered a small nod of thanks to the Vice Chancellor.

"I hope you will continue to share that wisdom with the Great Khans who follow in my footsteps for years to come." Manduul drew in a rasping breath.

When Mandukhai reached up to him from her seat, he waved her off irritably. She masked her concern with a warm smile. This was not the first time his breathing concerned her. Was he not telling her something?

"While I have not been blessed with sons of my own, I have been blessed to have such loyal and strong brothers. Having men like Bolkhu, Unebolod, Togochi, and Issama in my life has helped fill a void. Thanks to my brothers and lovely wives, my heart is full."

Mandukhai sank back at this, feeling the eyes of tribeswomen on her. Manduul had no heirs because of her and Yeke. While no woman would say as much around either of them, they certainly whispered of the queens' failure to produce an heir. She glanced at Yeke from the corner of her eyes. Yeke drank her *boal*, staring at nothing as if she could not even hear Manduul. Or perhaps she ignored him.

"With each year that passes, I become more aware of our impermanence under the Eternal Blue Sky," Manduul continued. Everyone listened attentively, waiting to see where the Khan was going with this speech. "I will not live forever. The line of Genghis Khan has weakened, but the wolves are still strong. Someday, Bolkhu will take my place." He chuckled as he said, "And hopefully by then he has finally settled down and produced sons of his own."

The congregation laughed at Manduul's joke. Bayan had quite a reputation around Mongke Bulag and had shown little interest in marriage or commitment of any sort—aside from his commitment to Manduul. Miraculously, none of the women Bayan bedded had conceived a child, either. Mandukhai did not understand how Bayan accomplished that particular feat.

"But no one can say what the future will bring," Manduul continued, sobering slightly. He took a drink from his cup, then scanned the crowd. "Step forward, Lord Unebolod."

Mandukhai's breath caught in her throat. All of this felt familiar in a way that she couldn't quite place.

Unebolod rose from his seat and moved with confidence through the crowd to stand before Manduul. For only a moment, Unebolod cast a glance past Manduul at her. This time she was certain she saw satisfaction in his eyes. *He knows what is happening already,* she thought as Unebolod dropped to one knee before the Great Khan.

Manduul set down his cup and placed a hand on the sword at his hip. "Let no man or woman present forget this moment. You are all witness to the will of your Great Khan, and our royal blood. You have all pledged your lives to me and to my heir, Bolkhu Jinong. You will all carry that pledge over from this day to Lord Unebolod, my brother and Lord of the Khorchin."

Mandukhai's eyes widened. A collective gasp rippled through the crowd gathered. No one dared to speak, though. It was as if the very air around them hung on Manduul's commandment.

"Should the royal line of our illustrious father, Genghis, die, should we produce no more heirs and perish from this earth, under the Eternal Blue Sky and with the divine authority as a descendant of Genghis Khan, I hereby install the line of Genghis's brother, Khasar, your royal khans. Lord Unebolod, do you accept this divine burden?"

Unebolod bowed his head before Manduul and spoke in a strong, clear voice. "I humbly accept the gracious offer my Great Khan has made on behalf of myself and my sons who would follow me."

"May you and your sons serve and protect me and Bolkhu, as well as his heirs, until such a time no heir of Genghis remains." Manduul placed his hand on Unebolod's head.

Mandukhai reeled in her seat, her head swimming as Unebolod rose. This announcement was everything Unebolod could have ever wanted, and if Manduul, Bayan, and any of Bayan's sons died, Unebolod would not have to fight for the title of Great Khan. It would simply be his to claim rightfully and lawfully. *And if Manduul ever dies, we can rid ourselves of Bayan and have a clear path to everything we ever wanted!* It could not possibly be this easy.

But why would Manduul name a second heir to the khanship? She glanced his way for a moment as he settled beside her with a huff. His eyes seemed darker than normal, clouded by some great secret. Yet they also shined with a light of hope. Mandukhai could not understand this decision. *The* boal *has gone to my head,* she thought.

Men and women cheered Unebolod's name. Music lifted high and jovial into the air like a bird. Drinks flowed and a great burden lifted from the capital. Mandukhai could not help mirroring that sense of hope as she downed her cup of *boal* and held it out for a refill.

Dancers began the traditional *biyelgee* dance in the center of the square as the horse fiddles rose to a crescendo. Mandukhai smiled and clapped along between drinks.

A voice echoed in her head, interrupting the jovial spirit with its dark, hard tone. *Only the one who carries the spirit can reunite the One Nation. Only he of my bone will have the might to hold it.* Her heart hammered in sudden fear. The drink in her hand nearly slipped from her fingers as alarm slammed against her chest. Mandukhai glanced around her, but no one looked her way.

It had been the voice of Genghis, speaking to her again, reminding her of his warning. He had spoken those words in her vision three years ago. A vision she had not told another soul about. For Genghis to come to a woman in such a vision was unheard of. No man would believe her.

Surely that warning did not mean Unebolod was unworthy. It couldn't. Unebolod descended from the line of Khasar, Genghis Khan's closest brother. Khasar and Genghis were of the same mother and father, which made Unebolod a descendant in his own right. It could not possibly mean that Unebolod, as Great Khan, would not have the strength to hold the Mongols together.

CHAPTER SIX

Sincerity and Sycophants

As the night wore on, Mandukhai heard the news that the Khorchin would return to their lands, led by Unebolod. The news had ripped out her heart. He was abandoning her again, and it felt like the deepest betrayal she had ever known. She tried to keep her spirits up and used *boal* to dull the pain, but as she watched women fawn over him—women who hardly had glanced his way before he had been confirmed for the line of succession—Mandukhai's anger flared, fueled by the honey wine.

Her face warmed from drinking, but she did her best not to show anyone else the anger or pain burning inside of her. Instead, she spent the evening conversing with Jaghan, who could hardly move with her pregnant stomach slowing her down. For hours, the two women chatted as Mandukhai watched woman after woman flirt with Unebolod.

Manduul had fallen deep into the drink nearly an hour ago, drunkenly groping at serving girls and making lewd jokes with whichever of his men were near enough to listen. Mandukhai could not have cared less what he did with himself that night. Her only concern was with Unebolod.

"I hear Lord Alayitung intends to offer his daughter's hand to Unebolod," Jaghan whispered conspiratorially, oblivious to Mandukhai's pain.

Lord Alayitung was a commander of the Borjigin, and his daughter was a dog. Unebolod would never accept. Yet, as an heir to the line of succession, Unebolod would now need to marry and have sons to carry on the legacy. And Alayitung was a good man of Borjigin blood. As ugly as his daughter was, Unebolod would have Borjigin blood in his children. Something Mandukhai could never offer.

As Jaghan mentioned this, a pretty, young Khorlod girl who had been chatting with Unebolod placed her hand on his arm. Her brilliant smile lit up the dark. Mandukhai wanted to punch that smile off her pretty face.

"It's a suitable match," Togochi said of Alayitung's daughter. He sat on Jaghan's other side, never far from her unless duty called him away.

Unebolod's stoic expression broke as he responded to whatever the girl said. His arm twitched where the girl's hand rested, causing the girl's face to heat. The corner of his mouth twitched upward in a way that made Mandukhai's heart hammer, and the *boal* went straight to her head.

"Excuse me," Mandukhai said politely to her two friends. "I need air."

Togochi's thick, bushy brows knitted together. For just a second, his gaze flicked to Unebolod, who eased the girl's hand off his arm. Mandukhai quickly looked away from Unebolod, aware of how hot her face was at the moment.

Jaghan rocked to her feet with Togochi's help. "I could use a walk as well. I will go with you."

Mandukhai nodded, then the two women strolled out of the Square arm in arm. Mandukhai let Jaghan guide her along, not really caring where they went, as long as she didn't have to see other women pawing on Unebolod. As they left, she felt his eyes follow her. Mandukhai held her chin high, hoping she didn't stagger as everything spun. Mandukhai drank more *boal* than she realized.

Jaghan made heroic efforts to engage Mandukhai in civil conversation. Not wanting to insult her friend, Mandukhai listened.

They passed a bonfire where the older children gathered—boys and girls all coming of age for marriage. Mandukhai thought it a miraculous thing that they all gravitated toward each other. Near a knot of boys, Esige stood tall and strong among them. Dirt covered her silk deel. Mandukhai and Jaghan watched for a moment as a boy advanced on Esige in a wrestler's pose. He reached for her arm, and Esige allowed him to grab it. But as he pulled her toward him, she used his momentum against him, swinging his body around and slamming a flat palm into his back, sending him sprawling on the ground.

"You were a bad influence on her, I think," Jaghan teased.

"I think she's glorious," Mandukhai replied, swelling with drunken pride.

The two women carried on, pausing to listen to a song at another fire. The song's melody placed further strain on her aching heart. The lyrics brought tears to her eyes. Two lovers, torn amid a war, saying a passionate farewell before he rode off to war and she never saw him again.

"Are you alright, Mandukhai?" Jaghan asked, startled as she turned her gaze to Mandukhai.

Sniffling, Mandukhai scrubbed the tears from her cheeks. "Fine."

A few others noticed her reaction to the song, staring. Mandukhai offered a friendly smile their way. "The combination of *boal* and beautiful lyrics. It's a lovely song."

The musicians nodded in thanks, not breaking rhythm. Before the music could affect her any further, Mandukhai turned away from the fire and headed toward home.

Along the way to Mandukhai's ger, Jaghan prattled on about her son and the upcoming birth of their next child. It only served as a bitter reminder of what Mandukhai had lost. And with the *boal* fogging her mind, Mandukhai momentarily lost her temper.

"I've heard enough about the baby, Jaghan," Mandukhai finally snapped. "I'm happy for you and Togochi, but I ..." Mandukhai choked off the sentence, unable to finish.

Jaghan adopted a sympathetic expression. "I'm sorry. How selfish of me. I should have known better."

Of all the women in camp, only Esige and Jaghan truly understood the depth of Mandukhai's sorrow over the miscarriage. Even if they did not know the truth about the father. Mandukhai had shared her pain with them in private a few times over the years.

For a while, she and Jaghan carried on in silence. As they passed some gers along the way to her own, Mandukhai could hear the grunts and cries of pleasure coming from within. The memory of her night under the birch tree with Unebolod flooded back, quickly chased away by the pitiful look of anguish he gave her after losing the child, then by the careless detachment in his eyes as he abruptly said goodbye before riding south with Bayan. Mandukhai shuddered at the memory.

Mandukhai wasn't really certain how they went from standing beside one ger to sitting inside of her own. She had simply drifted along with Jaghan chatting away, oblivious to the world. The next thing she knew, she was seated on her bed as Jaghan prepared salted tea to help sober her. Mandukhai didn't have the heart to tell her she didn't want to be sober.

Instead, she stumbled to her feet and grabbed a skin of black *airag* she had made for Manduul. He had his fill for now. She needed more.

Jaghan glanced over as Mandukhai fell back on the edge of the bed, taking a greedy drink from the strong alcohol. She made no comment as she continued preparing tea.

"You are fortunate, Jaghan," Mandukhai said, leaning back and tossing her royal *boqta* on the floor carelessly. "Togochi loves you." Her words slurred together a bit, but she hardly cared. Grief consumed her mind. She took another greedy drink of the *airag*. "And you got to marry him and have his sons. Not all of us get so lucky."

Jaghan pressed a cool cloth to Mandukhai's neck. "Manduul is good to you. And I see how he looks at you. He loves you."

Mandukhai snorted. "He loves his precious prince." Tears rolled down her cheeks. She swiped them away in alarm, unaware that she had started crying. Between the *boal* and black *airag*, she was quickly losing control of her wits. Something she never did, yet tonight heartily accepted. "It doesn't matter, anyway. I can never forgive him."

Jaghan frowned as she returned to the tea kettle. "Forgive him. For what?"

"For raping me and hitting me." Mandukhai touched the place on her cheek where he had left that mark four years ago. Sometimes she still remembered the pain of that blow to the face. Few women would call what he did rape, since he was her husband, but Mandukhai could not see it as anything else. She had refused him, told him no, yet he persisted.

This confession caught Jaghan off guard, making her spill hot tea on her hand. She yelped, nearly dropping the pot. Mandukhai hardly noticed the other woman's plight. Her thoughts had drifted to other places. The present moment felt more surreal than the past.

"When did he do this?" Jaghan asked, sliding down to sit beside Mandukhai with a cloth wrapped around her own hand.

"After we married." Mandukhai drank more *airag*. It burned down her throat. She coughed and sputtered for a moment. "He thought I desired another. His *orlok*."

"Unebolod?" Jaghan's eyes burst open with bright light, thrilled with the secret gossip. "Did you?"

Mandukhai's gaze fell on the bow that still hung beside the door. Her vision blurred as tears filled her eyes. Jaghan was a friend—her closest confidant outside of Esige. They often called each other sisters. Mandukhai had enough alcohol tonight that she did not even hesitate in her drunken state to tell Jaghan the truth. "Yes. I never told Manduul, though. He assumed on his own, and in a jealous rage, he ... hit me and forced himself on me."

The memory of that encounter haunted her still, making it impossible to love Manduul, while also equally hard to trust him completely. Mandukhai drew her knees up to her chest and hugged them tightly. Jaghan placed a hand on her shoulder. Mandukhai jumped, nearly swinging at her in alarm.

"Sorry," Jaghan murmured as she pulled away. "Has he done anything like that since?"

"I stopped resisting," Mandukhai said. A lump in her throat made her voice croak as she spoke. "He can't force himself on me if I don't resist."

Jaghan's expression made it clear to Mandukhai, even in her drunken haze, that she had never experienced such a thing, that she couldn't even fathom it. *Of course she wouldn't understand*, Mandukhai thought bitterly. *Togochi would never hurt her. He adores her.*

"Do you love him?" Jaghan asked softly, glancing at the doorway.

"No." Mandukhai flinched. Her gaze darted to the door as well, afraid Manduul stood there now. "I could never love someone who did that to me."

"No, I ..." Jaghan shifted. It took a moment to adjust her pregnant body around to the new position. "I mean Unebolod. You were staring at him all night. Do you love him?"

Panic rose in Mandukhai's chest as she realized through her drunken haze that she had said too much. "Jaghan, you can never tell anyone. Ever. Manduul will kill us if he thinks anything has happened."

"Has it?" The curious glimmer in Jaghan's eyes revealed her genuine curiosity.

"I ... I can't." Mandukhai dropped her face into her hands. "He's leaving and ..." Once the emotions poured out of her, Mandukhai couldn't stop herself anymore. "That will be the end of it."

Jaghan pulled Mandukhai's head toward her chest and stroked her hair, holding her close. "You poor thing. To love someone and be unable to be loved by someone. I cannot even imagine. If Togochi ..." She pressed her cheek to the top of Mandukhai's head. "It would kill me inside."

For a while they stayed that way, Jaghan stroking her hair and murmuring reassurances as Mandukhai finally released the tears. It felt good to let the emotions out. She had bottled them up for so long. When she pulled herself together again, Jaghan used the cloth from Mandukhai's neck to wipe the tears from her cheeks.

"You have to tell him, Mandukhai. Before he leaves. I have seen the way he looks at you. So has Togochi. There's a tenderness in his gaze."

"It won't change anything."

Jaghan tensed and lowered her voice. "It will if Manduul dies."

Mandukhai dipped her chin to her chest. For over four years she had waited for him to die, fulfilling her duty as his wife to the best of her ability. Short of killing him herself, she didn't know that he ever would die, and she could never kill him. She would never kill a Khan.

"I promise never to breathe a word of this to anyone. Not even my husband," Jaghan said, brushing stray hairs out of Mandukhai's face affectionately. "We are friends, like sisters. But you must promise to tell Unebolod how you feel before he leaves."

Mandukhai hesitated.

Jaghan took her face in a fierce grasp. "Please. You deserve better, and Manduul cannot possibly live forever." The intensity of Jaghan's instance, the affection on her face, made Mandukhai believe she meant it. She would not speak of it, and she firmly believed Mandukhai deserved better.

It would feel good to get the truth out in the open with Unebolod before he left. Mandukhai didn't see how it would make a difference; however, it was better than doing nothing. She couldn't allow him to leave believing she hated him.

"Okay."

"No. Promise me," Jaghan insisted.

"I promise."

"Good." Jaghan released her grip and rocked her pregnant body to reach the edge of the bed before awkwardly standing and making her way to the bucket of water. "Now let's get you freshened up and sober before Manduul arrives."

Mandukhai did not protest. Jaghan had been a genuine friend, like a sister, since the moment they met. It had been a natural fusing of their souls together. Hopefully, she could trust Jaghan to keep this most dangerous of secrets.

Unebolod had tried several times to slip away and speak with Mandukhai after Manduul's announcement, but the excitement of another heir had caught too much attention. Men crowded around to congratulate him, followed by a firm prayer for the strength of the royal Borjigin blood-line before him. It felt like a backhanded compliment to offer him praise in one breath and wish that new position would never come to pass in the next.

Women had pulled him aside in conversations, most of them single women or mothers of daughters old enough to marry. Again, they all felt false to him. The women wanted his position and the wealth that would bring to their families; he could easily see very few had an actual interest in him. Of those who showed genuine interest, Unebolod found he had none to return, though he did humor them to avoid insulting anyone.

He had given his heart away years ago. Though he knew he should marry and strengthen his line, especially now that he would become Great Khan, he waited. Manduul would die soon. Once he killed Bayan, Unebolod could finally propose marriage to Mandukhai. What were one or two more years after they had waited four already?

By the time he could slip away from the festivities, Mandukhai had already retired to her ger for the evening. He approached and nodded to the guards, then noted Manduul's dogs lying outside her door. His heart fell into his stomach. He had not touched her skin in years. Perhaps Man-dukhai had accepted Manduul and warmed to him. Perhaps she loved him now. Either way, Unebolod knew he could not intrude, just as Manduul had not interfered with his marriage to Odsar.

The next day, Unebolod began organizing his men and their families for the trek back to Khorchin lands. Some of his men were too young to remember their own tribe. As far as they were concerned, the men of this *tumen*, along with their wives and children, were their tribe.

Unebolod himself had not visited home for four years. That night, he dreamed of riding his strongest horse in the foothills of the northern Khingan Mountains, of walking along the rolling hills beside the Kherlen River. And there on the banks of the river, he and Mandukhai renewed their lost passion in the tall grass. He woke in the morning wondering if she would join him there when Manduul passed.

Duties to prepare for the journey home consumed his days until he found himself too tired to do more than collapse into sleep. Once, he was certain he saw Mandukhai nearby, watching him work, but when he turned to call her, no one was there. Had he imagined her presence? There had been a time when he could sense her nearby before she had even breathed a word.

Surely, she must have known he was leaving, yet the fourth day came and went, and she hadn't approached him. If she still cared for him, she would have found some excuse to visit him, as she had always done in the past. Yet by the end of the fifth day, he gave up hope she would even say goodbye. *Maybe it's better that way*, he thought with a grimace.

Issama visited several times over those five days, though Unebolod wished he wouldn't. Manduul trusted Issama, and the new *orlok* had done nothing Unebolod could point to as deceptive. Still, something about Issama didn't settle right with him. Bigirsen had sent Issama to help Manduul assert his position as Khan, but Bigirsen did nothing without some benefit to himself. Perhaps that was why Unebolod could not trust Issama completely.

"It will be good to return to your homelands, Lord Unebolod," Issama said.

The two of them stood beside a cart that had been filled with grain for the trip. One of Unebolod's men calculated the supplies as Unebolod waited, watching as another cart rolled to the eastern edge of the capital, close to where his *tumen* camped. The carts would begin the journey that night with a *jagan* of one hundred men to guard them. Tomorrow, his riders would easily catch up.

Issama examined a cart as it lumbered past, piled with silver and silk sent by Manduul to the Khorchin khan for his loyalty these past years. Unebolod swore he could see greed in those narrow eyes.

"I have found that returning to my homeland is revitalizing," Issama said.

Unebolod had no interest in making conversation and sought any excuse to escape. "I won't be there long. Manduul has given me a task, and I will see it done. In the spring, I will begin the journey south to visit the other eastern tribes."

"Perhaps you will finally find a wife along the way," Issama said. His tone suggested humor, and pleasure shined in his eyes.

Unebolod did not find it funny. Still, Unebolod could not keep from twisting a knife of superiority in Issama, so he said, "Yes. I suppose, as Bolkhu's heir, I should ensure that my line continues. Otherwise, where will the Mongol Nation be?"

Issama nodded in affable agreement. "I suppose, if both you and Bolkhu fail to continue the line, there will always be Bigirsen's son, Nemeku, who is, after all, born of a daughter of the royal line."

Unebolod resisted the urge to spit at Issama's feet for even suggesting a Uyghur Great Khan. He would do everything in his power to ensure that never came to pass. Borogchin had been a pleasant enough girl, and she was a princess of the Borjigin, but even she would agree that her child was not an heir.

"If it comes to that, I won't be alive for it to matter to me, should the Mongols become so desperate," Unebolod said. "Excuse me, Issama. I have a lot to see to before dark."

Issama dipped his head respectfully. "May your journey be blessed."

Unebolod grunted as he walked away. In just a few words, Issama always crawled under his skin. Yet he had never been able to tell if his own comments did the same. How had they survived a year together along the border?

He glanced once more at the horizon, shielding his eyes from the setting sun. It was the last sunset he would see over Mongke Bulag for some time. Perhaps, in the dead of the night, he could ride out to the birch tree. If Mandukhai wouldn't come to him, he could at least visit their favorite place one more time before he left.

CHAPTER SEVEN

Bitter Departure

After Mandukhai woke the morning following her confession to Jaghan, she worried that she had said too much. If Jaghan told her husband anything of what Mandukhai had said, it could be the end of both herself and Unebolod. In fear, she had ventured to Jaghan's ger to speak, but could not make herself knock or speak. Instead, she spent the next few days holding her breath, praying Jaghan had kept her mouth closed as she promised.

Thankfully, no one seemed the wiser. Jaghan only hinted that she remembered when she saw Mandukhai heading back from another failed attempt to speak with Unebolod. Jaghan cast Mandukhai a raised brow from a distance, but said nothing about it.

Mandukhai had been restless the night before the Khorchin were to depart. She had promised to speak to Unebolod, but hadn't summoned the courage, no matter what Jaghan might have thought. Twice she went to him, only to stop and observe from a distance as he carried out his preparations with his usual stoicism. She stood, frozen in place by fear of rejection, unable to take another step both times. Perhaps it had been too long. Perhaps they could no longer bridge the rift between them.

The second time she observed him, her feet almost moved. She had come close to mustering the nerve to confess her true feelings and desires. As her weight shifted, Genghis Khan's warning thundered in her mind, casting a cloud of doubt on her actions once more. Mandukhai knew the fate of the wolf was in her hands. Did that mean she could never have what she wanted? Did that mean she and Unebolod could never be together?

Genghis had promised her a litter of wolves. Unebolod was not a true wolf—not like Bayan. That didn't mean he was not of the blood. He was a descendant of Genghis's brother Khasar. That gave him royal blood ... didn't it? And then she also remembered the vision of Bayan dead in the desert. Was he about to die? Would she have his sons before that happened? Or would Unebolod's sons be the new wolves of the Borjigin? So much uncertainty once more turned her away from Unebolod.

On the last night before Unebolod's departure, Mandukhai stepped out of her ger. Her two night guards—Arslan and Torgus—stood at attention, but she hardly noticed them. Her attention fixed on something else.

A brown ring of long-dead grass was the only trace of Unebolod's ger that remained. She had known the structure had been dismantled and packed up earlier in the day, but as it happened so close to her own door where she could hear the men talking as they disassembled it, she had hidden inside to avoid facing the inevitable.

The ring represented the hole she felt in her heart. For a moment, Mandukhai paused at the edge, as if simply being near the space offered some solace. There would be no avoiding this vacancy. Unebolod's ger had been so close to her own that she saw this gaping void the moment she stepped out her door. She would continue to see it until the grass sprang back to life in the spring to erase the memory of him.

At first, Mandukhai did not know where she was headed when she stepped outside. Arslan and Torgus followed her until she waved them back. "Do you really believe that, with so many of the Khan's men around, anyone would dare to attack me? Take your leave for the evening. I'm sure your wives would appreciate your company."

They exchanged uneasy glances. Then Torgus bowed his head to her as he spoke. "My Lady, if you were harmed, and we were not there to guard you, the Khan would take our lives."

Mandukhai sighed in irritation. She knew they spoke the truth and did not want to be responsible for their deaths. "Fine. At least give me space. You can reach attackers well enough with a bow from a distance. I'm going for a ride."

"In the dark?" Arslan asked.

"Am I incapable of handling my mount?" Mandukhai asked tersely.

"No, my Lady," Arslan and Torgus murmured in unison.

Satisfied, Mandukhai headed toward the corral where Dust grazed with the rest of the Khan's horses. She sent Arslan back to fetch her saddle and blanket from her ger, allowing Torgus to accompany her. Arslan returned in just a few minutes.

She strapped the saddle in place and ran her fingertips along the dragons on the pommel. Manduul had given her this saddle and this horse, but Mandukhai had later discovered that it had been a gift from Unebolod. He had taken great care in seeing to the details on her saddle, and over the years, those very details became a reminder of what they'd shared and what she had lost.

Dust nuzzled her shoulder, and Mandukhai stroked his nose.

"We have come a long way together, my friend," she murmured to the stallion. "But we still have far to go."

In no time, the three of them were mounted.

Arslan held Mandukhai's bow and quiver out to her. "If you insist we ride further back, I thought it best if you also have your bow," Arslan explained.

She reached for them with solemn hands. Yet another gift from Unebolod. One that matched the saddle. He had given it to her hoping she would realize who had truly arranged for the mount and saddle; it hadn't taken her too long.

"Thank you, Arslan." Mandukhai turned east and kicked Dust into a trot.

Torgus and Arslan rode far enough back that she could hear their mounts' hooves, but not near enough for her to feel like a prisoner. Even if she didn't want them there, their presence was reassuring.

Dust wove through the maze of gers toward the east, through the Khorchin camp. Or what remained of it. Mandukhai was uncertain where Unebolod would be, or if he was even what she sought tonight. Her gaze lingered on a few of the gers, though most were already en route toward Khorchin lands. Khorchin riders lay under the stars, sleeping on the ground as if they were safely nestled in their beds. She found the men's ability to sleep anywhere intriguing.

As they passed the last groups of slumbering men—drawing only a few sleepy-eyed gazes—Mandukhai kicked Dust into a full gallop. They had traveled this path hundreds of times in the day and at night. Mandukhai knew this land as well as she knew herself—perhaps better. She knew where the hills crested and fell, where hazards might trip Dust or sprain a leg. And as they sprinted forward at top speed, Mandukhai glanced back over her shoulder. Torgus and Arslan fell farther behind. Their mounts were strong, but not as fast as Dust.

Without consciously choosing her destination, Mandukhai rode toward her favorite birch tree. The years had not been kind to it, and the scars deepened as it had attempted to heal old wounds. Mandukhai sympathized with the tree's plight, often feeling the same of her own scars. Tonight, of all nights, she wanted to sit on the grass and feel the peeling bark press into her back. She wanted to close her eyes beneath its embracing branches and remember happier days.

The moon shone brightly tonight. In the distance, she spotted a tall, broad-shouldered figure beneath the tree. Mandukhai stopped just as his ghostly silhouette entered her view. Dust slowed swiftly, prancing in a circle as she jerked the reins to hold him back. Only one man would be waiting there under that tree. Her heart leaped into her throat and hammered against her chest. Her head swam with excitement and terror.

Arslan and Torgus reined in beside her. As Torgus squinted into the darkness to determine who waited, Arslan strung an arrow and prepared the shot.

"Don't." Mandukhai placed a hand on his arm, drawing it down.

Arslan loosened the tension on the string and turned an uncertain gaze on her.

"I know who this is. He won't harm me."

"My Lady—"

Arslan began his protest, but Mandukhai barreled over him. "You will trust my judgment. Lord Unebolod would no sooner harm me than the Khan." Mandukhai nudged Dust into a slow canter. "Stay here. Keep watch. Do not engage him."

Even in the dark, Mandukhai could tell Unebolod watched them, aware of their presence. As she approached, his gaze came into focus beyond her at her guards. They remained far enough away that they could see her, but not close enough to hear.

"They will leave us," Mandukhai said.

"I should have known you would come here." Unebolod shifted forward a touch, as if he wanted to go to her, but his feet remained fixed in place.

"Is that why you came?" Mandukhai asked as she dismounted and allowed Dust to graze on the grass beneath the tree.

"I don't know why I came here."

Mandukhai's chest tightened. She hadn't known her reason, either. It was as if fate had inexorably pulled her to this place tonight. Perhaps it had done the same to him. Perhaps this conversation was inevitable. Perhaps this was a sign that she was right, that he could be Great Khan.

The two of them remained fixed in silence that flooded the air like water in a bucket. Neither moved toward the other, frozen in place by some unseen force. Mandukhai had never felt such a painful silence in her life. She feared she would drown in it. Over the past five days, she had turned what she wanted to say over in her mind again and again, churning the words like milk into butter. Now, all the careful planning evaporated as if it had never existed. No words could express how she truly felt: love, fear, hope, helplessness, passion, duty, grief, joy, sorrow. None of these words conjured cohesive thoughts.

A breeze blew between them, shaking leaves from the branches to flutter down as more kicked up from the ground. They swirled in a chaotic mass akin to Mandukhai's own mind. Once again, she felt as if the tree was trying to speak to her, understanding her plight. The breeze itself symbolized the gap that had grown between them. Mandukhai bowed her head, her hair falling in waves over her shoulders.

"Have a safe journey home, Unebolod," Mandukhai said, unable to summon more fitting words for the moment. She let out a shaky breath as she turned toward Dust. Standing here a moment longer would be the worst sort of torture.

"That is it?" Unebolod's sharp tone seized Mandukhai as surely as any iron grip. "After all this time, after everything, you have nothing more to say? Have we come back to such beginnings at the end?"

Mandukhai dipped her chin to her chest as tears flooded her eyes. *No! I have so much more to say, but none of it matters*, she thought. Her stomach churned. She pressed her palms against it as her hands shook. She drank in breaths that didn't quite fill her lungs.

Unebolod's boots rustled the leaves on the ground as he approached behind her. He stopped far enough away that she could not feel the heat from his body or the breath of his words. His touch didn't fall on her body. She wanted to turn, to face him, but she found herself unable to move.

"I cannot leave again with this pain between us," he said.

Mandukhai struggled to swallow the lump that swelled in her throat. "Yet you will," she whispered. "As you have done before."

"Mandukhai, now more than ever, I need your patience."

Patience? The very concept of waiting sickened Mandukhai. How long would she wait for her true purpose, for what she wanted and deserved? For him? She spun around, surprised to discover Unebolod closer than she had expected. The gap remained between them, but he stood close enough for her to see the agony in his eyes.

"You are abandoning me." Mandukhai felt her pulse quicken and her temper rise. It took a conscious effort to take deep breaths to calm down, but it didn't work well. "Again."

He flinched. "Abandoning you?"

"What else do you call this?" Her hand shook violently as she swung it toward the east.

"Duty."

Mandukhai whimpered as if he struck her. "Duty. Always duty!"

"Do you think this is easy for me?" Unebolod snapped. "Do you think I don't feel your grief, your pain? Mandukhai, you hold a power over me unlike any other. A power that could destroy our honor—destroy us both completely." He edged closer, but still did not touch her. "I have tried moving on, but you consume me. You have taken me, a mighty warrior, and reduced me to a love-struck boy. I am at your mercy."

"Then don't go. I need you!" Mandukhai's voice quivered. How had they gone three years without speaking like this? "Is that what you want to hear? I fear I cannot survive with that void in my heart."

Again, silence fell. Mandukhai didn't want to cry in front of him, but she found it impossible to hold back the flood of tears once they broke free. She gulped quivering breaths as the tears poured down her cheeks.

He wouldn't stay. Unebolod's hand twitched, half-rising before falling uselessly at his side. His inability to comfort her, even now, only enhanced her sense of loss. His gaze slid past her over her shoulder, reminding Mandukhai that her guards stood nearby. With some relief, she realized he didn't touch her because they were watching. For the two of them to speak was no strange thing. But if he touched her ...

"I have never known a woman like you, Mandukhai," Unebolod said. Tenderness and sorrow bled into his voice. "You are capable. You know what you must do to protect yourself. You don't need me. I'm not sure you ever did."

Didn't need him! The words filled her with anger. How could he dare say such a thing? Mandukhai's muscles tensed as she ground her teeth in fury. Did he not know her at all? Were they so distant now that he truly thought she didn't need him? All the resentment from him distancing from her since the miscarriage boiled over.

"How dare you!" Mandukhai slapped Unebolod hard enough to leave a red handprint on his cheek. Realizing the guards were watching this confrontation, she held up her hand to keep them from riding to her aid. "You are all I ever needed."

The pained expression on Unebolod's face, the shock in his eyes, burned into her soul.

"Ride, Lord Unebolod," Mandukhai said, her voice thick with heartache and anger. "In the name of your Great Khan, do your duty. No matter the cost. It is no less than you have always done." He would leave again. Abandoning her. Mandukhai understood now where his loyalty would always remain. She would never mean more to him than his duty.

"I will return for you."

"It will not matter. You have chosen your path, Unebolod, and it has forced me to choose mine." If he would leave to do his duty, she would stay and do her own.

Unebolod bowed his head and closed his eyes. The slope of his shoulders shifted downward. Several long moments passed in silence before Mandukhai huffed in disgust, turned on her heels, and stormed away, mounting Dust's saddle.

"Manduul is dying," Unebolod said in a hushed, desperate voice.

The words had their desired effect. Mandukhai turned Dust toward Unebolod, her chest heaving as she wondered if she heard him correctly. Perhaps this was a trick. Another way for him to buy a moment of her time.

"We all are," she said sharply.

"No, Mandukhai." He strode toward Dust, gripping the reins and placing the stallion between himself and the guards like a shield. "I mean he is dying. Now. He told me as much the day I returned."

Mandukhai didn't believe him. It was too much to hope for. After all these years, her prayer would be answered. Yet, if she thought about Manduul's behavior lately, it made sense. The coughing fits. The reduced appetite. But Manduul always had an excuse. "Why would he not tell me?"

"He doesn't want to worry you unduly, but he is preparing for his death." Unebolod glanced over Dust's neck at the guards, who were but silhouettes in the distant dark. "You cannot speak of this. You can't let him know you are aware. He will kill me for betraying his trust."

"How long?"

"A year. Maybe two." He placed a hand over hers on the reins, and she saw the hope and desperation in the depths of his soul. "I will gather other tribes to support me and come back for you. Please. Just be patient."

It was all Mandukhai could have hoped for. But if Unebolod gathered the tribes to support him over Bayan in *kurultai*, it could end in war. Perhaps this was what Genghis Khan had warned her about. Sorrow pressed against her heart. No matter what she wanted, she could not betray Genghis. "But Bayan is the heir."

Unebolod recoiled. "Does that mean we cannot be together? When Manduul dies, I will convince Bayan to release you from the bonds of marriage."

Perhaps that could be enough. But something told her Unebolod would never bend the knee to Bayan. And Bayan could not hold this fractured empire together on his own. *The strength of a man comes from the strength of the woman who guides him,* Genghis had said in the vision. Mandukhai opened her mouth to tell Unebolod, but she knew that the spirits were selective about whom they chose to speak with. She could not tell him. Not unless the circumstances required it. Not yet.

"Bayan will need me to help guide him," Mandukhai said, hating the words as they escaped her lips. She wanted Unebolod. She *needed* him. Surely Genghis had not meant for her to marry Bayan instead.

"He will have men to do that," Unebolod said impatiently.

"Men I do not trust." Mandukhai pictured Issama whispering into Bayan's ear, steering him into danger and war. Why Issama conjured such an image, Mandukhai had no reasonable explanation for.

"You would choose *him*? Now who is abandoning whom?" Unebolod stepped back, his jaw setting in anger.

"No. I am doing my duty." Mandukhai threw his own words back in his face.

Again, Unebolod recoiled as if she had slapped him. Why was it that every conversation they had turned into an argument these past three years?

Unebolod's spine stiffened. He nodded tightly, as if accepting her answer. How could he not? It had been the same excuse he had given her just moments before.

"I *will* return," he said firmly. "I swear this to you. And when I do, I will light your fire for you. Even if I have to wait until my bones are old. My blood will always burn young for you."

Mandukhai's heart leaped into her throat. The lighting of the fire was a sacred promise between lovers that they would be together, consumed in passion, and start the family they dreamed of. Swearing such an oath to her was not something to take lightly. Mandukhai realized undoubtedly that he did still love her, despite all that had happened between them. He would wait for her and take no other brides before her. No matter how long he had to wait.

As Mandukhai rode back toward Mongke Bulag, she felt a flicker of hope that perhaps, once she completed her duty, they could at last be together.

But to do that, Mandukhai would have to be certain Genghis Khan's warning about his bones did not include Unebolod as a danger. How she would determine that, Mandukhai did not know. However, if she could, she would find a way to be free of Bayan for good. Then she could finally have all she had wanted.

Until she could verify Unebolod's legitimacy in the eyes of the spirits, until Manduul died, she knew that duty would keep them apart.

Chapter Eight

Home

Leaving Mongke Bulag had been a bitter affair for Unebolod. As his tribesmen rode away, he struggled to not look back. For years he had remained at Manduul's side unless he rode out on campaign in the Khan's name. This was different, though. Unebolod likely would not see Manduul alive again. Yet it was not Manduul who caused the stone to sink into his gut.

The thumps of thousands of hooves and the lumbering creak of a handful of remaining carts had drowned out all other sounds. As his *tumen* reached the final hilltop east of Mongke Bulag, just before the capital disappeared from sight, Unebolod's instincts drew his attention toward the crest of another hill.

Two riders sat in saddles on that distant hill. Though their features were hard to distinguish at such a distance, the shapes of the two and their hair rippling on the breeze had given him no doubts. Mandukhai and Esige had ridden out to watch him leave. A lump swelled in his throat, and he forced his gaze forward, struggling to maintain a cold, impassive face.

The journey to Khorchin lands would have been only a week for a swift-riding *tumen*, but with carts and families in tow, it would take more than a month to reach the Kherlen River that marked the boundary.

Along the way, the memory of Mandukhai watching him leave haunted his sleep, mingling with her glib comment about her duty to help Bayan.

He knew what he must do to gain the power he had waited for all his life, to finally be free to have her. He had to kill Bayan without pointing a finger at himself. *I have completed my oaths to that runt. There is nothing to keep me from disposing of him now.*

The caravan rode along the southern edge of the Kherlen River, following the water northeast toward Hulunbuir. When it at last came into view in the distance, nestled against the Khingan Mountains, Unebolod called Soke—his second in command—to his side along the banks of the river.

He nodded toward the small city his father had established, now only half a mile away. "I will ride ahead to meet with my brother. See that the carts reach the city without trouble. Once that is done, the men are free to mingle as they please as long as they maintain their daily training. We will camp in Hulunbuir this winter, then ride south at the first signs of spring. When you are done, meet me at the palace."

Soke bowed from his saddle. "My Lord." Then he rode back to gather the *mingghan* commanders to organize their men.

Unebolod reined his mount beside the river and gazed at the water. Nearly ten years ago, he left his homeland to join the fight against Bigirsen and the Oirat. Unebolod had only returned twice in the years that followed. The last time was four years ago, when he came to retrieve Bayan from his brother. Now, Unebolod had returned home once more ... and again, not for long.

Letting out a slow breath, he nudged his mare onward. She bobbed her head as she crested a hilltop.

Unebolod smiled as the Hulunbuir grasslands spread out before him, dotted with thousands of Khorchin gers and stone structures. Eager to ride in among his people once more, Unebolod kicked his mare into a gallop as, behind him, his *tumen* escorted the carts.

The river twisted to the east again, fed by a lake. On one of the rocky cliffs of the lake, an impressive stone palace with a sloping red roof marked the home of his family, and the Khorchin khan. At its back, the Khingan Mountains rose hundreds of feet in the distance.

Unebolod had been a boy when the construction of the palace began, but a sense of duty and adventure had called him away before it was completed. He remembered his father giving him a good walloping when he and his best friend, Jochi, had taken those red roof tiles and used them in a throwing contest. Several expensive tiles had broken. It had been a well-deserved cuffing that had burned into his memory. His older brother, Bolunai, was the one who had told on him. After his father was through with him, Unebolod had taken the fight to his brother. They had beaten each other bloody, but Unebolod had won the bout and earned his older brother's respect.

Jochi had left the grasslands with Unebolod. He had died in a bloody battle on the edge of the Gobi against a *tumen* of Oirat warriors. The first of many friends he had lost to the Oirat and Uyghur.

An *arban* of ten Khorchin riders raced out to meet Unebolod. He slowed his pace to a trot. They met near the edge of the first cluster of gers and reined in at an arc around him. Unebolod sat stiff and straight in his saddle.

"Bolunai khan is expecting you, Lord Unebolod," said one man, the officer of this small group, no doubt. "He welcomes you home to the palace."

Unebolod inclined his head as custom dictated and rode amid them as if they were his guards and not the khan's. He had come with a purpose and showing these men weakness would hinder his goals.

Khorchin lands spread far to the north and south between the Kherlen River and Khingan Mountains. It was fertile land for grazing and water. Unebolod had adopted his love for swimming in rivers along these very banks. He could smell the river rock even from this distance, stirring nostalgia for his youth.

The peaks of the mountains would be covered with snow in the winter that then melted down into the Hulunbuir grasslands and turned them a rich green. He resisted the urge to reach down and run his hands along the tall blades of grass that nearly came to his mare's belly. He remembered how soft the tall grass could be on one side, and how rough on the other side of the same blade. *Much like women*, he mused.

The surrounding trees offered ample hunting grounds in the winter months. Unebolod had taken his first trip with his four older brothers when he was only ten. After the Borjigin butchering only three years later, only he and Bolunai remained. His brother had hardly been old enough to rule his family, let alone the whole tribe.

Aside from Karakorum, no other lands were as abundant for such a large tribe. While Unebolod had spent more of his life away from these lands than he had within the borders, it still filled him with pride to call this place home.

Families of the tribe gathered from all corners of the Khorchin lands for the winter. Camping together protected them against raids and offered resources when necessary. By spring, the clusters of families would spread out again. Unebolod admired the sheer number of Khorchin gers and wondered how many more would come before winter finally settled in. The tribe had grown strong in his absence.

They rode through the stone archway into the palace courtyard, where servants waited to take his horse. Unebolod deftly slid out of the saddle and handed his reins to a young boy who eyed him with open awe and admiration. Unebolod knew he had quite a reputation among the Khorchin—among most tribes, actually—but he often found such admiration uncomfortable. It created an itch of discomfort between his shoulders.

The guards also dismounted and escorted him across the trampled brown grass of the courtyard, up the wide staircase, and through the massive red doors.

Unebolod had been away for so long that the grandeur and permanence of the palace struck him as confining, as if he was trapped when his spirit wanted to roam free. Mongols were not meant to live in such permanent structures.

Massive red columns thicker than his own body rose at regular intervals along the wide, tiled corridor. As he passed over the gleaming red tiles, glimpses of thick red doors closed off passage on either side.

His nephew, a boy of fourteen, stood rather close to a young woman whose face Unebolod could not see past the layers of pearls and bells on her headdress. The body language was clearly flirtatious. Unebolod's lips thinned as he turned his gaze away.

Ahead, an arching doorway led to Bolunai's gathering space beyond. Unebolod spotted his brother sitting atop his gilded throne in that room as he approached the open doors. Behind the hulking form of Bolunai, banners of deep red and gold hung from ceiling to floor. The grandeur of it felt very un-Mongol to him. Unebolod preferred the simplicity of nomadic life. This was why he never bothered challenging his brother for the right to rule the tribe. Bolunai could enjoy his life here in the palace, tethered to one place, all he wanted. Unebolod would rather travel the land.

On a step below Bolunai, his oldest son, Tengghar, watched Unebolod approaching with sharp eyes. Tengghar had to be at least twenty now. There was something cruel about the young man's eyes. *Perhaps he can ride with me against Bigirsen*, Unebolod thought. Tengghar was old enough to join the fight.

"And so, the infamous brother returns," Bolunai teased as Unebolod reached the head of the room and bowed. "I was beginning to think you had forgotten your roots, Unebolod."

Unebolod straightened and clasped his hands behind his back. "The Hulunbuir grasslands have always been in my heart. I could never forget such a place."

Bolunai grinned crookedly. "It's good to have you home, brother." He stood and held out a hand which Unebolod clasped and gave a firm shake. "You've done well for yourself, I hear."

"For all of us," Unebolod said.

"Let's have a few drinks and catch up," Bolunai said, snapping his fingers. "Tengghar, you can leave us now. I'm sure you will catch up with your uncle another time."

A herd of servants rushed into action, setting up a heavy lacquered table with matching chairs, then covering the surface of the table with an assortment of food and drinks. As they worked in a flurry of activity, Tengghar stood, stretching his back casually.

As he passed Unebolod, Tengghar placed a hand on his uncle's shoulder. Tengghar had broad shoulders but still could not quite match Unebolod's height, no matter how tall he tried to stand. "I can't wait to show you around, uncle," he said. "I can share a few tips with you." The way his mouth curled up in the corner made his suggestion clear enough. Those tips involved women.

Instead of correcting Tengghar or outright refusing him, Unebolod gave a small nod of appreciation.

Unebolod took a seat across from his brother and relaxed back into the chair. Weeks of riding in the saddle had strained his back, and it felt good to have something to lean against.

As the *airag* flowed, so did the conversation. Bolunai opened the conversation with stories of their childhood, reminiscing about the glory days of his youth.

"But you always were the serious one, brother," Bolunai said.

"One of us needed to be," Unebolod teased.

"I thought for certain you would be Great Khan by now," Bolunai said. "Serious and strong as you were."

Unebolod grimaced. "My oaths have bound me to a different life."

"And your word is iron." Bolunai waved his hand, showing how little he thought of that. "I've heard it a thousand times. I wonder what father would say if he could see us now."

Unebolod grinned. "He would probably call you fat."

Bolunai chuckled, considered this, then nodded in agreement. "And call you lame."

The grin slipped slightly from Unebolod's face.

"It's been years, Une. Why haven't you taken another wife yet? I know you loved Odsar, but you have a legacy to continue."

Unebolod stared into his *airag*, watching the milky liquid wave and ripple with the smallest movement of his hand. Without meaning to, he slumped further down in his chair.

"If you prefer a boy, I can make those arrangements," Bolunai offered.

Unebolod's gaze shot up to his brother, expecting a joke to dance in Bolunai's eyes. Instead, he was met with a seriousness that made Unebolod's stomach twist. He squirmed, sitting up straighter as he glanced around at the servants lingering on the edge of the room.

Bolunai seemed to understand that he did not feel comfortable speaking freely in front of them. His brother's face turned deadly serious. Then he barked an order for everyone to leave the *airag* and leave them alone. In a few minutes, they were alone with two jugs of *airag*. Unebolod downed his drink, then refilled his cup.

"That bad, huh?" Bolunai asked. Though there was a hint of teasing in his voice, his expression remained stone serious. "Who is she married to, then?"

Unebolod had never felt so uncomfortable. Bolunai may have been apart from him for years, but his brother knew how to strip him bare with just a few words. Anxious, afraid of speaking the truth aloud, Unebolod finished another cup and refilled it.

Bolunai groaned and set his cup on the small table between them. "If he finds out—"

"He won't," Unebolod said quickly. "Because nothing will happen."

"Then why not take another wife?"

Unebolod swallowed the lump that lodged in his throat. "Have you ever tried to hold water in your hand? It's cool, refreshing—"

"Wet," Bolunai added with a crooked smirk.

Unebolod rolled his eyes. "And impossible to hold on to. Still, it soaks into your skin, and without it, you die."

"You are in serious trouble."

Unebolod didn't need his brother to tell him that. He understood it on his own. "It isn't Mandukhai's husband I worry about. It's prince. When

Manduul dies, his wives will transfer to Bayan. He won't care for the water unless it's wet."

"He always was a petulant, self-entitled little yak," Bolunai said tersely. "And a coward, too. I am not surprised he has not changed."

"I doubt the men would agree," Unebolod said with far more bitterness than he intended. "He has earned a lot of respect since Manduul raised him."

Bolunai snorted. "Raised him. *I* raised him. Our family swore a vow to Samur to raise him and see him safely to his place. I tried to harden the whelp, but he was far too soft. When I tried to push him, he ran away." Bolunai spit at the ground to show his true feelings. "I will never follow him."

Unebolod stared into his cup as his brother's words sobered him. "What about me?" This drew Bolunai's gaze sharply to Unebolod. "Would you support me in *kurultai*?"

Bolunai fell silent, studying his brother across the table with scrutiny. Unebolod had been certain his brother, at the very least, would support him at *kurultai* as he put himself forward as a candidate to become the next Great Khan. Now, as Bolunai considered him critically, Unebolod doubted his own confidence.

At last, Bolunai broke the silence. "What brings this question? Why do you think we should have this discussion now?"

Unebolod glanced around to be certain they were alone, then leaned closer and lowered his voice, just in case anyone listened. "You cannot tell another soul. Manduul trusted me with this secret and if it gets out, he will know it was me." Unebolod took another drink to help steel his nerves. "From his own lips, he does not have much longer. Which is why I am here. So I ask again, brother. Do I have your vote?"

Bolunai's brows shot almost comically up his wide forehead when he heard of Manduul's impending death. "Why you?"

"You and I are the closest blood ties to the line of Genghis once Manduul and Bayan are gone," Unebolod explained. "Manduul has already named me and my heirs in the line of succession. It is my duty to the people and the legacy of our Nation. And once I am Great Khan, we will finally remove the Uyghur-Oirat threat. You know I can do it with enough men."

Bolunai nodded tightly. "True. You are certainly more capable than any other men who might try and claim the title." He downed his drink. As he refilled it, he said, "You have my support, brother ... as long as this is not about the Lady."

Unebolod could barely keep his expression neutral. Mandukhai certainly was a motivating factor, but he had wanted this long before she had come into his life. "I would be lying if I said that was not a piece of it. But you know me, Bolunai. I have spent my life waiting for this opportunity. The time is right." He leaned closer. "Bigirsen has lost much of his control in the south and even now struggles to gain back his status. And Bayan ... well, we both know what sort of Khan he would be. He is weak."

"We cannot kill him, brother," Bolunai said over his cup. "We swore an oath to Lady Samur."

"And we have fulfilled that oath." Unebolod set down his cup and rested his arms against the edge of the table. "He is in his place, grown into a man. We have done what we promised. Now, we can finish him and take what we have waited centuries to attain."

Bolunai sighed and sagged in his chair. "Killing him will turn other tribes against you. You will make too many enemies. If you want to be Great Khan, you need someone else to take the fall for his death."

Unebolod grinned at this. "Let me handle that." Unebolod already knew of a Uyghur man he could set up to take the fall for Bayan's death. Then the tribes would blame the Uyghur and finish any remaining threats of control they had. The whole of *kurultai* would turn against the Uyghur. And then, when Unebolod became Great Khan, he would declare war on the Uyghurs in Bayan's name and finish them for good.

Bolunai pursed his lips and raised his brows. "And Mandukhai? Will she be trouble?"

Unebolod grinned again and shook his head. "No. She will support me with the full fury of a dragon."

Bolunai chortled, taking his comment as cockiness and deception when Unebolod had been perfectly sincere. "You sound confident. Let me guess. Once that is done, you plan to take this dragon queen as your own. Somehow, I doubt she will be so easily taken. I have heard stories about how stubborn she is."

"All true, I'm sure. But she returns the feeling. She is just as eager for this as me."

"That is why you are not married, then." Bolunai clearly understood Unebolod's intentions.

"She would never accept being second wife again." Unebolod downed his drink. "Nor should she."

"But what of Manduul's first wife?" Bolunai said. "Will you not take her as well?"

Unebolod sneered. "No. But I believe Mandukhai has plans for her. I won't interfere."

Silence settled between the two brothers as they drank their *airag* and mulled this over. Unebolod knew he had his brother on the hook. Bolunai was reasonable, but also just ambitious enough that he would take what served him best. That Unebolod was his brother would only solidify that loyalty. Bolunai had never been interested in running the whole of the Nation, only the Khorchin tribe. He had called it "too much responsibility." But that did not mean he wouldn't support the man with the best offer.

"When do we begin?" Bolunai asked, breaking the silence.

Unebolod smirked ever so slightly. "I will stay among the Khorchin this winter, and in the spring my *tumen* rides south to gather support."

"Why wait until spring?" Bolunai raised his cup to Unebolod. "I know a few khans who will travel here to meet with you, even in the winter. By spring, you will have the support of half a dozen tribes, if not more."

The suggestions surprised Unebolod. *Who would make the journey in the winter just to speak with me?* The prospect of beginning right here during the winter settled well with Unebolod. Warmth spread through his chest, fueled by too much *airag*. He leaned back in his chair as he refilled his cup. At long last, the khanship would be his. His patience had paid off.

"Now, tell me more about Manduul Khan dying," Bolunai said over the rim of his cup.

Unebolod shifted forward, grinning.

CHAPTER NINE

Inescapable Destiny

30 Miles North of Baotou – Late Winter 1469

Bayan's *mingghans* camped near enough to Baotou that Bayan's scouts could easily ride back and forth in less than a day. Yungei, the Khorchin commander Unebolod left behind to assist Bayan in the south, chose an excellent location nestled between hills.

As winter had pressed its chilling fist against the earth, Bayan and his men had moved with more caution along the Ming borders. Hiding the tracks of so many had proven an impossible task, so they only broke camp when necessary, remaining one step ahead of the Ming commanders tracking him.

Yungei had a critical eye for analyzing the landscape in ways Bayan envied. On Yungei's suggestion, Bayan occasionally had sent a *mingghan* of a thousand men back on the Ming's flanks to sting the pursuing forces when the land had offered the best advantage. Yungei's strategic strength had also led them toward the safest locations to camp. Such as this one.

Bayan never forgot how Yungei had glared at him with such animosity when he first arrived in the south to fetch Bayan and bring him to Mongke Bulag nearly five years ago. Though Yungei never disrespected him openly, he voiced his dissent when he felt it necessary. And Yungei's tone rarely offered amiability.

Without prompting, five *mingghan* of Chakhar had traveled with Bayan through the winter, giving him the full force of a *tumen*—ten thousand Mongol warriors. Chakhar families also moved with them.

Bayan stood outside the ger he shared with Siker, breathing in the cool air of late winter. He could almost taste the freshness of spring if he breathed deeply enough. It revitalized him and reminded him of the freedom he had enjoyed before joining Manduul.

One positive of the Chakhar presence had been the regular company of Siker. Bayan could have unearthed many young women eager to share his bed, but he found an odd sense of comfort from Siker's familiar presence. He spent his evenings in her ger, making it his own and dismissing her when he needed to meet with his commanders. The two of them had fallen into a familiar rhythm—comfortable and distant as they had been years ago, yet eager to please each other to ward off the frosty nights.

"Prince Bolkhu," Guden's familiar voice called to him.

Bayan groaned to himself and turned to face the Chakhar khan, who was accompanied by half a dozen of his guards.

Guden khan stopped beside Bayan and crossed his arms over his wide chest, gazing into the distance as if to see what Bayan stared at. In truth, Bayan stared at nothing and enjoyed the simplicity of it. Having Guden beside him spoiled the moment. Guden was the one who turned him over to Manduul's men nearly five years ago. While Bayan had thrived under Manduul's care, he never forgot how Guden had turned against him so easily. Since Guden joined him on this campaign, the Chakhar khan treated him like a child—while still offering deference to the Great Khan's heir. Bayan often sought escape from these conversations.

"Guden." Bayan heard the flatness of his own tone. "To what do I owe this early morning pleasure?"

Guden's lips thinned as if the question insulted him. "Several officers have come to me raising concerns." He peered sidelong at Bayan, who refused to glance in his direction. "Men and women are talking."

"They do so endlessly," Bayan commented tersely. "What sort of bug has gotten under their skin this time?"

"Your relationship with the Lady Siker."

Lady! Bayan scoffed. Were the people calling her Lady now? It hardly befit her station. Her father had been a nobody, which had been precisely why Bayan had hidden in their home for so long before Manduul finally found him. Who would think to look for him in the home of a nobody? "What of it?"

"You have spent these past months together as man and wife, yet you have not married."

"Nor will we. Siker and I agree on this."

Guden turned, dropping his arms as he squared off in front of Bayan. "This is not the first time you have used her."

Used. Bayan ground his teeth. Guden made it sound as if Siker slept with him against her will. Like he forced her into his bed.

"The Chakhar women are voicing their outrage to their husbands and fathers," Guden continued, either oblivious to Bayan's reaction or ignoring it. "If you do this to Siker, what will become of the purity of any other daughter of the tribes under your rule? And as the women speak, the men follow. The Chakhar cannot accept this any longer. You will marry and give her the honor of her place at your side, as she deserves."

Bayan's temper flared. He struggled to swallow it down as his fists clenched at his sides. The heat of his anger burned in his neck. "You would dare tell me what to do? Do you forget I am your prince, that when my uncle dies, I will be your Great Khan? You are in no position to make demands of me."

"Do not mistake me," Guden said, stepping closer with a menacing heat in his eyes. "When Manduul Khan passes, you will still face *kurultai*, where you must gain the support of the tribes and the oaths of the people to become Great Khan. If you sow discord among my people, who only make a simple request, word will spread. It will create a ripple of doubt that could cost you dearly. Do not make a hasty decision here, Bolkhu *Jinong*."

Bayan wished his sword was at his side, yet also felt a hint of relief that it was not, or he might have used it on this lesser khan. Inwardly, he quivered with rage and a hint of fear.

Bayan inched closer until he was nearly toe-to-toe with Guden. "Are you threatening me, Guden?"

Guden waved off his guards, who tensed for a fight. "I am warning you. For your own sake. This marriage is a small price to pay for your future."

"I should speak with Manduul before agreeing," Bayan said, hoping he had an escape. "After all, I am the heir to the nation. The Great Khan should have a say in this as well."

Guden shook his head. "Your reputation is well known. So much so that we have heard Manduul Khan has stated plainly in front of the whole of Mongke Bulag that he hopes you will find a wife soon. He will be happy you have formed such a strong bond with one of the southern tribes."

Was Guden speaking the truth? Could Manduul have made such a comment at Bayan's expense? Did he truly want Bayan married? Would Manduul be angry with him if his refusal made an enemy of the Chakhar?

Questions rolled through Bayan's mind as he debated the merits of this. Guden really didn't offer him a choice. Either he agreed to marry Siker, or the Chakhar would oppose him when he called for the Lords to vote for him at *kurultai*. And if the Chakhar had enough time, they could turn other southern tribes against Bayan as well. If he lost the south, he would lose the vote to Unebolod, who had control of the east.

Guden stepped back and said, "This is in your best interest, my Lord *jinong*. Her dowry was spent on the first marriage, but she still has a bit of wealth that will transfer to you, herds and valuables from her previous husband. The bride price will be your service to the Chakhar as Great Khan, when the day comes. I will make the arrangements for you. We will do it this evening." He strode away, surrounded by his loyal guards as if that were the end of the discussion.

The encounter left Bayan stunned. He remained in that spot as if his feet had taken root until the sun rose well into the sky. A Chakhar bride-price as Great Khan? It felt more like a hefty favor hanging over his head for future use. An ax waiting to drop.

Marriage. Bayan didn't want it. He had spent years running from it. Could Guden truly force him into this? Him, the Golden Prince? The urge to flee made his feet itch. He would rather face down the Ming army with only his sword than face down this night.

The tradition of constructing the ger for the newlyweds had been skipped since Bayan and Siker already shared a home, though Siker had been chased out of the ger by the women in her family. She tossed vicious protests at them as they pushed her out the door.

Bayan sat beside the open door, scowling in a way that drew occasional chuckles from Berkedai, which only fueled Bayan's irritation.

"This is my ger!" Siker snapped, attempting to spin away and dart back in the door.

Another girl her age—and much more attractive, Bayan noticed—grabbed Siker by the arm and pulled her away from the door. "We must leave to get you prepared as he readies himself here." The girl glanced at him, and Bayan instinctively flashed her his winning smile.

"Let *him* go elsewhere!" Siker shouted, glaring at him. "Stop looking at my cousin like that!"

Bayan averted his gaze. Then a flare of anger surged through him as he realized what she had just done to him. Ordering him around as if she were already his wife, making demands of him. And he obeyed. Bayan grimaced.

Guden's son approached. Upon seeing his tall, imposing form, Siker stopped struggling and fell silent. The women guided her away before she could kick up dust again.

Bayan stood and entered the ger behind the other man. He could not let Manduul down. If this was really what Manduul wanted, and if the Chakhar would fight him at *kurultai*, Bayan saw no way out. He could make a fuss like Siker, but it would only make him appear weak.

Guden's son to helped Bayan prepare, offering a sky-blue silk deel and breeches, with soft sheepskin boots. Along the trim of the deel, someone had stitched golden wolves sprinting out of a swirling cloud of mist. Though Bayan hated what these clothes would represent, he admired the elaborate and stunning work. Someone had been planning this for some time to create clothing representing the Borjigin.

As the sun began moving toward the distant horizon, Bayan stepped outside. Everyone would have collected to witness the event, and the celebration began before either Bayan or Siker made an appearance. It made his steps as heavy as blocks of iron.

"I can have your mount ready in minutes," Berkedai said as they made their way toward the gathering space where everyone awaited his arrival.

Bayan felt the itch between his shoulders to take Berkedai up on his offer. Riding off right now would be preferable to marriage. "How can I be so powerless to stop this?" he asked quietly, but with no less frustration.

"Why would you want to?" Berkedai raised a teasing smirk at Bayan, but he could see in his friend's eyes that Berkedai truly did not understand. "Having a woman always there to keep your bed warm and your stomach full, and to fill your ger with sons. What more could you want?"

Bayan glanced south, toward the city of Baotou. "Wives expect things from you, and I have no interest in having a woman tug at my reins like a broken pony."

Berkedai shrugged as they neared the already boisterous crowd. But Berkedai wouldn't understand. He had taken a second wife during the winter—a young Chakhar woman with the shoulders of an ox. His friend often boasted his appreciation for her strong, broad form. It promised good childbearing years. Bayan never would have chosen such a girl, one with a bigger build than himself. It would make him appear weak when-ever he stood beside her. Siker was a full head shorter than Bayan, and her shoulders were half as wide as those of Berkedai's wife. For Bayan, a woman's purpose was to keep him satisfied through the long winter. If she cooked his food and cleaned his clothes, all the better. But a wife ...

The crowd parted for Bayan to pass.

"At least you will have a wife who doesn't care about pulling at the reins," Berkedai said under his breath.

Perhaps. But Siker's command earlier cast a shadow of doubt over Bayan's mind. Before that, Siker had never nagged Bayan or tried to force him into anything. They simply went about their own business. Aside from sharing a bed and meals, they rarely interacted with each other.

Marriage was Bayan's worst nightmare. But if he had to have a wife, at least he would have one that cared for marriage as little as he did. At some point, he would have to have sons if he was to carry on the Borjigin royal line. Something Manduul clearly expected of him sooner rather than later. Bayan supposed that, at twenty, he had avoided marriage longer than most. Boys typically married between fourteen and sixteen. He had managed to wrangle an extra four years of freedom.

Berkedai patted Bayan sympathetically on the shoulders as he broke off, leaving Bayan to continue the long march toward the head of the gathering space—and his doom—where Guden waited with his own wives.

To the side, Siker's mother and stepfather watched with their three younger children. Murmurs of excitement rippled through the crowd as Bayan stepped up beside Guden and the fire was lit in the center of the space.

"You could at least pretend to be pleased," Guden grumbled under his breath.

Bayan grimaced. "I would be more pleased with death."

"That's always an option."

The words shot into Bayan's chest like a promise. It took every ounce of Bayan's energy to keep from showing his alarm. But killing Bayan would bring Manduul's wrath on their heads, and they would not risk that.

Siker entered the other side of the gathering space, dressed in stunning robes in an array of blues and yellows. The beaded crown on her head chimed with each step as she followed behind the Chakhar shaman who sprinkled mare's milk as a blessing of fertility. She passed between the two fires burning high in braziers on either side of the path. Men nodded their approval. Women murmured in admiration.

Bayan found Siker quite plain, even in such lavish trappings—hardly a woman befitting a future Great Khan. The set of her thin lips and furrowed brow clearly exhibited her thoughts about this situation. Bayan wasn't sure he had ever seen such a sour bride. To his surprise, the sight of her distaste filled him with warmth and excitement. *Perhaps Berkedai was right.* Siker was a preferable option to any of the other women Bayan had encountered.

Bayan stepped down and turned to face Siker in front of Guden. The ceremony itself was short. Guden offered a blessing of their marriage on behalf of the Chakhar and Siker's family. Each of them drank from a silver bowl of mare's milk. Then Guden pronounced the marriage loudly enough to make Bayan wince.

"With all your flock, raise thousands. May all your wishes come true," Guden said at last. "May the power of these marital ties strengthen your families and our nation. Go forth through the cleansing fires of marriage and into your shared future."

Bayan and Siker turned to face the crowd. He could feel the waves of irritation rolling off her as they trudged up the path together. Her hand rested delicately on his as they walked, and the crowd folded in behind them to follow the new couple to their ger.

Neither of them uttered a word, walking stiffly with their hands layered in a whisper of a touch. When they reached the door and ducked through, it was almost with a breath of relief that they closed it behind them. Music struck up in celebration. Bayan could hear the prayers outside the door as men and women of the tribes dipped their fingers in milk and swiped it over the felt lining the outside of the doorway to encourage fertility in the home.

He turned to Siker, who had already tossed her beaded crown aside on the table and loosened her hair. It fell around her shoulders at odd angles. She froze, staring at him as he stared at her. For a long while, they remained rooted in place, unable to look away. They had tried to escape this for years, but fate, it seemed, had other plans.

Neither spoke. Neither had anything to say. In a typical marriage, they would consummate their future together. But this was not a typical marriage. Their relationship was far more complicated than that.

Siker loosened her deel, letting it fall to the floor around her feet. Now that they were married, he found she lacked appeal. Before she could approach him, Bayan turned away and marched to the shelf where they stored the jug of *airag*.

"Put your clothes back on, Siker," he said, pouring a very generous cup.

"This is the only thing we have done well," she said.

He turned with the cup in hand, startled to find her standing right behind him, still naked. He grimaced. "I'm not in the mood."

"That's a first."

Bayan reached back and picked up the jug of *airag* in his free hand. Then he brushed past her toward the bench—away from the bed—and settled down with his drink.

Siker grumbled something under her breath as she gathered her clothes and slipped them back on. He didn't care what she said or what she thought. All he cared about now was the *airag* in his hand.

Bayan knew with certainty that there was no escaping his destiny. There had been a time when he had not wanted to be the next Great Khan, when he had not wanted to marry Siker. Now he walked the path of both.

CHAPTER TEN

Kicking the Hornet's Nest

Unebolod followed Bolunai into the tunnels beneath the palace with only a carefully sheltered lantern to guide their way through the dark. The walls of the tunnels were coarse stone, as if carelessly carved out from the earth itself. The air was so dry it made Unebolod's throat itch. They walked along the worn path in silence for some time. Unebolod did not know where his brother was leading him.

Unebolod hated being underground, preferring the wide-open sky above his head as opposed to dozens of feet of stone and packed earth. What would it take for the ground to collapse on their heads? Being beneath the ground like this caused the air in his lungs to come in shorter gasps, as if he were a drowning man gulping down each breath as he broke the surface. He had only been underground once before, when he and his brother initially hid from Esen's men during the Borjigin butchering. How could Bolunai stand this confining space again?

"Stop breathing like that," Bolunai grumbled as they turned a corner. "You sound like a dying yak."

"How would you know what a dying yak sounds like?" Unebolod ribbed back.

"Don't push me, little brother, or you may never come out of these tunnels again," Bolunai teased.

I already feel that's true, Unebolod thought.

Bolunai held the lantern high, casting a faint glow along the walls of the long tunnel. Unebolod gasped. Barrels upon barrels stacked along either side of the tunnel as far as Unebolod could see into the darkness at least fifty steps ahead.

"What is this?" he asked as he approached the nearest barrel, seeking clues.

"Gunpowder."

Unebolod yanked his hand back as if the barrel burned him, then retreated a few steps. "So much of it. Where did you come by all this?"

"The Jurchens across the mountains. They are easily bought and swayed. I've been building this collection for years." Bolunai puffed up proudly as he gazed at the plethora of barrels, the way a father would gaze at his son.

"Beneath your palace? Have you lost your senses? What if it explodes?" This much gunpowder could level a significant portion of the Hulunbuir grasslands.

"It is well protected, and only a handful of others know of this." Bolunai turned to Unebolod.

"Does Manduul know?"

"No. And I trust that, considering all you have told me these past weeks, you will keep your mouth closed." Bolunai's tone took on a rough edge. "Only the men I trust most know of this place, and only I have a key to get down here. The conditions are optimal to keep the powder stable. The only way this place will blow is if someone breaks in and does it themselves."

The explanation hardly put Unebolod at ease. His gaze swept the walls once more. If Bolunai had this wealth of gunpowder, what other eastern khans had something similar?

"I will have carts filled with it before you leave," Bolunai said. "If matters in Karakorum turn ugly, you may need this to secure your place."

"What would I even do with it?" Unebolod hadn't realized he had retreated even further back up the tunnel from the direction they'd come until his back bumped the wall.

Bolunai grinned like a boy. "Follow me, little frightened sheep."

Bolunai brushed past, and Unebolod flinched away from the lantern, suddenly very aware of the danger of dropping it in this space. It would be the end of them. His brother moved with quick steps that belied his age around the corner to a door they passed before. Bolunai extracted a large metal key and unlocked the door, then pushed it open with his big hand. The hinges creaked, and the scent of metal and earth rolled out from behind it.

Unebolod peered cautiously inside, now afraid of what he might find.

Dozens of long metal tubes were stacked in pyramids in the small room. It was hardly enough space to fit the stash.

"Are those hand cannons?" Unebolod asked, curiously brushing his fingers along the rough, pressed metal. Manduul had never been able to get his hands on these.

"Over fifty. I will send a cartload with you to use with the gunpowder. I would not want to be the man who opposes you." Bolunai turned to Unebolod, beaming with pride. "What do you think, brother?"

"I think I will need men who know how to use them safely. I assume you have those."

Bolunai grinned. "Of course."

Unebolod turned his attention once more to the stacks of hand cannons, admiring the metal finish and cool feel beneath his fingertips. A dozen would not be enough, but it would certainly slow his enemies down. The Uyghur would never stand a chance.

In the dead of night, Bayan stumbled out of his ger to relieve himself with his two guards in tow. Married or not, he still had drunk his share of *airag* until he could no longer stay awake. The *airag* still swarmed his senses, and he struggled to avoid stumbling into the urine-soaked ditch.

Behind him, one of his guards grunted, followed by the sound of steel against steel. As Bayan spun around, he lost his footing and fell backward into a mound of dirt on the edge of the ditch. At least his luck held out enough to keep him from falling in. One of his guards fell to the ground with a thump, his lifeless gaze peering at Bayan in the dark. Panic surged in his chest as the guard's face morphed into Nergui—now dead for almost four years.

The second guard fought off a swarm of soldiers. Bayan was too drunk to see them clearly or count their numbers, even as his guard killed them one after another.

"Go!" the guard barked as a sword sliced into his arm. He growled and tightened his grip, thrusting his own blade up into the man's neck. What was the guard's name? Bayan blinked through a haze of *airag*, unable to pull up the name from his memory.

Too many attackers outnumbered his lonely guard. A dozen? Maybe more. As valiantly as he held them back from Bayan, in seconds, they would surge past his last guard. Bayan scrambled drunkenly to his feet and ran, but the *airag* betrayed him. He stumbled as his feet hit a dip in the ground, making him pitch forward. Hands grasped Bayan's arms, wrenching them behind his back.

Bayan cried out a warning, calling to Berkedai—to anyone who could hear. His captors bound his arms behind his back so tight it made his shoulders scream in pain.

One of his captors hissed a command, and it took a moment in his drunken haze to recognize the Ming tongue. How had they snuck into camp without notice? The realization that he was being captured by Ming soldiers sobered Bayan quickly.

One captor stuffed a cloth in his mouth, then tied it in place. They heaved him up by the arms to drag him away. Bayan kicked his legs out wildly, taking one Ming in the kneecap and snapping the leg backward. The man fell with a scream.

Before his feet could touch the ground, Bayan kicked again. As they held his arms, he used their strength to hoist himself up as he added extra power to the kick. Both of his feet hammered into another captor's chest. The force of the blow knocked the man off his feet. The Ming soldier cursed.

The impact threw the two captors holding Bayan's arms off balance. Bayan slammed backward into the dirt. His head banged against the ground. He landed on his shoulder and felt it pop out of place, but with the gag in his mouth, he could do little more than scream in his throat. Tears stung his eyes.

After a moment of struggling with his own body, Bayan staggered to his feet. Hands tied behind his back still, Bayan sprinted away, praying his luck would hold out.

A glance over his shoulder revealed camp torches flickering off muted brown Ming soldiers. Still over a dozen remained, all in pursuit of him. Bayan was too far from his ger to outpace them. But if he could just get a little further, Berkedai would be close.

He shifted his course so abruptly it threw off the Ming soldiers chasing him. None of them made a sound, aside from the thump of their boots on the ground. If the Ming were discovered in the camp, Mongols would butcher them before they could escape.

Bayan took advantage of the silence and screamed as loud and hard as he could. The cloth in his mouth muffled most of the sound, but some of it surely would catch attention somewhere. He screamed until his throat burned.

Within feet of Berkedai's ger, a Ming soldier lunged at Bayan's legs. Bayan pitched forward, pinned to the ground beneath the soldier's weight. Bayan kicked and twisted as wildly as he could, making himself harder to capture and hold. He continued shouting through his gag.

As the soldier pinning him leaned closer, Bayan slammed his forehead into the man's nose. Blood gushed out. The soldier cursed and sat back, but kept his weight on Bayan, holding a hand over his broken nose. The soldier hissed a command, and Bayan knew his chances of escape were waning. Luck would not hold out much longer.

Four men steadied his thrashing legs, binding them together. Bayan shouted again for Berkedai through the gag. The commotion must have caught *someone's* attention by now.

As he pulled in another deep breath through his nose to prepare for another shout, the Ming soldier on top of him growled what Bayan could only assume was a curse word.

This is how it ends, Bayan thought as he watched the soldier raise his sword over Bayan's head. His luck would not hold after all.

The pommel of the sword hammered against Bayan's skull.

The thumping pain in Bayan's head felt like someone striking a hammer against an anvil. A ringing filled his ears. Bayan shifted his weight. Sharp pain lanced down his back from his shoulder. The gag muffled his scream.

It took a moment to recall what had happened. Bayan still lay on the ground, bound and gagged. However, the ringing he heard was not in his ears. It was all around him.

A dozen Mongols fought Ming soldiers in a ring around him. Berkedai stood at the head of the group. He barked orders to finish the soldiers off, leaving one for questioning.

Bayan lay on the ground and waited for the battle to be won. How long had he been unconscious?

It was over in minutes. Berkedai ordered the last remaining man bound as he kneeled behind Bayan and cut the ropes, then removed the gag. Yungei crouched on Bayan's other side.

"What happened?" Berkedai asked.

Bayan croaked as he tried to answer. His throat was sore and dry from screaming.

"Water!" Yungei barked, holding out a hand expectantly.

A Mongol warrior handed over a skin of water. Bayan sat up to accept the skin from Yungei, but nearly collapsed again as the pain from his shoulder burned through him. Using the other hand, he drank with greed, but it still took several attempts before he could find his voice.

"They attacked me ... when I went to piss ..." Bayan coughed as his raw throat chaffed at speaking. He took another drink before continuing. "Killed my guards."

"Go check on Lady Siker," Yungei commanded a handful of men who rushed off to obey.

"Your shoulder is out," Berkedai said. "We can get that fixed."

Bayan nodded, wincing as even that drew fiery pain. His gaze fell on the one surviving Ming soldier who glared at him. Even held under guard, the soldier radiated hate. "How did they get into camp without anyone noticing?"

"I don't know, but we will find out," Berkedai said in a vengeful tone. "Yungei, alert Guden khan. Let him know what happened and have men move around the perimeter. Send out scouts to search for dead watchmen, and to see if there are more Ming waiting nearby."

Yungei nodded and rushed off to carry out the orders. Bayan couldn't stop thinking about one thing as he watched the man leave.

"Berkedai, why didn't they just kill me?"

"Don't question your luck, Bolkhu," Berkedai said. "You may find it won't hold."

But his luck always held. Sometimes, it toed a bit too close to death for Bayan's taste. But it always held.

Bayan allowed Guden's men to question their Ming captor as he waited in his ger. Siker boiled water for salted tea and warm cloths to clean him. Guden had sent one of his men in to set Bayan's shoulder, and once it was done, the pain slowly subsided. Yet they could do nothing about the hammering in his head.

Berkedai entered the ger, closing the door behind him. He took a seat near the door. "It isn't safe here, Bolkhu," Berkedai said. He had organized a dozen guards around the ger for Bayan's protection. "You have kicked the hornet's nest, and now they are prepared to sting you with a vengeance. The wisest course of action would be to return home and let the work you've done here carry on in your name. You've done your job well. The Khan will be pleased."

"But they haven't revolted yet," Bayan said.

Siker prepared the tea and brought a cup to Bayan. "If I may offer my advice?"

Both men raised alarmed eyes to her. Siker never spoke up before. She usually quickly and quietly excused herself from all political and military affairs without comment. Had this marriage emboldened her? If so, it would prove a problem for Bayan.

Siker waited patiently for a response.

"Well, out with it then," Bayan snapped.

Siker scowled. "We could call upon the rest of the Chakhar. You could raise your black banner and call these southern tribes to your side as you attack back. You cannot let the Ming get away with such an insult."

On some level, he knew Siker had a point. The Ming would think him weak if he returned home. But Manduul had been clear.

Bayan waved her off. "I won't start a war without speaking to my uncle first. His command was explicit. Incite the people. Don't engage the bulk of the emperor's forces. We don't have strength for it yet. Even with the support of the southern tribes. The Ming still outnumber us."

Berkedai remained silent, looking away as Siker glared at Bayan. For a moment Bayan thought she would protest, but she wisely kept her mouth shut and soaked some cloths in the boiling water to clean his wounds.

"Returning home now could make me appear weak," Bayan said to Berkedai as if Siker were no longer present. "But I cannot attack the main Ming forces yet."

"This isn't their first attempt, Bolkhu." Berkedai glanced at Siker, obviously able to sense the anger rolling off of her as easily as Bayan could. "They have tried capturing you before. They will try again. As long as you remain in the south with only half a *tumen* to guard you, the Ming will strike again and again."

Bayan leaned back against the wall as he considered this. Berkedai had a point. He didn't have enough men to withstand these assaults repeatedly. Yet returning to Manduul after such an attack would offer little glory, despite his successful mission. The power of a Khan was in the power of his name. Bayan needed vengeance.

"Any word from the scouts?" he asked.

"There is a camp of about ten thousand Ming near the eastern wing of Baotou," Berkedai reported. "If we return home without engaging, we have to move through Bigirsen's territory to the west."

Bayan winced. He would rather face the Ming. At least they seemed eager to capture him. Bayan was certain Bigirsen would rather see him dead. Though there was another choice. Straight north. Through the Gobi Desert.

A shudder raced down Bayan's spine. He made that journey once before, when he was thirteen. Alone. Surviving the desert alone had been dangerous enough. This time, he would lead thousands.

However, should Bayan fall into the Ming emperor's hands, the future of the Mongol people would belong to the emperor. As much as Bayan hated returning to Mongke Bulag, he knew he had no choice. The fate of the wolf and the people depended on him surviving.

"What did we learn from the prisoner?" Bayan asked.

Berkedai shrugged. "Not much. He just keeps repeating the same words. The line of Khans will fall."

The truth was as bitter as Siker's tea. Manduul would die someday, and if Bayan had no sons, the line of Khans would indeed fall. If he didn't return to Mongke Bulag soon, he may never return. He could either face Bigirsen, face the Ming, or face the desert and return home. His odds were better with the desert.

"Fine." He sighed. "Give the command. We will return to Mongke Bulag today. Be sure everyone takes as much water as they can carry."

"Your will, my Lord," Berkedai said formally as he stood and bowed to Bayan, then left the ger.

Siker pressed a warm, wet cloth against the wound on the side of Bayan's head with less tenderness than he would expect from a wife. Her touch was rough, and she pressed into the gash without mercy. In irritation, he snatched the cloth from her hand and swatted her away.

"Start packing what you will take with us," he said sharply, wishing he could leave her behind. But now she was his wife. He had no choice but to take her along. "I can manage my own wounds."

Siker huffed and clicked her tongue in irritation, but quickly set to work packing up their belongings as he cleaned his own wounds.

What would Yeke say when he returned with a wife?

CHAPTER ELEVEN

The Best Laid Plans

MONGKE BULAG – SPRING 1469

Unebolod's departure made the winter months all the colder and more bitter to handle. Despite Esige's revitalizing company, Jaghan's friendly conversations and consolations, and Satai's regular ladies' tea gatherings, Mandukhai slipped further into herself. She began losing motivation to leave her ger unless necessary. Every time she stepped out the door, the snow-covered ring of space reminded her of Unebolod. Mandukhai found it increasingly challenging to put on her usual serene mask.

One evening, after a silent dinner, Manduul wiped his sleeve across his mouth and grimaced in her direction. "Sadness presses down on you. What is it?"

Mandukhai blinked slowly, forcing her focus back to the present. "The winter, I suppose. It feels so long. And in my morning and evening prayers, I find myself thinking about our lost child." Her throat tightened. It was not entirely a lie.

Manduul reached over and patted her arm. "I think about it sometimes, too. But we cannot dwell on dreadful things." He stood with some effort and kissed the top of her head on the way to the door.

That had not been the end of Mandukhai's cloudy mood, though. The knowledge that Manduul would die soon did nothing to ease her pain every time she saw the vacancy left behind by Unebolod's ger.

Not long after that dinner, Manduul requested that Mandukhai and Yeke no longer spend too much time together—not that the two women found themselves in each other's company often. "I fear her sour mood has been burrowing into your skin," he said.

Although Mandukhai's mood had nothing to do with Yeke, his judgment had brought something else to Mandukhai's attention. When Bayan left to head south with Issama and Unebolod, Yeke had drawn more and more into herself. Now, Mandukhai experienced the same sense of loss. The similarities reinforced what she suspected all along. Yeke had fallen for Bayan, just as Mandukhai had fallen for Unebolod.

The revelation put Mandukhai in a dangerous position in a few ways. First, Yeke would never accept Mandukhai after Manduul died. If Yeke held sway over Bayan as Mandukhai held sway over Unebolod, Mandukhai knew she could end up dead after Manduul died. Second, if she did not pull herself together, Manduul would put the pieces together and confirm what he had suspected years ago.

This shared remorse between the two women had awoken Mandukhai's senses, and she found the strength to put on that mask she had struggled so hard to wear. She was a queen. She would not curl up and cry over a man just because he left. She was stronger than that.

Today, as spring breathed new life into the grass and warmed the breeze, Mandukhai and Esige raced their horses across the plains around Mongke Bulag, as they often did. Esige's stallion gave Dust a challenge as they snorted, pushed on by their riders. These rides helped Mandukhai clear her head.

Once Unebolod had told Mandukhai that Manduul was dying, she began noticing his condition. The coughing was the most obvious, but Manduul always had an excuse. When he stayed with Mandukhai, Manduul's coughing would sometimes wake her in the night. Their walks around Mongke Bulag had ceased as the bitter cold gripped the area. Manduul had insisted he had no desire to freeze his balls off, but Mandukhai could see the exhaustion in his posture. At what point would he finally confess his condition to her?

Esige stood and guided her mount easily with her knees. Her body was tall and lithe, and Mandukhai could see the water in her eyes as wind whipped past them. Mandukhai herself felt the sting of the breeze on her cheeks and eyes as she rose in the stirrups in a natural, fluid motion. Her hair was braided behind her, and the braid bounced and fluttered, thumping against her back.

Esige whooped and whipped her stallion into a harder run. Her own hair was braided in layers in a way that clung to her back and shoulders as she rode. The girl was glorious, and again, Mandukhai envied Esige's strength and freedom. She was nearly fifteen years old now, and she rode with the fire of youth at her will.

The ring around Mongke Bulag was ten miles and worn in a wide path of dirt from years of men training. The horses kicked up clouds of dust in their wake. As they rounded the northern corner of the track for the second time, Mandukhai's felt legs tensed with exertion from the ride, but the sensation breathed a second wind into her. Such races would only make both her and Dust stronger. While she couldn't say why that felt important, somehow she knew in the months to come such stamina would be necessary. She needed to be able to ride as hard and long as any of the men. Esige had taken up the practice with just as much enthusiasm, always seeking new ways to show off her own strength.

Mandukhai squeezed her knees to tighten the turn around the next corner, gripping the reins with feverish determination to beat Esige across the finish line. Dust cut the corner tight, bumping Esige's stallion in the shoulder just enough to slow his step and allow Mandukhai the inside track. And the lead.

Esige roared in frustration as she attempted to close the narrow gap. Both horses frothed at the mouth, their skin gleaming with a sheen of sweat. Ten miles was not far to race, but the finish line approached.

At the last corner, Mandukhai yanked the reins and used her knees to guide Dust away from Mongke Bulag toward the river, never once slowing the pace. The thunder of hooves at her back was all the confirmation she needed to know Esige followed close behind.

The edge of the river was rocky, a danger for the horses at such speeds. Mandukhai kept her pace steady for as long as she dared. The shore raced closer. Esige called out a warning to Mandukhai, but she didn't slow. Within paces of the rocks, Mandukhai yanked the reins and shifted her weight back, squeezing her knees to turn Dust. The stallion skidded to a halt within a breath of the rocks, facing Esige.

The other girl trotted closer, her face flush from the exertion. "You really pushed your luck this time," Esige said, grinning from ear to ear.

Mandukhai dismounted and released the reins. Dust immediately turned to the river to drink. "Precision and patience are critical skills, Esige. I would think you had learned that by now."

Esige dismounted, and her stallion joined Dust at the river. "So you keep saying." The girl dropped to the ground and flopped on her back, then plucked a long strand of grass to chew on.

Mandukhai sat beside her, stretching out her tired legs. No one else was nearby. The two of them were blissfully alone. Mandukhai's usual guards often left her to run laps without following, but she knew that when the two of them didn't show up at the checkpoint by the finish line, someone would come looking for them. They had little time.

"You have trusted me so much these past years," Mandukhai said, watching Esige as the girl stared at the sky and chewed on the grass. "We are nearly there. I cannot tell you how I know this, but I can tell you with certainty that change is coming."

"About time," Esige muttered like a petulant child.

"Never forget what we are working toward, Esige. Our goal is to retrieve your sister and keep the Nation from falling apart."

Esige sat up, her gaze fixed with determination on Mandukhai. "We could achieve both with Unebolod."

"Perhaps. He is gathering support on the Khan's orders," Mandukhai said. Every time Esige brought Unebolod up in conversation, Mandukhai found herself unable to respond with any level of patience. He had his duty. She had hers.

When Manduul died at last, Yeke and Bayan would make a move against Mandukhai—possibly the same day. The only way to survive the transition was to strike first. Mandukhai had to turn Bayan against Yeke ... or kill them both. However, Bayan's death would need to be an accident.

The thunder of hooves approached. Their time alone was at an end.

"We have nearly crossed the finish, Esige. Keep faith in me. If Bigirsen learns we plan to act against Yeke, he will kill us both—and use your sister as bait."

Esige nodded grimly. Mandukhai knew the girl wanted to be the one to strike Bigirsen down. But Mandukhai had other plans for Bigirsen.

Issama waited as the shaman, Khosoichi, finished his work, then left Issama alone with Manduul in the gathering tent.

"You can't hide this much longer, Manduul," Issama said.

Manduul sagged on his throne, as if the mere act of sitting there exhausted him. In the middle of a meeting with Issama's army of scribes, Manduul had fallen into a fit of wheezing that drew too much attention. Issama had quickly dismissed the scribes and sent his trusted second, Nahai, to fetch the shaman, pressing discreet urgency.

"I will do nothing until Bolkhu returns," Manduul snapped, panting out the words sharply and breathlessly together. He pulled in a breath that made his body shudder. "Lord Guden insists he is on the way. Until then, we will not speak of this again."

"My lord Khan," Issama said, bowing apologetically.

"What of Unebolod?" Manduul asked.

Issama had noticed Manduul using shorter, clipped sentences the closer he marched toward death. How much longer did the Khan have?

"He spent the winter with the Khorchin and plans to take a full *tumen* south to gather Bolkhu's support once the weather there breaks, in accordance with your instructions."

Manduul nodded, then carefully drank more of the herbal mixture Khosoichi had given before he left them. Issama could not discern what herbal concoction Khosoichi had created to help prolong Manduul's life. Without Khosoichi's herbs, Manduul may have died already. The condition was progressing swiftly despite the shaman's best efforts. If Issama knew what was in it, he could slip in another toxin undetected to counteract the herbs. However, one wrong herb and all his plans would be for nothing.

Manduul's demise was no accident. Small doses of a salt-based intoxicant mixed into Manduul's *airag* over time had done its work even before Issama had left to head south. The line of Genghis Khan would end.

And Unebolod would never return to stop him.

"The Oirat?" Manduul asked.

Issama smiled to himself. He had connections to the Oirat—everyone knew that already—connections Issama had spent more than a year cultivating. Paisahan khan had no desire to be subjugated under a Borjigin Great Khan ever again. Such desperation and hate put Issama in a powerful position.

"I have been in communication with my contacts among the Oirat all winter, my lord Khan," Issama said, folding his hands in front of him and putting forward all the confidence and patience he could summon. "According to my men, your years of stinging along the borders have agitated Paisahan khan. He is worried about a large-scale invasion. He knows he is outnumbered and would not stand a chance against your forces. My contacts have reassured me this is simply a defensive precaution."

"I don't like them on our border," Manduul growled, which spurred on more coughing until he spit into his silver bowl. Issama could not see the contents, but he was certain blood tinged the spit.

"I understand your concern, but I have complete faith in the integrity of my men. The Oirat will not attack you." The words were a careful skirting of the truth. The Oirat would not attack Manduul. But once he died, all bets were off.

Manduul sending Unebolod away had played into Issama's plans to perfection, even if naming Unebolod in the line of succession had not. Without the Khorchin *tumen*, victory would be certain and swift. Fifty thousand strong and ready warriors against less than forty thousand of Manduul's unsuspecting men. There would be no escape. The people would either submit or be crushed—and he would allow but moments for them to choose.

"Very well," Manduul mumbled. "I trust you, Issama."

"I live to serve, my lord Khan," Issama said, bowing deeply. He knew when he was dismissed.

As he left, Manduul called in his servants.

The early evening air was cool, and Issama breathed in deep gulps. It tasted like freedom. It tasted like victory. He headed toward his ger, where no doubt his army of scribes would be waiting outside.

His plan was in action. Only one piece remained to fall into place, and for that, he needed the return of the Golden Prince.

Issama had spent much of his youth in the west, learning language and politics from the Arabs and Mongols in cities like Kashgar and Kabul. When the Moghul Khanate began fracturing, Issama joined the fight, using his cunning to work his way into Bigirsen's command tent. He had met Manduul Khan only a handful of times before Bigirsen had assigned him to this post—and that assignment had been no accident.

All around him, Mongke Bulag buzzed with activity. Children chased each other. Girls carried buckets of fuel for evening fires toward their family gers. Issama could have predicted the paths of everyone around him.

Once he had proven his political savvy to Bigirsen, Issama had laid his path all the way to the top—from the moment he'd suggested Yeke marry to Manduul so Bigirsen could maintain a tight hold on the Khan. Bigirsen was arrogant, proud, and ambitious. The arrangement benefitted him should his daughter produce a child.

As if summoned by his thoughts, Issama watched Yeke glide past, a ghost of a woman. She never stood a chance. Between her less than appealing features, too-long legs, and his meddling, Yeke had been doomed to a lifetime of misery from the start. She could never have a child. She just didn't know it.

Issama had seduced a young female servant in Yeke's service six years ago. The girl adored him and actually believed he would take her as a wife one day. It was a station a mere serving girl could never attain, but she never understood that. She didn't even know his real name. At his suggestion, she had continually mixed small doses of milk of the thistle into Yeke's drinks. If administered frequently, milk of the thistle would create permanent infertility. The girl thought she was giving a fertility treatment. Poor thing.

Issama had given Mandukhai a pouch of milk of the thistle on her wedding night, but she never took it to his knowledge.

Only a handful of clerks stood outside Issama's door waiting for him when he arrived. Issama gave a few sharp orders and sent each of the men on their tasks. This role as Vice Chancellor and *orlok* occupied much of his time, but at least he had an army of clerks to handle most of the work for him once he gave the orders.

Uingen smiled at Issama as he ducked into the ger. She had been a careful selection for marriage. Issama had studied several women in various subtribes loyal to the Uyghur, but Uingen had been the only one whose father held an actual position of power. Between her father and himself, they could handle Bigirsen's stranglehold on the Uyghur when the time came.

Uingen herself was a pretty girl, if not exactly beautiful, and she made for an outstanding wife. Her round face was appealing enough to stir his interest. Issama had courted her cautiously. She did not know the true power her husband held, and he was perfectly happy to keep it that way for now. One day soon, she would be a queen of the Mongols.

Unfortunately, Uingen had been unable to worm her way into Mandukhai's inner circle. He needed Mandukhai on his side, but she politely sidestepped Uingen whenever possible. It had not been overt enough to hurt Uingen's feelings over the rejection. But it was enough to make Issama wonder why his wife was not good enough for Mandukhai's elite circle.

"I know that look, my love," Uingen said. "You have had another good day." She brushed her hands on the front of her deel and turned away from the butcher block to face him. They had been married nearly five years now and lost three children. But he was not worried about heirs. Not yet. Still, he often noticed the ache in her eyes as she gazed at other children.

"All is well in our lives, Uingen," Issama said, resting his sword against the wall beside the door. He crossed the ger, then cupped her face in his hands. She beamed up at him in a way that erased any doubt about how she might feel about him. Issama did not love her as she deserved, but he enjoyed her companionship well enough. He placed a gentle kiss on her lips.

Soon, the prince would return. Then, everything would come together at last.

Mandukhai slid into bed beside Manduul, watching the way his chest rose and fell in his sleep. His breaths were shallow and raspy, and her concern grew with each passing day. The end must be near. *Just tell me the truth*, she thought as she lay back and curled under her own furs.

Mandukhai slept fitfully, dreaming of a life without Manduul's looming presence. Of Unebolod's arms around her. And of Bayan as he had been in her spirit walk ... dead in the Gobi.

CHAPTER TWELVE

The Devil's Blanket

The emperor sent a large force of Ming soldiers in pursuit of Bayan's five thousand men—over fifty thousand Ming. Even with the Chakhar nipping at Ming heels to distract them from full attack, Bayan's escape remained harried. After the first night of rest had cost Bayan nearly a thousand of his warriors in a midnight attack, it had forced him to travel day and night. Once he reached the desert, the Ming would not dare follow.

The Ming pursued him relentlessly, like a dog with the scent of the kill. Bayan feared he would not make it home again until, at long last, the rust-colored hills of the Gobi came into view. He plunged recklessly into the desert, and the Ming fell back, unwilling to attempt pursuit across the unforgiving landscape. Only a fool would travel straight through. Thankfully, Bayan had been through it before. He knew what he was doing.

The rocky hills became a vast sea of rippling dunes. Game was rare in the desert, and his warriors rationed their meager supply of food and water, improperly prepared for the seemingly endless desolation. During the day, Bayan ordered his men to cover their faces to protect against the harsh winds and sun. Only their eyes were visible beneath the cloth coverings.

This return trip consisted not only of warriors, though. Over the last year, several of the men had taken wives—himself included. Those women traveled back to Mongke Bulag with him. Many of them were pregnant or had newborn children to care for. Bayan worried about the welfare of those women and children. Warriors were hardy and could handle anything. Women and babies were much weaker.

As the days and nights dwindled on without an end in sight, supplies shrank. The warriors had filled as many jugs and waterskins as they could find with water before leaving the south, attaching it to the horses to carry. Mongol horses could dredge up food or grazing just about anywhere, but they were unaccustomed to the desert. They could only carry so much. Men hunted scorpions to roast for food. Water was rationed to a mere mouthful at a time.

Siker had complained about their course the first few days, but after the fifth day, she had stopped nagging him and remained with the cart in silence. Enkh, his servant, rode with Siker, keeping careful calculations on Bayan's personal food and water supply.

Yungei rode up beside Bayan on the sixth day. His frostiness contrasted with the heat of the sun hammering down on them. "I suggest we turn west," he said. "This course will lead us to our doom. My best guess puts Bigirsen's territory only a day or two in that direction."

Bayan scowled at Yungei. "Your best guess? I will not turn course because you have a hunch, Yungei. We go north to Mongke Bulag. I won't ride into Oirat territory." Nor would he enter Bigersen's camp and ask for help.

"*Jinong*—"

"No!" Heat and thirst shortened Bayan's temper. He fired a deadly glare at Yungei, daring the commander to challenge him.

Yungei's mouth curled up ever so slightly in loathing, but he nodded. "Your will, *Jinong*." Then he fell back into surly silence.

By the next day, Bayan could feel his own lips turn dry and brittle. He could not even lick them to add moisture; his mouth had long since gone dry.

What would Manduul think when he returned early? Would Manduul see it as a failure? Bayan could only hope his uncle would understand.

The temperature during the day should have been cool, but for the unforgiving sun. With no wind or cloud cover, it pressed against them all like a great mountain attempting to smother them all. Nights offered respite from the heat, but only for the first hour. After that, the cold became unbearable. Layers that were shed under the sun were heaped back on in the moonlight. No amount of complaining would change their fate, though Bayan heard the grumbles trailing behind him.

Each morning, Berkedai watched the horizon to be sure the sun still rose to their right, and that they hadn't veered off course in the night.

Two weeks passed, and the families following Bayan wilted. Though Bayan could not hear their complaints, he sensed their discord. They doubted him and his ability to lead them through the desert. Some newborns had not survived the heat, catching heat sickness only a few days in. The sickness took them within a week. The men blamed him for their lost children. Did they not understand that if they had remained in the south, the Ming would have killed the children instead? Those babies were destined to die.

But Bayan would get most of them through the desert. He had always been lucky with survival. He survived his birth when his grandfather wanted him dead. He survived his childhood under Bolunai's abusive hands. He survived his harrowing escape from Bolunai's care, and his last trip across the desert. He survived all the Ming attacks. In all of those cases, Bayan should have died. But fate had plans for him. Luck always saw him through.

This trip would be no different.

Berkedai cast worried glances over his shoulder at the men and woman following them. "The men are getting restless," he said, lowering his voice. "I worry they will revolt against you."

"And go where?" Bayan asked, sounding as exhausted as he felt. Even if they revolted against him, the only way out of the desert was straight through.

The conversation cut off as someone cried out from behind them. "Storm!"

Bayan and Berkedai both yanked their horses around, following the direction all eyes had turned.

In the distance, a rolling wall of tan spread along the eastern horizon, spinning straight toward them. Women cried out in fear. The devil's blanket rumbled toward them, inevitable, determined to swallow them all whole.

"Dismount!" Yungei hollered. "Huddle down under blankets. Lay the horses and bury their snouts!" His orders echoed up and down the line. Commanders shouted orders as the howl of the wind picked up.

Bayan slid from his saddle as Enkh and Siker rushed toward him carrying blankets. Sand began pelting them as the storm blew closer. Siker grabbed Bayan's arm and pulled him down as he laid Andayar on the ground. Before disappearing under a blanket with Siker and Andayar's head, Bayan spotted Berkedai doing the same with his wife.

Wind screamed around them, pressing against the blanket covering their backs. Siker clung to Bayan, but she didn't tremble. To Bayan's dismay, he did. Despite the covering over their head, sand kicked up, stinging his face and arms. It lodged in his nose. Air grew thin, recycled over and over as he, Siker, and Andayar shared the same air repeatedly.

Darkness descended. Wicked wind pushed the two of them over, forcing them to their hands and knees. The sound howled deafening in his ears. A great weight pushed against his back. Bayan pressed his forehead against Siker's neck as they curled tighter around each other. The space became confining as it shrank.

When at last the howling wind passed, no light penetrated their shelter. Siker pulled away from him but could only shift a few inches. Andayar's head moved in the darkness, huffing and whinnying in terror. The only sounds came from their own breath and the panicked horse.

"Berkedai!" Bayan called, his throat raw and screaming in pain.

"I can't move," Siker said, alarm in her voice.

Bayan tried shifting his weight. A mountain had pinned them down. No wonder the horse struggled. The air they breathed had gone hot some time ago.

Siker's panic penetrated his thoughts. "Bayan ..."

"I'm thinking!" Bayan snapped. He hadn't meant to lose his temper, but did she really think he would know what to do in only seconds? "Berkedai!"

Bayan pushed his back up, grunting, breathing in the hot, stifling air.

The storm had buried them.

"Stop sitting there and help me push up!" he snapped.

Siker made a noise of anger. However, a moment later, the two pushed in unison, their backs against the weight of the fresh dune over them. Their hands pressed into the shifting sand beneath them.

"Stop. Stop!" Siker called, panting hard. "We will burrow ourselves deeper."

Bayan sagged, feeling the weight of the sand on their backs shift. His face burned hot. He knew, were he not so dehydrated already, he would have cried. *Where is my luck now?*

"Bolkhu!" A muffled voice reached through the layers above them.

Bayan's heart lifted. Luck, it seemed, struck again. "Berkedai!"

"Here!" Siker yelled.

The sand shifted around them, freeing the struggling Andayar first. The horse snorted and pulled away, making more sand collapse around their heads. A minute later, the last of the sand on his back shifted away. A muscular hand reached down and pulled him from the earth as if he were reborn.

Berkedai clasped Bayan in a brotherly hug as Yungei retrieved Siker. Bayan blew the sand out of his nose, then rinsed it from his mouth with a meager supply of water.

"How many?" Bayan asked.

Berkedai shook his head. "No way to know yet. We have to uncover them all."

Bayan turned, scanning the bright horizon. "We cannot delay long. If we don't find survivors in the next hour, we need to move on."

Berkedai nodded.

"Those are loyal Khorchin men," Yungei argued. His anger bled through. "My men. Unebolod's men. We cannot abandon them!"

Bayan tried to stand as tall as he could while his entire body ached. "Those are *my* men, Yungei. But I will not risk everyone for the sake of a few."

"Unless it's your own skin," Yungei snapped. His shoulders tensed and he clenched his hands into fists.

Berkedai stepped between them, hand on his sword.

Siker scoffed. "Men. Perhaps you should stop wasting time fighting each other so you can help find more people."

Yungei glared at Bayan, then turned and stomped away. Loose sand shifted under each step.

"I don't like him," Bayan declared, watching Yungei continue searching for survivors.

"You don't have to like him," Berkedai said. "But he is a skilled commander and we need him."

As the second week bled on, one of the *mingghan* commanders—a Uyghur from Issama's *tumen*—suggested they shield the eyes of their mounts to protect them from the sun. They had tried, but the mounts bucked and complained until riders had no choice but to remove many of the blindfolds. A mucus began forming around the eyes and mouths of the horses, and if they didn't get fresh water soon, they would fall over dead.

"How much farther?" Berkedai asked as he rode at the head of the column beside Bayan.

Bayan wished he had an answer, but there was no way to know. He had only crossed the desert once before, and he had been alone. He didn't have to worry about food and water for everyone. Only himself and his stallion—and even that he had traded for supplies. Traveling with thousands of men and their new families proved far different. Two weeks of desert lay behind them. There would be no turning back.

Bayan wiped sweat from his brow with his arm and noticed how dark his skin had grown in the passing weeks, tanned and coated in sand. Sweat soaked everything, and the coarse dirt and sand stuck to his skin everywhere it could reach. He could not wait to dip himself in a cool spring river.

"It can't be much longer now," Bayan said, but he was certain his tone lacked real confidence.

Berkedai squinted into the distance ahead of them. "We are losing men, my Lord. If we don't reach the other side soon, we will return to Manduul Khan with no army—if we return at all."

Bayan clenched his fists and resisted the urge to slap Berkedai. The heat and exhaustion made his temper short, but striking the one man he trusted outside of Manduul would help nothing.

Despite the skins and jugs carried with them, their water supply had run out the day before. Bayan ordered the last of it given to the mounts. Without them, the *mingghans* would never cross the desert on foot.

Everyone moved much slower than they had upon entering the desert. Bayan counted over five hundred lost in the sands to hunger or thirst. Another thousand in the storm. By his estimation, they would return to Mongke Bulag three thousand short of the five they had left him with.

What would Manduul say?

Chapter Thirteen

Sand, Smoke, and Death

Unebolod spent his winter in Bolunai's small palace among the servants and Bolunai's wives and children. Yet he had not been idle. Bolunai sent messengers to three nearby tribes, offering rooms in his palace in exchange for their company. Two of the lesser khans had come, eager to see the palace and spend their time within its warm walls during the cold months. They were each received with a small banquet and private meetings, first between them and Bolunai—who would plant the seeds of change—then between them and Unebolod, where Unebolod would convince them to support Bayan. But in the event of Bayan's death, they would support Unebolod.

Convincing the first to support Unebolod had been simple enough. The lesser khan had close ties with the Khorchin and was eager to support the noble descendants of Khasar should the line of Genghis die off. Unebolod had to be careful how he collected these alliances. They had to believe they would follow him if Manduul and Bayan both died. They did not have to know that both would soon perish.

The second khan had been more apprehension, citing the support the prince had gathered in the south. It had taken quite a bit of reassurance that Unebolod would not make a move for the title if Bayan survived—which he would not, but the khan didn't need to know that. Unebolod even cited

Manduul's proclamation that the Khorchin nobles would be next in line should there be no Borjigin heir.

"The call to *kurultai* is coming," Unebolod had said, "and we must be ready to support the next Great Khan against outside attacks."

That has settled matters quickly.

Now, with spring arriving, he prepared his *tumen* for the journey south. A third khan would need his attention, and Unebolod could not afford to let this one slip away.

"Just remember, this is a dangerous game you play, brother," Bolunai said, as they checked the mounts he would send with Unebolod. The khan's stable was large, and the horses had to be taken out to graze by several expert herdsmen each day. "If you plan to do this thing, be sure it is done swiftly and with true aim."

"He won't escape me," Unebolod said confidently, taking the reins of his mare and guiding her out of the stable.

Bolunai walked alongside him. His brother winced so slightly it would have been easy to miss. "That boy is slippery. Don't underestimate him. His will to survive outweighs everything else, and he will do anything to survive even if it means aligning with your enemies."

"It will be quick. We cannot afford any less. I know the risks." Should Unebolod fail to kill Bayan and the prince figured out it was Unebolod who attempted the assassination, the boy would become Great Khan and send in all the *tumens* he could gather to sweep the Khorchin off the map.

Bolunai nodded solemnly. "You have worked for this your entire life. Let me keep my title and my lands, and you will have the full support of the Khorchin."

Sunlight broke over the mountains to the east, warming Unebolod's chilled skin. He mounted his mare to ride out and meet the army waiting to ride with him. It would be a good day. "Thank you, brother. I give you my word. You will keep control over our tribe while I control the Nation."

"And the queen," Bolunai said, a grin spreading across his face.

Unebolod grimaced. "I should never have drunk so much around you. I know better. Speak of her to no one, Bolunai. As long as Manduul still lives, he could still take my head." Not that his brother knew the extent of his relationship with Mandukhai. But Bolunai understood enough that it could condemn him to death.

"Our line will finally claim what we have waited centuries for," Bolunai said, bobbing his head in respect. "Who knew it would be at the hands of my obnoxious younger brother?"

"Should the High Heavens support our right and the sky father bless our path," Unebolod said. Though he spoke the traditional blessing, Unebolod didn't to feel it in his heart. The gods often found new ways to torture him.

He turned his mare toward the southern hill and nudged her forward.

"Don't start the fun without me!" Bolunai called as Unebolod rode away.

Unebolod chuckled as he guided his mount along the wide paths between makeshift homes and gers. Bolunai had built something wonderful here, but the nature of the Mongol people was that they would always be on the move. Such a place could never keep a tribe happy for long. They were meant to travel the countryside. *Unebolod* was meant to move across the face of the world. At last, his chance would come.

As he crested the slope of a hill, the mass of carts and horsemen spread out across the grassland south of the city, waiting to meet with their Kharchin cousins farther south. Soke, Unebolod's second in command, rode up to the crest of the hill to join him.

Several carts of gunpowder had been delivered in the wolf dawn to the *tumens* waiting to the south. Unebolod found the gunpowder unnerving and did not trust the men in charge of it. But Bolunai had insisted he take carts of it. One wrong charge and his own army could be destroyed.

"The khan has generously given us extra mounts and rations to make this journey," Soke said after bowing in his saddle. "We have an extra thousand men to help manage the gunpowder and cannons, on top of the warriors he has already given. The *tumens* are ready for your orders."

Bolunai had offered another full *tumen* to Unebolod's command, some of whom could work with the new materials he provided. The khan had insisted that Unebolod would need a show of strength to carry out his mission successfully. None but his brother knew his true intentions. Unebolod had been careful to gather support behind him without making it apparent he would oppose Bayan. He trusted Soke, but not enough to share the truth. It was too dangerous. Soke was a loyal Khorchin, but loyalty to the Great Khan often proved stronger in some men.

"Send the command then," Unebolod said. "We ride—"

A deafening concussive boom drowned out all other sounds. Thunder rumbled across the sky and the earth beneath his mare shook. For a moment, he could hear nothing but the roaring blast. Unebolod's mount kicked up in protest, her squeals smothered by the roar. A shockwave rocked her back a few steps away from the heart of the Khorchin city. The overpowering scent of sulfur and earth filled the air.

Plumes of thick black smoke continued to rise into the sky over the Khorchin city as debris of stone and earth rained down from the heavens as far as the hilltop Unebolod sat on. Some of the debris crushed men, women, homes, and horses in its path. A massive crater dipped into the foothills, surrounded by crushed or burning gers. The smoke continued to rise high into the sky, marking the grave its victims. In the center, nothing remained of the khan's small palace.

As Unebolod yanked his reins to maintain control of the mount, another deafening blast trembled the earth to the south. Unebolod had no time to gather his wits as the second explosion erupted in his camp to the south where his own men waited. He called out for Soke, but the thunder wholly swallowed his screams for action. A second shockwave hammered against his chest before he could catch his breath from the first.

The carts of gunpowder Bolunai had given him marked the graves of hundreds—if not thousands—of his men just as certainly as the crater in the city marked that of his family. All around him, smoke choked the air and blocked out the bright light of the rising sun.

Grief weighed down on Unebolod. For a moment, he was too stunned to think. Heaviness made his limbs hang at his sides. Sorrow rooted itself deep in his heart as reality hammered against his mind. Unebolod's brother and all his wives and children would be dead—which left Unebolod the most senior member of the tribe.

This is not time for weakness, he thought bitterly. Spinning his mare around, he charged toward Soke, grabbing the stunned man by the collar of his padded leather armor and yanking him close, nearly unseating him.

"Assemble any senior officers who survived," he shouted at his commander over the rumble of earth. "Send half into the Khorchin camp to collect survivors, and the rest to reorganize what remains of the *tumens*. Quickly!" He released his grip on Soke with enough force to send the other man's mount racing toward his *tumens* in the south.

Without hesitation, Unebolod kicked his mount toward the burning, smoky remains of the khan's palace. Disbelief rattled his cold warrior mask. In all his years, Unebolod had never witnessed such devastation. Nor had he lost everything in a moment quite like this. Without his family, with Manduul dying, Unebolod had only Mandukhai to cling to. He would be utterly alone in the world.

This realization only firmed his determination to confirm the truth. If Bolunai and his sons were dead, Unebolod needed to prove it to himself.

The army waned under the unforgiving sun as it continued following Bayan across the sands of the desert. More men and women had died, and more mounts had collapsed from exhaustion or dehydration. Though Bayan could not hear the whispers, he knew the men questions his ability to lead. Faced with doubt, he maintained his optimism; even when his own strength waned; even when his eyes dried and caked with abrasive sand; even when his mouth ran so dry and his limbs grew so weak he could hardly control his chestnut mare beneath him.

Bayan slid in his saddle as his body sagged, ready to give out. He slipped toward the ground. A large hand seized his arm and pulled him upright, then slapped him hard enough on the back to bring him back to alertness.

Berkedai rode beside him, holding Bayan in his saddle. The two men said nothing. But the way Berkedai stared at him, Bayan understood. As long as Berkedai had strength, he would continue to keep his prince alive, but even his own strength had diminished in the deadly desert.

In the distance ahead, waving in the heat, Bayan spotted a shallow pond of water. His dry mouth amplified the dehydration, and he picked up the pace. In moments, Berkedai caught stride, frowning at him.

"What is it?" Berkedai asked.

Bayan pointed at the shimmering water. As if in a nightmare, it continued to keep an even distance from him.

Berkedai squinted into the distance. After a moment, he shook his head. "It's nothing. Just sand."

"Water."

"It isn't real, Bolkhu."

Dismayed, yet still doubtful, Bayan sagged further in his saddle.

Enkh had delivered the last of Bayan's water two days ago. The servant appeared on the verge of collapse himself, in dire need of his own water. Bayan only felt bad for a moment before he finished his water. Enkh was a servant. Bayan was a prince. If only one of them could survive this, Bayan knew who it needed to be.

Without a water supply, the men resorted to nicking their mares for blood just to stay alive. However, even that task proved challenging, as many of the men lacked the strength to stand on their own feet. His hope had begun to vanish. Surely his luck could hold out just one more time ...

Unebolod had never heard thunder quite like what rolled across the hills. It echoed off the peaks and rolled down the valleys, amplified by the landscape. Riding into the remains of the Khorchin city brought bitter reality down on him so forcefully he had to cover his mouth with his sleeve to not only block out the smoke that stung his eyes, but to hold back the unexpected bile rising in his throat. Seasoned as he was, nothing prepared him for this sort of carnage.

A woman was rooted to the earth in numb shock as blood poured down a wide gash along one side of her face. More bodies than he could count littered the ground in heaps—many missing limbs. He trotted through the smoke, squinting to see as the black smoke continued drifting on the air. A child stood alone between the broken bodies of his parents, crying as fire consumed his tiny body. Unebolod dismounted, holding the reins tight in one hand as he drew his sword and put the poor child out of his misery. Fires burned all around him; embers catching on felt and wood. Were it not for the smoke stinging his eyes, he was certain the agony would pour out of him. The cold warrior's mask was replaced by deep lines of sorrow creasing his face.

Unebolod's heart pounded in his ears as he jumped back into the saddle and carried onward, sending survivors toward the edge of the chaos where, hopefully, his men could reorganize whatever remained.

Horses, men, women, and children all screamed in pain or terror. He did his best to follow those voices and guide people to safety as he carried on toward the palace. Those who would not survive, he mercy killed. *Was this the will of the gods? What sort of god would do such a thing? The Khorchin were good people.*

The scent of spent gunpowder mingled with the stink of burning or charred flesh. Any hope of finding a survivor among his family swiftly dwindled the deeper he rode into the heart of the Khorchin city.

By the time he reached the palace grounds, Unebolod's eyes burned painfully from the smoke. He could hardly breathe as it filled his lungs.

Unebolod dismounted, gripping the reins of his mare in a tight fist, guiding her to the edge of the foundation—the only thing that remained of the khan's palace. He poured out water on a strip of cloth he ripped from his deel and used it to create a mask over his nose and mouth.

The stones of the palace smoldered as he stood on the edge, staring into the gaping hole in the ground where the gunpowder had been stored. Everything had blown away from that space, leaving no doubt that this had been the epicenter of the blast. Flames licked at stone and earth here and there.

Unebolod's mare stamped her hooves and danced in protest, eager to ride away. He thrust his sword deep into the earth and tied the reins tightly to it. Then he wrapped his hands in cloth and eased down into the crater where the charred remains of a body lay in pieces. A lump formed in his throat. Control of his warrior's mask that he barely managed to wrangle a moment before cracked as he gazed at the remains of a man too small to be his brother.

He turned slowly in place, seeking any other clues. The gunpowder had done its work. If any evidence remained to explain the explosion, it had either burned, blown apart, or launched up and out of the crater. But it could not have been an accident. Not when the gunpowder in both the city and his own camp further from the city had happened so close to each other. The timing of both explosions was no accident. But who was responsible? And were they, too, dead?

Unebolod climbed out of the hole, coughing out smoke from his lungs as the air slowly cleared. A guard in black and red lacquered armor held his sword up to strike. The moment he saw Unebolod's face—or what was visible of his face behind the watered cloth—the guard dropped the sword and bowed his head, revealing a nasty gash across his skull. Unebolod noticed the guard's other arm was missing, but he had already wrapped the stump. The man could hardly stand on his feet. *How is he still upright? He must have lost a lot of blood already.*

"The khan?" Unebolod asked, already knowing the answer.

The man shook his head, then stumbled to the side. Unebolod turned. The khan's stable was little more than a single wall. The rest had been crushed beneath rocks that must have blasted outward from the explosion.

"Take my horse," Unebolod said, desperate for help as he untied the reins, knowing he would not get help from this man. "Go to my camp and get yourself help."

"My Lord khan," the guard said, giving a bow that nearly toppled him forward.

Unebolod grasped the man's shoulders to steady him, then helped him climb into the saddle.

Khan. The words would have filled him with excitement under any other circumstances. But this was not how he would have chosen to earn the title. Hearing such a proclamation only confirmed what he was not yet ready to accept, that his brother and his entire family were dead.

GOBI DESERT – SPRING 1469

Just when Bayan was certain he had led all of his men to their doom, the sand grew stiffer under hooves, then shifted into red rocks that bled into brown grass pastures and familiar rolling hills of the north. At first, he was certain his eyes deceived him, that this was some trick of the desert. But as men whooped with joy and found their strength renewed by familiar homelands, they raced forward as if the desert were death itself on their heels.

Bayan rode at a steady pace, afraid that too much jostling would dislodge him from the saddle. Berkedai gave a few commands Bayan only heard as a distant noise. In seconds, more than a dozen scouts raced out of the desert, fanning in all directions toward the north.

"What …?" Bayan asked, his voice raspy and his throat raw. He could not ask the question he wanted to ask. *What are the scouts doing?*

"I sent them to find water." Berkedai sounded weaker, but not as affected by the desert as Bayan had been.

He could only nod in response, which made his head throb.

The sun began moving toward the west before a scout raced back with news of a river. Without a second of hesitation, Bayan commanded the scout to lead the way, and the caravan followed. He only had two thousand men left, but at least *he* was still alive.

Failure, Fate, and Fortune

MONGKE BULAG – SPRING 1469

With the approaching spring had come news that had all of Mongke Bulag buzzing with excitement. The Golden Prince would return soon. Manduul's scouts had ridden for miles each day, moving back and forth with new reports of the cart-laden caravan, which had emerged from the Gobi. Mandukhai could not fathom what would possess Bayan to risk traveling through the desert. Surely there would be a good explanation.

Mandukhai had found some of those reports distressing. Far fewer people were returning than they had left with Bayan. Their condition was frail, forcing them to move at a slower speed as they recovered from their treacherous journey through the desert. Of those who remained in Bayan's charge, hundreds hung on the brink of death. Mandukhai worried about them all.

Yeke had thrown open her door to air out her ger once she heard the news. She also opened the smoke hole wide, to let in sunshine and fresh air. With each passing day, Yeke showed her face more frequently. Her demeanor had changed as well. Any doubt that remained about Yeke's relationship with Bayan had diminished swiftly. Mandukhai wondered if *she* would act the same if she heard Unebolod was returning.

As the caravan approached the capital, Mandukhai accompanied Manduul to the gathering tent to await Bayan. Manduul had wanted to ride out, but a fit of coughing made Mandukhai wonder if he could handle the activity, small as it was.

"I will go greet him," Mandukhai reassured Manduul as he slumped on his throne.

"No. Send my guards. I won't have him greeted by a woman when he returns from the campaign."

Mandukhai bristled, not bothering to hide her scowl. After everything, he still called her just "a woman." Had she not proven herself to be far more than that already?

"Very well," Mandukhai said, bowing to Manduul slightly before marching toward the doorway to give the orders. In moments, she had an honor guard assembled and riding out of Mongke Bulag to greet their returned prince.

By the time Mandukhai returned to her seat, Yeke rushed into the gathering tent. Her gaze swept the open space in a thinly veiled hope to see Bayan already standing there. The moment it was apparent he had not arrived, Yeke slowed her pace, then took her usual seat near Manduul. She carefully arranged her copper-colored silk skirt around her legs and sat with her back straight. As they waited, Yeke's gaze shifted to Bayan's empty throne.

Mandukhai also noticed that, for the first time since Bayan left, Yeke wore light powders and paints on her face again. It was a subtle change, but noticeable to her. How did Manduul not see such things? Was Yeke so invisible to him? Mandukhai was certain that, had it been *her*, he would have noticed immediately. Sometimes she wished she could be as invisible to him as Yeke.

Mandukhai yearned to learn what had happened to Bayan's people. When Issama had returned, he reported leaving nearly five thousand men with Bayan. Manduul's reports noted scarcely two thousand men, with their women and children in tow. How had Bayan lost so many?

Issama caught news of the men riding out to greet Bayan. He swiftly mounted his own horse and rode out to join them. Since returning from the campaign, Issama had gained more power as Manduul's *orlok* , and he would not be seen as lesser or weak by waiting in a tent with the Khan and his women.

The sheer lack of carts and horses trailing back along the landscape brought a thousand questions to mind as Issama rode out with the guards. Foremost, what happened?

The condition of the people shocked Issama. They appeared ragged, as if they had ridden without stopping the entire way north. Bayan's skin was several shades darker than it had been in the fall. *What would possess him to ride through the desert?* Issama wondered as he rode closer and spotted Bayan at the head of the column.

"Bolkhu *Jinong*," Issama said as Bayan reined to a halt in front of the line of Manduul's men. "Welcome home."

"It's good to be home," Bayan said, sounding exhausted. "I assume Manduul is waiting for me?" While he appeared fresh, there could be no doubt Bayan only put on the appearance of confidence.

"He is."

Bayan nudged his chestnut mare past Issama. Berkedai and Yungei followed the prince without so much as a nod to Issama. It grated under his skin.

A young woman with a flat face and large eyebrows rode behind Bayan and his guards. As she passed Issama, his gaze caught hers. Nothing about her struck him as familiar, yet he felt a link to her. She offered a weak, shy smile before ducking her head and following. *No, I could not have met her before. I would remember that face.* It certainly was a pleasant one.

Issama turned his mount and joined them as the Khan's guards closed around the prince in a protective ring.

Mandukhai struggled to remain patient as Bayan and his men dismounted outside the gathering tent. She squirmed in her seat and clenched her hands together in the folds of her sleeves. It took far too long before they at last ducked inside, following Issama. Spotting the contemplative expression on Issama's face, Mandukhai idly wondered what Issama was considering.

Then she saw the state of the three men and the young woman trailing behind Issama. While their clothing appeared clean and their faces washed, the exhaustion was clear on all of their faces. The journey through the Gobi had taken a toll on them all. Bayan was thinner than Mandukhai remembered, but taller as well. A glance at Yeke revealed the concern shining in her eyes as she studied Bayan.

To his credit, Bayan paused on the second step of the dais in front of Manduul instead of just marching to his own seat beside the Khan. Issama drifted to the side of the dais steps. Berkedai and Yungei—Bayan's guards and Khorchin men loyal to Unebolod—both bowed deeply to the Great Khan, as did the young woman with them.

Mandukhai studied the young woman. Who was she, and why was she here? Nothing about the woman stood out. She was young, perhaps the same age as Mandukhai, with a rather plain face. Her deel was a fine Chakhar cut, but nothing that marked her out as important.

"You look exhausted, Bolkhu," Manduul said, sounding much stronger than he had just minutes before. Mandukhai knew it was an act. "What brings you back to us early?"

Bayan stood straight, raising his chin proudly. "Your orders, uncle. Incite, but do not engage. The Ming learned our location over the winter months and chased us into the desert. I would have stood our ground, but your orders were clear. We had no choice but to return."

Mandukhai started with this news. *Ming? So far north? But how had they gotten past the Ordos tribes?* Even if they skirted wide, they would have met resistance, either from the Urainkhai to the east or Bigirsen's men to the west.

Manduul's expression darkened. "Berkedai, Yungei, what have you to report?"

Both men finally raised their heads, but still kept their gaze downcast as if ashamed. The young woman with them said nothing as she stood behind the men.

"We defended our prince, my lord Khan," Berkedai said. "The Ming soldiers seemed intent on capturing but not killing Bolkhu *Jinong*. One man we captured would only say that the line of Khan's would fall. They were quite relentless, and they outnumbered us. Even with the Chakhar's help, we would have suffered defeat."

Yungei grunted.

"Speak," Manduul barked.

"Our lord *Jinong* learned men were looting Mongol caravans in his name," Yungei reported. "He spoke with a Chakhar Lord and learned where these raids happened, setting a trap for the offenders. The battle was well-planned, but we learned it had been Ming disguised as Mongols. Instead of killing all the Ming, Bolkhu *Jinong* sent two Ming soldiers back as a warning. This drew the eye of the emperor our way. Only weeks later, the emperor sent an army."

Ming disguised as Mongols? Mandukhai had thought such a thing would be beneath the Ming, who considered themselves superior.

Bayan glared at Yungei. The two of them never had gotten along. How had these events strained their relationship?

Yungei continued his report. "During the first attempt to capture our Golden Prince, we engaged the Ming forces. They collapsed on our camp from all sides, forcing us to divide our *mingghans* to defend the camp. When the Ming closed in around Lord Bolkhu, the Chakhar disengaged. They eventually returned to chase away the Ming. But it looked a lot like desertion."

"And the Chakhar had nothing to say for themselves after turning away on the field of battle?" Manduul asked. Mandukhai could hear the heat of anger burning in his voice.

Bayan opened his mouth to speak, but Yungei barreled on without giving the prince a chance. "Lord Mingtau insisted they had another force to the south to fight first, but I believe something more deceptive was happening. They hesitated before joining us on the battlefield. The attack cost us a thousand men."

A thousand men! Mandukhai's gaze darted to Bayan, then to Manduul. *How many Ming had there been to kill so many skilled Mongol warriors? Have the Ming declared war on us?* The very idea made her heart clench with worry. They did not have the strength to stand up against the vast number of Ming soldiers.

Bayan cast a hateful glare at Yungei so fiercely that, if looks could kill, Yungei would have died a slow, painful death.

"We moved our camp, only stinging at the Ming when they came too close," Yungei said. "But their last attempt at kidnapping the prince came in the dark of night after the prince's wedding."

Yeke gasped just loudly enough to draw Mandukhai's attention. For a fleeting moment, Bayan glanced at Yeke, and Mandukhai was certain she saw an apology in his eyes. Yeke clasped her hands so tight in her lap that her knuckles turned white. Manduul glanced at Yeke, but did not seem to care. He quickly dismissed her by turning his attention to Bayan. *He probably assumes she is reacting to the news of the Ming attack so close to the camp,* Mandukhai thought.

Manduul's alarm at this newest development was written all over his face as his bushy brows climbed his wide forehead. Mandukhai herself could not help feeling a little alarmed along with Yeke—though probably for much different reasons. Bayan had been against any sort of commitment.

She gazed at the young woman hiding behind the men curiously. Hardly a great beauty. *Why her?* she wondered.

"What happened to the rest of my men?" Manduul asked Bayan, ignoring this latest news for the moment. "You have only returned with two thousand out of the five left to you."

Bayan dipped his head, his voice lowering in shame. "Between the Ming's endless attacks and the journey across the desert, many of them died, along with good mounts. I'm sorry for the failure, uncle. I worried about disobeying your command. We had no other options. The Ming had us pinned in."

"You could have gone to Bigirsen for aid," Manduul said sharply.

Mandukhai knew this would not have worked out much better for Bayan. Bigirsen fought near the edged of the Gansu Corridor to expand the Khan's influence. Bayan could have just as easily fallen to a different Ming force on his flanks.

Bayan said nothing, his gaze still downcast. The silence seemed to stretch on forever. Mandukhai wondered if, at last, Manduul would question Bayan's capabilities.

"I suggested we go to Bigirsen for help," Yungei announced. Had he just puffed up with pride that this had been his idea all along? "But Bolkhu *Jinong* felt we had better chances going straight through the desert."

"That is not what I said," Bayan snapped, fury burning in his golden eyes, as if kissed by flames themselves. "*You* could not be certain how far it would be. We were better off staying the course than risking your hunch was wrong."

Yungei didn't flinch. "It would have been a shorter path."

"We had no way to know that for certain." Bayan's hands clenched into fists at his sides. Mandukhai wondered if he would punch Yungei right there on the spot.

Manduul grunted, shifting slightly in his seat and drawing their gazes grudgingly apart. Who would win a fight between Bayan and Yungei?

"Well, we are relieved to have our prince returned." Manduul cocked his head to see past Bayan. "So, who is that magnificent creature hiding behind you?"

The young woman cleared her throat as Bayan stepped aside. Mandukhai noticed the grimace he did not even try to hide as she introduced herself. "Siker, my lord Khan." She bowed again. "Prince Bolkhu's wife."

Manduul chortled. "And about time, too. Come forward, Siker, so I can see you better."

Siker glanced nervously at Bayan before climbing the steps and standing in front of Manduul. Yeke stiffened as the other woman approached. Mandukhai watched her sister-wife out of the corner of her eyes. Yeke examined every inch of Siker from head to toe. Her expression became more detached, as it had been during Bayan's absence. Though Yeke masked her jealousy fairly well, Mandukhai knew what she was watching for. Mandukhai glanced at Bayan from the corner of her eyes and noticed him watching Yeke's reaction as well.

"Tell me," Manduul said as he looked Siker over. "How did you tame my wild nephew?"

Siker swallowed hard, glancing at Bayan before answering. "Lord Guden, of the Chakhar, convinced him, actually."

Manduul appeared impressed. "Is he your father?"

Siker dipped her head. "No, my lord Khan."

Mandukhai raised her brows in alarm. Why would a tribe leader push such a marriage if not to his own daughter? Unless there was a child involved. Had Bayan's promiscuity finally caught up with him? Or perhaps this marriage came with other promises ... of full support at *kurultai*.

"Have you any children, Lady Siker?" Mandukhai asked with a carefully welcoming tone.

"None that I am aware of, my Lady," Siker answered evenly.

Mandukhai frowned. A curious answer. How could a woman not know if she had a child? From the corner of her eye, Mandukhai noticed Issama relax ever so slightly. As Bigirsen's man, Mandukhai figured it would make sense that Issama would also want Yeke to have a son with Manduul before Bayan had any children.

"Is your father a Lord or commander serving Guden khan?" Manduul asked.

"No, my lord Khan. My father was a simple herder, killed five years ago," Siker said. For just a moment, she glanced at Berkedai and Yungei as if they had killed him. Again, Mandukhai found this woman intriguing ... and perhaps dangerous.

"Well," Manduul said, taking Siker's hand and patting it. "Either way, this is good fortune to us. A prince needs a wife, and you seem suitable enough."

Siker's face flushed. "Thank you, my lord Khan."

"We shall have to celebrate this union as a prince deserves," Manduul announced, then dismissed everyone with a gesture.

Mandukhai watched Siker with growing curiosity as the other woman turned and waited for Bayan to head toward the exit before trailing behind him. Bayan did not even bother reaching for Siker or looking at her at all, as Mandukhai would have expected newlyweds to do. Something was amiss between them. Siker had secrets. Mandukhai would earn Siker's trust and unearth them. Secrets in this court could be deadly—for Siker, or for Mandukhai.

Siker did not stare at the charming prince with the same admiring eyes as other young women. In fact, her gaze drifted to Issama as she crossed the open space. Issama met Siker's gaze in a way that made Mandukhai stomach twist. *What is he thinking about?* She could not even imagine.

Yet she could not deny that something had passed between Issama and Siker. Even if only for a moment.

Issama approached Manduul with a sheaf of parchments. In moments, the two were deep in business. Mandukhai slipped out of the gathering tent to find Esige. The girl could learn anything.

If Siker had secrets, Esige would discover them. Mandukhai needed her little spy.

Bayan wanted to collapse onto his bed and sleep the day away, but the ger was no longer his own.

Siker quickly slipped deep into unloading her possessions and reorganizing everything around him. Though he lay back and closed his eyes, her incessant questions about the purpose of this or the placement of that created an irresistible itch to escape. With a growl, he surged to his feet and stomped toward the door.

"Don't be late for the celebration," Siker called after him as he ducked out the door.

Bayan grumbled to himself. Manduul intended to celebrate Bayan's marriage to Siker that evening.

This situation with Siker would not do. He needed somewhere to escape. Just the thought of going back to sleep in the same bed with her filled him to the brim with irritation. He trudged off with no destination in mind, slipping his guards. He needed to be alone.

Fate, it seemed, was a terribly cruel punishment. Everything he struggled to avoid continued to dog his every step. He could escape Siker no more easily than he could escape Manduul. *At least I love Manduul*, he thought bitterly.

Had Bayan's grandfather not been Khan for half a stupid day, and had he not been brothers with Taisun Khan and blood of Genghis, Bayan may have been able to find a way out of all of this mess. Now, the Ming wanted him captured, Unebolod most likely wanted him dead, and who knew what other enemies he had yet to meet. Death loomed over his shoulder at all times in Mongke Bulag as surely as it had in the desert. Yet in the desert, he had known how to conquer death; in camp, he had no way of knowing. All he could do was hope that his luck would continue to serve him well.

The meandering train of thought and desperation to evade his ill fate brought Bayan to the bank of the Orkhon River. Bayan had dunked his entire body in the Ongi River when they had reached the northern edge of the desert, along with hundreds of others. They had soaked their skin in the water and scrubbed away sand from the Gobi. A dip in the Orkhon River brought further satisfaction.

Bayan stripped down, welcoming the chill in the late-spring air, and jumped off a ledge into a short waterfall. His backside scraped the bottom, but he didn't care. Water surrounded him, drowning out the rest of the world. Bayan broke the surface and breathed in the chilly air, swiping his long hair away from his face. For a moment, the weight of everything lifted off his shoulders as if the water had taken it on for him.

Yeke's familiar voice spoke softly from the riverbank. "I thought we had an understanding, Bolkhu *Jinong*."

Bayan started, spinning around in the water. Yeke watched him from the riverbank impassively—or at least what she probably thought was impassively. The corners of her mouth turned downward ever so slightly. Though her brows remained smooth, her eyes gave away her pain. She held his clothes and boots in her arms, hugging them against her chest. *Please don't leave me like this*, he thought desperately.

"We had an understanding, yet you come back with a wife?" Yeke clearly tried her best to sound angry, but he could hear how her voice wavered.

Bayan glanced around, but no one else was anywhere near them. No one else could see them so far from the capital.

"I had no choice," Bayan said, more afraid that she would leave him in the water with no clothing than he was of Yeke's anger or disappointment. "The Chakhar khan—"

"I heard," Yeke snapped. "But you are the Golden Prince."

Bayan heaved out a sigh. He hated being called that. Not because he didn't want the easy life, but because he didn't want the attention it had drawn toward him. He rose from the water, which came to his waist, and held out his hand to her.

"Siker means nothing to me. But if I had refused, the Chakhar would not support me in *kurultai*. And if they turned their backs on me, others would, too. I either had to agree or risk losing my claim to another."

Yeke tipped her head slightly, considering his words. At last, she said, "We both know who that will be." Her gaze swept over him before settling on his hand, as if debating whether to join him.

"Yes, and Unebolod has more support than you know."

"My father will support you."

Bayan scoffed. "We both know your father loathes me. Come here, Yeke. Join me."

"How do I know you mean it?" Yeke said, dropping his clothes on the ground and revealing a carving knife clutched in her fist.

Bayan licked his lips anxiously, chest tightening. "Mean what?"

"That she means nothing to you." Yeke's grip on the knife was far too tight for Bayan's comfort.

She wouldn't use that on me, would she?

Bayan waved toward the capital. "Ask Berkedai. He marched me to the ceremony. He offered to help me escape." He inched toward the riverbank. The water level lowered a couple more inches down his waist.

Yeke's father had too much power. Bayan was certain he would need Yeke to keep Bigirsen on his good side whenever the transition of power happened. Yeke would be the key to keeping himself alive.

Once more, Yeke's gaze swept over his body. She adjusted her grip and he could sense the hesitation.

"Please," he said gently, reaching further toward her. "I beg you. Believe me, Yeke. Join me."

Yeke remained frozen on the riverbank, forgetting the knife in her hand as she stared at him. The chill in the late afternoon air made bumps rise on his flesh as he waited, praying she would join him and abandon her knife. If she refused him now, he would have an uphill battle to regain her trust again.

At long last, Yeke averted her gaze from him, glancing around anxiously as she lowered the knife.

"No one else is around," Bayan reassured her.

Yeke chewed at her lip. "Turn around."

"Are you serious?"

Her brows shot up insistently.

Bayan sighed dramatically, turning from her, praying she wouldn't stab him in the back. After a minute, the water sloshed gently, making ripples that nudged his balance. Yeke slipped around him beneath the surface, her head bobbing as she moved deeper. Bayan cast one more glance around them to be certain no one else was nearby. They were blissfully alone.

Bayan grinned and slid deeper into the water with her. His hands easily found her waist, and he pulled her close to him, near the rocky wall of the waterfall where they would be harder to spot by any passerby.

"Do you remember the last thing I told you before leaving?" Bayan asked, leaning close enough that his breath rolled over her skin.

"That you would return successful for the sake of our future," Yeke said softly. She seemed so timid and pliable in his arms.

"*Our* future, Yeke." He brushed a kiss along her jaw. "Yours and mine."

"And Siker?" Yeke asked, her voice breathy with excitement as she clung to him.

"She is not part of my future," he murmured against her skin. "And when Manduul dies, everything will all be ours at last."

He kissed her neck as his hand slid along her skin beneath the surface. Her body immediately responded to his touch, and she wrapped her legs around his waist. Bayan had almost forgotten how desperate for human connection Yeke was. He was not about to waste a moment of it.

Enkh bowed prostrate on the ger's rug covered floor before Issama. The two of them were alone within the walls of Issama's ger. Outside, the festivities to celebrate the prince's marriage had already begun and Issama had dismissed his wife, Uingen, to enjoy herself the moment Enkh arrived at his door.

"You are certain?" Issama asked. The magnitude of this news would change everything in Issama's favor.

"I saw with my own eyes, my Lord," Enkh said from the floor.

"And you told no one else?"

"No one, my Lord," Enkh said. "I feared sharing the news with the Khan myself and thought you might direct the course of this news, as his Vice Chancellor."

Issama placed his hands on Enkh's shoulders, looming over the servant. "Listen to me very closely. You've done well coming to me." Now he could test the waters of all his hard work to see how susceptible Manduul was to the prince's weakness. Perhaps Bayan's failure would be Issama's fortune. But the Khan could be prickly concerning his Golden Prince. "You will tell him tomorrow. These words will have more wight from you than anyone else, as long as you repeat exactly what I tell you to say."

Fate had once more smiled upon him. Issama had been given another piece of fuel to use against the prince, and tomorrow he would see it ignited.

CHAPTER FIFTEEN

Changes in the Air

A messenger arrived before the sunrise. Manduul snapped at the guards who woke him to announce the rider, grumbling first about the hour, then about how exhausted he was. The marriage celebration the night before had gone deep into the night, which also meant he had drunk far more than he should.

Mandukhai sat up in bed, her interest piqued by the urgency of the moment. She prodded Manduul out of bed. The two quickly slipped on deels and stepped outside, where the rider swiftly bowed and held out the message. His exhaustion was clear on his face. Sweat discolored the messenger's clothes. Mandukhai could smell his pungent aroma even from a few feet away.

"Apologies, my lord Khan," the rider said. "But this was pressed as urgent news for the Great Khan only, from the Khorchin khan."

Manduul frowned so deeply it made creases in his sagging face. *Is he losing weight?* Mandukhai wondered. Manduul tore the seal and unfolded the parchment. Mandukhai stood close, peering over his shoulder. Her reading skills had improved over the past few months, and she recognized the handwriting immediately, though she could not get a good enough look to read the words.

"This is from Lord Unebolod," she said, gasping in alarm. "Not the Khorchin khan."

"I only deliver the words given to me, my Lady," the rider said.

Manduul's back stiffened as he read the message. "Go," Manduul commanded the rider, waving him off. "Get food, water, and rest. I will send a response before midday."

"What is it, Manduul?" Mandukhai asked. She burned with intense curiosity.

Manduul didn't bother going back into the ger to finish dressing for the day. Instead, he stomped toward the gathering tent with his belt loose and his deel half unfastened. Mandukhai had to gather her deel and rush after him in bare feet just to keep up with his brisk pace. The cool, damp earth pressed into the soles of her feet.

"Manduul!" Her patience wore thin at his lack of response.

"Lord Bolunai is dead, along with the rest of his family and half the Khorchin tribe," Manduul grumbled, gasping for breath as he slapped open the door to the gathering tent. "Apparently Bolunai had a significant store of gunpowder he never told me about. Someone ignited it. It's by fortune alone that Unebolod survived the attack."

Mandukhai's heart leaped into her throat. Was Unebolod injured in the explosion? *The rider called him their khan,* she thought as the reality suddenly hit her. While the title was not undeserved, the Khorchin khan was reserved for the man who led the entire tribe. With no heirs in Bolunai khan's line, that left Unebolod to take up the mantle.

"Did he mention who did this?" she asked as she waited for him to settle into his seat before taking her own.

Manduul read over the message once more, then shook his head. "There is no clear evidence." He crumpled the parchment in his fist and barked orders at the guards at the door. "Summon Lord Issama!"

Mandukhai and Manduul fell silent as they waited. An attack against the Khorchin lords could only mean whoever was responsible had something to gain from their deaths. Mandukhai imagined the man to most benefit from their downfall would be Bigirsen. Without the Khorchin lords and Bayan, Bigirsen could easily seize control unopposed once Manduul died. *Does Bigirsen know Manduul is already dying?* Mandukhai wondered, glancing at her husband. How he thought he was hiding his condition was beyond her understanding. Whispers had begun spreading when no one thought they were listening. How much longer could he have?

The gathering tent swiftly became a flurry of activity. Issama joined them, followed by his army of scribes. Manduul shared the news, and Issama frowned.

"It is a good thing that your sworn brother has survived this explosion," Issama said soberly. "But how do we know it was an attack and not an accident?"

"One explosion is an accident," Manduul said. "Two is a plot. We have work to do, Issama."

Issama nodded, then set to work with grim-faced determination, carrying out all of Manduul's commands as Mandukhai watched over the Khan and ensured all went smoothly.

"Unebolod will need support to investigate," Mandukhai proposed. "We should send some of our own men."

Manduul shook his head. "He insists we should send no one. He worries we will be next, and that this is a plot against Borjigin supremacy. If he is right, we cannot afford to send men to him or we risk weakening ourselves. He knows this, and he claims to have support in the east."

Manduul had named Unebolod next in line behind Bayan and any potential Borjigin heirs. As far as Mandukhai was concerned, Bayan himself could have been behind the attack. But Manduul would never consider such a thing, so she kept this to herself. Would Bigirsen's son be considered the rightful heir ahead of Unebolod? *No, the Lords would never support Nemeku at* kurultai *with a Uyghur father*, she thought, dismissing this option. *But Borogchin might know more.*

Mandukhai rose. "You need to eat, my lord Khan," she said, bowing to Manduul. "I will prepare something for you and return."

He waved her off, distracted by his own business.

Mandukhai moved as swiftly as she dared to her ger. A bit of ink and parchment was nestled in the corner of one of her chests, and she fished it out. It took her far too long to write in a clear, careful script so that her words could be understood. As she dusted the ink dry, sealed the parchment with a bit of wax, and pressed her ring to seal it, Esige strode into the ger.

"What is going on, Mother?" Esige asked the moment she set eyes on Mandukhai. "The gathering tent is buzzing. Are we at war?"

"Perhaps." Mandukhai stood and pressed the parchment into Esige's hand. "I need this sent to Borogchin immediately, but no one else can know we have sent it."

Esige's eyes burned with excitement and hope. "Is it time?"

Mandukhai hated to dash her hopes, but she could not lie to the girl either. "No. But perhaps soon. Be sure the rider is someone we trust. Allow no one to see you send it. Make the rider memorize these words. 'This is only for the hands of Borjigin loyalists, for Lady Borogchin alone. Burn upon reading to her.'"

Esige straightened with determination, repeated the words, and gave a stiff nod. The moment she slipped out, Mandukhai gathered a few items of food onto a tray and called Tuya to bring it along to the gathering tent. The rest was in Esige's capable hands. It could take at least a week for the message to reach Borogchin, if not longer. Then, at least as long again to get a response, but it was all Mandukhai had to work with at the moment.

When Mandukhai stepped back into the gathering tent, the atmosphere had thickened. Something had changed dramatically in her absence. Manduul's expression was like a thunderhead prepared to strike. She motioned for her servant to set the food aside where Manduul could reach.

Mandukhai resumed her position in her seat, staring at a servant prostrate on a rug before the dais. Though the man's face was pressed to the rug, Mandukhai could see the flush of color on his face. It took a moment to recognize this man as Bayan's personal servant, Enkh. Mandukhai didn't dare ask what had happened when Manduul appeared so angry.

"Summon Bolkhu," Manduul growled. "Tell him if he does not listen and come immediately, I will have his ears."

Mandukhai's eyes widened as shock rippled through her core. Manduul was angry with *Bayan*? *What have I missed?* she wondered, wishing she could just ask.

"If you are lying to me, boy, it will be the last words you speak," Manduul snarled at Enkh as a guard rushed out to carry out the Khan's command. Manduul's hateful gaze burrowed into Enkh.

The gathering tent fell into a hush. Only a dozen others, including Issama, occupied the space, yet not one of them dared move or speak. No one even dared glance up from the floor. The tension in the air was so dense Mandukhai felt it accumulating on her skin like humidity. *Has Manduul learned Bayan was actually responsible for the Khorchin attack?* She could think of no other reason for such fury in the Khan's posture. *What if Bayan does not come?* she wondered.

Several long, silent minutes passed. The only sound in the gathering tent was the ragged, wheezing breaths from Manduul.

When at last Bayan entered, he strode in with all his usual casual grace, as if they had not summoned him upon a threat, but he had come of his own accord without a care in the world. He frowned at his servant, who remained prostrate on the floor. Somehow, Bayan must have sensed he should stop, because he did not take his normal seat beside Manduul. Instead, Bayan stopped at the bottom of the dais beside his servant.

"Everyone out!" Manduul roared, his gaze burning into Enkh.

A dozen servants, advisors, and scribes jumped into action, eager to be the first out the door. Issama lingered nearby, but at a glare from Manduul, he bowed and strolled out.

"You too, Mandukhai," Manduul said.

"My love—"

"Now!" His command rolled off the felt walls like the roar of a monster.

Mandukhai jumped and rose from her chair, gliding out with her back straight and chin raised. She *had* to know what was happening.

Once outside, she slipped around the edge of the gathering tent until she reached a spot near the back of Manduul's throne. Hopefully, she could hear something through the wool and silk barriers between them. Though the layers muffled their voices, she could distinguish Manduul easily enough.

"Eavesdropping is beneath you, Lady Mandukhai," Issama said.

Mandukhai jumped and spun around, pressing a palm against her racing heart. "What has angered him so?"

"If he had wanted you to be a part of this, he would not have kicked you out of the tent."

Mandukhai straightened and glared at Issama. "He kicked you out as well."

"Indeed. Some matters are for the Khan alone."

Before he could insult her further, Mandukhai stormed off. She would find out what happened somehow.

CHAPTER SIXTEEN

Conspiracy of Lips and Nose

Bayan struggled to maintain a cold warrior's face and hide the fear pulsing wildly through him as he entered the gathering tent. Had Mandukhai finally told Manduul about Nergui? Or perhaps Unebolod had, and now that Bayan had returned, Manduul would exact his justice?

Bayan stopped short of the dais, staring down at the servant on the floor—*his* servant. *Enkh?*

The threat that had accompanied Manduul's summons set Bayan's teeth on edge already, but the absolute fury on his uncle's face made each breath feel as if a herd of horses trampled over his body. Just keeping his limbs from betraying him with quivers proved a monumental task. Did Manduul find out about his affair with Yeke? *He all but gave me permission years ago!* he thought, desperate to excuse his behavior.

Manduul sat in furious silence for so long Bayan was afraid Manduul would let him die of anticipatory fear. When Manduul broke the silence, his voice was so calm that it belied the wrath in a way that only increased Bayan's terror.

"I am most aggrieved," Manduul said at last, "by the news that has been brought before me. I thought you should be with me to determine the outcome of this treachery." He shifted his gaze from Enkh to Bayan, and a deep sadness belied his rage. "We swore a sacred vow in a sacred place. I have given you everything I have to give."

"As have I, uncle." Could Manduul see him trembling? What would Manduul do to him if he had not meant Bayan could actually sleep with Yeke?

"Yet, despite all of this, your servant tells me you are plotting behind my back. That you intend to do evil to me and rob me of my wife. By his own words, you are planning my death." Manduul tapped the arm of his throne.

Bayan could no longer control his emotions. Bewilderment replaced the fear as he blinked at his uncle, dumbstruck by this confession. All he could respond with was a stammered, "What?"

"According to your man here, you are conspiring to replace me." Anger burned in Manduul's face, and his hands clenched into fists. "Tell me he lies, Bolkhu."

"I would never do evil against you," Bayan said. He cursed himself for the tremor in his voice.

"So you are not trying to take over by taking my wife?" Manduul's eyes were like well-aimed arrows of death pointed directly at Enkh.

Enkh saw something and betrayed me? Bayan gritted his teeth. He also had no suitable answer for Manduul's question. While on one hand, he was in no rush to take Manduul's position away, on the other hand, he was planning his eventual takeover by using Yeke.

Bayan's hesitation lasted too long for Manduul's patience, and his anger erupted. "After everything!"

"It isn't what you think!" Bayan said. He sounded more like a child desperate to get his father to believe him than a man pleading for his life. A lump the size of his fist rose in Bayan's throat, and he fought to swallow it down. "Yes, I am making plans for the day I have to replace you. What prince would not? But I have never plotted against you. Ever. Manduul, I take our oath seriously. My devotion to you is pure and absolute. I would *never* dream of doing evil to you. You know my heart. I love no other as I love you."

"And you have not been sleeping with Yeke?"

Bayan opened his mouth to respond, but only a crack of sound escaped. The truth, at this moment, would sound completely damning, even if he thought his intentions had been innocent at the time—given with permission.

Manduul's face crumpled. "After everything?" he said again, but the sadness bled through each syllable.

The agony broke Bayan's heart. He cared for no one as wholly as he cared for Manduul, the father he never had, the family he always wanted. *I cannot admit to this. Not today.*

"Did Enkh tell you this?" Bayan asked, glaring at his servant. "He is twisting reality around to drive a wedge between us. Would you truly listen to such slander from a lowly servant?" Bayan shook his head, resolved now and standing straighter and more confidently. "It breaks my heart to even consider such a thing. I don't know what vendetta he has against us, but I promise you this. I swore a sacred vow and have broken nothing of it. Yet if you believe this man, this servant, over me, your blood, what does that make of us?"

Manduul hesitated, leaning back on his throne and stroking his chin.

Bayan had never fully trusted Enkh—he trusted none but Manduul—yet Bayan had assumed his servant understood there was a connection between them. Not trust, exactly, but something akin to trust. Enkh had seemed bitter and unhappy ever since they escaped the Gobi. Bayan had assumed that, in time, that would wash away as he returned to his life of safety and comfort.

Now, Bayan had no sympathy for him. Enkh had tried to drive a wedge between him and Manduul. His fate would be deserved.

"You make no plots against me then," Manduul said at last. He sagged in his throne.

"Never. I want you to live a long life, uncle. My only plans are for the inevitable future—as distant as possible. Believe me, I'm in no rush."

Manduul drummed his fingers on the arm again, then leaned toward Enkh. "Your conspiracy has failed. I cannot understand why you would tell such lies, but I can promise we will meet it with swift justice."

Enkh whimpered and lifted his desperate, tear-streaked face to plead with the Khan. "No. Please. I speak the truth."

The guards marched forward, their boots thumping against the wood. They seized each of Enkh's arms and dragged him to his feet as he struggled feebly in their iron grips.

"Your plot to create trouble between two brothers and to divide them has been revealed," Manduul said over Enkh's desperate cries.

Bayan did not flinch as Enkh thrashed against the guards.

Manduul raised his chin in disgust. "Take his nose for sticking it where it did not belong and his lips for spreading lies. When he has suffered this fate, finish him."

"No!" Enkh screamed and thrashed like a wild animal as one guard stepped in front of him to carry out the Khan's orders.

Bayan winced and turned his head away, unable to watch such violence as the guard hacked at Enkh's face. Bayan's stomach churned and twisted as Enkh's shrieks pierced the air and carried out of the gathering tent. Just when he thought he could not bear it any longer, Enkh's voice cut out. Bayan dared a glance. Enkh's body crumpled to the floor in a heap, his lifeless eyes and mutilated face staring back at Bayan.

Manduul grunted in satisfaction as Enkh was rolled up in the ruined rug and dragged out of the gathering tent. Manduul's massive hand clamped down on Bayan's shoulder. The prince jumped, terrified that he would be next.

"I hope you can forgive my doubt," Manduul said. All the fury had dissolved away. "I will give you the benefit of the doubt this time, and I will not so easily be fooled again. But don't provide me further reasons to question your loyalty."

The threat hammered into Bayan's chest. He nodded dumbly. The warning was clear. Next time, it would be him on the floor, mutilated and staring with lifeless eyes at his accuser. It took a moment for Bayan to recover from the terror making him shake in his boots. At last, he flashed his most charming smile and said, "I would never do anything to harm you, uncle. I hope you understand that."

Manduul sighed and sank back down on his throne, suddenly appearing very weary. "Sit, Bolkhu. We have urgent business to discuss."

Bayan hesitated, glancing at the red bloodstain on the wood. The servants would have a hard time getting that out. Shaking off the image of Enkh's demise, Bayan joined Manduul.

"I worry about the future of the Mongol Nation, Bolkhu," Manduul confessed. "You were left with five thousand men, an easily manageable number, and returned to me with only a fraction of that. What will happen when I am gone and you step into my place?"

"I only wanted to follow your orders," Bayan said. Would Manduul renounce the title now that he had failed the Khan? "And I worried about the future of the nation if I did not return at all."

Manduul nodded solemnly. "A fear I often share. But I need you to be stronger, Bolkhu."

Bayan flinched at the insult. Stronger? What did Manduul expect of him? "You have taught me well. As have your men."

"You and Unebolod are all that remain." Manduul fell into a fit of coughs that worried Bayan.

For the first time, Bayan noticed the changes in Manduul. The weight loss. The sunken eyes and slightly sagging features. The rings of exhaustion around his eyes.

"Manduul, are you well?" he asked, afraid of the answer.

The coughing fit lasted several more long, excruciating seconds before Manduul spit out a wad of phlegm into a cup and dabbed his mouth. Bayan noticed the blood. His heart seized.

"I'm dying, Bolkhu."

The world tilted. The entire confrontation with Enkh, the brutal death, the accusations ... all of it felt meaningless in light of this news. If Manduul already was dying, then what did it matter what Bayan had done?

Worse, what would Bayan do when Manduul died? Unebolod and Bigirsen would both be after his head the moment Manduul took his final breath. The only wall holding back the tide of death pressing against Bayan was his uncle.

And the only person he ever loved would leave him alone to die.

"How long?" Bayan asked. How much time did he have left to prepare himself? *I will need Yeke now more than ever. She can hold her father back and perhaps make him an ally.*

Manduul shook his head. "Not long. Months. A year at best. Khosoichi says my symptoms have worsened over the winter months. Nothing can be done. Except preparing for your future."

"They will all kill me the moment you die." The confession tumbled from his lips.

"Who?"

"Anyone who wants the title," Bayan said, his voice rising a pitch. "Bigirsen. Unebolod. Togochi. Any of the Lords who could put forward a claim to the title."

Manduul shook his head. "Togochi is a good man whose loyalty I would never doubt. Unebolod is a man of honor. My death won't change that. As we speak, he is rallying the tribes in the east to support you. Between the eastern tribes and Unebolod's expertise in battle, Bigirsen would never stand a chance, even if he was foolish enough to try. And I don't think he is. He knows he cannot take the title as a Uyghur."

Bayan wanted to believe Manduul, but he had seen the way Unebolod glared at him. The man harbored hatred for him. *Ironic, considering he is the one who saved me as a child.*

"I am preparing for a smooth transition," Manduul said. "I will not leave you to fend for yourself. But you will need a quick show of strength. And that may mean sweeping Bigirsen's power off the map. You need Unebolod to accomplish this. Unebolod and Mandukhai. She is wise. Listen to her advice. Consider her words. Treat her like a queen. Do that, and she will respect you."

The words seemed true but rang false. Mandukhai had no love for him either. In fact, she and Unebolod were friends. He worried about what that alliance could do to him. Yeke would be his key. He had to remove Unebolod. He needed Bigirsen to do that.

By nightfall, the guards had hung Enkh's body where everyone could see it as a warning to any who dared attempt to drive a wedge between the Khan and his heir. Mandukhai could not bring herself to gaze upon the body of the servant as many others had. Their fascination turned her stomach. She had suspected an affair between Bayan and Yeke, and this confirmed her suspicions.

Mandukhai heard the rumor. Enkh had told Manduul he saw the two together with his own eyes. However, Manduul had not cared about the infidelity nearly as much as the conspiracy against his title. Yet why Enkh thought he could turn Manduul and Bayan against each other was beyond her understanding. What had the servant hoped to gain?

As night descended on Mongke Bulag, Mandukhai realized the true depth of Manduul's deeply rooted affection for Bayan. Telling Manduul she agreed with Enkh, that Bayan and Yeke were engaged in an affair, would no longer be a possibility. Her best choice was to wait. Bayan, she could not touch, but Yeke she could.

Manduul stumbled drunkenly into the ger. He and Bayan had spent most of the day and night drinking in the gathering tent. Intoxicated as he was, Manduul practically collapsed on the bed. Mandukhai kneeled beside him and slid off his boots.

"You drink too much," she chided, dropping his boots on the floor.

"Doesn't matter," he said, his speech slurred. Already, his eyes were drifting closed. "I'm dying either way."

"I know, but there's no need to race across the finish line."

Manduul's eyes snapped open. "You know?"

"You do not hide it well, husband."

He stroked her cheek. "He will need you."

"I know. I will be here."

Manduul smiled, satisfied with this response. Within seconds, his breathing became heavy and uneven. Mandukhai sighed and pulled a fur up over him.

Would Unebolod keep his word to Manduul once he passed, or would he use his newfound power to challenge Bayan? Mandukhai closed her eyes and took a few steady breaths. She would not oppose Unebolod, but could she stand against Genghis's rightful heir after what Genghis had told her in the vision?

Issama stood before the mutilated, bloody corpse as the sun disappeared behind him. So much of this day had not gone his way. Somehow, Unebolod had survived the explosions. His men had not done their jobs effectively. Issama had given them one simple order: Make sure *all* the Khorchin Lords died. *Unebolod seems to have the protection of Lord Tengri himself,* Issama thought bitterly.

He had also underestimated Manduul's trust in the prince and their bond of brotherhood. The servant had been an excellent test of that strength, yet Issama now knew one thing with certainty.

If he truly wanted to drive a wedge between them, he would have to be sure he had the evidence himself. The Khan could dismiss the words of a servant, but he could not so easily dismiss the words of his chosen *orlok*.

But first, Issama had to be certain he could hear and see everything he needed, and to do that, he would have to learn more about the prince's new wife.

CHAPTER SEVENTEEN

New Alliances

I ssama observed Bayan and Siker's daily routine for two weeks, watching for patterns, tension, or Bayan's prolonged absences. His own ger's proximity to Bayan's allowed him to hear the muffled voices within. For newlyweds, the two constantly bickered. But only in private. In public, they maintained a cool distance from each other, interacting only when necessary. By the end of the second week, Issama could predict when Bayan would stomp out of the ger each morning to train his men—often accompanied by Berkedai. Issama also knew when Siker would head to the river for fresh water.

Using this knowledge, Issama rode to the river shortly before Siker's normal arrival. It was a fairly busy spot, offering the cleanest water. Several other women moved along the shore with their buckets, casting him only a cursory glance. A few recognized him and offered polite greetings. Issama simply nodded in greeting and said nothing back. Their station below him required only a simple nod.

When Siker approached with two empty buckets for water, her gaze met Issama's. He no longer doubted that there was some sort of connection there, yet he still couldn't place it. As she passed him, Siker bit her lip and averted her gaze toward the ground. *Did she just smile?*

His horse drank from the river and grazed on the grass nearby. He allowed the mount her freedom, pretending he waited on his horse to have her fill.

Siker kneeled on the riverbank, arranging her silk deel around her legs to avoid tangling her limbs. Though she wore trousers beneath, as everyone did, Issama still noticed how thick her calves were, a sign that she was used to hard work. *Where did Bayan dredge her up from?* he wondered as he watched her easily haul the full bucket to the shore and dip another to fill.

As she hauled the second bucket back to the riverbank, Issama could not help but appreciate her form. Her arms were muscular as well. The sharpness of her shoulders angled abruptly toward her narrow waist, then flared out with wide hips. *Like the tip of an arrow dipping into a bowl*, he thought. It was an intriguing form, and he hated where it sent his mind. He needed to remain sharp to pull this off.

Siker sank back on her heels and swiped her silk sleeve across her forehead, then pushed to her feet. Issama averted his gaze before she could turn and notice him staring. This was supposed to be a casual encounter.

Siker waddled past, clinging to the wooden grips on the bucket handles as she tried not to spill the water.

Issama gathered the reins of his mount and caught stride with her. "Lady Siker."

She glanced at him only for a moment, focused on her path.

"Allow me to help," Issama said, sliding his hand along the handle of one bucket.

"It keeps me balanced," she said in that always cool tone.

He admired the way she always sounded so unflapped and distant from her emotions. Few women bothered to control their emotions. In Issama's experience, women used their emotions like weapons.

"What sort of Lord would I be to allow the *jinong's* wife to struggle?" he asked. "I will take both and you can lead my horse."

Siker halted abruptly, staring at him. "Are you calling me weak?"

"Hardly." Issama forced out a laugh. "I'm simply being a gentleman for such an honored Lady."

Siker glanced down at his hand, still wrapped around one handle. "What do you want, Lord Issama?"

No nonsense in this woman, he thought, smirking to himself. *No wonder she and Bayan fight so often*. Again, he could not understand how the two of them came together.

"To help you."

Siker released the bucket, then set down the other and reached for the reins. Her countenance gave nothing away. The puzzle intrigued him. "I don't believe you," she announced as she waited for him to pick up the second bucket.

Issama edged in front of her and to pick it up. They were heavier than he had expected. "I suppose I am interested in how you and Lord Bolkhu met."

"It's a long story," she said sharply, resuming her march toward home.

"The best stories are usually the long ones. It's a long walk."

Her brow raised ever so slightly. Siker glanced at the buckets. "Don't spill them."

"Why do you not have your servant do this?" Issama asked.

"He does not trust servants anymore," Siker replied. The whip in her tone implied clearly enough that this had been the source of at least one of their fights.

"I cannot say I blame him." He glanced sideways at her. "Do you believe the accusations against him?"

Siker kept her gaze fixed forward, silent for several painfully long strides. "When he was thirteen, he practically fell out of the Gobi into my lap," she said, obviously changing the subject. "I had seen a lot of boys go into the desert, but hardly for more than a day, and never far from our camp. Most of them were all talk. But I could tell that he had actually traveled through it."

Issama couldn't help the disappointment that she clearly avoided his question, but it surprised him that her history with Bayan went so far back.

"I was a foolish girl," Siker continued. "And he had beautiful golden eyes. I had never seen anything like it before. I brought him home, healed him, hid him from the men hunting him. He never told me why they were hunting him, though. I suppose I guessed on my own. I had heard of the eyes of the wolf in stories. Men who descended from Genghis."

"He seduced you, didn't he?" Issama asked. "Apologies if that is not my business."

Siker shrugged. "He didn't have to. He was handsome. I was curious. None of the other boys in camp seemed interested in me. It just happened."

The handles pinched Issama's hands. He paused, setting them on the ground and rubbing his palms tenderly. Siker observed with casual curiosity.

"You are not used to long, hard labor," she noted.

"Perhaps," Issama teased. "But I am experienced in battle. For a Mongol, that is all that matters."

"But you are Uyghur."

"And you are Chakhar. Do you have a point?"

Siker studied him. No woman had ever truly picked him apart with their eyes the way she did. As plain as her face was, he found this quality of intrigue alluring. Dangerous ground to walk, considering who her husband was.

"He killed my father," she said as plainly as if she were talking about laying out rugs on the floor. "Berkedai, Yungei, and a handful of Manduul's men came to the Chakhar camp where my father had accepted Bayan into our home, fed him, and cared for him. As payment, Bayan cut his throat."

Issama hid his alarm at this. What a curious turn of events. "And yet you married him?"

Siker flushed and dipped her chin to her chest. He watched as she breathed in slowly. "You don't understand his power. He burns like a fire, brilliant and beautiful. Alluring. And you, a simple moth, know that you should not approach the flames. Yet no matter how hard you try to avoid his light, the desire to be part of something so beautiful draws you in. You cannot avoid the flames."

Issama glanced around them. Dozens of people milled through the area, but few only offered small bows or nods. No one passed close enough to hear her hushed confession. Issama picked up the buckets and resumed the walk back to her ger. Siker easily matched his stride.

"And he returned to the area, drawing you in," he continued.

"I was married before he came back," she confessed. "About a year after Bayan left the first time. My husband was killed by Ming soldiers only a year later. His family took care of me, but when Bayan returned as the prince, my husband's family knew of the connection I had with him. They encouraged me to speak with him. I tried to tell them it was a bad idea, but they wouldn't listen to me. I knew he would pull me right back into his flames. And it didn't take long.

"Before I knew it, he had moved into my ger, taken over, and we were living together." Siker released a shaky breath. "Then the Chakhar khan found out. People complained. The khan used it as an excuse to tie the prince to the tribe. Neither of us could escape it by then."

Issama had to admit, it certainly had been a stroke of genius on Guden khan's part to use Siker to tether Bayan to the Chakhar for good.

"And so I am the moth, slowly burning to death," she mumbled.

"You don't have to be."

Siker stiffened, casting a curious glance at Issama. "How so?"

"The brighter a flame burns, the faster it burns out."

Siker froze so suddenly Issama nearly tipped the buckets of water to stop as well. "That's treason," she hissed.

"What is?" Issama asked innocently. "I simply stated a matter of fact."

Siker's eyes narrowed suspiciously. "You asked if I believed the accusations against him. Why?"

"Simply making conversation, my Lady."

Siker hesitated, glancing around them. She lowered her voice. "And if I did?"

Issama feigned alarm, mimicking her lowered pitch. "You believe he is plotting against the Khan?"

"I know my husband very well," Siker said cautiously. "And I know he will stick his cock in any woman who spread her legs for him. He had scratches on his skin that did not come from me. And they certainly did not come from training, like he told me."

"I can help you, Siker," Issama said, edging closer.

"I don't need help."

"I think you do." He hesitated, watching for guards or men who might report him. "Because the brighter a fire burns, the faster it burns out. And you are a moth drawn toward the flame. The fire will consume you."

"What do you know?" Siker asked. Her gaze met his, and she didn't flinch or act shy as other women often did when backed into a corner.

"Not as much as you," Issama replied carefully. "But I have a sneaking suspicion. I don't dare discuss it in the open."

Siker's next words were little more than a breath. "You *do* think he is plotting against Manduul."

Issama shook his head. "I think he already has enacted his plan." Issama reached toward her, taking her hand and adopting a desperate look that he hoped she bought. "Please. If you tell anyone, I'm a dead man. And if I die, I cannot protect you."

Siker snatched her hand away, body tensing. "I don't need protection."

"You do. Because if the rumor about Lady Yeke is true, she will kill you to take your place the moment he becomes Great Khan. I can help you."

"Enough." Siker thrust the reins against his chest, dropping them before he could take them from her. She then picked up the buckets.

Fear rushed through Issama. He had overreached too fast. Siker would report him and Manduul would have his head.

"We will talk later," she said, adjusting her grip. "Until then, do not contact me."

Siker marched forward, forcing him out of her path.

As she rounded a ger, Issama bit the inside of his cheek to avoid grinning like a fool. He had her on the hook. While he trusted few, he couldn't help the surge of excitement that rushed through him. Bayan's inability to control his own impulses would be his downfall.

CHAPTER EIGHTEEN

Cowards and Conspiracies

MONGKE BULAG – SUMMER 1469

S pring swiftly faded into summer, and Mandukhai could feel the days melting away. She had dedicated significant time to befriending Siker. The woman was terribly cold and dismissive of most things, her husband included. It had taken Mandukhai several weeks of casual encounters and invitations to tea to get a grip on how the woman operated.

Siker never divulged much, though when Mandukhai pressed her on it—along with Esige staring at Siker with wide-eyed eagerness—Siker had grudgingly shared the story of how she had met Bayan, and it went much further back than Mandukhai had expected. Before he had come to Man-duul, Bayan had lived with Siker's family. The two were man and wife in all but official title, but she admitted she knew that he had spent time with other women even then.

"Some horses need to remain free or you risk breaking their spirit," Siker said one summer day as the three of them wove their way through the maze of gers with no particular destination in mind.

Mandukhai ached a little inside at this statement. Perhaps she and Bayan were not so different. "True," Mandukhai nodded in agreement, "but some stock are meant for breeding to ensure a strong and fruitful herd. So why did you not join him when he came to Mongke Bulag five years ago?"

Siker shrugged as if it didn't matter. "That was not our arrangement."

Mandukhai waited for her to elaborate, but Siker said nothing else, as if that explained everything.

Siker halted so suddenly Esige nearly bumped into her. The woman's eyes locked on a young boy who couldn't be much older than five or six. Mandukhai watched Siker curiously as Siker's gaze became almost distant. Then she stiffened her spine and continued walking as if it had never happened. Esige cast a slightly bewildered glance in Mandukhai's direction as she once again continued behind Siker.

Mandukhai understood that look. She had caught herself staring at Jaghan's son much the same way several times—and Satai's. *She lost a child,* Mandukhai realized. Perhaps there had been a child involved, after all. If Siker lost that child, it would help explain the distance between her and Bayan. Mandukhai understood how such a loss could strain a relationship.

"Bolkhu never truly chose me," Siker said. "We just sort of fell into each other, then we were forced together. I married after he left the first time, but the Ming killed my first husband. We never had children. Then, when the Ming came for Bolkhu ..." She shook her head and Mandukhai could not decipher what this woman was thinking.

"I can tell he prefers the company of another, though," Siker said.

"Oh? Do you know this woman?" Somehow, Mandukhai already knew the answer, or hoped she did.

Siker bit her lip and frowned, then huffed. "I dare not say, for fear I am wrong. I would hate to cause trouble where there is none."

So Siker knows about Yeke, Mandukhai thought. Who else would she fear could cause trouble? Everyone in Mongke Bulag gossiped about the accusation mounted against Bayan and Yeke, though Manduul's brutal response kept any other from daring to question the prince's loyalty again. Somehow, Siker must have suspected some truth of the rumor. Or she knew more than she let on.

Siker shrugged it off. "It does not matter in the end. I am his wife, and one day he will take another. Perhaps even you. It is the way of men. Besides, as you say, sometimes strong stock needs to be bred for a stronger and more fruitful herd. My place is where it is, and I will have children as I should."

Mandukhai fought off a shiver at the idea of having a child with Bayan, or even allowing him to force himself on her. It was not his appearance that put her off. He was handsome, without a doubt, but his personality certainly lacked appeal. He was not strong stock, but he was the last of it, and having his son would give her back any power she would inevitably lose during the transition. If she had Bayan's son, they would have no further need of him. Would Unebolod accept Bayan's son as his own if it meant becoming Great Khan? As detestable as the prospect was, it would offer her and Unebolod legitimacy they would otherwise have to fight for.

The three of them meandered back toward Siker's ger, and Siker excused herself to her duties.

Esige shuddered the moment Siker was out of sight. "Everything she says is so cold and distant, like she is stating facts and not living life. Her soul seems devoid of any form of desire."

"She is married to our next Khan," Mandukhai said calmly. "And I may be forced to become her sister-wife. If I become friends with her now, we will get along with each other much better later. We don't have to like her, but we need her to trust us."

"I do not believe that woman trusts the air not to suffocate her or water to quench her thirst," Esige said, then tittered at her joke, glancing back as if afraid Siker stalked silently behind them even now. "I would rather trust a rabid wolf."

"That may be the alternative if we are not careful."

Mandukhai stopped short as she spotted a messenger waiting outside her own ger.

The rider bowed to her and held out the message. "From Lady Borogchin, my Lady."

Esige gasped eagerly as Mandukhai snapped the message away and read it, waving the rider away to get much-needed rest and food. Esige peered over her shoulder.

The writing was terrible, and it took Mandukhai several passes reading it to decipher what it said. Bigirsen was tangled deep in the Moghul khanate revolution. Borogchin had prodded him for information about the Khorchin explosion, but Bigirsen did not know of it, stating good riddance. Borogchin claimed to read him fairly well and believed his reaction was genuine.

Mandukhai thrust the parchment at Esige. "Burn that in the stove now. No one else can see it."

"She has been there too long," Esige said as she snatched the parchment from Mandukhai and pushed her way into the ger.

"I know." But Mandukhai could do nothing about it yet. Part of her had hoped Bigirsen had been behind the Khorchin attack, and she could use that as an excuse to spirit Borogchin away from him. If he had nothing to do with it, and no knowledge of it, that revealed two facts to Mandukhai.

Bigirsen's network of spies was dwindling.

Someone else wanted the Khorchin dead.

If not him, Mandukhai could only think of the Oirat tribes or Bayan himself, but such an attempt seemed beyond Bayan's capabilities. Issama had connections everywhere, and he and Bayan were friends, but he had seemed alarmed by the news as well.

At least Bigirsen could not ride in quickly for *kurultai* if she could push Bayan or Unebolod into position fast enough. Unebolod would gather the support they needed and bring it back. Manduul had sent him for just that purpose. They would need to rally the tribes swiftly to avoid outside interference.

Since the attack, Unebolod had only sent one other rider, assuring Manduul he had everything under control in the east and would soon ride to gather support. He sent nothing to her. His oath to her the night before his departure still seeped into her dreams more often than not.

"Lady Mandukhai," Arslan called from the door. "Lord Togochi would like to speak with you."

Esige had been stoking the fire, ensuring the message from her sister properly burned. At this announcement, she turned her wide eyes to Mandukhai. "Does he know?" she hissed.

Mandukhai shook her head, but was uncertain. Togochi could have spotted the messenger, or perhaps noticed something suspicious in her behavior.

"Let him in, Arslan," Mandukhai said, raking through her mind to dredge up any clues she might have left for him to find regarding her plans.

Togochi ducked through the door, sliding off his hat and bowing to her. "Sorry for the intrusion, but Manduul will not answer me."

Mandukhai's heart leaped into her throat. Was he dead?

"I don't mean to cause distress, but the men are talking and I have no answers for them," Togochi continued. "Manduul appears ... unwell. When I ask about his health, he will not tell me anything. But if there is a threat to his life, or Bolkhu's, I need to prepare the men. There are ... whispers." He shifted feet, clearly uncomfortable with this conversation. Togochi stared at the floor. "I come to you because you and my wife are such close friends, and I sort of see you as a sister. Some men are doubting Bolkhu's capabilities as a leader, and if Manduul is unwell, we could have upheaval on our hands soon."

Mandukhai glided toward Togochi, placing a hand on his arm. "I see you as a brother, as well. You are my family, Togochi. Esige and I have heard the same whispers as you. But please trust me. Everything is under control."

Togochi grimaced. "That is exactly what Manduul keeps telling me."

"Because it is true."

He shook his head. "The attack on Unebolod was no accident."

"It was not," she agreed.

His gaze snapped up to meet hers. "What do you know?"

Mandukhai knew this must have been torture for Togochi, to be the one in the family who did not understand what was happening around him. "He survived, and could find no evidence leading to a conspirator. Which you already know. You are worried about the fate of the Nation, and what will come if Manduul ever dies. This is natural, Togochi. Manduul named Unebolod, and he is working on support for Bolkhu. Everything is under control."

Again, Togochi grimaced. "But Manduul is not ill?"

Mandukhai offered a sweet smile. "Let me worry about my husband. If you want to help, then protect him. Stop these rumors from spreading and weakening his reign."

Togochi seemed skeptical of her words. The deepening frown clarified her words offered no consolation at all. But until Manduul shared his condition with Togochi, Mandukhai could say nothing more. He nodded stiffly.

It hurt to see Togochi's shoulders sag as he marched back out the door. Togochi was a good man. One of the few good men left in this cruel court.

Issama stood as Siker entered her ger. Bayan and Berkedai were training their men, so Issama was confident he would not be interrupted. Uingen could not find her way into Mandukhai's inner circle of trust—for reasons he still could not understand—but Siker had done so swiftly. He found it irritating that this acceptance came so easily to Siker because she had married the prince, yet Uingen was simply the wife of the *orlok*, a prestigious position in itself. Was his position worth nothing to his wife in this court? Women played a different game than men, and he found it infuriating to decipher.

Siker did not seem to care much for her husband, but she also cared little for the idea of a queen trying to steal her husband away. Yeke had swiftly made an enemy out of Siker. Between the bitterness that Bayan chose Yeke over her, the fact that she was forced into this marriage, and that she still harbored anger about her father's death, Issama had made a swift ally out of her. More than an ally. Issama trusted her more than most. She had just as much to lose in this game as he did.

Siker didn't even spare a second glance at Issama, as if she had expected him to be there when she returned.

"You are fortunate she did not insist on coming in for tea," Siker said as she set the water on to boil.

"Coming in here would be beneath her," Issama said.

Siker pulled out the tea and set it into the pot. "She knows about Yeke." At last, she glanced at him, and her face bore her usual impassive expression. "I could see it in her eyes. Yet she won't speak of it."

Issama fought off a smirk and only nodded, as if he expected as much. Mandukhai knew of the affair, but was wise enough to keep it to herself. If he played this game well, he could get Mandukhai to confirm this affair to Manduul and support Issama. But the situation was delicate, and he had to be careful how he approached the Khan so that Mandukhai felt obligated to offer Manduul advice when the time came.

"She will tell him, under the right circumstances," he said confidently.

Siker poured tea and offered him a cup. "I have not yet found what you believe he may have used on Manduul."

"It is alright," Issama reassured her, patting her on the arm. "I'm sure he would hide it well. Perhaps not even here. It could be in Yeke's ger. Who would look there?"

"Why not just search her ger, then?" Siker asked, staring at his hand on her arm. She didn't pull away.

"Because that will implicate her and not him. We need Manduul to see what Bolkhu has done."

"And if we are wrong?" Siker inched closer. "Issama, what if this is just the natural course of things, and has nothing to do with Bayan?"

"Then you are caught in the flames, little moth." He slid his hand along her arm.

Siker flushed, slipping away from his touch. "Then we will need Bayan?"

Issama nodded. She didn't need to know the whole truth, and she was not wrong. They needed Bayan. But not as Great Khan.

Coward. No one had dared say it to Bayan's face, but he had heard the rumors milling around Mongke Bulag even if men tried not to speak of it around him. When the Ming had pursued, he hadn't taken a stand, but had fled through the desert, risking death and losing good men. Hundreds of the survivors who returned with Bayan had fallen ill and died within weeks of reaching Mongke Bulag, weakening his position. Now, thanks to Enkh, all of Mongke Bulag knew of his affair with Yeke, though no one else admitted to seeing or hearing anything of it. Instead, they ridiculed him behind his back for allowing Enkh—a servant—to be mutilated and killed for his crime. Bayan was losing ground with the men in the capital. Coward, they were calling him behind his back.

Degghar, Siker's father, had made a promise just moments before his death, and it haunted Bayan. *One day*, he had said, *they will all learn what sort of man you really are. And when that day comes, may the sky father strike you down.*

Bayan sat in his saddle on the training field south of Mongke Bulag, staring at his clenched fists as they tightened in rage. *I am not that man anymore*, he thought bitterly. So much had changed since he had left that encampment with the Great Khan's men. He had grown stronger and more powerful. Bayan had never asked to be the prince or to become Great Khan. It was his fate, hurtling inexorably closer while his uncle gradually died.

Bayan signaled the command to his *mingghan* commanders to switch their routes, and their response was sluggish; not because they were incapable of the swift maneuver, but because they had little faith in him after he had lost so many men to the Ming and the desert. Their deaths were his failure. Bayan watched his warriors sweat through their clothes as they rode through the bow-horn maneuver.

Genghis Khan. The name was still worshiped with almost god-like reverence, even so long after the legendary man himself had passed on. Bayan often found it hard to believe that he came from the same bone, that the same blood pumped through his veins. Genghis Khan, the man who had brought warring tribes together in a great nation with his brute force of strength and will; the legend who had crossed impassible mountains to conquer other nations and expand the Mongol empire; the man who had preferred a nomadic life of simplicity over cities and extravagance. Bayan was nothing like him; Bayan was nothing like any of the heroic Great Khans of the past. The only reason Bayan would become Great Khan, he was certain, was simply because no other from the legendary bloodline lived to challenge him. He was their last hope.

Yet they called him a coward behind his back.

Bayan raised the horn to his lips and blew the signal to draw the men back. If they wanted to call him a coward, he would work them until they were on the brink of collapse. What would they think of him then?

CHAPTER NINETEEN

Unexpected Consequences

KHORLOD TERRITORY – SUMMER 1469

The explosion in the palace had slowed Unebolod's schedule significantly. It had taken two days to sift through the rubble and confirm the death of Bolunai and his family. Then another month to organize the survivors and prepare the entire Khorchin tribe to move with him. The commanders and nobles had easily fallen in behind him.

No one had called him khan until Bolunai's family was confirmed dead, but the day they were found—or what remained of them—the men began calling him khan almost immediately. Unebolod took on the title as if they had pressed a yoke against his shoulders. It was a burden he would bear, and only one of many to come, he was certain.

Not that Unebolod did not want to be khan. But the circumstances under which he had attained this title were far from ideal. He would rather have his family alive. As thousands of others must understand, having lost loved ones as well.

The attack on his *tumen* had taken nearly five thousand of his men, a devastating loss, but not nearly as many as the deaths around the palace. No one could be confident of the exact number. But Unebolod was certain they only rode away with half the tribe. The deficit burned in his heart. He had uncovered no clues as to who was responsible.

If the explosion had only been in the palace or the army's camp, he could have accepted it as an accident—such things happened where gunpowder was involved—but the fact that both explosions happened nearly in unison made it clear they had been calculated attacks. The men who had set off the gunpowder had likely died in the explosions and left no evidence behind. *Someone* gave the order. They could not have acted alone. Men gave their lives for a cause they believed in—or a person they worshipped. Both dangerous prospects for him.

Unebolod could only hope that Mandukhai remained safe in Mongke Bulag. Would Manduul or Bayan be next, or was this targeted at Unebolod's tribe alone? Unebolod knew Bigirsen had a deep loathing for the Khorchin; all the Uyghur did. But Bigirsen was thousands of miles away. He could not have gotten an assassin to Hulunbuir so quickly. Issama was Bigirsen's man, and he likely had the means. Could he have found such loyal men so quickly after Unebolod left Mongke Bulag? Somehow, the Uyghur had to be behind this, but how could he prove it? Someone would have to pay. He could not let this go unavenged.

Unebolod had told the remaining Khorchin families that they could remain in the grasslands until *kurultai*. However, most of the families preferred the safety of numbers. The attack had shaken the Khorchin to their core, and they looked to Unebolod to lead them to safety. He prayed he would not let them down. If only he believed the High Heavens had his interests at heart.

After nearly two months of preparation at the edge of Hulunbuir, the carts and horses and herds of livestock flowed south. Unebolod would meet with the Tabun tribe's khan personally. To do that, the Khorchin would pass through the territory of two other tribes. Unebolod had sent messengers ahead, so the massive caravan of Khorchin riding through their lands did not threaten the Kharchin and Khorlod tribes.

Soke rode beside Unebolod. When they stopped for rest, gers were set with incredible efficiency. Before sunset, fires were burning, and they consumed meals. In the wolf dawn, everything was swiftly packed back up and they would be on their way again by the time the sun finished rising. Unfortunately, with so many in tow, Unebolod's men moved much slower than he had hoped. A trip that should have only taken one month took nearly three.

By the time they finally stopped to set up camp a mile from the Tabun khan's camp, Unebolod had received multiple messages from Manduul. He dismounted as his servants—newly gained after the explosion—busied themselves setting up his ger. He preferred lying beneath the stars, as he had done with Odsar and Mandukhai. It helped him feel closer to them, though he could not be with either.

Manduul's messages offered some reassurance—and some disappointment. Mongke Bulag was secure, the prince had returned safely from the south, and preparations for Manduul's death were underway. Mandukhai now knew of Manduul's condition, according to the messages, but that had been the only mention of her. He yearned to see her again, or to hear more about how she was doing and what she was up to. Would she understand what he planned? Did she feel the same excitement as him, that soon they would be together at last?

He couldn't help a small smile as he called for a messenger. Hope was dangerous, but he could not help himself.

A boy rushed up, his face flushed and excited.

"Send word to the Tabun khan and let him know I will visit in the morning," Unebolod commanded. "I believe he is expecting me."

The boy bobbed his head and took off at a sprint. He couldn't be over thirteen and carrying messages like this at such an age gave boys like him purpose. They learned how the army worked while serving a function before they were old enough to fight themselves.

"We are bordering on dangerous ground," Soke said as he watched the boy sprint off. "Bigirsen has quite a hold on this territory. The Urainkhai are within a throw from here. If we aren't careful, we could end up clashing with them, and they would significantly outnumber us now."

"I know." Unebolod turned to his ger as the final felts were layered over the top. "But Bigirsen has ten tribes firmly in his grasp. If he can oppose Bolkhu or myself at *kurultai,* he will. But he is not from the blood or bone of the royal line, and Manduul has made his succession clear. We can only hope that such a thing will still matter to the tribal Lords when the time comes. That is why we are here, Soke."

Soke snorted. "You speak as if you know *kurultai* comes soon."

Unebolod shifted away from Soke and pulled his bow from the saddle hook. At some point, he would have to tell his commander the truth. Soke was a sharp man, and he would suspect what Unebolod was up to eventually.

"I'll see that the commanders have their men organized to protect the camp," Soke said, bowing to excuse himself.

Unebolod rubbed his mare's neck and turned to see the expanse of Khorchin settling in. Already, they had finished his own ger, and when he stepped through the door, a servant had prepared mutton for him.

Unebolod set down his bow and sword, then set to work pulling out his maps. During the months of reorganizing the Khorchin and traveling south, Unebolod had kept his nights busy with messages to far-off khans who were only distantly part of the empire anymore. He had maps marked out with movements of the tribes under Bigirsen's rule—information he received from his spies. He had calculated how long it would take all the tribal Lords to arrive and support him against Bigirsen. There was still every chance Bigirsen would simply make his move for control and start another bitter civil war, even if Unebolod won the *kurultai*.

Sleep tugged at Unebolod as the night wore on, and he rubbed at his eyes. For weeks, young women had been sent to his ger to entice him. Some were lesser noblemen's daughters eager to marry a khan; others were slaves and possibly spies. Unebolod had sent all of them away, some more politely than others. A few of the young women had made a scene until his guards had to remove them. A handful had broken down in tears, claiming they had no family left to return to. These women he employed as servants or offered to his men—depending on the woman's social status. For some of the Ladies from lesser nobles, Unebolod had spoken directly to their families. He needed loyalty and did not want to insult the Khorchin Lords, but he had no interest. Sometimes, he arranged for those young women to marry his highly ranked men. Then everyone was happy.

These estranged young women had been an unexpected consequence of the explosion and his rise to Khorchin khan.

As he stifled a yawn, the usual knock on the door drew his attention. Unebolod groaned inwardly and shuffled toward the door.

The young woman on the other side was striking, despite her poor clothing and dirty face. Something in her eyes reminded him of Mandukhai. She bowed respectfully. "My Lord khan."

Unebolod's lips thinned. "Please tell your father that I appreciate the gesture, but I'm busy tonight."

She dipped her head and her dark hair fell around her shoulders, reminding him of the night Mandukhai had nearly run away from Manduul. That seemed so long ago now.

When she gazed up at him again through her long lashes, he couldn't help but notice the sorrow in her eyes. Unebolod groaned and rubbed his forehead. He knew that look. This was the sixth girl to come to his door with no father.

"In the explosion?" he asked, sounding just as exhausted as he felt.

"Yes, my Lord khan." She bit her lip as if she wanted to say more, but perhaps feared she shouldn't.

"Out with it."

"I have nowhere else to go," she said. A quiver crept into her voice. "My brother is all I have left, and he told me ..." A tear slipped out, and she gritted her teeth and swiped it away, clearly frustrated at showing such emotions. "He said if I fail to ... to share your bed, not to come back at all."

"I assume he threatened dishonor on the entire family if you fail," Unebolod said, leaning against the doorframe. Not the first time he heard that line.

She nodded and, to his surprise, raised her chin as if hopeful that he would change his mind. He hated to crush her hope. But he would.

"People will make assumptions if I let you in," Unebolod said. *What would Mandukhai think?*

"I understand." Her shoulders slumped, giving her disappointment away. "I'm sorry to have bothered you, my Lord khan."

She turned and started away.

Unebolod groaned inwardly. She would have nowhere to go tonight if he turned her away, and it was far too late at night for her safety. "Wait."

She paused and turned back to him.

"What is your name?" he asked.

"Odgerel."

The name struck Unebolod with irony. Starlight. And just as he had been thinking of such things with Odsar and Mandukhai.

Without responding, Unebolod ducked back inside and left the door open behind him. After a minute, the door remained ajar. *I'm going to regret this*, he thought.

"Odgerel, it's getting late, and I would prefer my door closed."

Her boots scuffed the ground outside as she approached. As she ducked in, Odgerel placed her slender hands on the door and closed it slowly, watching him with clear apprehension. Unebolod gave her more than enough space to move around without having him too close. Her hands shook as she began removing her belt.

"Stop." Unebolod held up a hand. "That's unnecessary. Just—" He waved the hand toward the bed. "Get rest. I'll sleep on the floor."

"My Lord, will you not share the bed with me?"

"No. As I said, I will sleep on the floor."

"I could never steal your bed from you!" Her eyes grew wide as saucers, and he wondered if she was playing a game with him.

"Fine. Then *you* will sleep on the floor. Tomorrow we will find you more appropriate accommodation."

Odgerel inched deeper into the ger, her keen eyes always on him. Unebolod had to admit, had he not given his heart so fully to Mandukhai, Odgerel would sorely tempt him. The way she moved was graceful. Despite the dirty clothing, he could see the enticing curves of her hips and chest. And her eyes took in everything with sharp interest. Perhaps too sharp.

Unebolod turned his gaze away, almost ashamed of the thought of sharing his bed with this girl. He had given Mandukhai his word, and his heart was hers, no matter how long he had to wait. Yet he was still a man of flesh and desires, and it had been so very long.

He buried himself under his furs and laid on his side facing the wall to avoid seeing Odgerel as she curled up on the floor beside his bed.

Chapter Twenty

Excessive Desires

The air was pregnant with the anticipation of rain. It clung to Unebolod's skin like sweat and made him itch under the arms. How he wished he could remove his armor, but he was not foolish enough to enter this meeting with no form of protection. Albeq's men had already taken his sword.

Albeq, the Tabun khan, was wary of Unebolod despite their history. The two of them had fought together years ago, before Manduul had become Great Khan. At the time, Albeq had thrown his support behind Unebolod, but when Manduul became Great Khan, Albeq distanced himself as if afraid of retribution. The fear was reasonable. Who would want to risk the ire of a new Great Khan? Looking back, Unebolod now knew that fear had been misplaced. Manduul was a simple man who appreciated a simple life.

Unebolod settled on a bench in the tent across from Albeq. The sides of the tent remained open for all to see, even if only a handful of Albeq's guards remained close enough to hear anything. Beyond the open walls, a sea of Tabun gers dotted the horizon in all directions. The Khingan Mountains barred the eastern horizon.

Unebolod had deduced easily enough that Albeq still feared Manduul might lash out for showing loyalty to Unebolod years ago. Leaving the tent open would leave witnesses. However, Unebolod needed Albeq and was counting on old alliances to strengthen his position. War was inevitable once *kurultai* came around.

Albeq sat silently as his wife poured tea and offered it to both men—a formality that Unebolod recognized. He accepted the tea in his right hand as custom dictated and took a sip graciously.

"How is Lord Togochi faring in Mongke Bulag?" Albeq asked.

The Tabun were a smaller tribe whose allegiance followed the Khorlod. Albeq had likely not seen Togochi in at least six years.

"Happy, married, and well-respected," Unebolod answered. "Aside from myself and the Golden Prince, Togochi holds the most power and respect in the capital."

Albeq nodded. "He continues to uphold his word and undo the mistakes of his predecessors, then."

"And then some. But the winds are changing, Albeq khan," Unebolod said.

"You've come a long way to be refused, Unebolod," Albeq said, holding his cup casually. Unebolod knew he had the speed and strength of a viper.

"I have not even addressed the reason for my visit," Unebolod said, amused at Albeq's swift denial.

Albeq scowled in a way that pulled his thick brows into a straight, tight line. He sat in silence for a moment, then nodded. "Speak then, so I can give the same answer again."

In the war against the Oirat years ago, Albeq had fought against Bigirsen's *tumens*. Albeq would have lost that battle had Unebolod not joined with his own men. The only thing standing between the Tabun and the defeat that surely would have folded them into Bigirsen's growing ranks had been Unebolod's swift thinking. Albeq's freedom had come at Unebolod's hand, and he was owed a debt.

Knowing Albeq, Unebolod understood he must tell his old friend the simple truth of their situation. He sipped his tea, watching the old khan over the rim of his cup. As he lowered it, he straightened his spine. "As I have said, winds are changing. We will face *kurultai* soon. Perhaps within the next year."

"What plot is this?" Albeq asked suspiciously. His broad shoulders tensed visibly.

"No plot, Albeq." Unebolod lowered his voice. He would tell Albeq the truth, but no others could hear him. "What I tell you now has come from the lips of Manduul himself, and you should not utter it to another soul no matter how you trust them. Not your wife or sons. Not your generals."

Albeq's lips thinned.

"I come to you on Manduul Khan's orders," Unebolod said, hoping that would ease the tension in the old khan.

Albeq narrows his eyes, then gave a tight nod. "If you are here on Manduul's orders, you have my word. I will keep this secret so long as there is no doubt it comes from the Khan of khans."

Unebolod glanced around, keeping his voice low enough that none of the guards would hear him. He took an enormous risk admitting this to Albeq, but he knew the Tabun khan would not listen if he didn't understand what headed their direction. "Manduul is dying. He fears Bigirsen's reach, that the Uyghur will grab for power the moment he passes. Especially now that Bigirsen has a son from the Borjigin princess Borogchin. Soon, we will need to unite against Bigirsen."

Albeq's face fell for just a moment before he regained control of his emotions and resumed a stony face. He gave a tight nod. "That leaves us with his prince, Bolkhu, yes?"

Unebolod grimaced. Bayan would never become Great Khan.

Albeq seemed to read his mind, leaning forward as if on the verge of saying more, then clamped his jaw tight enough to make the muscles in his neck twitch.

"Speak, old friend."

Silence settled between them, making the air seem even thicker in the humidity. Albeq studied Unebolod thoughtfully for quite some time before speaking at last. "Even from afar, I have heard the rumors, that the two of you have never been friendly. I think your pride is too strong to follow a boy half your age. Yet if you stand against him, you will be destroyed."

Unebolod pressed his forearms against his knees. "Then what am I to do? I cannot stand against him or he will gather his power and destroy me. Yet according to you, I cannot follow him. And even if something happens to him, I will still have to face off against Bigirsen's power. He has gained most of the southern tribes behind him. His *tumens* are much larger. Whether it is I or the prince in charge, Bigirsen will not sit back and watch another Great Khan sit where he thinks he belongs."

Albeq smirked. "You haven't come to me for answers. You already have them. What bothers you most is not knowing for certain if the winds will blow your way. And you want me to tell you. Unebolod, you have always been a man of vision and strength, but not of excessive desires."

"And I should instead allow the tribes, the Nation, to fall into the hands of a weak, small man with no vision?" Unebolod was careful to avoid using Bayan's name. While they spoke in lowered voices, someone could still overhear. "He has a quick tongue, for certain, but the Nation needs someone of intelligence to lead, and we both know he lacks the necessary qualities. Bigirsen will use this against him. Can you look me in the eye and tell me you genuinely believe the prince would make a good Great Khan?"

Albeq snorted. "I've crossed paths with him in the past. He would make a terrible Great Khan. The power of the Nation would wither away. The Oirat would take control under Bigirsen's Uyghur forces. But *you* are not as weak as you would have everyone believe, attempting to reforge old alliances and upend the proper order of things. And so I fear I must repeat myself, Unebolod." Albeq's hard gaze penetrated Unebolod. "You have come a long way to be refused."

Of all the khans he had spoken to these past months, Unebolod had been confident Albeq would support him. Perhaps the distance and the years had driven the older man further away. Unebolod set down his cup of tea. "I thank you for your hospitality, old friend."

He stood to go, then paused after a few steps and faced the Tabun khan again. "Before I go, can you tell me what your tribe plans to do once Bigirsen has swept our Golden Prince away? As you have said, the Vice Regent's power has grown quite vast, and our prince does not have the experience or understanding we have collectively. Bigirsen will not take the oath to the prince. He will attack. He has waited too long for this opportunity. And when he has defeated our Golden Prince—and we both know he will—he will come for the rest of us. He will not be satisfied until he has conquered us all."

Albeq had stood when Unebolod made to leave. Now he remained rooted in place, staring at Unebolod bewildered. The words were bold, but honest.

"I am too old for this," Albeq said, his shoulders sloping. "One day, we will all die, and what will remain?"

"What we build." The answer was obvious to Unebolod. "Perhaps one day, even that will be reduced to dust, but it will outlast us either way. What we build today will create a foundation for the future of our Nation, just as it did when Genghis united the nation under his white banner. If we leave it to lesser men, the Nation will wither away. When I am dust, and people walk over my bones, I will be satisfied with my life knowing I have worked to build something for them. Even if they forget my name."

Rebuilding the Mongol Nation would allow Unebolod to move on in peace. To do that, he would have to become Great Khan and smash the power Bigirsen grasped with all the force he could gather. If he could subjugate or kill Bigirsen's forces, Unebolod would have his united Mongol Nation.

Albeq was silent for several long seconds before he finally spoke. "Do you know what our most valuable possession is in this life, Unebolod?" When Unebolod gave no response, Albeq pressed on. "Our honor."

Unebolod's back stiffened. Either he was about to declare for Unebolod, or he would have him killed in the name of the Khan for daring to speak against the prince.

"I swore an oath to Manduul Khan, just as the rest of the tribal Lords and their heirs did," Albeq said, standing straighter. "Honor also binds me to him, but also to you. I have not forgotten the debt owed."

Holding on to hope felt too much. Unebolod held his breath as he waited for Albeq to declare for him. "All I ask is that, should the Golden Prince fall, you support me as Great Khan as Manduul has proclaimed. Then, we will remove the Uyghur boot from our throats."

Albeq stepped toward Unebolod, and the two grasped arms to shake. "You have my word still, Unebolod khan. The western dogs will fall but be wary of the prince. Should he rise to power, you will need to earn his trust."

Unebolod smirked. "I already have something more powerful to sway him." *A knife to his throat.*

"Then go with the blessing of the High Heavens," Albeq said. "And we will see each other soon, united."

Unebolod bowed respectfully to Albeq and ducked out of the tent. His guards closed in around him and followed close on his heels. Now, with the Kharchin and Khorlod khans, as well as the Tabun, declared to support him and his own khanship, alongside Manduul's proclamation that he would be heir after Bayan, Unebolod could almost taste his future. And it was as sweet as good *boal*.

When he returned to his camp and strode with confident steps into his ger, Unebolod encountered Odgerel still beneath his roof. She had not left since spending the night on his floor the previous night. She bowed deeply as he entered, her cheeks flushed. Unebolod could not help admiring the curve of her hips or the way her simple deel hugged her chest. Exhilaration pumped through his veins and stirred his blood. Overcome by excitement from his victory and her alluring form, Unebolod approached Odgerel, forcing her steps back until her back pressed into the butcher's block. The warmth of her body seeped into his clothes and his breaths heaved with elation from the day. Unebolod brushed his fingers along her neck, leaning close.

Odgerel's breaths came in swift succession as well, rolling over his face. "My Lord," she murmured breathlessly. Her eyes fluttered, gazing at him through those long lashes.

His own gaze locked on her full lips. She was beautiful, perfect. Her skin was so smooth, reminding him of the feel of Mandukhai's skin against his own. *Honor is our most valuable possession.* Albeq's reminder pulled Unebolod back as guilt surged through him. Odgerel's eyes shined as she gazed up at him, and he turned his head away, taking a step back.

"Have I disappointed you?" Odgerel asked, her voice quivering.

Unebolod turned away from her and spotted the pot on the stove. "I need someone who knows how to make proper *buuz* and curds," he said briskly. "Can you handle such a task?"

For a moment, he was met with silence. Though it had only been a night and Odgerel had spent the entirety of it on the floor, Unebolod heard the whispers. People were curious about the girl who slept in his ger. Mandukhai would surely hear about it in time. Even though nothing had happened, it would crush her. He needed to keep his oath to her. One more year, and it would be done. He could marry Mandukhai. What was one more year after so many already passed?

Unebolod worried Odgerel would not respond. Part of him wanted her to refuse. Then he could turn her out and no longer face the temptation. Why had he made the offer? *High Heavens help me, she must say no,* he prayed. But the gods were never on his side.

"If that is what my khan requires of me, it would honor me to take on the task," Odgerel said, and for a moment he was certain he heard excitement bordering on sultry yearning.

"Good." Unebolod snatched his bow off the hook near the door. "You will sleep with the rest of my servants as of tonight." At least he could keep her out from under his roof.

Her voice trailed away as he trudged out the door again. "Your will, my Lord."

Hunting would help relieve some of his tension. At the very least, it would keep him away from her.

MONGKE BULAG – SUMMER 1469

"Are you certain no one saw you?" Yeke asked, resting her hands against Bayan's chest.

Bayan grinned at her concern. Ever since the accusation mounted against him—and Manduul's reaction to it—Bayan had been confident in his status of invulnerability. Let the men talk about him however they wanted. Manduul would never turn his back on Bayan, and he would turn a blind eye so long as Bayan was not plotting his premature demise. With Manduul on the edge of death, Bayan saw little point in plotting anything. And when Manduul died, he would purge any who doubted his right. It was the only way he could protect himself.

"You worry too much," Bayan said as he slid his fingers along her neck and pulled her closer to him. He pressed his lips insistently against her own.

Yeke pulled away, frowning at him. "But Manduul—"

"I scouted this very spot earlier today," he reassured her. "No one will find us here."

The surrounding briars provided enough cover to block them from sight to anyone without first revealing themselves. Bayan had tested the theory himself. This particular briar patch curved against a rock wall. He had brought along felt to lie on the grass and dirt so nothing would stick to them. He had even placed a small jug of honey wine on the felt for their enjoyment later. His men thought he was hunting with others, and no one would come looking for them all night. They had all the time they could want.

"You have said as much before," Yeke said, glancing over his shoulder as if someone could appear behind him at any moment.

Bayan kissed along her neck, sliding the silk deel off her shoulders. Already, he could feel his desire overwhelming his senses. Yeke gasped, and he grinned against her skin. She could deny him all she wanted, but she wouldn't do so for long. Yeke was too starved for affection to deny the only person to shower her with it. In no time at all, she spread out beneath him on the felt-covered ground. Then her limbs twined around him as she gave in to her own desires.

Issama had just finished dinner when someone knocked on his door. He frowned and called for them to enter, not surprised to see Nahai dipping his head respectfully. Nahai was a good and loyal retainer. His wit was just sharp enough to be of useful service without being so sharp he could outwit his superior. Issama had befriended Nahai three years ago when he learned how much the other man hated Bigirsen.

"What is it, Nahai?" Issama asked as Uingen busied herself cleaning up the mess from dinner.

"I have done as you asked, my Lord," Nahai said.

Issama stood, his heart thumping with excitement. For months, Nahai had carefully watched and followed Bayan and Yeke. He had missed a few opportunities in the past that had earned him a harsh dressing down from Issama, but Nahai remained loyal. If Issama had to trust anyone, he would trust Nahai, who understood what they had to gain and wanted it just as Issama did—though not nearly as bad.

"Now?" Issama asked, hoping he did not sound as exhilarated as he felt.

Nahai nodded.

"Show me." Issama rushed toward the door, snatching his hat and popping it on his head to help mask him in coming darkness. He debated bringing his sword along, but the noise could alert others to his presence, and he had no intention of using it. This mission simply required him to observe.

Uingen said nothing as she watched Issama disappear through the doorway. He had not told her about his business, nor did she need to know. This concerned the fate of the Nation, and women need not play a part in the politics.

Nahai had a horse ready for Issama and held out the reins as soon as they were outside. Issama frowned as he mounted. Would they go so far that they must ride? Nahai guided them away from camp toward the north. They moved with no haste. Riding hard would have caught the attention of the men on watch or the scouts, but Issama regularly rode around the perimeter at a canter. No one would look twice.

As they rounded a hill, Nahai dismounted and tied the reins of his horse to a tree branch. Issama followed his lead, and the two of them crept forward on foot, careful of making noise. Nahai motioned toward a briar patch butted against a rock wall. It was a good place to hide for such a rendezvous. No one would look twice unless they were searching, as Issama was. He only had to take a few steps before the muffled grunts and moans of pleasure reached him, along with the slap of skin. There could be no doubt what was happening within the briar, but he had to witness it himself to give true credibility to his allegation.

Issama motioned for Nahai to stay still, then picked his way closer to seek a weakness in the briar he could see through. It took several minutes before he found a space between briar branches and a rock just large enough to squeeze through. That must have been where they had entered. Issama shifted back and peered through the branches cautiously. They mustn't see him looking on or it would ruin his plan.

At first, all Issama could make out were the tops of their heads and their bare bodies. The woman lay on her back on a blanket of felt, but he could not see her face. The man on top of her could have been any wiry man, and her chest and his own hair masked his face. When he rocked against her, her head pitched back. Issama could not mistake that enormous nose and ugly face for anyone other than the Khan's wife, Yeke.

For a moment, he feared she had spotted him, but her eyes slid shut. She swallowed a moan. Bayan lifted his face, giving Issama just enough identification as was necessary before the prince pressed his lips against hers.

Satisfied that he had all the confirmation he needed, Issama silently slipped away, not bothering to hide his grin.

At long last, he had witnessed Bayan's indiscretion himself. Now he could plant the evidence for Siker and the guards to discover, then deliver the news to Manduul with absolute certainty. The words were spinning in his head as soon as he mounted his horse to ride back to his ger alongside Nahai.

Now, the Golden Prince would fall.

Chapter Twenty-One

Cold Thoughts

After returning from his rendezvous with Yeke, Bayan had promptly fallen asleep in his bed beside the snoring form of his wife. Siker had woken early, nagging at him about the dirt his boots had tracked in on the rug, which again turned into a full-blown argument. How did that woman ever expect him to have sex with her again if all she did was criticize everything?

The morning had offered the promise of a good day for hunting. Bayan mounted up with his personal guards and Berkedai to take an extended hunting trip. Escaping the suffocating mass of Mongke Bulag—and Siker—offered relief.

As he raced across the plains with his men, Bayan breathed in the warm summer air. They already had killed several marmots brave enough to stick their heads out of their holes to discover what made the ground rumble so. The dogs barked with delight, running alongside the mounts, their furry manes rippling along their heads and down their backs like black and brown waves. While Bayan despised warfare, he enjoyed hunting. It felt liberating, as if he were free of any cares he could have in the world.

Berkedai's bowstring snapped and Bayan watched the arrow whistle through the air and catch a bird in flight. He grinned as Berkedai whooped in delight. One dog raced ahead to collect the prize in its jaw.

By nightfall, they all stretched out on felt bedrolls beside a campfire and feasted on their kills from the hunt. Bayan tossed scraps to the dogs, who devoured the morsels of meat with slobbery delight. As he tossed a bone toward two dogs, they snatched it simultaneously, nearly biting each other as each grabbed an end of the bone in their teeth. The two tugged back and forth until one emerged with the reward. The other dog snarled, then the two wrestled over the dry ground.

Berkedai gave a sharp whistle, and the dogs stopped immediately, settling down on the ground. The loser of the fight rested his massive head on his giant paws and watched with sad eyes as the other dog gnawed on the bone, sharpening his teeth. The sadness should have bothered Bayan, but such was the way of life. The strongest always won.

Indeed, it was a good day to be alive, and Bayan stretched out beneath the stars as Berkedai shared a tale of their battle against the Ming imposters with the guards, as if the other men had not been there. His enthusiasm was contagious. Bayan closed his eyes and smiled.

MONGKE BULAG – SUMMER 1469

Everything came together as Issama had hoped. The morning after witnessing Bayan and Yeke together, Nahai arrived with the wolf dawn and reported that Bayan had left with his guards to go hunting. Issama moved through the shadows toward Bayan's ger. He waited for the guard posted at the door to move away to check the perimeter of the ger before gently rapping on the door.

Siker opened the door a crack, then pulled Issama through and quickly closed it behind him. "He snuck off again last night," she said, keeping her voice low so the guard patrolling around the ger would not hear them.

"I know."

Her eyes widened. "Did you ..." She swallowed, and her lower lip trembled. "Did you see them ... together?"

Issama did not respond, but the sympathetic expression he bestowed upon Siker was answer enough. She leaned against his chest, pressing her cheek to his shoulder. Issama wrapped his arms around her and stroked her back.

"So that's it then," she murmured against his shoulder. "You were right."

"For what it's worth, I'm sorry. You deserve better."

"And you will tell the Khan?"

"I have to. I gave an oath. I'm duty-bound to tell him."

Siker pulled away and turned her back to him, hugging her arms against her chest. Issama wanted to reach out and offer her more comfort, but he knew this opportunity would only last a few seconds. He could not waste it.

As Siker stood with her back to him, Issama tiptoed back a few steps toward Bayan's open chest. The pouch of poisonous herbs slid down his sleeve into his palm, then he casually dropped it into the open chest. It thumped, and he tensed, waiting for her to spin around and accuse him. Instead, Siker dipped her chin against her chest.

Issama crouched, watching her cautiously for signs of movement as he nudged the pouch deeper into the chest, beneath a stack of fine silk deels. If it just lay on top, someone might wonder why it had not been found sooner.

Siker pulled in a shuddering breath. *Is she crying?*

Issama found this distressing. He had expected Siker to experience some remorse, but mostly anger. He rose and glided silently toward her, placing a hand on her shoulder. "It will be okay, Siker. I told you I would look out for you, and I meant it. I will make sure Manduul sees you as innocent in all of this."

Siker spun around, tears streaking her face and an iciness in her dark eyes. "And then what, Issama? I will be widowed. Again. I will be pushed into another marriage with another man who doesn't care for me, but who offers the Khan some sort of political leverage. I didn't ask for any of this."

Issama cupped her face in his palm and brushed his thumb across a river of drying tears. "There is me."

This is not part of the plan, he warned himself. Yet seeing her state, Issama found himself alarmed at how much he truly wanted her. *She would be a valuable piece to my plans going forward*. Already, his mind spun with new webs, all with her at the center.

Siker leaned closer. Fear churned cold in his belly. Issama pressed his thumb to her lips as he stepped back. Siker wanted to kiss him. He could sense it just as easily as he could breathe. But it would end in disaster.

"No," he said. "We could end up no better off than him. Be patient. And remember, you are the innocent party in all of this. Make sure everyone sees that. Especially the Khan and Mandukhai."

Before Siker could draw him toward her again, Issama slipped out, wary of where the guard might be, and left Siker alone. *Another interesting turn of events*, he thought as he slithered away. Taking the prince's wife would lend Issama even more legitimacy when the time came.

By the time the sun rose, Issama had begun his daily duties. With his army of scribes, he carried out the Khan's orders and attended to daily tasks. Mandukhai was present for most of the morning as well, watching everything with her sharp eyes and sharing wisdom when necessary.

As afternoon came, Mandukhai excused herself to attend to other responsibilities. Issama dismissed his scribes to various chores until eventually only he remained with Manduul and the Khan's personal guards. Issama clutched one final parchment in his hands, chewing his lip pensively as he gazed at the flowing script.

"What bothers you?" Manduul asked, settling back in his seat with a fresh cup of *airag*.

"I hate to bother you with this, my lord Khan," Issama said, bowing his head shamefully. The way he presented this information to Manduul was critical in the success of his plot, and he played the part of an anxious servant to the Khan well.

"Clearly the news has you troubled. Out with it."

Issama released a shuddering breath. "I have a report here from Mingtau, of the Chakhar."

"Have the Mongols risen against their Ming oppressors?" Manduul asked, and excitement shined in his dark eyes.

Issama cleared his throat and read from the parchment. "I regret to share with the Great Khan that, during his time among my tribe, Bolkhu *Jinong* spoke of his own reign as if the day were upon us already, and before he departed, requested my personal support in *kurultai*."

Manduul frowned, stroking his chin as his gaze turned inward. Silence fell over the wide, empty gathering tent before the Khan spoke at last. "I sent him to inspire confidence in the future glory of our empire so those Mongols under Ming thumbs would have the backbone to thrust off their shackles. And we both know what is coming for me." Manduul coughed as if to punctuate his point, and Issama paused until the sound subsided enough for his voice to carry to the Khan without being heard by others.

"There ... is more, my lord Khan." Issama waited for Manduul to wave impatiently through his fit of coughing. Manduul wiped his mouth, and Issama noticed the red on the cloth. Issama dipped his head and lowered his gaze before speaking. "I hesitate to say this, after what has already happened. But ... I have learned something disturbing myself, and witnessed it with my own eyes, my lord Khan."

"Stop blathering and speak already!" Manduul snapped between coughs.

Issama suppressed a grin and adopted a frightened, concerned expression. "Of course. I do not say this to spark conflict, but simply to inform you because you have a right to know," Issama informed the Khan. "I have seen the prince and your first wife together. The charges that servant made against the prince were, in fact, true. I suspected something amiss, and so I followed Bolkhu out to an isolated place, and the Golden Prince and your wife met in a conjugal embrace."

As the words slowly and carefully slipped past his lips with the most regretful tone he could muster, Issama dared a glance up at Manduul. The Khan appeared confused for a moment. Then, as the pieces came together, Manduul's face fell.

"You saw this yourself?" Manduul asked, lowering the bloody cloth from his lips.

"I did, my lord Khan. Just last night."

"You are friends with Bolkhu, are you not?" Manduul asked, his voice suddenly weary.

"Yes, but I am loyal first to the Khan." Issama bowed deeply. "I regret having to bring such news to you, but I felt it my duty to remove the veil of deception to reveal the truth. I fear that what I saw, combined with what Mingtau has reported, does not bode well. In fact ..."

"What?"

Issama's shoulders tense. "I just wonder what brought on your illness."

"Are you accusing my nephew of poisoning me?" Anger marred Manduul's sagging features.

Issama stepped back, dipping his head. He pushed too far, too fast. "Not exactly. I just think that, with this new evidence of adultery, it cannot hurt to search his ger. If nothing else, to clear his name for good. If he is only sleeping with your wife, that is for you to decide punishment. But if I were in your place, I would want to be certain he was innocent so no one could doubt him again."

"But you are not in my place!" Manduul roared, then wheezed for a moment.

"Of course not, my lord Khan."

The flash of anger transformed into sorrow that creased the corners of Manduul's eyes. Whether or not he cared about the adultery, the betrayal from Bayan clearly stung deep. Issama had nurtured the seeds of doubt. Now he just needed to wait for those seeds to sprout.

Manduul nodded, but he appeared distant. "You did the right thing telling me."

Issama took a tentative step back, rolling up the parchment in his hands and setting it with the others for Manduul to review himself. It was a forgery, but Manduul would never know. Mingtau would be dead before Manduul could verify it. Mingtau's death would only substantiate Bayan's guilt—assuming Manduul did not die before that.

"I will leave you to decide how you think best to handle this news, my lord Khan." Issama waited for Manduul to dismiss him, then slipped out of the gathering tent, fighting to hold back a grin.

Manduul kicked off his boots with a sluggishness Mandukhai had not seen before. Everything about the way he moved was not only weaker, but strenuous, as if he did not have the strength to control his muscles much longer. She frowned as he collapsed against the bed without asking for his usual drink. Mandukhai padded over and sat on the edge of the bed beside him, feeling his forehead.

"You are freezing, Manduul," she said. A warm cloth on his forehead would help. She moved into action. While she had no love for the man she had married, she had developed a co-habitable relationship with him over the years. His death would be her freedom—or her curse. She was not yet sure how Bayan would respond to her once Manduul passed. Or if Unebolod would make it back in time to save her from Bayan. She could not refuse the prince once Manduul passed. Bayan would inherit her as a wife just as certainly as the title of Great Khan.

"My mind is heavy with grief," Manduul muttered. "And I am having cold thoughts. Perhaps that is why I am freezing to touch."

Mandukhai returned with a cloth she had warmed on the stove and laid it across his forehead. "Grief? Over what?"

"My nephew has been accused of betraying me again," Manduul said, his voice weak and bone-weary. "With Yeke. And that he is working against me even as I die."

Someone else had come forward against Bayan? Who would dare after the previous accusation, and why would Manduul believe it this time? Mandukhai stared at the stove as her thoughts turned over.

"This is the second time I have heard the charges," Manduul grumbled. "I cannot let this pass a second time. I warned Bolkhu last time to be cautious."

Mandukhai's breath caught. She had no desire to see Bayan become Great Khan, but she also knew that he was the last heir of Genghis. It was a terrible sort of limbo. "What have you done, Manduul?"

"Nothing." He grimaced and pressed a hand to the warm cloth. "Yet. I should speak to him, get answers, but he is gone hunting with his men."

Mandukhai picked at her nails, afraid of saying the words that came to her tongue. Speaking against Bayan and Yeke could remove the other woman from power, but it would also condemn Bayan. She hated him, but the Mongol Nation needed him. Then again, without Bayan, they would still have Unebolod, and he was more than capable of leading. Perhaps that was best for all. At least he was still of the royal bloodline, even if he was not from Genghis.

Manduul narrowed his eyes to suspicious slits as he watched her consider all of this. "What?"

"I just ..." Mandukhai bit her lip. "I have suspected this for some time. Yet with no proof for myself, I did not dare accuse the prince."

Manduul shot up, grabbing her arm in a weakened grip. "Suspected what?"

"That he had some association with Yeke. As I said, it was speculation. I could prove nothing. Except, he may have also been responsible for Nergui's death. Unebolod found a single painite stone with the bodies of the gambler and his wife. Bolkhu's belt was missing a stone."

"No one bothered to tell me?" Manduul asked, clearly more hurt than angry.

"We did not want to upset you," Mandukhai said. "And you loved him so much. I worried the stone would not be enough."

Manduul's grip tightened until it pinched her skin, and Mandukhai winced. Then, just as suddenly, he released her arm and dropped back on the bed as if the life had gone out of him. For a moment, she feared the worst, and her breath hitched until reason took over. Manduul had not just dropped dead. He was simply overcome with grief.

"Did I know him at all?" Manduul muttered.

"Sleep on this, husband," Mandukhai said, pulling a blanket over him. "No righteous judgments come from rash actions."

Manduul muttered something incoherent as he closed his eyes.

Mandukhai shuttered the stove and turned off the oil lamp before settling down herself, trying to think through this logically.

Without Bayan, perhaps the empire could once again unite under a powerful Great Khan. Perhaps she should advise Manduul to punish the prince for his disloyalty, but doing so felt like a betrayal to Genghis. Would Genghis's spirit forgive them for killing Bayan? *Lord Tengri, guide us*, she prayed as she closed her eyes.

Shattered Oaths

EAST OF MONGKE BULAG – SUMMER 1469

Before the sun rose the next morning, Issama and Nahai rode out of Mongke Bulag with a handful of men. Bayan had gone east to hunt in the rolling plains. It would not be hard to track them down. No one would try to hide their passage. Issama left under the guise of taking his own men hunting with the promise of returning before nightfall. Hopefully, Manduul would not put the pieces together. It was a risk he had to take.

Bayan left a clear trail in his wake—ground trampled by hooves, patches of blood from the kills, a recently smothered campfire surrounded by the remains of their feast. By late morning, Issama and his men rode up to the prince, calling out a greeting to avoid alarming them. Bayan turned his chestnut mount toward the newcomers and grinned as he saw Issama, waving at him. *Such a gullible boy.* Bayan had been easy to trick into friendship. Now, Issama would use that trust against the prince.

"Issama, what brings you so far from home?" Bayan asked, beaming brightly as Berkedai whistled at the dogs who nipped at Issama's mount.

"Can we speak privately?" Issama asked, casting untrusting glances at Bayan's men.

Bayan frowned, as if he didn't understand the question. "I trust these men with my life. Speak freely, Issama. They will never utter a word of this. What worries you?"

If this all happened according to Issama's plan, these men would be witnesses to him warning the prince. They could not know what he said. If they overheard, he would have to kill them all or risk having Manduul learn the truth.

Issama still edged his mount closer to Bayan's and lowered his voice. "I rode out early this morning to warn you. Manduul knows the truth of your affair with his wife. He is furious. If you have allies, now is the time to gather them. Manduul intends to do evil to you to prevent you from forcefully removing him."

Bayan sat statue-still in his saddle, staring at Issama with no obvious reaction. Were it not for the rise and fall of his chest—increasing with each passing moment—Issama would have assumed the news had shocked him to death where he sat.

Issama's gaze slid past Bayan to Berkedai, who edged closer, his hand on his sword, sensing something amiss. At last, Bayan's blank expression cracked. The corner of his mouth curled up slowly until he broke into laughter.

"He would never do evil to me," Bayan said, shaking his head. "And I have no intention of removing him. What would be the point?"

Issama leaned forward with urgency, glancing suspiciously at Berkedai as he lowered his voice. He spoke with all the seriousness he could muster. "Would I have ridden out to warn you if I were uncertain? You trust me, don't you?"

Bayan's mirth slowly faded, and he appeared uncertain, cocking his head slightly to the side. "Yes ..."

"Then heed this warning. Be cautious and ever watchful. Your uncle's suspicion will be evident soon enough. It was hinted that you may have poisoned him to this sickness." Issama did not know how Manduul would handle the news, but he knew Manduul well enough to be confident in this next part, at least. "He will send a messenger to question your loyalty. Mark my words, Bolkhu Jinong. The Khan will try to deceive you into revealing yourself. I promise to do what I can to help you, but you must be careful who you trust."

Bayan had a reputation for keen survival instincts. Issama actually hoped Bayan's natural paranoia would make the prince believe the Khan was tricking him, even if Manduul's questions were innocent. If Bayan believed Manduul truly was angry and he fled to avoid certain death, it would only confirm his guilt and condemn him, even if Manduul had been prepared to declare him innocent. Issama needed Bayan to doom himself to push the final wedge between the two.

He placed a brotherly hand on Bayan's shoulder and gave it a squeeze. "May the sky father protect you."

Issama turned his mount and rode back toward Mongke Bulag, content that he had done all he could for now. For his plans to come to fruition, he had but to wait and hope that Manduul and Bayan would react as he expected.

Bayan was too stunned to speak as Issama rode away with his men. Berkedai rode up beside him, eyeing Issama and his men suspiciously with a hand on his bow, as if expecting an order to kill them all. Bayan gave no such order. His mind reeled from the news. Could Manduul truly have such designs against him? Did he think Bayan had poisoned him to his death?

"What was that all about?" Berkedai asked, keeping his gaze fixed on the men as they disappeared over a hill.

Bayan swallowed the lump in his throat. *Be careful who you trust*. Bayan shook his head. "Nothing."

Bayan had given an oath to remain loyal as long as they lived, and he had kept his oath. They were brothers, one blood and the last of the wolves. Yes, Bayan had slept with Yeke frequently over the past several years, but Manduul had seemed very careless about her years ago. In fact, Manduul himself had first brought up the idea. Could he truly be upset now that he knew it had, in fact, happened?

Something else must be amiss. Some detail Issama did not know or share. Manduul could forgive Bayan for sleeping with Yeke, the wife he cared nothing for. Bayan had attempted nothing of the sort with Mandukhai, knowing Manduul preferred to share her bed.

Manduul's casual warning after butchering Enkh right in front of Bayan resurfaced. *I will give you the benefit of the doubt this time, and I will not so easily be fooled again. But don't provide me further reasons to question your loyalty.* His heart hammered against his ribs.

Until Bayan knew more of what had transpired in his absence, he could not return to Mongke Bulag or he might find a dagger in his neck. His hunting trip would have to be extended.

"We will stay out a few extra days," Bayan announced, turning his mount south.

Berkedai frowned, but did not question the command as his horse followed alongside Bayan.

For the first time since arriving in Mongke Bulag five years ago, Bayan no longer felt safe. The wind itself could blow him into the earth and swallow him whole, for all he knew. Danger lurked in all things. Bayan glanced at Berkedai from the corner of his eye. Could he still trust his friend, or was Berkedai loyal first to the Khan? Enemies could now surround Bayan no matter where he ran.

Mandukhai escorted Manduul into the gathering tent the following morning and helped him into his seat before taking her own. Waking him had been a challenge, and his sleep had been fitful. Mandukhai knew everyone would notice the dark circles around his sunken eyes. The exhaustion was clear to all who laid eyes on him. He sent away servants, then ordered his guards to stand outside.

Only Togochi and Yungei attended Manduul this morning, waiting before the dais. They clearly sensed Manduul's dour mood, standing tense and silent. Issama had not answered his summons. After waiting several painfully long minutes, Boke returned to the gathering tent and reported that Issama had taken some of his men hunting. Manduul excused Boke with a grumble.

"No one will breathe a word of this meeting to another soul," Manduul said. "What we discuss here will be only between the four of us and Lord Issama. If anyone else hears, I will know who to question."

Yungei straightened. Togochi cast a questioning glance at Mandukhai after offering a nod of agreement.

Mandukhai understood the need for secrecy in this matter. Manduul would want to be certain of the accusations against Bayan before anyone else heard of it. Mandukhai trusted Togochi, but she was not so sure about Yungei or Issama. Again, she found Issama's absence suspicious after delivering the news to Manduul himself. If Issama warned Bayan or Yeke—and he very well could—then Manduul's secrecy had no meaning.

Manduul perched on his throne like a man prepared to jump off a cliff to his death. He dipped his head and his shoulders sagged.

"Charges have been raised once more against Bolkhu," Manduul said at last. The words seemed to deepen the surrounding silence.

Togochi glanced at Mandukhai as if for confirmation. She only gave a small nod.

"The prince has deceived me," Manduul said. "As far back as the early days of his arrival in my court."

Togochi's eyes widened as Manduul listed the charges. Mandukhai could not decide how she felt about this turn of events. For so long, she had wanted vengeance for what Bayan had done to Nergui. Now, it simply felt surreal.

Manduul sighed. "It is time for the truth. I myself am not in good health. I am without male descendants, and after I am dead, my queens will be his." Manduul lifted his head and met the curious gaze of both Togochi and Yungei.

Mandukhai held her breath as she waited. Manduul had been unwilling to discuss the matter with her before the meeting, and she did not know how he would respond to the charges. Hopefully, he would use calm logic, but she had little faith he possessed the skills for it.

Manduul's countenance revealed his pain and weariness as he continued. "I am aware of the rumors that have swirled around the prince since that first accusation. Maybe I believed, deep down, the rumors were true."

Mandukhai forced herself to remain calm. What Bayan had done with Yeke was abhorrent, but it wasn't illegal since Yeke was above his station. Younger men would sometimes bed the wives of their older brothers to help produce sons if the husband had difficulty in this. However, usually this was done with permission. Bayan could face a lesser punishment for this offense, but Yeke, as the wife, faced much more severe consequences. Somehow, Mandukhai suspected there was more to the charges than Manduul had admitted.

"I have turned a blind eye to his misgivings with an old man's foolish hope that I could guide him toward the right path. Now, I fear he may be rushing too quickly ahead. I have given him power and *tumens*. I have given him commands and a throne of his own. I have pushed him toward this fate, and perhaps he believes he has already replaced me or need offer no respect toward his Khan any longer."

Replaced him? Mandukhai thought. Had she underestimated Bayan's ambition? Perhaps he was much better at the political game than she had given him credit for. Mandukhai supposed it was possible for him to have made his own plans to seize power. It would be no less than any other man she had known. If Manduul had evidence of treason against the Khan, it would be enough to sentence Bayan to death.

Not for the first time, it relieved Mandukhai that Manduul had never learned the truth of her affair with Unebolod, or her true feelings for him. If Manduul was so despondent about Bayan and was considering punishing the prince, he surely would have killed both her and Unebolod if he had learned the truth. *Or perhaps he would have forced me to watch as he tortured and dismembered Unebolod.* The thought made a shiver race down her spine. The horror of witnessing such a thing!

"Bolkhu *Jinong* has been accused of murdering a queen's guard, stealing my first wife from me, and plotting my death and his takeover as Great Khan," Manduul said, listing the charges as if they were the heaviest words he had ever spoken. He straightened. "It is bad that, starting now, he should have such excessive desires. However, we cannot act further until we are certain of the truth of these allegations. I have sent a rider south to learn of Bolkhu's alleged evil plots from Lord Mingtau, who sent a message warning me of Bolkhu's plans. It will be some time before I receive word back from him."

Evil plots ... Mandukhai wondered just how much she had missed. Manduul must have some other evidence that Bayan had conspired against him, and from the Chakhar, which means this plot at least stretched as far back as Bayan's campaign in the south.

"The prince is out on a hunting trip, and he must defend his charges," Manduul said, turning his gaze to the two men he summoned. "Togochi, Yungei, I am sending you out to find him and reaffirm his loyalty. Ask him this—and only this—and bring his answer back to me immediately. Ask him—" Manduul's voice cracked with sorrow. He clenched his jaw to regain command of his emotions before that control slipped away. "Ask him what reasons does he have to be against me? I must have an answer." His face drooped. "I fear our oaths of brotherhood have been shattered, and only his answer can shore up this breech in my dying soul."

Mandukhai could not help but wonder what Bayan could say that would fix this. Even if he proved his innocence, that trust had already been broken. With Manduul's days numbered, Bayan would not have time to earn that trust back.

Togochi bowed. Yungei stepped forward, and Mandukhai was certain she could see happiness on his face for just a moment before he bowed deeply. Yungei was a loyal Khorchin man—and Mandukhai knew he worshiped Unebolod. Doubtless, this turn of events pleased Yungei beyond his wildest dreams. Because without Bayan, Unebolod would be next in line.

"Your will, my lord Khan," Yungei said with all the loyalty of a trained hunting dog.

"Speak of this to no one," Manduul repeated. He paused as he struggled to suppress a cough. When he spoke, his voice wheezed. "I will not have rumors flying before I hear his answer. Yeke can know nothing about any of this until I decided what to do with her. I cannot allow her infidelity to go unpunished."

At the final comment, Togochi cast a glance at Mandukhai that made bumps rise on her arms. She could not look away, trapped in his gaze. Togochi suspected her and Unebolod. His gaze only lasted a few moments, but it was long enough for her to recognize it for what it was ... comprehension.

Manduul could contain the cough no longer. It surged past his lips, making him double over. Togochi and Yungei left Mandukhai to tend to the Khan.

Mandukhai fetched a damp cloth for his mouth and a cup of wine. His lungs rattled as he struggled to breathe. She waited patiently, rubbing his back as Khosoichi had shown her. When at last he had regained control, his sad, sunken eyes stared distantly at Bayan's seat beside him. Raising the boy so quickly had been rash, but Manduul had tried his best to teach Bayan all he could. Mandukhai had observed and advised for years. Now, all of that hard work could be undone.

And what of Yeke? Mandukhai loathed her sister-wife, but did she wish death on the other woman? There would be no way to warn Yeke of her impending fate. If Mandukhai even tried, Manduul would know, and Mandukhai would be punished as well. Yeke's fate was not worth the risk.

"What will you do if his response confirms the allegations?" Mandukhai asked, staring at the empty seat as well.

Manduul shook his head. "It's treason, Mandukhai. If he is plotting against me, and has orchestrated my demise, I have no choice. Law dictates my actions, and I cannot make an exception for him." He ripped his gaze away from Bayan's seat, and the grief in his eyes punched Mandukhai's heart. "I have to kill him."

Chapter Twenty-Three

False Securities

Mandukhai could think of a thousand things she would rather do than have tea with her circle of women, but change was coming, and she needed these women to support her. With Bayan's allegation and his potential death looming on the horizon, Mandukhai needed allies more than ever before. Until Unebolod returned, Mandukhai would be exposed and utterly alone. With any luck, Manduul would at the very least strip Yeke of any titles and possessions for collaborating with Bayan.

If Mandukhai survived the transition of power, she could summon the lesser khans at *kurultai* to support Unebolod. Then she would finally marry him and get everything she had worked so hard for. It was all so close now.

Esige poured Mandukhai another cup of tea and settled in beside her. Across the table, Jaghan shifted uncomfortably beside Lady Satai, pressing a palm against her belly. Togochi would fill his ger with sons in no time at the rate he and Jaghan conceived. Already they had two, and now another was on the way. Jaghan seemed to be in a perpetual state of pregnancy. Mandukhai ached to have a child of her own. *Soon enough, Unebolod and I will be married and we will fill our own ger with children.* The thought filled Mandukhai's heart with hope and happiness.

"I just don't understand why he rode off in such a hurry this morning," Jaghan said, shifting again in her seat. "Togochi would say nothing. Not even how long he would be gone. Only that he was on business for Mandu-ul Khan and would return when he could. What if this child comes before he returns? What if he doesn't return at all?"

Lady Satai huffed in irritation. She had little patience for Jaghan's whining about her husband, as Mandukhai had learned fairly early in the friendship. "If it was our business, we would know of it," Satai said sharply, but her gaze fell on Mandukhai as if she were expecting some sort of answer.

Mandukhai simply sipped her tea and pretended not to notice. After a moment, she lowered the cup and smiled at Jaghan. "Togochi will return."

"How do you know that?" Jaghan asked, despairing.

Mandukhai reached forward and placed a hand over Jaghan's on the tabletop. "I just do. You trust I would not lie about this, yes?"

Jaghan chewed her lip, and tears shimmered in her eyes, but she nodded. Her emotions seemed to be more chaotic with this pregnancy than either of the others.

Siker strolled into the ger as if she were not nearly an hour late. She bowed respectfully to Mandukhai before taking an empty seat.

"Kind of you to join us at last, Lady Siker," Satai said. Though her words were innocent, there was an edge of disapproval in her tone.

"A wife has duties to perform even when her husband is away," Siker said, completely unfazed by Satai's tone. "I would not want Bolkhu to return to ill-kept herds or improperly churned *airag*."

"Isn't that what you have servants for?" Satai asked, raising her thick eyebrows and scowling at Siker. The two women were too much alike in some ways, and that similarity constantly raised feathers between them.

"He has little trust in them anymore, as I'm sure you can understand," Siker said calmly. "It is best if I oversee the duties in his absence."

Mandukhai could tell Esige bit her tongue and struggled not to smirk. She frequently joked about just what she thought those servants "duties" were when he was not absent. Mandukhai had to admit she had not realized how many of his servants—aside from the now-dead Enkh—were women until Esige had pointed it out. Siker must have been aware that he was sleeping with all of them.

"We appreciate you showing up all the more," Mandukhai said, setting her cup on the table. "Finding time for tea with us when you have so much to do must be trying."

Siker smiled at Mandukhai, but she wore the smile like a mask, as if it were never meant for her face. Did she have any idea of the danger her husband was in? Would she care if she *did* know? "I will always find time for tea with you, Lady Mandukhai."

Mandukhai nodded respectfully toward Siker and noticed how Siker was careful to name her specifically and not say "tea with her queen," as that would include Yeke. The two women had such bitter hatred toward each other, often cloaked in polite words meant as insults to anyone who knew better. *I suppose I would hate the noblewoman sleeping with Manduul behind my back as well,* Mandukhai thought. It was not so much that she would care who Manduul slept with as it would be the issue of trust and deception. A servant was one thing, because a servant could not replace her. But a noblewoman could.

Satai had turned her attention to studying Mandukhai with those hawkish eyes, always digging for gossip. "You know what orders the Khan has given Togochi and Yungei, don't you."

It was not a question. Mandukhai could tell Satai knew the answer already, so she did not bother giving one.

"One of these days someone will shave your nose clean off your face for sticking it where it does not belong, Lady Satai," Siker said tersely.

Satai flashed an astonished glare at Siker and worked her jaw. "Well, I ... You ..." She straightened in her chair and raised her chin proudly. "Our job is to care for our families, and we cannot do that if we do not know what is going on around us."

Siker rolled her eyes and poured herself a cup of tea. "If that excuse helps you sleep at night, what right have I to shatter your illusions?"

Esige stifled a giggle. Mandukhai shot her a hard stare, and the girl dipped her head. It was rare that Esige found Siker amusing. The girl often called her cold and soulless. In these rare moments, Esige revealed just how much she despised Satai.

"Mandukhai, if I may, I have a personal question to ask," Jaghan said, spinning her cup between her fingers over the surface of the table. The nervousness in her countenance piqued Mandukhai's curiosity. "One Togochi insists he has no answer for, yet I know he wonders the same. And I have heard others talk."

"You can ask, but I cannot promise I can answer," Mandukhai responded.

Jaghan glanced at Satai, and for a moment Mandukhai wondered if the other woman had put her up to this. "Is Manduul ill?" Her next words came in a rush, as if afraid Mandukhai would condemn her for even asking the question. "I only wonder because he seems to be losing weight, and his skin is sagging around the eyes and ... well, the coughing has caused Togochi some concern. That paired with the fact that Manduul often disappears into either his ger or yours far earlier than he used to ... The commanders are worried."

Mandukhai did not know what she had expected Jaghan to ask, but she found herself unprepared for this question. The Khan had only told a handful of people about his illness, and those he only told out of necessity. Mandukhai was not even certain if Yeke knew the truth. Though if Bayan did, and he truly was working to replace Manduul, then he surely must have told Yeke. Mandukhai glanced at Siker to see if the woman gave any sign she knew the truth, but as usual, her face was a mask of impassive emotions. Would Bayan have told her? Mandukhai doubted as much. Their marriage seemed to be more of a convenience than one of genuine interest.

"My husband has expressed concerns as well," Satai admitted. For once, her face was not lit with delight at gossip. Instead, she appeared almost ashamed to admit it. Her husband, Unige, held a position of respect among the Khan's men, and as much as she loved gossip, she would not want to shame him in exchange for juicy words. "He says the men are talking."

"Men are always plotting something," Siker said.

"But she is right," Jaghan said as she shifted again. "Togochi said the same. He worries that the Khan's influence is weakening."

"The Khan's influence is still far-reaching," Mandukhai interjected, drawing all eyes to her. "Perhaps more so than ever before. We cannot put too much stock in rumors. Manduul turns in early now because he has taken to prayer at the altar with me after dinner." A half-truth. Manduul did pray more often now. But not nightly. "And he loses weight because he is preparing for the fight against the Ming."

"So, he is well?" Jaghan asked.

"Well enough to run the empire, and that is all we need to concern ourselves with." Mandukhai did not enjoy lying to her friends—particularly Jaghan—but she could not tell them the truth. She had to protect her own interests, or she could wind up dead.

If the Mongol Lords discovered the Khan was, in fact, dying, Manduul faced removal. Bayan may even deem the Khan unfit and seize the title before Manduul died, thus giving him exactly what Manduul suspected him of. The Mongol Lords would support Bayan if Manduul's illness was known.

Then Mandukhai could lose everything.

80 Miles South of Mongke Bulag – Summer 1469

Issama's warning bothered Bayan deeply. He had been certain of Manduul's love for him and of his complete disinterest in his first wife. Even after the issue with Enkh, Bayan assumed Manduul was angrier about the alleged plot against the Khan than about Yeke. Now Bayan wondered if he had been wrong all along. Perhaps he had misunderstood when Manduul said they shared everything. Perhaps that did *not* include Yeke. *I will give you the benefit of the doubt this time, and I will not so easily be fooled again.* Manduul would not forgive him a second time.

That night, Bayan could not sleep. Every sound from the surrounding wilderness jarred him awake and made his heart race all over again. He had taken his men farther from Mongke Bulag on the hunting trip. Berkedai had asked him what Issama had said to him and swore he heard nothing, aside from Bayan's own laughter and confidence in Manduul. But could he trust Berkedai? Was the man trying to trick him? *No. Not Berkedai. Not after all we have been through together.* But the doubt would not stop nagging at his heart.

Before dawn broke over the horizon, Bayan woke the men and insisted they travel further south. All the while, he considered where he could go that would be safe from Manduul's reach. Perhaps if he stated his case to Bigirsen and expressed concern for the Vice Regent's daughter, he could find an ally in Bigirsen. Yeke could be Bayan's pass to salvation. If Bigirsen thought she had a chance to wed another Borjigin heir, Bayan could use that to his advantage if he had to run. *I won't run. Manduul won't try to kill me.* Yet he could not be certain of Manduul's intentions. How angry would he be?

Perhaps Bayan could turn to the Ming. They seemed bent on capturing him alive. If he went to them, he might be able to bargain with them in exchange for his life. That was, after all, the only thing he really cared for. *No, that is a desperate move for a desperate man. Bigirsen will help me.*

Around midday, Bayan insisted they dismount and break for lunch. His stomach rumbled. He had not earned the battle-hardened belly of men like Berkedai, who could ride and eat at the same time, snacking on dried meat. Bayan allowed Andayar to graze freely around them, watching to be sure she didn't wander too far.

The thunder of hooves brought up several heads. Berkedai barked out commands, and everyone surrounded Bayan, bows ready. The riders crested a nearby hill. Bayan squinted at the approaching figures and recognized them almost immediately. His heart sank into the pit of his stomach. *This can't be a good sign*, he thought.

Togochi and Yungei rode closer.

Togochi was Manduul's man through and through. Yungei served as Bayan's guard, but he was a staunch Khorchin commander. The man had despised Bayan since that first trip to Mongke Bulag five years ago.

"Why do you suppose they are here?" Berkedai asked, obviously recognizing the two men as well. He lowered his bow.

Bayan swallowed the lump in his throat. "Be ready for anything."

Berkedai's brows shot up his forehead at this command. He waited for more, but Bayan gave him nothing.

Bayan's heart pounded in his chest, making his head swim. He could not hide his agitation. His hands fidgeted at his side, and he began sweating. Manduul would send someone to trick him into revealing himself. Issama had warned him, and Bayan became certain these two were sent to do just that. Manduul knew Bayan trusted Togochi, and that Yungei served Bayan. These two choices could not be coincidence.

As the two slowed to a canter, Bayan adjusted his silk deel and golden belt, then wiped his sweaty palms on his sleeves. The dogs growled at the newcomers, and Togochi called for them to hold their dogs. Berkedai gave a sharp whistle. The dogs settled back on their haunches but watched the two men with clear suspicion.

Togochi and Yungei dismounted, leaving their bows and swords on their saddles as Togochi approached Bayan. Yungei waited beside the horses, observing every movement Bayan made.

"What brings you so far from Mongke Bulag?" Bayan asked, cursing himself for allowing his voice to waver as he spoke.

"I came to speak with you," Togochi responded.

Togochi stopped far enough away from the guards that Bayan would have to approach if Togochi lowered his voice. It felt like they were drawing him away from his guards. Bayan waited, praying his hands did not shake as badly as he thought they did. No one spoke. No one moved. Yungei stood behind Togochi, holding the reins of both horses and watching with a cold face.

Horses snorted and stomped their hooves. The dogs shifted anxiously, sensing the tension. The longer Bayan stood there, the more agitated he became. His gut churned painfully enough that he feared he would spill out his lunch on the ground. His palms sweated so badly he was certain he could not wield a sword or bow. He had not been this frightened since Bolunai had sent his men after him eight years ago.

"Shall we stand staring at each other in the sun all day?" Bayan asked, laughing nervously. "I prefer bows over swords, Togochi."

The joke drew a few chuckles from Bayan's men—the joke insinuated the difference between men and women.

Togochi grinned, then lowered his voice. Bayan had to edge closer to hear the words. "I bring you a question from the Khan."

He is *drawing me in.* Bayan's heart raced so quickly it made his head spin. *No. No, it can't be!* He thought in sudden wild panic. Until this moment, he held on to the hope that Manduul would forgive him. That Issama had been wrong. For the first time in his life, Bayan's words failed him. His skin tingled as the hairs rose into the air and he swallowed repeatedly against the lump in his throat. *Come on luck, where are you now?*

"The Khan asks, 'What reasons do you have to be against me?'" Togochi asked quiet enough that Bayan knew his guards could not hear.

Bayan tugged at the collar of his deel, which suddenly felt stifling in the summer heat. He worked his mouth. "Against?" he asked, his voice rising several pitches too high. Bayan glanced in every direction, probing for a means of escape. His chestnut mare, Andayar—the gift from Manduul—grazed too far away to jump on and race across the plains. Sweat rolled down his temples.

Togochi's lips thinned, and his shoulders sagged. "You have no response for the Khan?"

Fury at his own inability to calm down and just answer the question burned at Bayan's flesh. If he said nothing, it was as good as admitting the truth of the question, and it simply was not true. Manduul had not asked if Bayan had slept with Yeke. Only if he was against him. Which he was not. But Bayan's agitation won out and he could find nothing coherent to say.

"Against?" Bayan blundered again. "I ..."

Togochi shook his head. "I had hoped for better from an heir of Genghis. But the men were right about you."

"What?" Bayan had never hated himself more. How could he not form the right words?

Togochi turned away, taking the reins from Yungei, who glared at Bayan with intermingled hatred and satisfaction. Togochi turned his mount toward Bayan, muscles tense as if expecting a fight. "You have no answer for the Khan?"

Bayan's chest rose and fell in shallow breaths, and he wanted to scream out, to say something, anything, to redeem himself. Yet Issama's warning echoed in his head, clouding his thoughts and freezing him in place as certainly as if he were stuck in the dead of winter.

Before he could break himself out of the cursed spell, Togochi shook his head in apparent disappointment. He and Yungei galloped away, leaving Bayan with only his guards.

Berkedai stepped forward, but Bayan could not meet his gaze. He could not look at any of his guards.

"What has happened, Bolkhu?" Berkedai asked, scowling at the retreating men and gripping his bow in a fist.

Bayan had half a mind to command Berkedai to kill them before they escaped, but that would do him no good. Manduul would learn of it and still assume his guilt. Unless he could come up with an explanation for their deaths before returning to Mongke Bulag.

"Wait!" he called, trembling.

But the hammer of the horses' hooves against the hard ground drowned out his voice. Bayan released a shuddering breath. If they returned to Manduul, and he kept to his previous warning ... It was their lives or his own.

"*Alakh*," he commanded the dogs, his voice quivering as he gave the kill command.

The dogs took off after the two men. As the dogs understood the command, so did Berkedai. He fired his bow so quickly Bayan hardly noticed him raise it. The moment the rest of Bayan's men noticed Berkedai's action, they mounted and raced off after the pair. Berkedai's arrow struck Yungei's mount, and the animal squealed as it pitched forward, taking the rider down with it.

This is it. Bayan thought as he watched his guards ride off.

Berkedai turned to him, and the confusion was clear on his face. Asking no further questions, Berkedai collected the horses. Bayan and Berkedai set off after Bayan's guards as well.

Andayar raced beneath Bayan, but he hung back far enough for his guards and dogs to do the work for him. Yungei stood with his sword raised as the dogs closed on his mount. They attacked the horse's legs, ensuring it could not stand again. One of Bayan's guards aimed at Yungei, and the man stood his ground, holding his sword ready. Bayan knew Yungei intended to bring the mount down, even if it meant taking an arrow. As the arrow struck Yungei in the shoulder, it threw him off balance, but he still sliced the guard's mount in the flank before his body twisted all the way around.

Bayan yanked on his reins, afraid of pulling in too close. Togochi twisted in his saddle, firing back with deadly accuracy at the guards. One he took in the eye. Another fell to an arrow in his unarmored chest. On the hunt, they had been unprepared for such an attack, and none of them wore proper armor. None but Togochi and Yungei. In a matter of heartbeats, three of Bayan's five guards lay dead on the ground. Only two remained, along with Berkedai.

"Go!" Yungei shouted at Togochi, ripping the arrow out of the gap between his armored plates.

Bile rose up Bayan's throat, and he kicked Andayar to race after Togochi. With a sharp whistle, the three dogs howled alongside Andayar as she raced over the rolling hill. Togochi glanced back, leaning close to the neck of his mount for more speed. An anger like Bayan had never witnessed before—even in the eyes of Bolunai Khan—burned in Togochi's fierce gaze.

Knowing he had no other choice, Bayan unhooked his bow from the saddle strap and took careful aim, guiding Andayar with his knees. The dogs closed the distance.

As Bayan released his arrow, Togochi fired at the dogs, taking each of them down with well-placed arrows of his own in such rapid succession his movements were almost a blur. Bayan's arrow glanced off Togochi's armor and grazed his neck, lodging in his mount. He yanked it out and used it to return the fire back at Bayan, who ducked behind his own mount for cover.

The race lasted only a mile before Togochi reached into a bag attached to his mount and tossed something on the ground in his wake. Bayan hardly had a chance to yank the reins and keep his own mount from running over the small spikes of metal. Andayar would suffer an injury that would keep her from walking for weeks if he tried to force her across. Togochi continued the race, not bothering to glance back as if he knew he had escaped. And Bayan knew he was as good as dead now. Along with his men.

He wheeled Andayar back and rode past the dead dogs. One of his guards, Onc, caught up to him, clutching his side. Bayan swallowed a lump of sickness back down his throat. When he returned to where he had left the others, Berkedai and Yungei circled each other, shouting insults.

"You follow a coward," Yungei snarled.

The heat of anger rose in Berkedai's voice as he spoke. "He is your prince! From where I stand, only one of us is acting a coward."

"Throw down your weapon and come back with me, before it's too late," Yungei offered.

Berkedai roared. "Lies from the lips of a dog!"

Then he lunged for Yungei's heart, but Yungei was smaller and faster. His own sword ripped into Berkedai's side, leaving a nasty gash that instantly began spilling copious amounts of blood on the ground. Berkedai staggered, and Yungei raised his sword for another blow, but Berkedai's move appeared to be a feign. He thrust his own sword up through Yungei's chin. As he ripped it out, Yungei's body crumpled to the ground.

Onc went pale, pressing against his side, just as Berkedai did. Bayan was in serious trouble. The dogs were dead, and his last two guards were on the edge of death themselves. He jumped off Andayar and rushed to Berkedai's side as his only remaining friend staggered sideways. Bayan tried to catch him, but Berkedai's considerable mass was too much for him and they both collapsed to the ground.

"He said ..." Blood poured from Berkedai's mouth, and his accusing gaze fell on Bayan. "The Khan ..."

Bayan clenched his jaw to hold down the despair and sorrow washing over him. Berkedai reached up and grasped the side of Bayan's head, pulling him close and pressing his forehead to Bayan's.

"You ..." He coughed up thick, congealed blood that spattered on Bayan's face. "Brother ... You are my brother." He struggled to get the words out in a coherent sentence.

"Hang on, Berkedai," Bayan said, unable to keep the grief from his voice. But he knew it was too late. His friend was dying. How had he doubted Berkedai's loyalty?

"Go with ... with the gods," Berkedai said, his voice growing weaker. "Ride ... your luck ... Go ..."

Berkedai's hand slipped free as his body went limp in Bayan's arms.

"Onc!" Bayan called to the last remaining guard and twisted around as a thump sounded behind him. Onc lay motionless on the ground beside his mount as it nibbled at the grass.

All around, his guards lay dead. Only careless mounts moved. For the first time since arriving in Mongke Bulag, Bayan realized he was completely alone.

And Manduul Khan would come.

Manduul had been a father to him and had lulled Bayan into a sense of false security. But he realized now he had never been safe, just as Bolunai had warned. Why had he not listened? It must have been stubborn pride and youth getting in his way, but now the veil was lifted. His life was never truly his own.

In a sudden panic, Bayan shoved Berkedai away, wiped his bloody hands on Berkedai's deel, and began moving around the area to scavenge for anything of value. He collected all the food and water, tethered the mounts together, retrieved all the arrows, and even stripped Yungei of his armor. The stench of loosened bowels and death surrounded him.

Andayar whickered and stamped away when Bayan attempted to mount. He clucked soothing words to keep her from running off. Rocks weighed down Bayan's stomach as he climbed into the saddle, and his sweat turned cold.

Togochi would reach Mongke Bulag before nightfall. Bayan could not stop to rest. He would ride Andayar as far as he could, then trade for a fresh mount from his tethered line. *I have done this before*, he thought as he gathered the reins.

"Chuh!" He kicked the mare in her flanks, holding the reins of the lead packhorse. Andayar lurched into motion.

Bayan headed in the only direction in which he might have an ally. South. As long as he avoided the main messenger paths, he might reach Bigirsen in time to save himself. Then he could strike a deal and gather Bigirsen's support under the guise of protecting Yeke before Manduul did anything drastic to her.

Chapter Twenty-Four

Treasonous Breaths

Mongke Bulag – Summer 1469

The hour was late when Boke—Manduul's commanding royal guard—entered Mandukhai's ger to wake Manduul. She sat up, rubbing her eyes and frowning at the intrusion, resenting Boke for interrupting perfectly good sleep. Yet she also knew he would not wake them unless it was urgent. Boke's youthful face shined with sweat even in the ger's darkness, and the memory of Nergui's death surged to the surface. Who would it be this time?

"My lord Khan, sorry to wake you, but it's Togochi," Boke said in a rush.

Mandukhai's heart leaped to her throat. She had insisted Jaghan trust that Togochi's task was safe, but the way Boke sweated made her wonder if something had gone terribly wrong.

"He has returned," Boke said.

Manduul did not wait for further explanation. He threw off the light blanket and stepped into his boots, then flung on his deel and belt as he marched toward the door. Before falling asleep, he had tossed and turned, worrying over how Bayan would respond to the question he had sent Togochi and Yungei to ask. He expressed his worry in ways that clearly had pressed the weight of a mountain down on his shoulders. This morning, Mandukhai was also eager to hear Bayan's response. She moved quicker than Manduul to dress, then followed him out.

Boke stomped along with brisk steps as the rest of Manduul's guard closed in a ring around them. Mandukhai glanced around in alarm when she realized Boke did not lead them to the gathering tent, but to Togochi's ger. Her stomach revolted. *Please don't let him be dying!*

The stench of sweat and blood saturated the air within the ger so thickly that Mandukhai gagged on it the moment she stepped through the door behind Manduul. The stove roared with life and lamps lit the cramped space as Jaghan barked orders at her servants. Khosoichi tended to Togochi. Manduul's guards remained outside to avoid filling the cramped ger.

"Get me the silver bowl and a bandage," Jaghan snapped at one woman, then, as an afterthought, added, "and the silver shavings."

Manduul pushed his way through the crowd to where Togochi lay on the bed. Mandukhai held a breath as she noticed the blood covering Togochi's side, flowing down from his neck. How much of that blood was his? What had happened?

The moment Togochi spotted Manduul, he pushed away the shaman as Khosoichi cleaned the wound in Togochi's neck. Manduul's face drained of color, and Mandukhai rushed to his side, afraid his weakening body would give out.

"He has lost a lot of blood, my lord Khan," Khosoichi said, bowing back out of the way.

"I'll live," Togochi snapped. Fury burned in his dark eyes.

"Who did this?" Manduul asked, his voice shaking.

Togochi clenched his jaw, wincing as he pressed the cloth to his neck. "They attacked us, Manduul."

"Who did this?" Manduul asked again. A dangerous hush consumed his tone. Mandukhai knew Manduul realized the answer but had to hear the name spoke aloud to believe it. "And where is Yungei?"

Jaghan marched over to the bedside with silver in hand and nudged Manduul back so she could help Khosoichi work, pressing the cold silver to the wound and rolling it along the gash. Blood soaked the pillow and Togochi hissed through his teeth.

"Dead," Togochi growled. "Killed by Bayan and his men."

He killed Yungei? Mandukhai placed a hand on Manduul's arm, worried about his condition as her own heart beat harder. That Togochi called him Bayan instead of Bolkhu was enough to confirm his complete loss of respect for the prince.

Manduul shuddered beneath her touch, and she tightened her grip on his arm to offer what strength she could. No one—not even Mandukhai herself—had stolen Manduul's heart quite like Bayan. This betrayal must have shaken Manduul to his core. As if to confirm just how stunned he was by the news, Manduul appeared unable to formulate a response.

The ger fell oddly silent. Only Jaghan's whispered reassurances penetrated the stifling air as she and Khosoichi tended to Togochi's wound.

"Lady Jaghan, would you please see that your husband is properly bandaged and healed, then bring him to the gathering tent to share the full report with the Khan," Mandukhai said in her gentlest tone.

Jaghan shot back a glare that ripped at Mandukhai's heart. The other woman needed to say nothing for Mandukhai to comprehend. Jaghan felt betrayed. Mandukhai had insisted Togochi would be fine, and now here he was in bed with a serious neck wound. It was a wonder he had survived to return to Mongke Bulag. But Mandukhai never would have guessed Bayan would react this way.

Bowing her head, ashamed of how she had failed Jaghan, Mandukhai escorted Manduul back out the door. Togochi first needed to be healed. Once that was complete, they could hear a recounting of events.

Mandukhai caught Boke's attention as she and Manduul stepped outside. "Assemble the Khan's council to the gathering tent. All men of noble rank or command are to report immediately, along with scribes, on the Great Khan's orders. Search Bayan's ger personally, Boke."

Boke glanced at Manduul as if for confirmation, but as stunned as Manduul was by this news, he could only offer a brief nod. Boke bowed before swiftly marching off to give the commands to his men.

In all the commotion, Esige emerged from her ger and watched curiously as Mandukhai shepherded Manduul toward the gathering tent. The girl seemed to pick up on the urgency of the situation, because she sprinted over to assist Mandukhai.

"Esige, I need you to fetch the Khan's servants—all of them—and have food and drinks brought to the gathering tent," Mandukhai said. She glanced at Manduul from the corner of her eye. "In the top drawer of my chest, you will find a red pouch of herbs. Mix two pinches with our best batch of *airag* and bring it to Manduul immediately."

The herbs were a mixture from Khosoichi, to help stave off the effects of the illness that ate away at Manduul. What was to come would not be easy for any of them, and he would need his strength to make it through the day.

Esige rushed off, holding the hem of her skirt up to avoid tripping in her haste.

Moonlight shined through the opening in the roof of the gathering tent at an angle, glowing directly on Bayan's seat as if mocking the current mood. Though the hour was early, with the wolf dawn still a couple hours away, the servants busied themselves lighting the copper pots on each side of the dais to heat the space and offer light. Mandukhai passed them without comment and escorted Manduul to his throne, helping him ease down. Manduul sank into the cushioned seat with a defeated breath.

The two sat in silence. Manduul's guards took up position near the door. Was Manduul truly safe, though? The guards she trusted. But who among the nobles or commanders would choose someone younger and in better health to lead them? Any of them could decide Manduul's reign was at an end, that it was time for Bayan to step up and take over. Would they ignore Bayan's act of treason in favor of his youth and health? Perhaps one of Bayan's supporters would attempt to kill Manduul prematurely. She could not take that risk. She needed Manduul, at least until Unebolod returned.

"Arslan!" Mandukhai barked, calling for the head of her personal night guard.

Arslan rushed in and kneeled in front of them. He understood that whatever was going on, the matter carried urgency.

"Send in six of your best men to guard the Khan," Mandukhai commanded. "Only men you would trust to protect him with their lives. And we need them all immediately."

"Yes, my Lady," Arslan said, then rose and rushed out the door, glancing at Manduul only for a moment.

"What did I do wrong?" Manduul muttered, the agony ringing out clear as a bell in his voice.

"Nothing. You loved him. You supported him. You gave him everything. Without you, he would have nothing at all. Don't question your decisions. Question his."

Manduul nodded weakly.

Esige rushed in with the *airag*, crouching in front of Manduul as she offered it. He accepted it absently, not even acknowledging Esige at all. The girl cast a worried glance at Mandukhai.

"That will be all, Esige," Mandukhai said. "Thank you." Manduul slouched forward in his throne, pressing a hand to his forehead and holding the cup in the other.

"Drink, husband," Mandukhai said soothingly. "You will need your strength today."

"I fear there is no strength left in me," Manduul said.

Mandukhai wanted to slap some sense into him. How could he allow himself to slip so fully into despair when this was a time for strength and action? Illness could not excuse this weakness. His death would come, but until then, he remained Great Khan.

"You are Khan of khans," Mandukhai said tersely, which drew his gaze to her. Tears brimmed his eyes, and she felt a momentary swell of revulsion at such weakness. Who *was* this man? "Now more than ever, your people need you to be strong and fight. Death may be coming for you, but it is not here this day. And until that day, you will rule the Mongol Nation amid crisis. You cannot succumb to the weaknesses of mortal men when you are so much more. Drink and use that elixir as fuel for your pain to channel strength."

Manduul raised the cup, but before he drank, he said, "You will rule well as Queen Regent once I am gone, until a new Great Khan is named at *kurultai*."

Mandukhai studied him as he drank, realizing for the first time that the day would actually come. Manduul's body betrayed him more each day, and with Bayan and Yeke facing potential death for their treason, it would leave only Mandukhai until the tribes came together at *kurultai* to choose their new Khan. Unebolod had been named successor in Bayan's stead, but Mandukhai knew that would not be so easily won should the Oirat tribes would gather against Unebolod. And Bigirsen controlled several of the southern tribes. Somehow, Mandukhai would have to hold the Mongol Nation together using her political savvy. *And then Unebolod and I will be together*, she thought. Her desired future was within her grasp.

In no time, an army of servants moved throughout the gathering tent, setting out freshly cooked meats and jugs of *airag* on tables lining either side of the room. It was a simple feast, but enough to fuel the men who would gather. Mandukhai called for chairs to be placed behind the tables at even intervals for the Lords, and benches near the door of the gathering tent for the commanders. They had designated Togochi a seat close to Manduul's dais so all could see him and clearly hear his report.

Through all the preparations, Manduul remained in the same slumped posture on his throne, gazing at the dancing flames of one of the copper firepots. Only once, as seats were first brought in, did he speak, commanding the prince's throne to be removed.

Lords and commanders filtered in. Ladies of the court took positions behind their husbands. Some men and women were well-dressed, as if they had been up for hours. Others rubbed their eyes, fought off sleep, or wore rumpled deels. The wolf dawn was well underway by the time the gathering tent filled with the Khan's court.

Whispered speculation swirled around the open space. Mandukhai ignored all of it as she sat straight in her seat. The commotion must have woken Yeke, but she would not attend this meeting. Manduul had her under strict watch since the news about her infidelity had been delivered to him two days before. Yeke remained free to move around Mongke Bulag, but the guards were ordered to observe and be sure she didn't flee. So far, Yeke seemed oblivious to the danger she was in.

Boke marched in and approached the dais with a handful of his men and Manduul's shaman. Boke kneeled at the bottom step. Manduul waved him forward.

Mandukhai observed the stiffness in Boke's movements as he climbed the stairs. He offered a pouch of some sort to Manduul and leaned close, whispering in Manduul's ear.

Manduul paled considerably and his gaze darted to Khosoichi, who only gave a grim nod. The news could not be good. A hush fell over the gathering tent as everyone noticed the way Manduul sagged during the exchange.

Issama glided in with his wife trailing behind him. Mandukhai was not sure what to make of Uingen. The few times they spoke, the other woman was so quiet and reserved that Mandukhai wondered how she ended up with Issama. The woman was weak—not as Mandukhai would have expected from any woman who would marry Issama. As the two of them made their way toward his place near the dais, Issama paused to exchange brief words with a few of the commanders and a couple Uyghur Lords. Mandukhai pressed her lips together. What was he up to?

Siker entered, and Mandukhai tensed, glancing at Manduul. He didn't seem to notice Bayan's wife joining them. Siker rolled through the room like a storm followed in her wake. Was she angry that her ger had likely been turned inside out by Boke's men? Siker hesitated when she realized her seat near Bayan's throne was gone. But she quickly recovered with a grace that Mandukhai admired, taking a vacant space across from Togochi's seat.

Togochi arrived last, with Jaghan assisting his pale form toward his seat. Mandukhai waved for a servant to bring a seat for Jaghan, which was placed next to Togochi's within moments. A hush fell over the gathering tent as men witnessed Togochi's state. None of them knew what task Manduul had sent the general on, but Togochi's condition did not go unnoticed, nor did the absence of Bayan's throne.

As Jaghan took her seat with Togochi, she cast a hateful glare at Siker. The other woman averted her gaze, bowing her head. *She must know something about what happened.*

Manduul straightened, resting his palms against his thighs as his gaze swept the crowd. The slight hunch of his back reminded Mandukhai of a man bearing the weight of a mountain on his shoulders. Sweat beaded on his forehead, but he made no move to wipe it away. Servants poured drinks for the men gathered, then melted into the background.

"Two days ago," Manduul said, and his voice carried through the space with strength that startled Mandukhai, "allegations once more were made against the prince, that he was, in fact, plotting against me and attempting to steal away my wife, Yeke."

Only the swish of cloth against cloth penetrated the deep silence at this news as men shifted in their seats. No one would dare interrupt the Khan.

Mandukhai glanced at Siker, but the woman's face was a cold, impassive mask.

Mandukhai knew what Manduul would have to do, and she hoped he took strength from her presence.

"One day ago, I sent two men I trusted to speak to the Golden Prince and allow him the opportunity to defend himself," Manduul continued. "This morning, only one of those men returned."

All eyes shifted to Togochi, who remained rigid and vigilant in his seat despite his pallor. Siker did not gaze at Togochi, as the rest of the congregation did. Mandukhai caught her glancing at Issama. But why?

"General Togochi, tell me what happened when you found the prince," Manduul commanded.

Togochi stood, despite the hushed admonitions of his wife. "Commander Yungei and I rode out, as you instructed, my lord Khan," he began. The weakness from his injury bled into his voice, but his words still bore strength. "We tracked down the prince and his guards while they were hunting. Before I even spoke, the prince appeared agitated. He fidgeted and sweated excessively. When I asked what reasons he had to be against you, as you commanded, he gave no direct answer, but began glancing around as if seeking escape. The only coherent words he spoke were clearly in anxious fret—against. I pressed once more, asking if he had no answer for you, but again he spoke in broken words—against, I, what. Knowing we would get nothing more, Yungei and I mounted to return and report to you."

Though Togochi reported with expert ease on the events, the sorrow in his voice was apparent to all. "That was when Bayan's men and dogs attacked."

A ripple of shock spread through the men gathered. Mandukhai couldn't suppress a small gasp herself. Bayan had never seemed capable of such a thing. Attacking Manduul's own men unprovoked? It was so unlike him. The only time Bayan ever acted out was when he felt trapped in a corner—which could only mean one thing. His guilt could no longer be in question, and Manduul would have no choice but to order Bayan's execution. Her heart hammered.

The outrage in the gathering tent turned into mixed feelings.

"Bring him back to answer for his alleged crimes," one Lord called.

"He committed treason and should be killed!" another demanded.

Most of the responses offered the same sentiments.

Togochi pushed on, not waiting for the crowd to hush. "The prince and his guard fired their arrows at us. The dogs killed and ripped apart Yungei's mount. He fought off the rest of the prince's men so that I could escape, but not before the prince himself fired his arrow at me and nearly took out my mount."

This confession only intensified the outrage of the court. Togochi ignored them all, raising his chin proudly and lifting his voice above the crowd. "My lord Khan, Yungei died an honorable death."

Manduul's jaw twitched. He drummed his fingers on his thigh. Togochi fell silent, waiting for Manduul to ask further questions before he took his seat again. Manduul waved at Togochi, who sank into his chair as the Lords and commanders raised their own voices to a crescendo. Mandukhai could no longer make out the protests, but she understood their sentiments well enough. They wanted Bayan's head.

The sigh that rolled out of Manduul seemed to shake the gathering tent. It silenced the angry mob. He stiffened and raised his chin. "So it is like this." The sadness rang out in his voice, but something else lay beneath it, like the tinder of a fire about to catch. "It is true that he has evil intentions toward me."

Mandukhai observed the gathered nobles and commanders, attempting to spot any who might secretly align with Bayan. A few bowed their heads in shock or sadness. Most stared at Manduul as if wondering what the Khan would do next. Only one observed the proceedings with a cold face.

Issama sat near Togochi, surveying the room just as Mandukhai did. When his gaze fell on hers, he gave away nothing of his emotions. The

Khan's new *orlok* had always unnerved Mandukhai, but this void that stared back at her worried Mandukhai far more than ever before. Issama was friends with Bayan. Yet he was also the one who had informed Manduul. With his position at court, he stood to gain a lot from Bayan's downfall. Mandukhai knew he had not lied to Manduul about Bayan's affair. She had suspected Bayan and Yeke for some time, but treason felt out of nature for the prince.

Mandukhai had always doubted Bayan's ability to lead the nation, but never his loyalty to Manduul. Something about Issama's calm observance of the gathering forced Mandukhai to reconsider everything that had happened these past two days. Did he somehow have a hand in all of this? Surely Issama was not so conniving. He certainly was a clever man, but to frame the prince ... *No, he and Bayan are friends. He would not go that far.*

"It is no secret to any of us that the Mongol Nation has struggled to mend alliances that were ripped apart centuries before any of us were born," Manduul continued. "Since the beginning of my reign, we have maintained a tenuous peace between tribes. To preserve that peace, we will need a firm hand to guide us. We will need a cool mind to work as a balm to sooth raised tempers. I have no heirs to raise as Great Khan. The blood of Genghis will die with me."

Mandukhai watched Manduul carefully. Saying such made clear enough that he already considered Bayan dead to him and the nation.

Manduul swirled his drink, then downed it before continuing. "A nation without a Khan is like a horse without a master. It will run wild and chaotic, with no purpose. For without a Khan, the tribes will fall apart. They will begin fighting over scraps and lands again. The vision of Genghis will, once and for all, disappear into history. We cannot allow that to happen. Not after we have shown the world our superior strength." Manduul's words caught in his throat, and he coughed.

Mandukhai held her breath, afraid he would fall into another fit of coughing in front of the assembly. It would reveal his weakness with certainty. A weakness which now was only rumor. The Lords might turn against him in favor of Bayan if they knew their Khan was dying. Thankfully, Manduul regained control fairly easily this time.

"Only strength can save the nation," Manduul continued. "Sadly, the boy has strayed too far too fast. He is too impulsive and reckless." Sorrow burned away as Manduul's face reddened in anger. "The people do not need a ruler like him!" He slammed a fist against the arm of the throne, making several people—Mandukhai included—jump at the booming thump. In his fat fist, Manduul clenched the pouch Boke had brought to him. "Tell me, Khosoichi, what this is."

Manduul threw the pouch on the ground at the shaman's feet.

Khosoichi jumped back, then picked it up and examined the contents. "A slow-acting poison, made to affect the lungs and liver."

Manduul sneered. "The prince has broken sacred oaths and committed treason against his Khan. He has, in fact, been working against me. Perhaps from the very beginning. He is Bolkhu the Golden Prince no longer. All rights and titles are forfeit immediately. I want riders sent out to every corner of the Mongol Nation!"

The redness in Manduul's face worried Mandukhai, but she dared not interrupt. She had seen him in a rage before, but this was different. She honestly feared that anyone who would dare to stand against him look alone would strike dead. His usually weak arm muscles quivered as his hands clenched into fists. His chin shook as he fought to control his anger. Mandukhai found herself unable to watch him any longer for fear that anger would turn on her.

"Bayan is to be brought to me for punishment," Manduul roared. "Any who give him quarter will be declared traitors to the Mongol Nation!" Manduul surged to his feet, and everyone bowed their heads, Mandukhai included. He began pacing. "What is taking so long?"

For a moment, the tent seemed frozen in time. Then, as Manduul barked out his next command, the tent erupted with activity. *"Send them now!"*

His entire body trembled with pure rage. In seconds, scribes raced out of the tent with parchments in hand to send word with the riders.

Manduul stabbed a finger at the nobles as the scribes scrambled away. "If any of you wish to support Bayan, lay your heads at my feet now and save us all the trouble!"

No one moved. Mandukhai gazed at Manduul in wide-eyed shock as he threatened dozens of commanders and Lords gathered around him, stalking up and down the aisle like a caged tiger eager for blood.

Like everyone else, Mandukhai was too stunned to speak or move. For months she had assumed Manduul too weak to do anything, but now, for the first time since their marriage, she saw the visage of a Great Khan, of Genghis himself, and she respected him for it. Why could he not have been this strong from the start? Why was it only in the face of death and betrayal that this side of him finally emerged?

"Bring my wife!" Manduul growled.

Mandukhai's blood ran cold, as if she had suddenly been plunged into a frozen river. It took a moment for her to realize Manduul meant Yeke and not her. *What will he do to her?* Mandukhai had seen Manduul in a jealous rage before. She had felt the sting of his wrath. But this was different.

Three of the commanders left the tent immediately. All eyes turned toward the doorway, awaiting Yeke's appearance. A few cast curious glances at Siker, as if trying to see how she was reacting to all of this. To the woman's credit, she gave nothing away. Siker was as frosty as ever.

Mandukhai suddenly understood the horrendous danger of this situation with terrible clarity. Even if anyone had wanted to support Bayan before, no one would dare to do so now in the face of the Khan's wrath. But that did not mean there were not Lords who would rather have Bayan in charge.

If Manduul killed Yeke, how would Bigirsen react? Would he charge north to fight Manduul, or accept that Yeke's infidelity was shameful and side with Manduul? Bigirsen certainly would be happy to have Bayan out of the picture, but that would put Unebolod in danger. Bigirsen had *tumens*. Far more than Manduul commanded. And the Oirat already waited on their doorstep as if they knew this day approached. *Did* they know?

Mandukhai's chest heaved with anxious breaths. What would happen to her if Bigirsen killed Manduul? Could she get word to Unebolod quickly enough to bring more men to Manduul's side? Would she survive to see him again?

As the door opened and Boke dragged in a startled Yeke alongside another royal guard, Manduul held out his hand. Arslan placed a sword in it. Yeke's eyes shot wide. Her entire body quivered, and she attempted to pull away from the men holding her. Her certainty of her fate read clearly on her face. Her limbs appeared ready to give out as Boke and the other guard forced her forward.

"Kneel," Manduul snarled.

A few gasps rippled through the gathering tent as Lords and Ladies realized what was about to happen. No one defended Yeke, though.

Yeke seemed too stunned to obey and cast an imploring gaze at Mandukhai. Did she truly think Mandukhai would rescue her from this, after all the hatred she had thrown at Mandukhai over the years?

Mandukhai stiffened her own back. The small action had a significant effect. Yeke collapsed, bowing prostrate at Manduul's feet with a guard on either side.

"You have been found guilty of treason against your husband and Khan," Manduul said in the coldest voice Mandukhai had ever heard him use.

Yeke trembled violently, unable to control her own body. She appeared like an animal left out in the freezing cold. Manduul's grip on the sword tightened so much Mandukhai could see the whites of his knuckles.

"Have you anything to say for yourself, woman?" Manduul asked.

Mandukhai shifted forward in her seat, eager to hear any response Yeke might give. To her surprise, Yeke raised her gaze in open defiance. Tears rolled down her cheeks, but the disgust and hate she threw at Manduul were apparent to all.

Yeke's voice quaked despite the seething hatred in her tone. "My husband abandoned me years ago. Another offered me comfort, as my absent husband never could. I have betrayed nothing. A woman alone cannot be blamed for seeking the company of another."

Mandukhai watched in horror as the slope of Manduul's shoulders shifted downward. She had seen that slope before. She knew what came after. She had to do something. Terrified of how he would react, Mandukhai licked her lips and drew in a measured breath to collect strength.

"My lord Khan," Mandukhai said as firmly as she dared.

He turned slowly, a hulking mass of fury with a sword ready for death. She shuddered.

"By law of the High Heavens, you cannot spill noble blood," Mandukhai said, praying her tone was soothing enough that he would not strike out at her just for speaking up.

Everyone in the room remained stone silent, watching Mandukhai in awe.

To spill noble blood in the sight of the gods could incur their wrath ... something neither she nor Manduul could afford.

"She will die for what she has done," Manduul snapped.

Mandukhai nodded once. "Of course she will. And there are many ways to die."

In a fury, Manduul hurled his sword to the ground near Arslan's feet and stomped back up onto the dais to reclaim his seat.

"Take Yeke to her ger," Manduul commanded Boke. "No visitors. No food or drink. She will remain there until I decide how to carry out her execution."

Yeke did not cry out or plead for her life as Boke dragged her to her feet. She did not threaten her father's wrath, as Mandukhai had expected in those final desperate moments before imprisonment. Instead, Yeke moved with a quiet dignity toward the exit.

"Choose wisely, noble Mongol Lords," Yeke said in an icy voice, unable to face the gathered court despite tugging to free an arm. "The Khan hides his coming death from you all!" Yeke disappeared out the door.

All eyes shot to Manduul at this proclamation, as if seeking confirmation. The rumors flew through the capital. Manduul could easily tell the Lords those were simply the words of a bitter wife, using the rumors to sow her final discord.

Manduul stood tall, glaring with such fury at doorway as if Yeke were still there. Mandukhai could see the subtle signs of fatigue, but he did his best to hide them all in the face of Yeke's proclamation.

Either Yeke's words would be cast aside as ravings of a desperate woman

...

Or they could shift the allegiances of all the Lords in the gathering tent. Mandukhai examined the faces of the Lords to see how they reacted. Most were too stunned by all the news to differentiate their reactions.

But Issama almost seemed to smile.

And Siker glared at the door with just as much fury as the Khan.

CHAPTER TWENTY-FIVE

Ripples in the Water

J aghan clutched her swelling belly as she paced the floor of Mandukhai's ger. Manduul's declaration against Bayan and Yeke had left Jaghan dizzy, and Esige had escorted her home for rest. An hour later, the woman had come knocking on Mandukhai's door in a fury. The guards had nearly sent her away until Mandukhai reassured them it was fine and welcomed Jaghan inside.

"You insisted Togochi would be fine," Jaghan said for the hundredth time.

Mandukhai grew weary of her irritation. "And he is."

Jaghan rounded on Mandukhai so suddenly the motion threw the pregnant woman off-balance, and she grabbed the center post for support. "He barely made it back! I hope the prince dies a brutal death."

"He is no longer the prince," Mandukhai corrected. She maintained her calm composure and tone, but inside she just wanted this emotional woman to leave her be. Without Bayan, Mandukhai had a thousand plans to prepare to ensure all would be ready for Unebolod's ascension when the time came. She had sent a private message to Unebolod along with the rider who carried the Khan's message regarding Bayan's new status.

"Brutally!" Jaghan howled. She finally ceased her pacing and sagged as she gazed at Mandukhai. "He lacks honor."

"Brutality is an act for men," Mandukhai said. "Are we bloodthirsty men? No. We are intelligent women. I do not wish brutality on Bayan, nor should you. I simply wish for justice."

Jaghan edged closer and lowered her voice. "You should wish for him to die a brutal death, too. If he does, you will finally be with Unebolod."

Mandukhai grimaced, worried who might overhear. Yet her heart also soared. Bayan's death meant Unebolod's rise. "Yes. I know that. But keep it to yourself, Jaghan. I have no desire to end up like Yeke."

Jaghan snorted and nearly spit until she realized she was in someone else's ger. "At least Unebolod has honor."

"Jaghan, I understand your anger and worry," Mandukhai said. She rose and took the other woman's hands. "But there is another innocent in all of this, and we must think of her at this terrible time. Lady Siker will need our support. Her husband's treason will cost her everything. It is our duty to protect her."

Though Siker had never said as much, Mandukhai understood Siker was as pleased with her marriage to Bayan as Mandukhai had been with her own to Manduul. She sympathized with Siker's fate. It created an urge to help the other woman, as she would want someone to help her if the roles were reversed.

"Her husband nearly killed mine!" Jaghan snapped.

"Is that her fault?"

Jaghan raised her chin as if prepared to say yes, then slumped. "No. But what can we do for her, Mandukhai?"

A smile crept across Mandukhai's face. "I have already invited her for tea. We will speak with her and find out first what she needs from us. If left to his own devices, Manduul would strip her down to nothing and send her on her way. We cannot allow that. Lady Siker was betrayed just as my husband was."

This seemed to calm Jaghan's rage. By the time Siker arrived at Mandukhai's ger, Tuya had already set the tea and been excused from the ger. Jaghan slouched in a chair Mandukhai had brought in for her. Sitting on the floor was no simple task with a child in her belly.

Siker appeared uncertain as she entered, as if afraid Mandukhai might slip something in her tea. Instead, Mandukhai stood and waved to a vacant seat for Siker to join them. At first, no one spoke. Siker clearly did not know why she was there or what to expect, but under the circumstances, she was in no position to refuse Mandukhai's invitation when her fate hung in the balance.

"Peace, Lady Siker," Mandukhai said after a moment. "Lady Jaghan and I would like to support you through this horrible time. I'm certain you had nothing to do with any of this. We want to help."

Siker sniffed the tea before sipping it, confirming Mandukhai's guess that Siker suspected ill intentions.

"Tell us, Lady Siker, what we can do to help you," Mandukhai said. "Perhaps if I understood your situation better, I could appeal to my husband's softer side. He may seem a grumpy old brut, but he does have a heart." She leaned forward and placed a hand on Siker's arm. "You are no more guilty of your husband's actions than I am for my own husband."

Siker glanced at Mandukhai's hand as if uncertain how to react. "I'm afraid my story is not exciting."

"We are not looking for an exciting tale," Jaghan offered kindly, but Mandukhai could hear the strain in her tone. Even if Siker was innocent in this, it was not something Jaghan could easily excuse when it had nearly cost her husband. "We only want to understand your role in the marriage. To help you. Bayan had quite a reputation long before you came here. No one would blame you for falling into his web."

Siker's lips thinned. A gentle fury rolled in her eyes, much as the sky threatened a coming storm. "I never asked for any of this," she said coldly. "Not even marriage to him. Yet he drew me in to him like a moth to a blazing fire. He had this ... way about him that always pulled me in. Before I knew it, things had spiraled out of control."

Mandukhai offered a sympathetic smile and patted Siker on the arm. "I can understand how frustrating that could be. Some women have no control over their fates, but simply make do with the fate that is given to them. It's a pity you never had a child, though. We certainly could use another Borjigin heir right now."

"A pity you haven't, either," Siker retorted sharply.

Mandukhai flinched despite her best effort to keep a neutral face.

"It isn't ... entirely true." Siker averted her gaze, staring into the depths of her teacup. "There was a son."

The confession drew sharp gazes from both Mandukhai and Jaghan.

Bayan had a son? Mandukhai tried to recall the day Siker had come to Mongke Bulag. Something the woman had said that day caught her interest. Mandukhai strove to grasp at it, but it rolled away from her like ripples in water. The prospect of another heir of Genghis terrified Mandukhai. What would this mean for Unebolod? Fear swelled in her belly. She had to learn more. Mandukhai straightened, setting down her cup as her gaze pierced Siker.

"Was?" Mandukhai breathed.

Siker shrugged, as if losing a child was of no consequence. Mandukhai wanted to slap her. What she wouldn't give to have her own child back, and Siker acted as if losing a child mattered no more than the death of a lamb.

None that I know of. The words sprang back to Mandukhai's mind. When she had asked if there was a child involved in the marriage, Siker responded with "none that I know of." A curious statement since it was impossible for a woman not to know if she had a child, unlike men. Which could only mean that child had not necessarily died but been lost in a much more earthly sense of the word.

"What happened to him?" Mandukhai asked, unable to mask her curiosity.

Siker rolled her eyes and glanced around the ger as if probing for an escape. "Bayan and I were never in love. We simply enjoyed certain pleasures. Unfortunately, after the first or second go, I ended up pregnant. My father was furious. He insisted Bayan enter bride-service to the family so the child would not be born a bastard. Bayan never agreed. He probably would have run away if he had anywhere else to go. The baby was born sickly, twisted, and thin." None of this confession seemed to bother Siker on the surface, but Mandukhai remembered how Siker had stared at a young boy not long ago.

"Manduul's men showed up, and Bayan refused to bring the two of us along. I resented him for a long time. Not because I wanted to come along, but because he left me with that child, and I could not handle it alone. My mother remarried, claiming Batu was her son, but her new husband refused to provide for a twisted sickly boy. No one wanted the boy. He was a burden."

Jaghan's face paled as her jaw slowly lowered in disgust. Mandukhai could not imagine such icy disdain for a child. It filled her with anger. Siker did not know the fortune she had been given. She spoke of the events as if they had no emotional impact on her. *Perhaps Esige is right, and this woman is soulless,* Mandukhai thought.

"I left Batu," Siker said at last. "I had no other choice. I could not handle him in his condition."

Jaghan's jaw suddenly snapped shut. Her face blanched, then she heaved, pressing her hands to her mouth. Mandukhai moved swiftly to retrieve a bucket before Jaghan vomited on the rug. She barely made it to the poor woman in time. Mandukhai crouched beside Jaghan and rubbed at her back, gazing at Siker as she would a wild beast. *Who is this woman? What sort of mother would abandon a child? What else is she capable of?*

"What happened to Batu, Siker?" Mandukhai asked again, this time more forcefully, struggling to contain the anger boiling within.

"Dead, I assume," Siker said, as if noting a change in the weather.

Mandukhai gritted her teeth, then drew in a careful breath to temper her rage. "Where?"

"Southeastern edge of the Gobi, near the Tohom red cliffs where my tribe lived." Siker's thick brows pulled together as she glanced from one woman to another, as if just now noticing their reactions.

Mandukhai surged to her feet once more and threw open the door. The guards jumped at her flushed expression, hands on their swords as if expecting trouble within her ger. She needed answers. The sooner the better.

"Bring me Seguse immediately," Mandukhai commanded. Seguse was one of the few men Mandukhai trusted. He had carried messages from Borogchin these past few years, traveling back and forth between the Uyghur camps and Mongke Bulag.

The guards blinked at her.

She narrowed her eyes. "Now! I need him at this very moment. Send him straight in the moment he arrives."

"Yes, my Lady," one guard said before rushing off to carry out her orders.

"What are you up to?" Jaghan asked, her face still pale and her eyes watering from vomiting in the bucket. Or perhaps she was just crying. It grew harder to tell with Jaghan's constantly shifting emotions.

"If this child still lives, we must know about it," Mandukhai snapped over her shoulder as she paced the few steps back and forth in front of the doorway. On impulse, she rushed to her chest. She removed parchment and other supplies, then set to writing out an order that would bring the child back to Mongke Bulag no matter where he was ... assuming he still lived. Her handwriting needed work, but it would do. "How old would he be now?"

Siker closed her eyes as if trying to picture his birth again. "Five? Nearly six?"

Mandukhai finished her order and waved it dry as she waited for Seguse. She briefly considered having Jaghan summon Togochi for this task. But Togochi could not leave without Manduul's notice, and Mandukhai had no intention of telling him this news until she knew how he would react. In his current state of anger, he was just as likely to kill the child as rescue him. Mandukhai could not take that chance. Not until she could determine her own course of action.

"Do you know how to sign your name?" Mandukhai asked Siker.

The other woman frowned and shook her head. Mandukhai thought it a bold assumption. She herself could not read or write upon arriving in Mongke Bulag. But as it became important for her to help Manduul with his reports and respond, he brought on a scholar to teach her. Only high-ranking men learned such skills. She would have to see that remedied when she became Queen Regent.

"Mandukhai, he was in very poor health," Siker said. "There is no way he survived. He was only one."

"You will have to forgive me if I will not hang the fate of our Nation on your assumptions, Siker," Mandukhai snapped.

She tested the ink, satisfied to find it dry. Mandukhai folded the paper, sealed it with wax from one of her candles, then pressed her ring into the wax. The ring bore no sigil as Manduul's would. It was a simple gold piece with a dragon on it—a gift from Manduul when he had assumed she favored the creature. His inability even now to understand the significance of the dragon cut Mandukhai deeply. Unebolod knew before he even met her.

Seguse ducked in and bowed to the women.

Mandukhai pressed the parchment into his palm. "Nothing, and I mean *nothing*, is more important than this, Seguse. Do you understand?"

He frowned at Mandukhai's intensity, but nodded stiffly as his hand closed around it. "Where shall I take it?"

"I don't know."

He blinked. Then his gaze slid past Mandukhai to the other two women in the ger before snapping back to attention. "My apologies, Lady Mandukhai, but how can I deliver it without knowing the destination?"

"All I know is that, four or five years ago, he was at the red cliffs of Tohom." Mandukhai turned to Siker, pleading with her gaze.

"It's a fool's errand, Mandukhai," Siker said, almost desperate to stop Mandukhai. "He is dead."

"That is for me to determine," Mandukhai responded. Her patience with this woman was wearing thin.

Siker trembled as she wiped her mouth. She put on a cool front, but Mandukhai could see the resignation, the sorrow Siker buried beneath the surface. *She has already grieved this child and accepted his death*, Mandukhai realized. *And now my search gives her hope that she doesn't dare feel.* Mandukhai's heart went out to Siker. It could not be easy to have another woman dredge up such a loss. But Siker had abandoned this infant. *His death is on her head. If he is indeed dead.*

"I expect you will only find the bones of a child, though," Siker said as she finished detailing where she had left the infant.

Seguse faltered, glancing from one woman to the next, clearly bewildered and confused. "I am to give this to a child?"

Mandukhai placed a hand on his arm. "No. If there are no bones, track him down. Begin with the Chakhar. Find out who is caring for him, where he is, and give this to whoever has the boy. I will accept nothing less than his safe return, assuming he still lives. If he does not, I want to know for certain where and how he died."

"This could take months," Seguse said. "Or longer."

"Take all the time you need, but know this, the fate of the Mongol Nation could rest on his life. And no one can know of this investigation. Not even my husband." Mandukhai adopted a cold face to be sure her point had gotten across clearly.

Seguse stiffened. Mandukhai understood what she asked of him. Keeping secrets from the Khan was dangerous ... but only if Seguse was caught. He bowed and turned to go.

Mandukhai tightened her grip on his arm and pulled him back. "If anyone asks, you were ordered out as another rider to spread news of Bayan. That is all they need to know. They should not question any orders from Mongke Bulag right now. You cannot, under any circumstances, utter a word of this to anyone else. We do not know who we can trust." Mandukhai released her grip and nodded. "Take any supplies you need and leave immediately. Travel as fast as you can."

With his orders in hand, Seguse slipped out of the ger.

Mandukhai rounded on Siker and Jaghan, her hands clasped together as if in prayer to the High Heavens.

"Speak of this to no one," Mandukhai ordered them both. Jaghan nodded, but Mandukhai scowled at her. "Not another soul. That includes your husband."

Jaghan tensed, but vowed to keep it between them until Mandukhai was prepared to share the truth herself.

Mandukhai did not yet know what she would do with the boy if he was found. If the child lived, he presented an obstacle to Unebolod's claim on the title. The Mongol Lords would always choose a Borjigin royal over one of a lesser noble's blood. She could not have Batu grow to challenge Unebolod's rule or have anyone else use the boy against his claim.

Before *kurultai*, she had to know if Batu survived. Otherwise, the Lords might raise the black banner of war. *They very well could do so regardless.*

Manduul grumbled under his breath as Mandukhai strapped on her *boqta*. In the past two days, he had become quite sullen. She had asked this morning if she could speak with Yeke before the execution. He had agreed, but not without persuasion.

"Perhaps I can learn something useful," Mandukhai said, turning to face her husband.

Manduul's complexion was unnaturally pale today. He wiped dinner from his mouth and stood. "I don't see how it will change anything."

Mandukhai took his arm as they ducked outside together, more to give him support than as a gesture of affection. The march to Yeke's ger took far longer than it should have, considering it was only two doors away. She knew she could not stop Manduul from killing Yeke—nor was she sure she wanted to. But she worried about how Bigirsen might react. Would he exact revenge by killing Borogchin? Was the girl in greater danger now?

When they reached the door, Manduul ordered the guard to allow Mandukhai in, adding a firm, "and no one else" before he withdrew and left her alone. A guard opened the door and Mandukhai ducked in.

The inside of the ger reeked of body odor and urine. Manduul had not even allowed Yeke out to relieve herself. They had imprisoned her in her own home. They had forcibly removed all traces of food or drink from Yeke's ger after her outburst in front of the court, along with all knives, glass, or anything else she could use as a weapon. The last days of the queen's life were doomed to isolation with no hope even to kill herself. Mandukhai knew she would have preferred suicide over waiting for judgment like this.

Tomorrow, Manduul would carry out the execution. Today, Mandukhai hoped to gain some insight from Yeke, or at least offer the woman some consolation.

Yeke uncurled herself from where she sat on her bed. Her *boqta* had been destroyed, strewn across the rugs in bits and pieces. Mandukhai picked her way toward the other woman, breathing carefully to avoid the stench.

"Have you come to twist the knife?" Yeke asked, her voice cracking in grief over each word.

"We could have been friends, Yeke." Mandukhai moved a dirty deel from the edge of the bed and settled carefully beside the other woman.

Yeke snorted. "You have been on his pedestal since he laid eyes on you. No matter how hard I tried, I could not knock you off." She sniffled and scrubbed the sleeve of her deel across her face.

Mandukhai noted the reddened eyes and rosy cheeks. Yeke had been crying. Her face was sallow. The hunger clearly affected Yeke.

"I find my fate unjust," Yeke said, and anger burned in her voice. "You were sleeping with his *orlok*, yet there you sit."

Mandukhai flinched. Yeke had known about her affair with Unebolod?

"Even when I told him what was happening behind his back, Manduul thought you too precious, too devoted to dare." Yeke's hate radiated from her.

Mandukhai wanted to reach over and rip Yeke's hair straight out of her scalp. She had told Manduul about the affair? Was that before or after he had raped her? Was his surge of anger and jealousy Yeke's fault?

"Bolkhu would have been mine soon enough anyway," Yeke said, oblivious to Mandukhai's sudden anger, "and we plotted none of Manduul's demise, no matter what he might think or how much I desired driving a dagger in his fat heart. Bolkhu never would agree. He worshipped Manduul."

"Bayan was never yours," Mandukhai said. In her anger, she could not give Yeke this small piece of happiness. Yeke's confession about reporting Mandukhai's affair with Unebolod stripped away Mandukhai's sympathy. She wanted to hurt Yeke. "He belonged to Siker."

"He hates that woman. He loves me!" Yeke shouted. Her eyes enlarged in rage and her face turned bright red.

"Oh, Yeke, you poor thing." Mandukhai reached out and stroked the side of Yeke's head, smoothing out rumpled hair. "He used you."

Yeke smacked Mandukhai's hand away. "What do you know?"

"Bayan only loved three things," Mandukhai said. "Sex, Manduul, and himself. Everything else was simply tools, us included. He used you because he feared your father. You offered him two things he loves. Sex, and a shield from your father. That's all you were to him."

Yeke gasped so deeply that her breath hiccupped in her throat. She shook her head, stunned and clearly in denial. "You are a hateful woman."

Mandukhai rose, headed toward the door. "Your death is set for tomorrow." She paused at the door before opening, gazing at the visage of a broken woman. "Remember, Yeke. You aren't a helpless woman. If you want to take his power away, stop wallowing and walk out of here tomorrow like what he has done has no effect on you. Don't let him have that piece of you. You are a queen." Mandukhai repeated the words Yeke had spoken when Manduul first assaulted Mandukhai. An assault that probably had resulted from Yeke's meddling.

As Mandukhai opened the door, Yeke gaped at her.

"We had nothing to do with your child," Yeke said softly. A final peace offering from a dying woman. Or perhaps a final lie.

Mandukhai hesitated, turning to gaze at Yeke one more time. She would not give Yeke the satisfaction of driving in a final knife. Instead, she would pretend she already knew the answer. "I know."

She ducked out and closed the door behind her.

The next morning, a small group of Manduul's guards ushered Yeke to the water. Yeke held her head high and walked as if they were her escort and not her prison guards. The river alongside Mongke Bulag flowed with a strong current downstream where it would feed into a small lake several miles away. Manduul had Yeke gagged and bound at the wrists so tight Mandukhai could already see red marks on the woman's arms. The skin had swollen around her usually thin fingers to something almost unrecognizable. When they reached the edge of the riverbank where the water ran deepest, Boke bound Yeke's ankles together.

Drowning. Mandukhai stared into the churning abyss of water with some sympathy for Yeke's plight. At one time, Mandukhai had expected this would be her own fate—particularly if Yeke had successfully convinced Manduul of Mandukhai's own infidelity. Having once had such fears, she could understand how Yeke must feel as she stood on the banks of the river with tears in her eyes and her chin held high.

Only a handful of others accompanied them on this trip downriver. Togochi, Issama, and a handful of Manduul's personal guards crowded the riverbank to witness Yeke's death. Two men stood beside Yeke to prevent her from throwing herself into the river before it was time. Yeke shivered against the cool summer morning air, but otherwise maintained her quiet dignity in a way that Mandukhai admired. Yeke had clearly taken Mandukhai's advice to heart.

Yeke's servants were bound beside the river as well, along with Bayan's—seven servants in total all bound at the wrists, and most were women in Bayan's service. No doubt he had slept with all of them. The women cried, pleading to Lady Yeke, professing their devotion to the Khan. But Mandukhai knew Manduul needed to sate his bloodlust for this betrayal, and he could not take Yeke's head. Sadly, these women were there to whet his appetite. While Manduul could not shed the blood of nobles without risking the wrath of the gods, he could do so to the servants who might one day betray him as payment for their master's punishments.

Mandukhai had tried to talk Manduul out of killing the servants, but he insisted no other punishment would relieve them of their conditioning. Too many had loved the Golden Prince, and he could not allow a shred of Bayan to remain. Mandukhai wondered if that was truly to purge Bayan's presence from court or to protect himself from the pain.

Manduul's men began working their way down the line. One by one, the crimes had been laid out. Stealing from the Khan, aiding in a conspiracy to supplant him, covering for the queen and prince's deception. None of these charges could be proven, but no one would dare attempt to disprove them either. Manduul had made his wrath clear the night he had stripped Bayan of all titles and rights.

Mandukhai could not watch as one of Manduul's young soldiers—most likely some son of a noble Lord who had paid handsomely for this right to help the Khan exact justice—lobbed the first servant's head off. She closed her eyes against the cries of the two women in the line and struggled to hold down her breakfast. The next in line was condemned and killed, on down the line until reaching Yeke. Her death would not be as swift.

Yeke stood statue-still throughout the executions, only flinching at the crunch of necks breaking as heads were cut off, or the thump of the head as it hit the ground and rolled. Yeke's gaze remained fixed across the river. She didn't even flick a gaze to any of the men and women pleading for their lives.

The stench of blood permeated the air. No one moved.

"Yeke, you are charged with treason for conspiring with the prince against the Khan, and for committing the act of adultery." Issama read off the charges with a casual business tone, as if recounting the current stock of sheep.

He asked if anyone wanted to step forward in her defense, and Yeke shot a glance at Mandukhai. Did she honestly believe Mandukhai would defend her, particularly against charges such as these? And after what Yeke had confessed yesterday? Mandukhai raised her chin and gave no response. Yeke sniffed and returned to staring at nothing across the river.

As Yeke was lifted off her feet and laid out on a rug, Mandukhai noticed how violently Yeke's body quivered. She twisted against the ropes binding her and whimpered, probably at the pain from the raw skin. One man began rolling Yeke in the blanket, then held her feebly squirming form still as two more men used thick leather straps to bind the felt closed so there was no chance of Yeke escaping. They fastened the buckles tight and waited for Manduul to give the signal to roll her into the river.

Mandukhai held her breath as Manduul nodded, and the two men rolled the bundled queen toward the deep waters. The river splashed and for a moment, Yeke howled through her gag as the felt slowly sank into the cold water. Then the bundle slipped beneath the surface, leaving behind nothing more than ripples to mark her passing.

Unebolod lay on the banks of the Xilin River to dry out after a much-needed swim. In the distance, along the hills of the basin, he could hear the horns of his generals and commanders practicing drills with the men. Unebolod no longer needed to oversee every practice maneuver. His men reported to him with striking accuracy regarding the state of his forces.

Unebolod passed the summer on the edge of the river, bartering for support with the Ongud khan, Korgiz. Now, fall closed in on him and the negotiations with Korgiz grew frustrating, if not infuriating. Unebolod had not expected such resistance from a khan whose tribe daughter served the Nation as the Great Khan's wife. Mandukhai's people were maddeningly stubborn, always prodding him for their own advantages.

Every time Unebolod had made Korgiz an offer, the old man had pressed for some other gain—higher social ranks for Korgiz's sons; a wealth of horses that could nearly wipe out Unebolod's own herd, among other requests. At one point, Unebolod had even spoken to the khan's son to get Korgiz to see reason, but that had only created trouble. Korgiz summoned Unebolod and verbally assaulted him for going behind his back and attempting to undermine his authority. Unebolod had wondered if perhaps the Ongud tribe was secretly serving Bigirsen, as many of the southern tribes seemed to do. He had hoped that appealing to their tribe ties with

Mandukhai might shift alliances toward him. Sadly, he had been grossly disappointed in the Ongud response.

Odgerel approached, along with another of Unebolod's servants, to bring his lunch. He sat up, thankful he had already pulled his trousers back on. Odgerel sat on her legs and bowed her head, holding out the tray they had prepared for him. He accepted *buuz* before leaning back on his arm.

Odgerel had attempted to entice him in very subtle ways—and some not so subtle. First, with a deel that hung open ever so subtly to reveal more than ample cleavage. When that failed, she would move close to him when carrying out tasks, just brushing his arm or back or, in one case, his bottom. One night, when he drank too much *airag*, she tried a more direct approach and simply entered his ger and shed her clothes to offer herself. Unebolod had pushed her out the door and thrown her clothing at her, warning her to never attempt such a thing again. After that, Odgerel had remained demure and servile, reverting to the subtle maneuvers.

Today, Odgerel's hair was braided over her shoulder and her deel buttoned up tight around her throat. Unebolod chewed the *buuz* thoughtfully as the other servant poured his *airag*. Odgerel must have felt his gaze lingering too long, because she chanced a glance up at him.

"Will you require anything else, my Lord?" she asked, watching him through her long lashes.

For a moment, he considered just throwing caution to the wind and giving in. Would it be such a big deal? It wasn't as if such an act constituted any real promises, and she was only a servant.

Before he could decide, the rumble of hooves against the ground brought Unebolod to attention. His guards charged toward the river, surrounding another rider whose saddle jingled loudly. *A messenger*, he thought, standing suddenly and wondering what could be so urgent. Had Manduul passed at last?

The rider dismounted and rushed toward Unebolod, with an escort of guards tight around him, ever watchful.

"Lord Unebolod," the rider said, clearly winded from hard riding. He held out two folded slips of parchment. "From Manduul Khan for your eyes only."

Unebolod accepted the parchments and noticed two different seals on them. One belonged to the Khan, but the other was of a dragon. His breath caught. He opened Manduul's first, though he ached to read what Mandukhai had sent.

The orders stunned him so much Unebolod had to read it several times. His chest rose and fell in excitement. He no longer had to worry about killing Bayan. If the boy stumbled across the path of Unebolod's men, they would capture or kill him by order of the Khan. *Have the gods finally ceased punishing me?*

Swallowing the lump of excitement that rose in his throat, he carefully opened the message from Mandukhai, brushing his finger over her tight script. *I fear for our lives. Return now. Bring all your supporters. We need men. I need you.*

Forgetting about the women on the riverbank, Unebolod tossed on his deel, belt, and sword, then mounted his mare in haste.

At long last, the time had come. He would return home, rescue Mandukhai, kill Bayan, and become Great Khan once Manduul passed—which couldn't be long now if Mandukhai urged his swift return.

Chapter Twenty-Six

Reparations

Moonlight illuminated the fog surrounding Mandukhai, making the world seem to glow despite the late hour. The fog swirled around her ankles as an eager dog would at the return of its master. For a moment, she stood breathless, trying to remember where she was or how she had arrived until the fog parted and bent around the branches of the Mother Tree, which shone in the moonlight like a pulsing star. *This is a dream*, she thought, stepping forward in her thin silk nightgown and placing a hand on the bark. It was cool to the touch and smooth, like silver. Like the tree that was rumored to have once been a focal point of the old Mongol Empire capital, Karakorum.

The last time Mandukhai had stood before this tree, the spirit of Genghis had come to her. She spun around, swirling mist around her ankles like the skirt of a dancer spinning out and away. Some part of her had expected him to appear again, but she stood alone on the hilltop, her only companions the tree and the fog.

A brief flash of light pierced the fog. Mandukhai glided toward it, surprised by the level of calm her nerves maintained in such unusual circumstances. As she approached the spot, the fog shifted like a coiled serpent up and around a silver post in the ground that came past her knees. As the fog serpent released its misty grasp, Mandukhai immediately recognized the wolf-head sword with its horsehair tassel. The sword of Genghis Khan. Once more, she turned in place. The fog rolled away.

Instead of finding Genghis, Mandukhai stood before a hunchbacked child curled up in the fetal position, coughing and wheezing. *Batu?* Mandukhai's heart lurched at the state of this boy. She reached out to him, but her hand slipped through him as if he were nothing more than the fog itself.

Could this vision show her where the boy lived? Mandukhai quickly scanned the horizon, seeking clues. Surely it meant he still lived *somewhere* in the empire. The darkness penetrated everything, as if the moon only shared its light with the boy. She glanced down, but the boy was gone. She stood alone beside the sword of Genghis.

Mandukhai slid the tips of her fingers along the hilt, afraid it would be as impossible to grasp as the boy had been, but the leather wrapping around the hilt felt solid beneath her fingers. For a moment, she wondered what it would feel like to hold his sword, even if only in a dream. She flexed her fingers anxiously. One by one, she wrapped them around the leather hilt. It creaked as she tightened her grip. Licking her lips, Mandukhai yanked the blade upward, and it sprang loose of the soil with ease.

This sword represented Genghis himself, a relic of the past, and it should be little more than that. Yet as she held it up in front of her, the moonlight shined on the polished steel, and Mandukhai could have sworn she felt the power of Genghis rush through her. Was this what it had felt like to hold his sword?

She swung the sword experimentally a few times, monitoring her stance, like her father had taught her, to avoid losing her balance. The sword was perfectly balanced, guiding her through the movements instead of jerking her along as some swords did. Like an extension of herself. As the tip of the sword arced downward, the eyes of the wolf-head pommel burned bright yellow as if suddenly alive and studying her. Mandukhai did not flinch. She cocked her head and pulled the sword closer, gazing curiously into the eyes of the wolf.

Just as suddenly as she had found herself in the dream, Mandukhai woke, her heart racing faster than it had in years. She had not felt such power since her previous vision when Genghis spoke to her about the future of the Nation four years ago.

Mandukhai did not sweat, despite the warmth pulsing through her skin, the same warmth she had felt as the power of the blade had moved through her.

The wolf dawn was coming when the sky shifted to lighter hues of blue before the sunrise. Mandukhai was alone in her ger, but she did not feel alone in spirit.

Ever since Bayan's judgment, Manduul had drawn away from Mandukhai; where before he had spent his nights with her since the onset of his illness, now he spent all his time in his own ger until duty called him to the gathering tent. Each morning, Mandukhai worried about his condition. Not because she did not want him to die; she simply could not afford for him to die yet. His growing resistance to duty, his increasing isolation, and his noticeable despondency could speed up his condition. She feared Unebolod would not return in time.

Mandukhai hastily dressed to head to Manduul's ger to check on him. Arslan and Torgus promptly rose to attention as she opened the door. They followed her to Manduul's door, where his own guards bowed to her.

"Has he woken?" she asked.

"He has not slept, my Lady," one guard replied. The concern for the Khan's condition was clear on his face, as well as that of the other guard. "He is awake most nights."

Mandukhai worried about Manduul all the more. If he refused to sleep, or it refused him, how much longer could he last? She pressed through the door, startled to find Manduul sitting at his lacquer desk, hunched over and resting his cheek on his fist as he wrote. Lines of age creased his sagging face, and the circles around his eyes had darkened significantly.

"Husband, you cannot do this to yourself," Mandukhai said firmly. She attempted sneaking a peek at what he wrote, but Manduul's arm blocked her view.

"I have heard nothing," Manduul mumbled. The exhaustion bled through every word as if some unknown force dragged them from his lips. "I had hoped to hear something, but it's been a week. Bayan disappeared. Just as he suddenly appeared. He is a wizard or a ghost."

Mandukhai crouched beside Manduul, placing a hand on his knee. "He is a boy afraid for his life and nothing more."

"I know what I must do." Manduul's voice had never been so miserable. "It pains me in ways I have never felt before." He raised his heavy head, dropping his fist to the desk as if it had no life of its own. Manduul's chin trembled as he worked his mouth to speak the words. Then he heaved out a sigh so heavy she wondered if any air remained in his chest.

"You need sleep, Manduul. You cannot go on like this. Your men need you. Your Nation needs you ..." She placed a tender hand on his cheek and tipped his head to meet her gaze. "*I* need you." For once, she meant it. Until Unebolod arrived, she needed him alive and functioning. If he wanted to give up after that, she would not stop him. But Mandukhai needed an army, an *orlok*, and a Khan.

Manduul barked out a mirthless laugh. "You have never needed me."

"What would I be without you?" The sincerity alarmed Mandukhai. She would be nothing. Not a queen. Not a woman of power. Not a future Queen Regent. Were it not for Manduul, Mandukhai would have been nothing more than a herder's wife. She did not love him; she never did. Yet she had grown to care for him all the same.

Manduul put his hand over hers and pressed her palm against his cheek. "I leave the Mongols in your capable hands until a new Great Khan has been chosen, and I do not worry over the future with you guiding the way."

Mandukhai started. It was one thing to be Queen Regent until *kurultai*. It was a different thing completely to be given control. She instinctively pulled her hand back, but Manduul held it fast, sliding it from his cheek. His grip tightened.

"Do not let the Mongols fall into Uyghur or Oirat hands," he said, and for the first time since Bayan's judgment and Yeke's death, fire burned in his eyes.

"I swear it," Mandukhai said solemnly. "I will fight their bid for power to my death."

Manduul nodded, and the fire slipped away as he sagged forward in his chair.

Mandukhai yelped as his weight fell against her. She stumbled backward, pressing her hands to his chest. "Help!"

The guards rushed in to help ease Manduul into bed. Mandukhai breathed a small sigh of relief as she noticed the shallow rise and fall of his chest. She brushed her hands on her deel and turned to the guards.

"No one is to disturb the Khan while he rests," Mandukhai ordered. "I do not care if Bayan is dragged into the heart of Mongke Bulag. Bind him, guard him, and make him wait for the Khan of khans to rise. Only Khosoichi or I are permitted in or out. No exceptions."

The guards glanced at each other uncertainly, and Mandukhai raised her chin and stared down her nose at them.

"Will we have a problem?" Mandukhai asked tersely, fingering her father's horn-handle knife in her belt.

"No, my Lady," they both said, bowing to her.

"Good. Double the guard if you need."

Manduul's time on the earth was limited, and this morning showed Mandukhai for certain that he would not survive long enough for Unebolod to arrive. He was deep in Ongud territory and it could take months for him to reach Mongke Bulag. She could not wait for a man to come to her rescue. It was time to ensure Boke and Togochi's loyalty to the Khan ... and to her.

500 MILES SOUTHWEST OF MONGKE BULAG – GOBI DESERT – SUMMER 1469

Avoiding riders had proven much more difficult than Bayan had anticipated. He crossed their paths at least twice each day, forced to veer so far off track he was uncertain he would reach Bigirsen at all. The journey had taken its toll on the mounts Bayan had collected after the attack. He had been most cautious with Andayar, riding her only when necessary, removing her blanket, saddle, and armor and forcing the other mounts to carry her burden. Just looking at her beautiful, shining chestnut coat reminded Bayan of the vow he had made to Manduul. He had kept his word, yet Manduul had still turned against him.

The horse beneath him squealed and stumbled a step. Bayan tried to force it along with his knees and a whip, but the animal was spent. He'd hardly removed his feet from the stirrups before the horse's front legs buckled forward and it lay on the ground, snorting. After just one week, Bayan had put over five hundred miles between himself and Mongke Bulag. But the fast pace had cost him two of the mounts.

Now, he had only Andayar and one other, and he knew he could not ride the second mount and have it carry the weight of Andayar's load. The second would have to be his primary pack animal. His pace would slow significantly.

Bayan collapsed on the edge of Baatsagaan Lake, laying his back against the dune that pressed against the edge of the water. The two remaining horses grazed on the tall chutes of sparse grass and drank from the shallow lake.

Bayan closed his eyes against the blazing sun overhead as it hammered against his skin. Sweat poured from him, seeping through his clothes as the desert sand sucked him dry.

He rode the horses too hard. With a grimace, Bayan sat upright and sifted through what remained of his possessions. He could only take food, water, and anything worth silver or gold at this point. The rest would be too heavy for his horses to carry.

High Heavens, if you are watching over me and sharing your luck again, I sure could use a heavy dose of it soon, he thought as he pushed himself to his feet again. Bayan frowned at the dead horse. It was good meat he couldn't afford to cure and carry.

If he did not reach Bigirsen soon, he never would. *My luck will hold out. It has to.*

MONGKE BULAG – SUMMER 1469

Issama spent his morning attempting to gain an audience with the Khan but Boke doggedly obeyed Mandukhai's command and insisted no one could enter. The Khan needed rest. Bribing them had been out of the question, leaving him with only the choice to wait. His curiosity churned the wheels in his mind as he tried to surmise what the Khan was up to, or if maybe he had already passed away and Mandukhai was trying to hide his death from the Lords of the Khan's court. Time would give that away. Manduul's body would bloat and smell rapidly in the late summer heat.

Issama struggled not to preen with pride as his plans began falling into place. Bayan was on the run. Unebolod was far from Mongke Bulag, among the Ongud far to the southeast. Manduul was dead or near enough to it. The Oirat were ready to strike the moment they received his order. With Yeke out of the way, Issama had only Mandukhai to contend with. Thankfully, despite his wife's failure at infiltrating Mandukhai's circle of ladies, Lady Siker had completed the task almost effortlessly. According to Siker, Mandukhai was eager to help save her from ruin.

So far, Manduul had done nothing with any of Bayan's property, nor had he forced Siker to give up her position. Issama had to be certain he controlled the circumstances. He had hoped to do that today.

Uingen sat in silence across from Issama as they ate dinner. She had not asked, but he could tell she sensed a change in him. Perhaps she attributed it to the Khan's unpredictable behavior as of late. Uingen smiled and laughed more than she used to, feeding off his positive energy.

Issama beamed at his wife as she chewed another piece of lamb. Frequently since Bayan's judgment, thinking of how perfectly everything had come together for him generated intense arousal. Most of the time, he bestowed that desire on his wife. A few times, he had compelled a servant to pleasure him when Uingen was unavailable. And on more occasions than he could count, he thought of Siker as he did. Uingen didn't know Issama's plans, but she knew he considered Siker potentially as another wife. Uingen had seemed agreeable enough to the prospect.

The growing power was heady and often left him swimming in a sea of euphoria. Even now, as he watched Uingen eat and considered what he would propose to Manduul once he could get an audience with the Khan, Issama's desire filled him to almost intoxicating levels.

Boke called out, then ducked into the ger, startling Issama from his fantasy. "Manduul Khan will see you now," Boke said.

Issama adopted a calm expression as he rose, hoping he did not appear too eager gathering his stack of scrolls. He followed Boke to the gathering tent.

Manduul perched on his throne at the head of the gathering tent, his hard gaze fixed on Issama as he approached. The coldness in Manduul's gaze gave Issama a chill. Did he know? Until given other indications, Issama would assume his usual position, sitting in the chair near the dais, at the side of the room where he could work as he conferred with the Khan.

Mandukhai's chair had moved closer to Manduul. Was this a power play, or was she closer to help care for him more easily? Her face was an impenetrable mask. Issama had never met a woman like Mandukhai before. She commanded respect better than any woman he had ever known. It unnerved Issama.

"Put aside your scrolls," Manduul commanded after Issama had taken his seat.

Though Manduul's deteriorating health was apparent to any who gazed upon him, somehow the Khan maintained a powerful presence. This crisis brought out something in Manduul that Issama had not seen before.

"My lord Khan?"

"I have a task for you that is more urgent than anything you will learn from those papers," Manduul said. His voice carried, but beneath it Issama could sense a weariness.

Perhaps he only needed rest.

"I have selected a new Vice Chancellor to take your place."

Issama's heart skipped. What urgent matter could remove him from his position? As Vice Chancellor, he could send messages all over the empire with no one thinking twice. If he lost that power, they would surely notice his messages to his web of spies. But what choice had he? Issama could either obey Manduul or kill him, and the latter could be costly if he did not kill Mandukhai as well. *My plans could come undone without this position!*

Issama reined in his worry. "What could be more urgent than maintaining your network of information?"

"I had hoped that my messengers would reach the other tribes and lesser khans and uncover the prince," Manduul said. "But it has been a week, and the prince has disappeared from the face of the earth."

Issama wondered if Manduul hoped Bayan would simply return and plead for his life. The love between the two men certainly would warrant such false hope.

"I have waited long enough," Manduul declared. "You are *orlok*. Take my army, leave the Khorlod *tumen* to protect us, and track down the prince. He is a traitor and a rebel, and he needs to be dealt with before he can cause further trouble for my empire. I would prefer him returned to me alive, but if you must kill him, be sure you bring me his head so I can see it for myself."

Issama straightened with intense interest. While he would likely be away when Manduul died, Issama could still seize power. Who could refuse the man who controlled the armies on Manduul's authority? But leaving with Manduul so clearly close to death would make it harder to capture control quickly, especially if he crossed paths with Bigirsen. Hopefully, Bayan was dim enough to leave a trail for him to follow so he could return to Mongke Bulag promptly.

This also presented Issama with the opportunity to kill Bayan, no matter the circumstances. Manduul would never know if Bayan gave himself up. Issama could kill the last heir of Genghis under the Great Khan's orders. None of this was according to Issama's plan, but if he proceeded with caution, it didn't have to undo his hard work.

"Not Lord Togochi?" Issama asked in smooth, even tones. Togochi had been a close brother to Manduul. So why would he not choose Togochi first for the task?

"I need Togochi here," Manduul said. "This is your task as my *orlok*."

Issama nodded. "I will gather our best trackers to find his path," Issama said. "The prince will not escape, Manduul. There is no corner of your empire where he would be safe from your men."

Manduul nodded, as if it really didn't matter to him. "Just see it done."

"Your will, my lord Khan." Issama bowed deeply.

Issama glanced at Mandukhai to gauge her reaction to the news, but her expression remained unchanged, unreadable as she studied Issama. *Perhaps she already knows of Manduul's plans.*

"If I may make one request?" Issama asked.

Manduul waved for him to continue.

Issama stepped eagerly forward. This was his chance. "When I bring him back, I would ask for the right to all his property, less your due share, of course."

"If you bring him back, you can keep it all."

Issama tried not to sneer at the "if." After all, Manduul had just made him a very wealthy man. Bayan was known to all as a lover of beautiful baubles, which meant he had gained an excellent collection of wealth. That did not even include the herds that belonged to the prince.

Mandukhai's lips thinned. Obviously, she did not appreciate this turn of events. *What will she think of my next request?* he wondered.

Issama bowed thankfully to Manduul. "My lord, I also understand that Lady Siker is in quite a unique position, being an innocent party in the prince's traitorous behavior. What will happen to her?"

Mandukhai stiffened. The response had not surprised Issama, based on what Siker had told him.

Manduul frowned, leaning back and rubbing his chin as he considered. At last he said, "You would not ask for no reason. What is it you want?"

"Her."

Mandukhai gasped.

Manduul snorted, not noticing or perhaps not reacting to Mandukhai's alarm. "As a servant? I don't see her as the type to obey."

"No. I could use a second wife."

"That's ridiculous," Mandukhai said tersely.

Manduul laughed. "My wife here calls her empty. What sort of wife would she be?"

Mandukhai's eyes widened at Manduul's confession of something she clearly thought had been a trusted secret between them. Issama heartily disagreed with Mandukhai's assessment of Siker.

"I believe she is simply ..." Issama cocked his head to the side as he considered. "Misunderstood. But she has served the prince well enough as a wife, and she was loyal to him even when he was not loyal to her. Uingen could use a bit of a break from me, I think. She would receive this well enough."

Manduul shook his head. "You do not understand women if you believe that to be true. I assumed as much about my wives, and they hated each other to the bitter end."

Issama glanced at Mandukhai. Her jaw had clamped so tight he wondered if Manduul could hear her grinding her teeth.

"If you truly want Lady Siker, you have my blessing. You can take her as your wife right now, for all I care. At least she would have a purpose while you are away."

"Manduul, I must protest," Mandukhai said, shattering her tense silence. "Does Lady Siker—?"

Manduul cut her off with a sharp gesture. "It is done. A woman needs a husband, and Issama is a loyal servant to his Khan and the Mongol Nation. He is *orlok*. What more could you want for her?" Manduul dared Mandukhai to speak again with a strong gaze. "The marriage is done."

Mandukhai seemed to understand there was no point arguing further, but the disapproval radiated off of her like heat from a bonfire.

Issama offered heartfelt gratitude to Manduul. He certainly would enjoy this evening. "Before I leave the capital to hunt the prince, I would like to know how you plan to handle the transition should anything happen while I am gone. Who will you put in charge until a new Khan is chosen?"

"I have left orders with my wife," Manduul said.

Mandukhai preened ever so slightly at this, her pride masked only by her anger.

"My orders were explicit," Manduul continued. "In the absence of an heir of Genghis, Unebolod and his line will take our place. However, I trust her wisdom. Therefore, any man who wins her over and proves themselves worthy has a chance at claiming my place."

All the anger melted off of Mandukhai at that moment as she turned a stunned gaze on Manduul. *She didn't know this.* Issama found the twist interesting. And it opened the road to his own legitimacy.

Win, like a game. Yet Mandukhai was unlike any opponent Issama had ever faced before.

Already, the wheels in Issama's head began spinning, trying to sort out plans. He and Mandukhai had never gotten along very well, though she did not seem to dislike him entirely, either. Yet somehow, he suspected she would not have any desire to be a third wife, nor *his* wife. Not unless he had something better to offer her. If he was to win her over, he would have to do it with political savvy. Siker had suddenly become more important than ever, and Manduul had just blessed their union.

"Is there anything else, my lord Khan?"

"No. Prepare your men. Enjoy a night with your new wife. You leave at the wolf dawn."

By the time Issama had the men notified and the army gathering and preparing for a morning departure, the sun was setting. Issama's mount danced beneath him and he absently stroked her neck as he stared south across the rolling hills, breathing in the scent of campfires.

A dozen of the best trackers in Mongke Bulag waited beside Issama for their orders.

"Go tonight and find the prince's trail," Issama commanded. "Report back to me in the morning. We will cut across his path in the most direct manner."

The trackers mounted and rode out of Mongke Bulag.

Issama dismounted outside of Bayan's door, overcome with heady excitement. This could not have worked out more in his favor, even if he was to leave Mongke Bulag. Manduul would not last long, nor would Bayan. Issama would not bring the prince back. He would take Bayan's head no matter how the prince surrendered.

Without announcing himself, Issama pushed the door open, startling Siker as she cleaned her tea set. A cup shattered on the rug. Siker pressed a hand against her chest as her gaze locked onto his. Issama thrust the door shut behind him, then removed his sword from his belt, and set it beside the door.

Siker's hair hung around her face, freshly released from a braid so it fell in waves around her shoulders. Issama stalked toward her, excited by his own success, certain he was on the brink of becoming Great Khan.

"Is it done?" she asked.

He brushed the back of his fingers along her cheek. Siker didn't flinch at the touch. Her breaths came in heaves that made her chest rise and fall in notable excitement.

"Manduul bought it all," Issama said, leaning close enough to feel the warmth radiating from her skin. "I promised to protect you, Siker. And now we have the Khan's blessing."

Siker wet her lips.

"Tomorrow, I hunt down the traitor," he said, noting the flush of her skin. "But tonight—"

Siker's lips slammed against Issama's. Her body pressed so hard against him that he stumbled back into the *uni* pole supporting the roof. It trembled from the force. All his careful work to earn Siker's trust had paid off with overwhelming force. He grinned as he ripped at her clothes, popping off the buttons that secured the deel in place. Siker breathed heavily against his neck as she yanked at his belt. As his deel fell open, Issama grabbed Siker's arm and tossed her down on Bayan's bed. He was going to enjoy this thoroughly.

CHAPTER TWENTY-SEVEN

Impeding Fate

Unebolod rode toward the Ongud camp with purpose. If he received the message about Bayan from Manduul, surely the Ongud had as well. Unebolod's days of playing mouse and elephant were at an end. Years ago, Unebolod had advised Mandukhai to be like the small mouse and show the elephant that she was mighty. At the time, he had been referring to her relationship with Manduul, yet the principle of that message worked in his current situation. It was time to press his only remaining advantage.

Unebolod dismounted as the Ongud men watching the camp's perimeter approached. They escorted Unebolod to Korgiz khan's ger—as they had several times already—where the khan's personal guards insisted on Unebolod relinquishing his weapons before entering. Unebolod handed over everything but his sword, and the men stiffened, blocking his passage.

"I will tie the hilt to my belt to your satisfaction," Unebolod offered, "but I will not, as a khan and an heir to the Nation, relinquish my blade to lesser men. I have come in peace and am a guest in Korgiz khan's camp. Breaching that sacred trust would raise a black banner of war. Do you really believe I am so foolish?"

A guard ducked into the ger. As he waited, Unebolod used a leather strap to secure the hilt to his belt, wrapping it around repeatedly in varying directions to ensure the blade could not be drawn. By the time he finished, the guard emerged and nodded. Unebolod scowled at the man and ducked into the brightly lit ger.

Korgiz sat on a bench as if it were a horse, one leg straddling either side. His graying hair was pulled back into a knot on the top of his head so tight it made the lines on his face appear stretched and deeper. Unebolod wondered briefly if the khan thought drawing his face back in such a way would make him appear younger. It certainly did not.

The khan's eldest son, Boragan, straightened and ceased pacing the moment Unebolod entered. The Ongud heir was only a few years younger than Unebolod, with a family of his own. His wide shoulders told Unebolod how skilled an archer he must be. Boragan could have taken over the tribe years ago, but his father refused to step down. Today, Boragan's countenance bore a stiffness, and his hand fidgeted on the hilt of his sword. Was he anxious over the news regarding Bayan? Did he assume Unebolod would be foolish enough to strike out?

"I assume you received the news as well," Korgiz said, breaking the silence.

Unebolod took an urgent step closer. "I cannot delay here any longer, Korgiz. I do not know what the prince has done to earn the Khan's wrath, but whatever it was, I am needed in Mongke Bulag. Manduul Khan needs my support through this challenging time. Will you support him, as well?"

Korgiz rolled the parchment between his hands as he studied Unebolod. Boragan watched the two with quiet interest, all the while keeping his hand firmly wrapped around the hilt of his sword as if he expected to draw on Unebolod. *I would like to see him try*, Unebolod thought. Unebolod didn't need his sword to floor any of these men before they could touch him.

"It isn't support for the Great Khan you seek any longer, Unebolod," Korgiz finally said. "You would have us support you."

"I serve the Great Khan by sacred oaths, just as you do." Unebolod's hands twitched, but he did not dare even make a fist with Boragan watching him like a hawk. "I serve his wife, a daughter of the Ongud, as well."

"Mandukhai was a stubborn, headstrong girl," Korgiz grumbled. "I had hoped marriage to the Great Khan would teach her what her place truly was."

Unebolod struggled to maintain a cold, impassive face, finding himself amused by the khan's assessment of Mandukhai.

He nodded. "I believe it has," he said truthfully. Mandukhai certainly had come into her own position of power since arriving in Mongke Bulag.

She had carved out her place in the Nation as a strong and wise woman. Korgiz must have heard as much after so many years.

"You can reassure Manduul Khan that he has our allegiance still," Korgiz said after a brief pause. "And when the time comes for *kurultai*, the Ongud will be there to support the next Khan."

Unebolod did not miss the unspoken "whoever that may be" at the end of Korgiz's statement. Again, he wondered if the Ongud alliances lay with Bigirsen.

"Return to your camp, Unebolod," Korgiz said. "I will arrange a tithe to return to the Khan with your men, as a show of our support. Then you can return to Mongke Bulag."

Being dismissed in such a manner chaffed at Unebolod's nerves, but he was a guest and could do nothing more than offer his gratitude and extract himself from the ger. As he walked his mount to the edge of the Ongud camp, he could not help but wonder how long it would take Korgiz to send the tithe to Unebolod's camp. Instinct warned him that Korgiz was stalling for time, and Unebolod was helpless to stop him. He had also carefully skirted offering Unebolod direct support in Manduul's stead. Considering how poorly conversations with Korgiz had gone, Unebolod refused to tell the old khan the truth of Manduul's condition. *If he does not support me at* kurultai, *he will fall with Bigirsen.*

Fall had arrived early, which also promised a swift and bitter winter. Unebolod breathed in the crisp air as his mare cantered toward the Khorchin camp. The sight of so many gers in one place, all those people following him, made Unebolod wonder momentarily whether he should bother returning to Mongke Bulag at all. With so many, he could sweep across the southern tribes and snatch Bigirsen's power away from him. Without Bigirsen to challenge him at *kurultai*, Unebolod would become Great Khan with no opposition. Only one thing kept his eyes to the north. One thing that challenged his ambition.

Mandukhai.

If he abandoned her when she sensed danger around her, Unebolod was certain he would never receive forgiveness—from her or from himself. He gave her his oath, and now more than ever, he yearned to touch her again. For the first time in his life, Unebolod discovered he craved for something more than the title he so long coveted. He would give all of it up for her.

Thankfully, he would not need to.

DRAGON'S SPINE – WESTERN GOBI – FALL 1469

Ranks of men and carts stretched back for miles behind Issama, far from Mongke Bulag. Manduul had given Issama command of all but Togochi's *tumen*, which he had kept behind to guard the women and children. Mongke Bulag would be vulnerable to attack the moment the Khan died. No one would come to their aid. Unebolod was too far away. Manduul was a fool to think his capital would be safe after his death. Issama only hoped he made it back in time.

When the hunt for the prince had begun, Issama had expected Bayan to head east and seek sympathizers, perhaps Lords or lesser khans who had no love for the Uyghur presence or for Manduul's reign. To his surprise, the trackers guided the column of men away from the east, cutting through the Gobi before heading south. The prince had gone deep into Uyghur territory. It made Issama wonder how Bayan had survived as long as he did. The boy was not terribly bright. *Perhaps he headed to Bigirsen hoping to appeal to Bigirsen's love for Yeke to save his skin. Foolish boy.* Bigirsen would not turn against Manduul, even for Yeke's sake. Besides, Issama had already sent Bigirsen a message informing him of Yeke's execution. It would only inflame Bigirsen's rage. Surely Bigirsen had received that message already.

Bayan had a week's head start on the *tumens*, but with Manduul's proclamation spreading to all corners of the Mongol Nation well ahead of Issama's army, there would be nowhere for Bayan to hide. Wherever he went, Issama was confident they would find him.

Fall winds swiftly swept over the *tumen* column after only a week. Once snow fell, Bayan would only be easier to track, and the cold would slow him down more than the well-prepared men with Issama.

The column had stopped for the night, and gers popped up all across the brittle ground, built by the servants brought along behind the army to take care of them. Issama had considered bringing Siker along to warm him on the cold nights—a few of the men had brought their wives, expecting a longer campaign—but Issama had left Nahai behind to watch over his wives. Soon enough, he would seize the title of Great Khan. And if Siker played her part well, she could only help Issama's efforts even while he was away.

Before ducking into his ger, Issama eyed a pretty young servant girl with alluringly wide hips. A grin spread across his face. He would not be cold in the winter, even without his wives. The girl tried to hustle past, but Issama snatched her arm. She yelped and stumbled, barely catching her balance.

"Wait in my ger," he said.

Her face paled. "But I have—"

"No one here outranks me, girl, and I have given you orders. Go." Issama released her arm with a shove toward his door. She staggered on her feet, eyes downcast as she disappeared inside. Issama stood straighter, beaming with pleasure.

"*Orlok* Issama," a warrior called out as he rushed over. "We found a homestead nearby. A single ger, poor by the looks of it. Only an old woman and a young boy with a couple of sheep."

Issama need not deliberate long on this. The old woman could spread word of their forces, which would alert Bayan to their location. The sheep would help feed his men, and the boy could serve the *tumens*. "Kill the old woman, bring the boy and sheep to me, burn the ger."

"The boy appears to be crippled," the warrior said.

Issama grimaced. "Then kill him, too." A crippled boy was utterly useless to anyone.

The warrior bowed and rushed off to carry out the orders. Issama lengthened his interlaced fingers high above his head, stretching out the kinks from riding and feeling the satisfying pop of joints.

Orlok, Issama thought with some satisfaction. Achieving such a high rank at only twenty-five was not unheard of, but it was rare since the position often went to more senior generals in the Khan's army. Manduul had made Issama field commander, the *orlok* overseeing all the *tumens* given to his command. Perhaps he was one of the youngest *orloks* in history. *Soon, I will be the youngest Khan without noble birth*, he thought as he turned to the door.

The girl trembled inside his ger, hugging her body tight, knees drawn toward her chest.

Issama crouched in front of her, tilting her face toward his and smiling reassuringly. "There is no need for tears. What is your name?"

"Qolotai," she moaned pitifully.

Issama's insides flipped with excitement at the sound. "I promise to be gentle, Qolotai."

She whimpered as he leaned forward and kissed her soft lips. Perhaps, if she proved supple enough to his needs, Issama would consider making

Qolotai his third wife. And a future Khan would need many wives to produce many sons.

Bayan lay on his belly, peering over the edge of the rocky cleft with an arm on Andayar's neck to keep her lying beside him. He tethered his spare mount to a boulder half-a-mile back, along with his supplies. Below, a collection of seven gers nestled together. He spotted them a few miles back from the puffs of smoke rising out of the smoke holes. At first, Bayan had hoped they might take pity on a lone traveler and offer him milk and mutton.

As he crawled on his belly, a banner rippled above the gers. The sigil on the banner was hard to make out as a stiff wind battered his face and made the banner undulate in his direction, but the moment he recognized the mark, Bayan kissed Andayar's nose.

"My luck still holds," he said to the horse.

Bigirsen's wives and children moved between the gers. Bayan had met them only a few times—one wife was his cousin. She should take pity on him, if anyone. *What was her name?* he wondered as he patted Andayar's neck to keep her quiet.

Yeke had told Bayan of his cousin's previous marital arrangement to Unebolod, and how Manduul had gone back on his word and married her off to Bigirsen instead. Would his cousin be bitter toward his uncle for breaking off the marriage to Unebolod? Bayan could only hope. He could not go much farther without more food and water. Not with the sands of the Gobi at his back.

Before Bayan entered the camp, he needed to know which ger belonged to his cousin. Bigirsen had four wives, so the rest of the gers must have been for his personal guards. He also needed to find out how far Bigirsen's family was from any of the rest of the army. They had to be nearby somewhere.

Soon, the sun would set behind him. Bayan needed to get up and move before then or risk his shadow falling over the small camp.

Bayan scrambled back from the edge, holding Andayar's reins. She snorted as she rocked back to her feet, and Bayan kept a careful eye on the camp below as he moved his mount away from the rocky ledge. The moment they were out of sight, he leaped into the saddle and kicked Andayar toward the slope down into the cleft, always watching for Bigirsen's men. This had to work. He had to gain Bigirsen's trust and support. His luck wouldn't bring him here for nothing.

DRAGON'S SPINE – WESTERN GOBI – FALL 1469

Issama sat on a stack of saddles outside his ger, wrapped in layers of silk, leather, and fur against the chill of the fall evening. The desert could become bitterly cold at night. Above, clouds marred the sky, making it difficult to see the stars. Did stars sleep when he could not? Issama grunted and took a long pull at the *airag* in his fist. It coated his belly and warmed his insides.

Inside, Qolotai slumbered huddled beneath a wealth of furs he should not have brought along on such a journey. He closed his eyes and leaned against the wall of the ger, picturing her smooth, bare skin in his mind again. Her father, it turned out, was the officer of an *arban*. Not highly ranked, but it was a respectable enough position for him to take her as his third wife.

All three women were markedly different. Uingen was respectful and demure and only spoke her mind when he asked her to; Siker was cool and distant on the surface, but soft and supple with him, and they had a bond of goals that led them down the same path; Qolotai was much more reserved than the other two, but when she had let go of her fear and given in to him, her focus had become centered on him. Three vastly different women. All three would need to learn their proper place once the transition happened, but he knew he had three women who could handle the task in their own way. A man could take as many as four wives. Issama had space for one more, and he had a suspicion who that would be already.

Footsteps crunched the dry, brittle grass nearby. Issama cracked an eye to see one of his men approaching—the same one he had sent to burn the ger as they set up camp.

"Well?" Issama snapped.

"We killed the old woman, burned the ger, and brought back the sheep, but the boy was gone."

Issama sat up straighter, cocking his head curiously at the warrior. "Gone?"

"Without a trace. Only a few of his toys remained as a reminder he had even been there," the warrior said. "Should we track him?"

Issama swigged more *airag* as he considered this. How could a crippled boy just disappear? "No," he said after a moment. "He's just a boy. A man does not mourn the loss of nothing when it has no bearing on him."

"*Orlok*," the warrior said, bowing and leaving Issama to his drink.

Gone ... Issama could not say why it bothered him to have a crippled boy just disappear without a trace. Surely there would be tracks somewhere to show where he had gone.

I have a different boy to worry about, Issama thought as he lurched to his feet. Tracking Bayan was far more important than some random broken boy. He scratched himself and stumbled back toward his door, warmed by the notion of Qolotai in his bed.

The sun set early, a sure sign of the coming winter. Bayan needed more than just supplies if he wanted to survive. He needed shelter. Gobi nights could freeze a man, and Bayan had no furs to keep him warm. If his luck held out, Bigirsen could offer shelter, furs, and life.

Bayan scouted the area surrounding the camp. Around the southern edge of camp, behind a rise of red cliffs, thousands of gers dotted the landscape for as far as Bayan could see. Herds moved around the dead space, foraging for food. Should this go poorly, Bayan had no choice but to escape into east the Gobi. If he headed west, he would be deep in Oirat territory; south would have him crash into Bigirsen's *tumens*; north would take him back into the arms of Manduul. If Manduul died, Bayan could petition to Mandukhai's smarter and softer side, but he couldn't take the chance while Manduul lived.

Bayan watched Bigirsen's camp from a crevice between cliffs with Anda-yar stuffed in behind him and muzzled to keep her quiet. Having her make noise when a guard passed would not end the way he wanted. After more than an hour of observing the men move around the small camp, Bayan was confident he knew when and where the best place to slip into camp would be.

Borogchin had only one son of her own, and the two of them moved around the camp with a rhythm that Bayan found simple to track. Near to camp, a shallow river fed past the area. Bayan had chosen his spot carefully. He wanted to be near enough to speak to Borogchin, but not visible to anyone else. He had watched two other women come to the very spot to fill their own buckets with water, and no guards had followed anyone, as if they all believed no one could get so close to Bigirsen's family without notice.

The sun set swiftly once it began its descent, and Bayan squinted into the darkness, watching the flow of the guards moving in the same pattern they had all evening. He did not know if she would come to the river, but Bayan had not seen her or her son visit all day. They had to retrieve water sometime. He just had to wait.

Nearly an hour after dark, Bayan received his reward for patience. Borogchin strolled to the river with her bucket in hand. Bayan waited for her to reach the shore and fill her bucket before clearing his throat and stepping out.

Borogchin squeaked and nearly dropped her bucket as Bayan revealed himself, a finger pressed to his lips. Her eyes grew wide as she recognized him. Then she shook her head.

"You should not be here," Borogchin hissed, glancing over her shoulder toward the camp.

"I need your husband's help," Bayan said, disappointed with how rough his voice sounded. It cracked over the words. "Please, cousin. I have been wrongfully accused, and Bigirsen could help me clear my name."

Borogchin took in every detail of Bayan's current state with deep calculation, and her lips compressed much the way Mandukhai's did when she thought he was acting foolishly. It was a comparison he found unnerving. Borogchin remained silent for so long, Bayan thought she would refuse. His pulse quickened. If she turned him away, Bayan knew he would die soon after. His life hung on his cousin's mercy.

Borogchin sighed heavily. "You need food and drink. It would be rude of me to refuse that much, at least." She headed back toward camp, holding the bucket to the side. "Come along, Bayan. You can carry this."

Bayan jumped forward eagerly, holding Andayar's reins in one hand and the bucket in the other.

Neither spoke as they walked to camp. Borogchin seemed to understand the danger of this situation. She took him into camp away from one guard. As they passed another, the man's eyes widened, and he reached for his sword. Borogchin leaned forward, placing a hand on the guard's wrist, and whispered something in his ear. He frowned, but let go of the weapon and turned his back on them.

Bayan observed the exchange as if watching some magic trick. *I think I've made a terrible mistake*, he thought as they approached her ger. Borogchin reminded him so much of Mandukhai that he wondered if she would kill him the moment he stepped inside. She could claim he had forced his way in, and she acted in self-defense. Borogchin felt far more dangerous now than she had minutes before.

Bayan loathed releasing Andayar's reins, afraid that he would lose his only means of escape, but the scent of cooked mutton made his stomach grumble. He ducked inside after her.

Inside, Borogchin's four-year-old son perched on the butcher's block, swinging his feet. His cheeks were puffed out as if he had squirreled something away in his mouth.

"Nemeku, I told you those were for your father," Borogchin admonished, but Bayan could hear the affection bleeding through.

"I didn't do it," Nemeku said around a mouthful of evidence. Despite his predicament, Nemeku eyed Bayan curiously.

Borogchin held her hand out in front of the boy. "Out."

Nemeku slumped and spit several sweet curds into her waiting hand. Bayan's nose curled. For the moment, the boy forgot about Bayan. "You can't give 'im them ones now," Nemeku said with a wiseness beyond his years. "They're icky with my slobber." He giggled.

Borogchin waved for Bayan to place the bucket on the block. Then she grabbed the little boy under the arms and pulled him down. Nemeku immediately coiled his limbs around her and cocked his head at Bayan. "Who's that?"

Bayan set the bucket on the butcher's block, then realized his sword was still in his belt. Removing it would be polite, but Bayan also feared being unarmed.

"We are playing a game, Nemeku," Borogchin said. "With your father. Do you remember the top-secret game?"

Nemeku nodded, grinning from ear to ear.

"Good. Daddy is it again." Borogchin placed a few strips of dried mutton in Nemeku's hand. "Jangi is playing eagle outlook this time. Take this him and tell him to warn the wolf if the lion approaches." She smirked, then gave him back one of his curds. "Remember. Top-secret. If daddy finds out we have a guest, we lose."

The boy nodded, hopping toward the door with his chest puffed out on this self-important task. Bayan watched him go, wondering what such a childhood must have been like; to have a loving mother and not fear every shadow that lurked around the corner. Bayan had never known such a life.

"My husband will not listen to you, Bayan," Borogchin said as she offered him a cup of tea.

Bayan accepted the tea and took a sip. The flavor burst over his taste buds: salt and rich bitterness with just a touch of honey to smooth it out. It had been weeks since Bayan had tasted anything so wonderful.

"If Manduul found out I brought you into my home, he might kill me and my son," Borogchin said tersely, sinking down on the edge of the bed across the ger from him. "So you understand the danger you have put us in?"

Bayan took another long drink of the warm tea before setting the cup down and leaning forward on the bench. "It isn't true. I have done nothing against Manduul."

"Tell that to Yeke," Borogchin snapped.

Her sharp tone made Bayan wince. "I would, if she were here."

Borogchin's expression softened, and for a moment the rest of her froze stiff. "Oh, Bayan." His chest tightened as he realized what she would say even before the words slipped out. "She is dead. Killed for conspiring with you."

Bayan's knees bounced. He rubbed his hands against his legs as the reality of his situation sank over him. Air rattled out of his lungs, and for a moment, he felt like a man drowning. Yeke's death did not bother him too much, but what her death meant for him certainly did. Unable to rein in the fear coursing through him, Bayan leaned forward and laced his fingers behind his head.

"I didn't ..." Bayan fought for each breath as some invisible weight pressed down on his chest. "I didn't ..."

Borogchin sank down beside him and rubbed at his back. "Listen to me very closely, Bayan." Her voice was reassuring, yet firm, reminding him once again of Mandukhai. "I cannot tell you how I know this, but Manduul is dying."

"Oh gods ..." Bayan sank further down until his forehead pressed between his knees. He knew Manduul was sick, that his death was coming someday because of the illness. But something about the way Borogchin said this made his stomach twist in knots, as if Manduul could be dead already. Manduul was like a father to him. No matter what had happened, that would never change. Bayan *loved* him more than he had loved anyone else in his life.

"You need to survive, Bayan. You are the last of my cousins. The last Borjigin heir." Borogchin slid her hand under his chin and forced him to sit up and meet her gaze. Every muscle in her body set with determination. "My husband is gathering his strength. He knows something is happening, but he doesn't understand the depth of it. Mandukhai has sent me word. If my husband knew what I knew, he would have already raised the black banner against you, Unebolod, and anyone who opposed him. If you can make it through the desert and survive until spring, you need not worry about the men hunting you. You can gather your strength to take what is yours."

"What men?" Bayan asked, his voice giving away his anxiety by cracking right in the middle.

"Manduul has sent Issama and the *tumens* to track you."

"What?"

Borogchin pressed her hand over his mouth. "Go straight through the desert and you could impede fate's grasp. But you cannot stay here. Bigirsen blames you for Yeke's death. He is angry with Manduul, but he is furious with you. If he finds you anywhere near us, he will kill you without a second thought."

Nemeku burst through the door, panting like an overtaxed dog. "Father ... the lion! He approaches the wolf!"

Borogchin's shoulders rose as tension bled through her. She surged to her feet. "Hide him, Nemeku. Remember, top-secret! The lion cannot learn the secret or we lose."

"Wait!" Bayan stood. "Where are you going?"

"To buy you time to hide," Borogchin said, smiling for the benefit of her son. "Nemeku! The place I couldn't find you when we played this spring. Remember it?" She waved him toward something, and the little boy nodded eagerly as she disappeared out the door.

Nemeku grasped Bayan's hand, and he realized how cold he had gone when he felt the warmth from the boy. "I know all the best hiding spots," Nemeku said, grinning from ear to ear.

CHAPTER TWENTY-EIGHT

Death and Nightmares

Two days after his meeting with Korgiz, Unebolod had meant to warn Korgiz to send the tithe, or he would leave without it. But Unebolod woke in a cold sweat. Just the effort of rolling out of bed and walking to his door made every muscle in his body scream in protest. A sheen of sweat covered every inch of his skin. Unebolod pulled open the door, groaning as his arms trembled from the effort.

The colors around the Xilin River began changing to brown, red, and yellow. Mandukhai awaited his return, but Unebolod knew he could not ride in this condition. *This is some cruel joke by the High Heavens to keep me from her,* he thought bitterly, furious with the gods for once more punishing him at the worst possible time. It was hard to have faith when it seemed the High Heavens continued to hold him back.

Odgerel froze, her eyes widening as she saw the state of him. She approached as she did every morning with the tray of food. "My Lord, what is wrong?"

"Nothing."

The terse response seemed to snap her out of her alarm. She hustled over, resting the tray on her hip so she could free a hand. Before Unebolod could withdraw, she pressed the back of her hand to his forehead.

"You are burning," she said, wiping his sweat off her hand. "Get back in bed."

Unebolod wanted to protest, but he was too weak to conjure the strength, and his mind felt stuffed with wool so he could not think straight. She nudged him inside. Though her touch had been gently insistent, Unebolod's knees nearly buckled. Odgerel slid the tray past him to set it on the table near the door, catching him under the arm deftly. He loathed how much he needed to lean against her just to shuffle back to bed.

Once she had him tucked in under his furs again, she set to work soaking a cloth in his cold bucket of water.

"I need to talk to Soke," Unebolod insisted, but even his voice sounded weak.

"You need to rest so we can bring this fever down before it boils you alive." Odgerel folded the cool cloth over his forehead. It hit his skin like ice. She brushed her hand over his eyes to close them.

Unebolod wanted to swat her away, but found his body betrayed his mind. His arms would not move. His hand would not even twitch, weak as he was. *Curse you, Tengri. I cannot die now.*

"Unebolod ..." Mandukhai reached toward him, sliding her hand along the scar down his face. Her fingers barely grazed his skin.

Unebolod reached for her, pulling her close to him, burying his face in her hair. The more he clung to her, the harder it was to hold on.

"I needed you," she whispered against his skin, her voice cracking.

Unebolod pulled back. Instead of holding Mandukhai's warm, supply body, he held her in death.

"No..." Terror clenched his chest.

In his hand, a wolf-head sword dripped with blood. The air in his lungs evaporated.

A shadowy form flitted past. Unebolod blinked, but his vision was blurry and the ger was too dark.

"You must leave him," an unfamiliar male voice said. "His life is in the hands of the High Heavens now."

"If we leave him alone, he will die." Odgerel's voice trembled.

Odgerel ... Unebolod reached for her. Or he thought he did, but his body had not moved at all.

"If you stay, you could be next," the mysterious man said.

"I will not leave our khan to die," Odgerel snapped.

Unebolod did not understand what was happening, but he was too weak to ask questions. Once more, he plunged into fevered nightmares about other men capturing Mandukhai, raping her in front of him, stealing his title ... Then they cut off his head as Mandukhai watched in tears, her hands cradling her belly, swollen with another man's child. And then the Mongol empire burned.

Two weeks after Odgerel had put Unebolod in bed, he broke through the fever and regained enough strength to shuffle out his door. His appearance drew alarmed gazes in his direction from the men. A moment later, as they realized he had not died—which at some point they must have assumed—they cheered the survival of their khan.

Soke edged closer, maintaining a distance from Unebolod's doorway. "I have never been so happy to see your face, my Lord."

"What—?" Unebolod's hoarse voice cracked and gave out before he could ask his question.

Soke's face fall and he wiped sweat from his brow with his sleeve. "A plague, my Lord. It is sweeping through camp. As soon as I realized what was happening, I ordered the families to spread out and keep their distance from each other as much as possible. But there was no stopping it. We thought we had lost you already."

Unebolod swallowed several times to gather the strength to speak. "Odgerel ..."

Soke frowned, glancing at a nearby ger. "She refused to leave you, even when she had been warned against it. Her swift action and care in those early days is likely what helped you pull through. But after the fifth day, she fell ill."

Unebolod frowned. Why had she stayed at his side when it could have killed her? *It still may*, he thought. He shuffled toward the ger, each step trembling as his knees shook. How long before he was well enough to ride again? And how many of his people would survive to ride with him? *The Khorchin are cursed.*

"My Lord, I would advise against entering her ger," Soke called, rushing over but still keeping a distance from Unebolod. He wouldn't touch

Unebolod and risk getting the illness as well, which also meant he wouldn't stop Unebolod. "Please. Unebolod, stop."

"If I still have the illness in me, then I can't catch it from her," Unebolod said. He pushed open her door, wincing at the stench of urine and body odor that rolled out.

Soke swiftly shuffled away from the open door.

Unebolod took as deep a breath as his weak lungs could hold, then stepped over the threshold and closed the door behind him.

The inside of the ger was dark with no fire in the stove to warm the space. Unebolod added fuel to the stove and struck the flint to light it. As it blazed into life, the light illuminated Odgerel's pale skin, glowing as the firelight reflected off the layers of sweat. He edged closer, using the bucket of water to wet a cloth, as she had done for him. Once the cool cloth was on her forehead, Unebolod set to work removing her clothes. They were covered in her own filth. She had clearly done the same for him.

After he finished removing her soiled clothes and wiping her clean, Unebolod laid a fresh deel over her body, then covered her with blankets. The shallow breathing concerned him as well. For a few minutes, he stared at her as she drew in ragged breaths.

Then she stopped breathing altogether.

No. You aren't dying on me. Unebolod leaned toward her, tipping her chin up to the ceiling. *Mandukhai, forgive me. This is nothing.* Unebolod opened Odgerel's mouth and pressed his lips against hers. She tasted like death, reminding him of the nightmare he had of Mandukhai. One careful mouthful at a time, he breathed for her, pressing air into her lungs.

For hours, he remained at her bedside, intermittently breathing for her until she seemed to gain the strength to do it herself again. Hopefully, that was a sign that she would pull through.

Two days after he entered Odgerel's ger, Unebolod emerged again. No one had even knocked on the door. Who would risk contact just to check on him? When he stepped into the sunlight, Unebolod sought Soke, praying his general had not fallen ill as well.

"The gods are your wings, Unebolod," Soke said as he rounded a corner with a handful of clean blankets.

"The gods hate me, I think," Unebolod replied.

Soke gave Unebolod a curious look, but said nothing more.

Unebolod longed to ride to Mongke Bulag, but he knew he did not yet have the strength. How long before his tribe was ready to ride again? Somehow, Unebolod knew that if he did not return to Mongke Bulag by spring, he could lose his chance to become Great Khan—or his nightmares about Mandukhai would come true.

The weeks bled away as Unebolod recovered his strength and the number of people who contracted the plague dwindled, then dropped off. As he waited, Unebolod had sent a message to Manduul, assuring him that he had scouts out watching for Bayan. Before the messenger left, Unebolod gave him a verbal message to deliver to Mandukhai.

"These words are for her only. If you utter any piece of it to anyone else, I will know, and you will pay dearly." The messenger understood the urgency and vowed to speak it to no one else. The message was simple: "The gods stall me, but I am coming."

Yet another two weeks passed, and the weakness of his tribe continued to bother him. He wanted to leave them behind, but would they forgive their khan for abandoning them? Would they choose someone else to take his place if he left them?

Korgiz khan had not yet sent his tithe to the Khorchin camp either. Unebolod had assumed at first that it was because he feared the plague would spread to his own tribe. Now, he grew certain Korgiz had simply stalled to flex his own muscles.

A surge of anger coursed through Unebolod as he munched on his breakfast and considered the day's tasks. Unable to contain his frustration, Unebolod threw his cup across the ger. The metal rim dented as it crashed into the doorway. Odgerel—who had only just returned to his service a week before—flinched as she straightened up the breakfast mess. Unebolod surged to his feet as the guards dashed in, scanning the ger for threats.

"Begin packing," Unebolod barked at Odgerel.

He had waited long enough. If Manduul died before he returned, he could still ride into Karakorum and become Great Khan. If Mandukhai was captured and forced into another man's bed before he returned, he would burn the empire, beginning with the Ongud khan, while challenging the High Heavens to stop him. *I wait for no man*, he thought as he stomped out the door to give orders.

The fate of the Ongud rested in Mandukhai's hands now. He would give her a chance to bring them to their senses, or he would bring armies to wipe them off the face of the earth. Who did Korgiz think he was, anyhow? Unebolod would be Great Khan; he would marry Mandukhai; Korgiz would kneel or pay, and that tithe would be seized in due time.

Soke trotted up to Unebolod as he stomped along the paths. "Are we leaving?"

"Yes. Now. I want everyone packed up and prepared to head toward Mongke Bulag within the hour. If they are not well enough to travel, they can meet us in Mongke Bulag. Send word quickly."

Soke offered a rare grin. He knew Unebolod had grown tired of Korgiz. With a murmured acceptance of the orders, Soke rode away to send out the command.

"My Lord," a man said softly from behind him.

Unebolod turned to face him, surprised to see an Ongud shaman awaiting with his head bowed respectfully. "If it pleases you, I would request permission to travel to Mongke Bulag with your men."

Unebolod raised an eyebrow at him. "Korgiz will not send his tithe, but he will send a spy?"

The shaman shook his head, making the graying hair sway. He met Unebolod's gaze with clear eyes and a strong sense of purpose. "I have spoken to the spirits these past weeks. Lady Mandukhai will need my services soon. If I cannot go with your men, I will journey there on my own, though I would prefer traveling within the safety of your *tumens*. An early, harsh winter is coming our way."

"What have the spirits shown you of her need?" Unebolod asked. Mandukhai's message had been so urgent, and he had delayed far too long already. Fear for her clenched in his chest.

"I'm afraid I cannot speak it," the shaman replied. "I mean you no disrespect, my Lord, but the spirits are very deliberate with whom they choose to speak. It is a sacred responsibility to speak with a spirit and be trusted with their secrets. Those entrusted with their guidance can only share their advice when the time is right."

Unebolod itched to burn the truth from this shaman's tongue, but he dared not anger the spirits. His situation was dire enough already. He could not take further risks. "What is your name, shaman?"

"Getei, my Lord," he said, dipping his head again.

Unebolod hesitated a moment. Despite his own shaky faith in the gods, Mandukhai had always maintained a steadfast belief in them. She would be furious with Unebolod if he left Getei to his own fate instead of protecting him.

"Mount up then, Getei. We ride the moment camp is broken."

Getei gave his thanks and rushed off to prepare himself for the journey. Unebolod watched him trot away, his mind buzzing with questions about Mandukhai's fate.

Mongols were terribly efficient at breaking camp, and in less than an hour, all the gers were loaded into carts and the *tumens* lined in ranks. Unebolod rode alongside Soke north to skirt the edge of the desert. With so many and such weight, it would take months to arrive in Mongke Bulag, through the heart of winter, but Unebolod still felt invigorated. He was returning to her, and then to Karakorum.

And then everything would change.

CHAPTER TWENTY-NINE

The Boy in the Basket

Nemeku revealed a hole beneath one of the great chests in Borogchin's ger. The hole was more than large enough for Nemeku's small four-year-old body, but far too small for Bayan to fit easily despite his wiry frame. Even after Bayan helped Nemeku move the chest to make a space big enough for Bayan to squeeze in, he had to fold his body up tight and curl into the hole with his knees up to his ears and his legs pressing so close to his chest that it compressed his lungs.

Nemeku grunted and pushed and pulled to move the chest back into place, slowly plunging Bayan into near darkness. Bayan struggled to keep his breaths even with his legs pressing so hard against his chest. His arms were pinned down against his sides, unable to move more than a hair at a time. Only a small gap between the chest and the hole revealed any of the ger, but he could hear everything clearly. Making noise would attract attention.

Bigirsen was not alone when he returned to camp. Bayan couldn't be sure how many of those boots outside were the same people milling around the small camp, but he was certain that at least ten men searched the camp. Muffled voices of men and women mingled in an argument. Children cried to their father—presumably Bigirsen. His wives demanded to know why his men tore the camp apart.

Boots stomped into Borogchin's ger and crossed the rug-covered floor. Bayan heard the groan of hinges and clatter of pots; the creak of furniture being shifted around. He held his breath as the boots stopped in front of the chest. For a moment, he feared he had been discovered. Then the lid of the chest rasped open, and Bigirsen tossed wads of cloth to the ground as the man shoved around the contents of the chest.

"You have lost your mind, Bigirsen!" Borogchin snapped. "Treating your wives and children in such a way, setting your men to sack our homes like enemies. What has gotten into you?"

The clunk and thump of objects shifting in the chest ceased abruptly, then the lid slammed down with such a thunderous crash that Bayan's ears rang and buzzed. He let out a small, slow breath and struggled to maintain control so Bigirsen would not hear him breathing. Bayan watched Bigirsen's boots stomp across the floor, and he dared to shift his head as close to the gap as he could to get a better view.

Bigirsen towered over Borogchin on the other side of the ger, backing her against the edge of the bed so she stumbled and sank down onto it. "I have seen that fancy chestnut mare out there. Everyone knows that horse. The prince is here. Where is he hiding, Borogchin?"

To her credit, Borogchin didn't shy away from Bigirsen's hulking mass towering over her. She stood, straightened her back, and adopted an expression of confusion so sincere Bayan almost believed her himself. "If he comes around me, should I hand him over to you?"

Bigirsen's shoulders quivered with rage. His hands clenched into fists at his side as if prepared to strike her. When he reached out and grabbed her arm, Borogchin barely flinched.

Trapped in the hole, Bayan's muscles cramped. His shoulder ached, but he would not move again and risk Bigirsen hearing him.

Enraged, Bigirsen leaned so close to his wife that their noses touched. She raised her chin in stubborn defiance.

"If I see him near you," Bigirsen growled, "I shall eat his flesh and drink his blood." He released his grip on Borogchin and turned toward the door, giving Bayan just a glimpse of the pure mania in his red face.

Bigirsen stormed out, and for the first time, Bayan heard the quiet sobs of Nemeku coming from elsewhere in the ger. Borogchin trembled the instant the door slammed shut behind Bigirsen. For a moment, she stood stunned, her face had grown pale.

The cramping in Bayan's limbs intensified, but he knew there was no way he could leave this hiding place until Bigirsen was long gone from camp. If the sky father had blessed him at all, Andayar would still be waiting, hobbled outside when he emerged.

Borogchin shook herself out of her stupor and crossed the ger to scoop up her son. Bayan could only see the back of her deel. "Shh, do not cry. We won the game. You hid him well."

"Why does father hate him?" Nemeku asked, his hushed voice shaking. "The man was nice to me."

"Because power corrupts the hearts of greedy men, Nemeku. Those who are worthy achieve power because of skill, and because they earn it. Those who seek power will never be strong enough to hold it."

Nemeku frowned, tipping his head to the side as he considered his mother's words. "Father is not strong? But I've watched him lift great weight, and he can fire a bow better than any man alive." Nemeku's voice revealed awe for his father that only reminded Bayan of how alone he had been all his life. Nemeku pulled back his arm as if drawing an imaginary bow, then released the invisible arrow.

"True strength comes not from the body, but from the spirit. Remember that, Nemeku. You must have strength of spirit, and if you are worthy, power will come to you. Do not seek it."

"But father commands *tumens*," Nemeku said, his voice rising in excitement. "Thousands of men! And I heard him tell Ibara that the Khan and *orlok* both follow him."

Borogchin kissed Nemeku's forehead. "One day, you will understand."

Bayan squeezed his eyes closed as tears threatened to flow. Was he such a man? Certainly, he had never sought power, but he heard what others called him before fleeing Mongke Bulag; a coward, little more than an easily frightened boy.

"It is time to sleep," Borogchin whispered. "Your father is angry with me, and he will not return tonight." The last, Bayan was certain she intended for his benefit, hoping he would heed her words. But sleeping in this position seemed a monumental—if not impossible—task.

Borogchin tucked in Nemeku, then closed the lamp and curled up with her son. Soon enough, the sounds from the camp died down.

A hollowness sank into Bayan's chest as he struggled to sleep. Despite exhaustion, the aches in his limbs screamed at him every time he tried to drift off. Briefly, he considered digging himself out of this hole and allowing Bigirsen to kill him. What was the point of all of this after everything he had gone through? Even better than submitting himself to Bigirsen's violent whims was the tempting prospect of just allowing the ground to swallow him whole here and now.

Bayan wanted to shift, to relieve his aching limbs and stretch out, but perhaps such confinement was no less than he deserved. While he had not betrayed Manduul or had any intention of stealing the title from him, Bayan *had* stolen one of his wives, which was a betrayal of sorts, even if he had misunderstood their shared connection.

All his life, Bayan had been defiant, entitled to the point of punishment. It began years ago, in Bolunai Khan's court. The khan had beaten him, but Bayan had done things that would leave the khan with little other choice. Perhaps, deep down, he had wanted to be beaten because it was no less than he deserved.

Bayan had never asked for any of this. He had wanted none of this. Those early days with Siker had been so much simpler. At the time, Bayan had balked at the idea of living the life of a herder or marrying Siker, but now he wished he had just accepted that simple life. No one chasing him. No court politics. No deception. But a taste for something better, something sweeter, had sunk its teeth into him. Bayan had been unable to let go once Manduul had accepted him into his family. *Maybe I enjoy the danger more than I want to admit*, he thought as tears rolled down his cheeks and soaked into his knees.

His grandmother and mother had gone to great lengths to save Bayan as a baby, and he had done nothing in his life to deserve such a sacrifice.

Unable to hold back the longing for someone to hold him as Borogchin held Nemeku, intense loneliness stole away the last of his strength. Bayan silently wept in that hole in the ground.

The prince found himself packed in a cramped space now, just as he had been as a baby when his great-grandmother's men had attempted to hide him from Esen Khan. To Bayan, it felt as if he had returned now to where he began, and that this was where he would end.

A boy alone in a basket.

Mandukhai's voice reached through Bayan's misery, admonishing him for cowering in a hole like a marmot instead of standing up like a prince. Bayan saw nothing through the darkness. The sound of grinding steel against steel shook the very ground beneath him. Bayan shifted, but his limbs resisted. Her hand rested on his arm, urging him to move.

"Get up, Bayan," Mandukhai hissed, gently shaking him. "Get up."

Bayan moved a stiff arm and opened his eyes. Just the act of uncoiling his limbs created a massive, blinding wave of protest in every muscle in his body. The joints ached so badly that he whimpered against the pain.

"Get up."

It took great effort to focus and recognize Borogchin crouched in front of him, with Nemeku peering out the front door a few feet away. Bayan opened his mouth to speak, but his dry mouth betrayed him and instead, he croaked.

Borogchin frowned at him as Mandukhai often had. Bayan rolled toward the opening above him, clawing at the dirt-covered by rugs. Borogchin grumbled and grabbed his arms, helping to haul him out of the hole. Once he settled on the rugs, she set to work wrapping warm cloth around his limbs as she straightened them. Bayan breathed sharply through clenched teeth with each movement. The warm cloths helped ease the aching muscles.

"My husband has taken his men hunting," Borogchin said as she massaged his calf over the warm cloth, working the heat into his muscles. "You cannot stay. He will be back, and you will never be safe here." She reached around her and grabbed a skin of *airag*, helping him drink it when his cramped hands refused to grab the bag. He gulped the drink down thankfully. "The wolf dawn approaches. You have a few minutes to regain feeling in your limbs and go."

Neither spoke for several minutes as she continued easing his aching muscles and offering food, which Bayan devoured with savage hunger. He didn't realize how long it had been since he had last eaten until the savory scent of cooked *buuz* filled his nose and made his mouth immediately water, craving the salty meat.

After regaining enough strength to stand and flex his joints, Bayan accepted a pack of cheese and meat from Nemeku, who watched him with an intense interest in the way only a child could. Borogchin sent the boy out to retrieve her guard, Jangi, as she stuffed another pack with supplies.

"Why are you helping me, Borogchin?" Bayan asked, setting down the pack and raising his hands above his head. The stretch pulled the length of his body. Bayan could feel his back pop back into place in several spots.

She paused, eyeing a knife on the bed beside the pack. He wondered if he had pushed his luck too far. Perhaps she would use that knife on him now to save herself from Bigirsen's wrath. At last, she said, "You are my kin, and my only tribe brother. Bayan, you are the last heir of Genghis. That has to mean something. And I believe, deep down, Mandukhai knows this as well."

He snorted, scratching an itch he could not touch all night long. "You don't know her as I do. She likely held sway in Manduul's judgment. Mandukhai would never want me to live. She and Unebolod have formed some sort of friendship and I'm a threat to him."

Borogchin stiffened for a moment, eyeing Bayan.

"You *do* know that Yeke believed Mandukhai and Unebolod were having an affair, too," Bayan said.

Borogchin blinked. Her face drooped. Bayan knew they had promised his cousin to Unebolod before Manduul gave her to Bigirsen. Did she still harbor feelings for Unebolod? Was this news a betrayal of Mandukhai's trust?

She shook her head, then returned to her task, tucking the knife into her belt. "She is the reason you have lived so long, Bayan. When the men thought you were a threat to the Khan's position, she convinced him to take you in and treat you as a son. If not for her, he would have had you killed years ago."

The news should have surprised Bayan, but after everything he had suffered these past months, nothing could shock him any longer. Still, picturing Manduul considering such a fate back in the early years felt out of place. Manduul had opened his arms before Bayan had even stepped foot into Mongke Bulag. He had listened to him and taught him and joked with him. They had been so close that this sudden turn was the worst sort of betrayal he could have ever imagined.

Perhaps there was no escaping fate. Even as a baby, Bayan had been hunted. The shadow of other Khans stretched over his entire life, forcing him into the shadows. Bayan had never truly known any other life. *Except with Manduul*, he thought bitterly.

"You have a way with people, Bayan," Borogchin said, closing the second pack. "Use that to your advantage now. Perhaps you did not betray Manduul. Perhaps you did. I will not judge you either way, cousin. He is a vile man. But if you are to be blamed for these crimes, rise against him. What have you to lose?"

He could lose everything ... or nothing at all. Bayan had nothing left but Andayar and the clothes on his back. Manduul could only take his life—the hardest of all to lose.

Jangi ducked into the ger, dragged along by the hand as Nemeku led the way. "Lady Borogchin, I have secured the camp. The other three women have done as you asked and will keep their promises."

"Do you have the saddles prepared, Jangi?" Borogchin asked, turning away from Bayan as if he were not there.

"As you instructed." Jangi's gaze swept suspiciously over Bayan. "Has he been hiding here all night?"

"Inconsequential," Borogchin waved the question off, then thrust the second pack at Jangi. "Ride hard, Jangi. Take him straight north and avoid the edge of the Gobi. Issama has several *tumens* riding this way. I will not have him falling into his hands."

"Now wait just a moment," Bayan interrupted, stepping toward her. Jangi snapped his grip around his sword in an explicit threat. Bayan raised non-threatening hands. "I'm not going back there to challenge him directly. You must be out of your mind."

Borogchin scooped up Nemeku and strode toward the door. "Jangi isn't taking *you*."

The words froze Bayan in place as she swept out the door with Jangi on her heels and Nemeku clinging to her neck. After shaking away the shock, Bayan snatched up his pack and rushed out after them.

The small camp remained dark, with no signs of movement from the other six gers. Bayan could not see, but he knew there would be guards and spies all around, watching for his escape. Andayar grazed nearby. Bayan breathed a sigh of relief. Losing his mount now would be the end of him for certain.

Jangi fastened the pack Borogchin had given him to the back of the saddle, watching Bayan from the corner of his eye.

Borogchin boosted Nemeku into the saddle on a small but strong pony, then strapped him in place as was the custom for young children on long, hard rides. *She is sending her son away*, Bayan thought, and his stomach sank like a lead ball as he realized this was his fault. Nemeku was only a year older than Bayan had been when his own mother sent him away. Would he suffer the same unfortunate life because of Bayan?

Without waiting to be ordered around, Bayan unhobbled Andayar and climbed into the saddle, tying the pack down securely. Borogchin had not given him much more than food and drink, but it was far more than he deserved.

"You should ride with us, Lady Borogchin," Jangi said.

"Mother?" Nemeku frowned when he realized his mother had not mounted behind him.

Borogchin stroked the nose of Nemeku's pony, a small, sad smile on her face. "I cannot. Bigirsen would hunt me. But if I stay here, I will buy you time to get my son to safety. Then I will finish what I have started."

"He will kill you if he finds out what you've done for me," Bayan said, edging Andayar closer.

She nodded.

Bayan gaped. "Mandukhai will protect you. She adores you."

"I owe everything to her. But I have suffered these past five years with a clear purpose. I will not run from it now." Borogchin turned a fiercely determined gaze on her son, and once more she reminded Bayan of Mandukhai and her stubborn will. "To protect you, Nemeku, I must send you away. Mandukhai and Esige will care for you as I would. They are your family now. Remember, always, what I told you last night, Nemeku."

The boy sniffled as tears rolled down his cheeks. For one so young, Bayan admired the way the boy's jaw mirrored his mother's determination as he swallowed his sorrow. He nodded.

"Go." Borogchin tossed Nemeku's reins to Jangi. Their mounts trotted away from the ger, toward the north.

She turned to Bayan, swiping a tear from her cheek. "If you ride straight through the crevice in the rocky cliffs, you will find yourself in the Gobi. It is not ideal, but it is the best route to escape notice."

The cramps in Bayan's muscles tensed up painfully as he considered this fate. Bayan shook his head, heart hammering against his ribs. "No. I can't. I've been through the desert before. Three times. And each time I almost died. I won't make it again."

Borogchin bit her lip, struggling to rein in her emotions. "You have no choice. If you go in any other direction, you will certainly die. If you go through the desert, you at least have a chance." She cocked her head as she studied him. "I do not know if you are worth all this trouble. But I *do* know that I believe in the Borjigin and the line of Genghis. I would rather face my death having supported the heir of Genghis than risk facing the wrath of the High Heavens when I die."

"Borogchin, ride with me," Bayan pleaded selfishly. Her death would be on his head, but more than that, he did not want to be alone anymore. "He will hunt us both, but together we can gather support and rise against them." Not that Bayan had any idea how to go about it.

Borogchin stubbornly shook her head. "I will not run, Bayan. I have unfinished business with my husband. He will know the truth of it, and of the strength of the Borjigin, before I die." She smacked Andayar on the flanks, forcing the mare forward.

Bayan rode east, away through the darkness, watchful for spies or guards. When no call came and no hooves thundered in pursuit, he spared a glance back at the camp as wolf dawn began lighting the night sky.

For the fourth time in his life, Bayan would have no choice but to cross the desert to save his own life.

And he did not know what he would do once he reached the other side.

Chapter Thirty

Bones of Winter

Fall gave way to winter, with Issama continuing to send updates to Manduul and Mandukhai. The prince had been spotted in Bigirsen's camp, but before they could capture him, he had fled into the desert.

Manduul surged to his feet as they read the report to him, throwing his cup across the gathering tent. It hammered into one of the support posts hard enough to make the roof quiver and dent the cup beyond repair. Mandukhai clasped her hands in her lap to keep from jumping at the sudden movement. She clenched her jaw and raised her chin.

His moods could swing from sullen silence to pure tenderness to manic anger to impenetrable grief within a matter of minutes. It terrified Mandukhai, though she showed none of her fear to him or anyone else. Bayan's betrayal had ripped out some piece of Manduul. These fits of emotion took a toll on his weakening body as the illness ate away at him. And the people had noticed.

"Am I surrounded by incompetence?" Manduul roared. His shoulders shook, and his usually pale face burned red with rage. "How could he escape *two* of my field commanders and the *entire* Mongol nation?"

Alayitung, the Borjigin commander Manduul had made Vice Chancellor after Issama left, dipped his head in shame, as if he were the one who had failed Manduul. Mandukhai knew Manduul's anger came from a place of pain, and she wished she could ease some of that pain. Yet as his illness grew worse and Bayan continued to evade the *tumens*, Manduul pulled further and further away from her.

"I will ride out and find him myself," Manduul growled. "Ready my horse."

Mandukhai's gaze shot up to him. "My love," she said in carefully soothing tones, "we need you here. You know the risks of riding out after him yourself."

Manduul stiffened and turned toward her with the slow grace of a wolf on the hunt. Her heart hammered under that icy gaze. As if to punctuate her statement, Manduul's legs nearly gave out beneath him. He stumbled back to his seat as a fit of coughing wracked his body.

Alayitung averted his gaze, pretending not to notice, but his eyes met Mandukhai's for just a moment. She saw the unspoken question, the doubt. Alayitung was in his late thirties, and a good man of Borjigin birth. Mandukhai had made a point of learning as much as she could about him these past months. His father had been part of Esen's Borjigin Butchering. Alayitung had been ill and missed the alleged celebration. When he recovered, he became part of the revolt against Esen, fighting with her own father. "I have a great deal of respect for your father," Alayitung had told her. "As I do for you."

Manduul's coughing fit carried on longer than any of the others as he gasped for breaths and spit blood into a cloth.

Mandukhai worried over Manduul's condition. She heard nothing from Unebolod. Had he abandoned her in her time of greatest need? A messenger brought her news from Unebolod that he promised to come to her. Yet nearly two months had passed before they received word that the Khorchin were on the move again. Why did he delay so long? She would need warriors to secure her place. She needed *him*.

Several painfully long minutes went by where the only sounds were of Manduul's ragged breaths and rattling coughs. When at last the fit passed, Manduul slumped in his seat, his eyes watering from the labor.

"Leave us," Manduul wheezed at Alayitung.

The stocky man gathered his stacks of reports and bowed. As he exited, Alayitung once more cast Manduul a worried glance. Surely he, of all people, knew that Manduul was dying. It would be hard to hide such a thing from a man who spent most of his day with the Khan.

Manduul breathed in and out with cautious, strenuous breaths. His chin dipped to his chest, and Mandukhai waited in silence. Flames from the copper pots flickered and kicked out puffs of smoke as they heated the space. The pine used in the pots emitted a woody fragrance that reminded Mandukhai of simpler days. She had been born a Lord's daughter, had married a Khan, and soon enough she would have to hold the nation together. How had this fallen on her shoulders? Mandukhai did not know if she could bear the responsibility. Yet what choice did she have?

"Have I made a terrible mistake?" he asked at last, his words so soft Mandukhai had to strain to hear them.

"You said so yourself, Manduul," Mandukhai responded, offering her best reassurance. "The law is the law. Bayan has broken it."

"And when he dies, and I die, the line of Genghis dies with us." Manduul rubbed at his forehead, making the sagging skin easily shift beneath the pressure and wrap around the tips of his fingers. "I have left nothing."

"Browbeating yourself will solve nothing," Mandukhai said. She yearned to ease some of his pain, but she knew his moods to be fickle. While today he might eagerly accept Siker's lost son as a beacon of hope, tomorrow he could send men to kill the child. She could not tell him.

Manduul rose to his feet, and the weakness that plagued him nearly forced him to the ground. Mandukhai rushed over to help him as he gripped the arm of the throne to keep from falling, but he waved her off.

"I can walk on my own, woman!" He pushed himself upright again and shuffled toward the exit.

Mandukhai followed behind him, ready to ignore his protests should he stumble again. If he wanted to be stubborn when they were alone, she would bear it; however, she would not stand by in sight of the men to allow them to see his weakness.

Mongols were used to moving in the winter, but snow fell in sheets so unnaturally thick that the deep drifts hindered the wheels of the carts. Unebolod ordered boys and men to clear paths, but the work was exhausting. Some men ended up with frostbite on their fingers that had to be healed; others fell ill from the flu. A few died.

With each obstacle and each death, Unebolod became more certain that the gods worked against him. Though he had tried to live his life with honor, he had clearly made some grave error that the High Heavens saw fit to punish him for.

Soke had urged making camp and resting. Unebolod had balked at the idea initially. Making camp could slow their progress even further, and there was every chance they could end up snowed in wherever they set up their gers. He had feared he would be stuck in snow forever while a new Great Khan was chosen in Karakorum without him.

Families stopped as he carried on. Unebolod did not mind at first. A few families would not hurt. But in a matter of weeks, he had left a trail of warriors he needed in Mongke Bulag and beyond.

Then the wheels of the carts cracked under the bitter conditions. He had no choice. Unebolod ordered the families to set up camp. The men and oxen needed rest. The horses had weakened.

Women and children busied themselves setting up camp as the men collected firewood. Finding enough dried dung in the winter would be difficult until they had established their camp.

Unebolod's servants had his ger constructed with the stove burning away the cold within an hour of stopping, thanks to Odgerel's calm, expert guidance. He stomped his boots in the doorway to shake off the snow. Heat from the stove quickly burned away the chill that had set into his bones. Unebolod slipped off his boots and marched toward the stove to warm his hands.

After their shared experiences with the plague, Unebolod and Odgerel had struck a natural, easy routine. She did not press her advances nearly as often and did her job with efficiency. Today, she had somehow turned dried strips of mutton into a savory stew by the time Soke knocked on Unebolod's door.

Unebolod welcomed his general into the ger, sharing his meal. The two settled into a comfortable silence as they ate. Soke's wives surely had prepared food for him—meals Unebolod often shared with Soke's family—but sometimes the two men needed to be away from Soke's wives and children.

Soke was the first to breach the stillness. "Unebolod, something is driving you onward at reckless speed. The men have been asking me questions I cannot answer. You know I will follow you into any fire, but it would help if I knew what that fire was before we reach it."

Asking his general to remain in the dark forever had never been a realistic expectation, and Unebolod knew it. Soke had followed him from Mongke Bulag to the Khorchin lands without question. His loyalty had never been in doubt. But more than a year had passed since they had left Mongke Bulag, and Unebolod had shared none of his motivations. If he could not trust Soke, whom could he trust?

"I know you have no love for the Golden Prince," Soke continued after a drink of *airag*. "And I don't disagree. But we are not hunting him for the Khan. The prince no longer needs support, and we are headed back to Mongke Bulag. I don't think I have ever questioned your motives before. But this reckless haste through the bones of winter worries me. Why are you in such a rush to return? What waits for us there?"

Unebolod leaned back against the thickly felted wall, cradling a skin of *airag*. His gaze flitted toward Odgerel as she cleaned. "You can go now, Odgerel. I will survive until morning."

Soke watched her with clear envy in his eyes as she bowed, slid into a thick layer of furs, and slipped out without allowing too much of the bitter cold outside to penetrate the ger. Soke released a sigh that gave away his admiration. "How can you resist that?" He shook his head and returned to attention. "Something about her feels familiar to me."

Unebolod grunted. He often had the same sensation, but now was not the time to discuss it.

"Soke, there is much I have not told you, and some I still cannot," Unebolod said. "Soon, you will know everything, but we must reach Mongke Bulag first." He glanced toward the door to be sure they were alone, then leaned toward the general. "You know Manduul has named me next after the prince."

Soke nodded.

"Before I left, Manduul gave me grave news. I trust you will not repeat a word of it. To do so would be an act of treason. Do you understand?"

Soke sobered and his muscles tensed with excitement. "I swear it."

The words still struggled to come forward; not because he did not want to speak them, but because he had guarded the secret for so long now that he found it difficult to even say. "He is dying."

Soke choked on his drink, thumping a fist against his chest to dislodge the *airag*. "What?"

"An illness that cannot be cured, he told me. He can't have much time left on this earth. I received a message from Mandukhai that they need us to return swiftly. Something is wrong, and I believe their lives are in danger." He carefully skirted the truth behind her urgency. Soke did not need to know of their relationship. He only needed to know that Unebolod was next in line.

"You believe someone else will try to steal the khanship," Soke said.

"And we both know who that will be." Unebolod grimaced, feeling the scar on his face burn at the prospect of meeting Bigirsen in battle once more. How he longed to stain his sword with that man's blood again.

Soke nearly spit in disgust before glancing at the floor of Unebolod's ger and thinking better of it.

"Help me smash Bigirsen's stranglehold on the tribes," Unebolod said with firm sincerity, "as my field commander."

Soke did not flinch. He reached out and clapped Unebolod on the shoulder. "As I have said, I will follow you into any fire."

Unebolod returned the gesture with a solemn nod. "Then may we both make it out the other side unburned."

MONGKE BULAG – MID-WINTER 1470

Yeke's ger had been dismantled months ago. Seeing the space there still surprised Mandukhai each day. When the ger had been taken down, the black ring of earth had remained dead through the late summer and fall, as if the ground itself had died with her. Now, in the bones of winter, snow covered the ring. Soon enough, spring would come, and the grass would bounce back, leaving behind no trace that a queen had once lived there.

Mandukhai gazed at the open sky where Yeke had lived as she turned on the worn path toward home. A bitter wind blew past, snapped at Mandukhai's fur-lined clothing, and stiffened her cheeks. The breeze seemed to draw Mandukhai around to the empty spaces where Bayan's and Unebolod's gers had been. It left a massive gap of open space in front of her own home that only reminded her of how alone she was. Unebolod's vacancy yanked at Mandukhai's heart. If the High Heavens blessed her at all, she would see his stern, scarred face soon.

Snow crunched beneath Mandukhai's boots as she turned toward her ger, head tucked down against the cold and arms deep in the sleeves of her fur-lined deel. The paths were worn from frequent use, but regular snowfall this winter had left a packed, slick layer of snow and ice between gers. She could almost sense the history of the capital by where those paths were deepest or smoothest, like the telltale signs of a battle by where the tracks moved and the bodies lay. Except this battle was political, and vacancies around the Khan's ger replaced the bodies. Were it not so cold, Mandukhai might have cried at the comparison.

Two mounts Mandukhai did not recognize nosed through the thick snow near her ger. Their hooves were hobbled to keep them from wandering. Hoping for another message from Unebolod, Mandukhai rushed to her door as quickly as she dared over the slick ground and pushed inside. In an instant, her hope vanished. Her heart fell into the pit of her stomach.

Esige clutched a small boy in an embrace as he cried. Mandukhai recognized him almost immediately. *Nemeku!*

Esige's own tears rolled down her cheeks, but she held her grief in as best she could to comfort Nemeku. A tall warrior stood beside the door with his head dipped as he wrung his fur hat in his hands. Mandukhai thought she remembered him from Borogchin's last visit to Mongke Bulag two years ago. Jangi.

Mandukhai's sudden appearance drew Esige's gaze. Grief and hate mingled in Esige's eyes as her jaw twitched. The hateful gaze burned at Mandukhai, but she knew it was not directed toward her. Esige loathed few with such burning passion, and this went far beyond anything Mandukhai had seen in her eyes before.

Where is Borogchin? Mandukhai thought, swallowing her grief and as she struggled to remain calm and push her own fury down. She already knew the answer.

Mandukhai turned to Jangi as she closed the door. "Tell me everything. Leave no details out."

Jangi nodded, and she could see just how weary he was by the way his entire body drooped, as if it took great effort to keep himself upright. How hard they must have ridden! Mandukhai hustled to make tea and offered the boy treats on a wooden plate, though he showed no interest in the food as he clung to Esige.

As Jangi relayed the tragic tale, Mandukhai listened in horrified silence. *Bayan had gone to Bigirsen for help? The boy is a fool!* Mandukhai thought bitterly, though she could only blame him for his part. Borogchin had been foolish enough to take him in and offer help when the *tumens* scoured the empire for him.

Mandukhai wished she could have been there in Borogchin's final moments to hear what she had to say to Bigirsen. She longed to see Bigirsen's face when Borogchin defied him! Borogchin had not shared everything with Mandukhai, but she heard enough to know that somehow Borogchin had undermined his authority among his own men and his other wives.

No doubt Borogchin had spent her last moments condemning him and promising his downfall. Mandukhai closed her eyes to picture the scene, but the grief spilled over. She pressed a hand to her mouth as a sob attempted to escape.

"He will come for Nemeku," Jangi said sadly, gazing at the boy as if he were already lost. "Perhaps without Borogchin's influence, Nemeku will be given to one of Bigirsen's other wives to raise."

Mandukhai's eyes snapped open, and she once more swallowed her grief. Yet as she opened her mouth to speak, Esige snarled out her own warning.

"If he tries to take this boy from us, I shall eat his flesh and drink his blood," Esige said, repeating the threat Jangi had said Bigirsen made toward Bayan. So much vehemence seeped from Esige's tone that Mandukhai did not doubt for a moment that she meant every breath. The hairs on Mandukhai's arms and neck arose from a chill.

"He is gathering his own strength," Jangi reported. "So he will not mount yet. If he wants his son back, he will send other men to retrieve him first."

Mandukhai understood. If they could hold Bigirsen off long enough, Nemeku would be under the protection of the next Great Khan—Unebolod. Bigirsen would have to start a war against Unebolod just to get his son. "We will be ready."

Esige sniffled and scrubbed a sleeve against her eyes.

"Thank you, Jangi," Mandukhai said. "You will be well rewarded for your loyalty. You are a guest in our camp for as long as you choose to stay."

"I will stay with Lord Nemeku as his personal guard, if it pleases you," Jangi said.

Mandukhai nodded. "Of course. Go now and get the rest you need to recover from the perils of your trip."

"Thank you, my Lady," Jangi said, bowing deeply. "Lady Borogchin was right about you."

Esige stroked Nemeku's bare scalp. He had stopped sobbing, but still clung to Esige as he slowly chewed one of the sweet curds. How would Manduul react when he found out Mandukhai protected Bigirsen's son? *I will appeal to his softer side*, Mandukhai decided. Manduul owed her for sending Borogchin into that horrible marriage. The princess's blood was on Manduul's hands. Protecting Nemeku was the least he could do to make up for it.

KHORLOD-KHARCHIN TERRITORY – GOBI DESERT EDGE – MID-WINTER 1470

Unebolod loathed winter more than ever before. He had never seen snows like this in all his years. Getei had warned him of a harsh winter, but how could so much snow fall from the sky? Where did it all come from? *Lord Tengri, I curse the High Heavens for this unnecessary delay.*

Every day, his men moved further out to find areas where the animals could forage.

Despite his best efforts to keep the people together, they began spreading further apart to move closer to wood and grazing spaces. Mongols were hardy people who knew how to survive harsh winters, but usually they could select their location and set up the camp to prepare before winter closed in around them.

Because of the excessive snows, no messengers would come his way unless they had urgent news. He prayed not to hear the bells of a messenger. Bells would bring with them news of Manduul's death. Nothing else would bring them out under such conditions. *Please let him stay alive a little longer*, he prayed.

As Unebolod returned to his ger after relieving himself, Getei caught up and followed him to his door.

"You cannot leave them," Getei said, as if reading Unebolod's mind.

Unebolod paused at the door, scowling and huddling tight against the bitter wind. "Keep your witchcraft to yourself."

Getei shook his head. His breath rolled out in clouds. "To all things, there is a purpose. You must have patience and trust the will of the gods."

Unebolod spit at the ground. "The gods can take their will and shove it up their asses." He threw open his door and stomped inside, slipping off his boots.

Getei slipped in behind him before Unebolod could close the door in his face. The shaman shook his head. "They beg your patience, my Lord." He closed the door behind him to ward off the winter wind.

"They can get in line," Unebolod snapped. He shook fresh snow off his fur cloak and tossed it over the chest beside the bed. "Everyone wants my patience, but I've had enough."

"There is a reason to all they do. I cannot tell you your destiny—"

"But you know it."

Getei did not confirm this. Nor did he deny it.

"Tell me, shaman, what reason did the gods have for the Borjigin Butchering, where my father and brothers were murdered?" Unebolod snapped. As he spoke each word, his rage mounted. "What excuse do the gods have for sending a plague into our camp that wiped out over *three thousand* of our people?" He stalked toward Getei, his shoulders tensing as if preparing to strike. "Or for creating such a vicious winter that more of the Khorchin people have died? What excuse do they have for taking the lives of my wife and sons?" He stopped toe-to-toe with Getei.

The shaman stood his ground without flinching.

Unebolod lowered his voice, growling out his final words as his muscles twitched and his breaths heaved. "Tell me why the gods saw fit to blow up my entire family and half of my tribe."

Getei raised his chin. "These things had to happen to get you where you need to be."

"Lies," Unebolod hissed. "Either the gods enjoy torturing me in the worst possible ways, which would make them cruel and unworthy of my worship ... or they do not exist at all."

Getei's eyes widened, and Unebolod took immense satisfaction from distressing the ever-calm shaman.

"Get out of my ger," Unebolod snapped, turning his back and storming toward his jug of *airag*. "You can travel to Mongke Bulag with us. But unless you have something useful to say, I don't want to see your face again."

The hinges creaked and a bitter wind blew in, matching Unebolod's sour mood.

"You will find your faith before this is over," Getei said.

Unebolod spun around, throwing his knife toward the door. Getei had already closed it behind him, and the blade thumped into the door, vibrating from the force.

Red rocky outcrops had fallen prey to winter just as surely as any other place in the Mongol empire. Bayan had stumbled across a small family early on his trek and waited until the camp was empty and the family left to complete their daily chores. Then he sneaked into their camp and grabbed furs to pad his clothing. The family likely had little to help them survive the winter, but he was an heir of Genghis. His need was greater. Bayan took as much as he dared from their food supply, but could find no spare arrows ready to use. Only a few amid creation.

This wasn't really stealing. If he survived, Bayan would become Great Khan and could seize whatever he wanted.

Just as silently as he had arrived, Bayan slipped out, careful to cover his tracks so they would not hunt him down when they returned.

Bayan had months to consider his options. Borogchin had seemed certain that, if he could just survive, Lords who still followed the old ways would support him as Great Khan once Manduul died. Becoming Great Khan was the only way Bayan could think he might survive. But where would he gather support? Bigirsen clearly wanted his head, and he had control of the southern and western tribes. Unebolod would want his head as well, and he had control of the eastern tribes. Bayan's best chance was among the Lords in the north who had fought with him and known him these past years. But as long as Manduul lived, Bayan could not go north.

And Issama ... they had been friends. Perhaps not terribly close, but Bayan had always trusted Issama. Now, under order of Manduul, Issama hunted him. Clearly, Bayan's trust had been misplaced. How could he ever contend with men like Bigirsen, Unebolod, Manduul, or Issama?

The Ming, he realized.

It was a stretch, he knew. But the Ming had tried to capture him multiple times, not kill him. Which meant they wanted him for something. Perhaps he could leverage that to get what he wanted. If they helped him take over the Mongol Nation, he could rule in alliance with them. The Mongols would not need to conquer the Ming, nor the other way around. And with the support of the emperor behind him, Bigirsen, Issama, Manduul, and Unebolod combined could not stand in his way. They would all have to die.

The thump of hooves crunching pebbles drew Bayan's attention. *I cannot be discovered. I have to hide.*

Bayan found a crevice in the red cliffs to hide in. His arrows had all been used to hunt food so many nights that the shafts had eventually broken under the strain. Only one remained.

As the rider approached his hiding place, Bayan took careful aim, drawing back with an inhale and slowly releasing the breath as he fired. The rider's mount reared as the arrow whistled near, and it struck the rider in the leg instead of the chest where Bayan had aimed. The impact had not unseated him. The rider raced toward Bayan's hiding spot—now revealed.

Bayan cursed and jumped onto Andayar's saddle, hooking his bow in a smooth motion and pulling his sword with the other hand. *Lord Tengri, share your fortune once more*, he thought.

The rider—a Uyghur man, judging by his clothing—raised his bow and fired at Bayan. He ducked low to Andayar's neck, causing a near miss. Battle had never been Bayan's gift, but he had been well-trained. And no one was as lucky as him. As the other man released a second arrow, Bayan seized his opening and yanked Andayar's reins to the left, causing the mare to jerk closer to the mount charging toward him. He needed the arrows and any other supplies this man had on him.

As the mounts crossed paths close to each other, the rider traded his bow for his sword, swinging at Bayan's neck. Bayan's heart hammered against his ribs. But he had prepared for the strike, as Berkedai had taught him. This would be a dangerous trick, and if his luck didn't hold out, he could end up trampled. But he had to unseat the scout.

With the reins now wrapped around his arm and his feet hooked in the stirrups, Bayan slid from the saddle dangerously close to the rider's mount. He needed the animal, and so he was careful to cut only the strap of the saddle, but his blade caught the back of the scout's heel as well, jarring Bayan's arm.

The scout's mount reared. The saddle slid loose. The scout slammed into the rocky ground as Andayar surged past him.

The muscles in Bayan's arms protested as he used all his strength to pull himself upright in the saddle once more. Bayan guided Andayar back around toward the scout, whose mount now raced away from the fray. The Uyghur scout staggered to his feet and screamed in pain, nearly crumbling again to the ground before he pressed all his weight into his uninjured leg.

Bayan grinned. He had not meant to hit the scout's heel, but clearly it benefited him. Andayar crashed into the Uyghur with the ease of a well-trained warhorse. The mare's hooves trampled his body. His legs were broken, shattered in several places. His chest compressed from the impact of Andayar's hooves. Yet somehow, the scout survived, feebly raising his sword in defiance as he lay on his back. His arm quivered violently under the weight.

Confident that the Uyghur could not escape now, Bayan reined in Andayar and jumped from the saddle. To his surprise, the scout dragged himself into a seated position. Bayan arced his sword toward the man's neck, but the scout blocked with enough force to make Bayan's arm tremble from the impact. *Where does he find such strength?*

The Uyghur's sword slid up, pushing Bayan's away. Before Bayan could recover, the man brought his fist crashing hard into Bayan's knee. Bayan pitched forward, hardly catching himself before his face slammed into the ground. As he pushed upright, a fist hammered into his ear, leaving him stunned and temporarily blinded by the pain and a ringing in his ears. The scout's sword trapped Bayan's own blade against the ground, twisted it around, and disarmed him. Then the scout rammed his first into Bayan's ribs.

Somehow, in a matter of seconds, this crippled, dying man had disarmed Bayan. The two wrestled on the frozen rocks and sand of the desert. *Lord Tengri, I cannot die here!*

The Uyghur, pinned beneath Bayan and unable to move him with his legs broken, yanked at Bayan's belt to hold him in place. Bayan pressed his advantage, pinning the scout beneath him so he couldn't even claw his way free. A fistfight he could handle.

The two exchanged hammering punches to the ribs. Bayan's chest ached, bruised from the vicious blows. But a wild rage took over. He heard the crunch of ribs, followed by the scout screaming in pain as the rib pierced his lungs. He gasped for breath. Bayan released a fierce scream as he grasped the scout's head, pounding it into the unforgiving rocks until the Uyghur's grip went slack. Bayan gasped for breath before climbing off the man.

This fight would cost Bayan dearly. His ribs were bruised, which would make riding painful. Rocks had gashed his arms during the scuffle, and his knuckles were bleeding. He needed time to heal, and the winter would not allow it. The searing pain in his chest made it hard to breathe as he staggered toward Andayar.

The moment Bayan reached for his saddle, a hand wrapped around his ankle and yanked him off his feet. Bayan hardly had time to grab his bow before his face smashed into the ground again. Blood poured from his nose, but the Uyghur did not relent. He clawed at Bayan's body and pulled him closer.

Bayan kicked out at his head, desperate to break free. The Uyghur jerked his head aside so Bayan's foot connected with his shoulder instead, dislodging it from the socket. The scout screamed.

The only weapon Bayan had in hand was the bow. In a panic, he lunged at the scout, wrapping the string around his throat. Sweat rolled down Bayan's temples and along his spine. His labored breathing was like a hammer against his ears. The two men wrestled. They rocked back and forth. They punched each other, fighting for control. Bayan wrapped his legs around the scout's body, trapping his arms against his sides. Increasing the tension, Bayan leaned back as far as he could. The string on the bow sawed back and forth against the scout's neck. The bow cracked and popped under the strain. Bayan's muscles strained against his layers of clothing. His face heated.

Bayan prayed for his luck to hold out as he summoned all of his strength, stretching back as far as his body could go. A scream ripped from his lungs.

At last, the scout's body went limp, followed by the gargles of death. Blood poured from his throat.

All the strength in Bayan's body evaporated in an instant. He released the ruined bow, kicked the dead man to the side, and collapsed back on the ground gasping for breath. His fingers burned. His ribs ached. The muscles in his arms and legs refused to respond to any of his demands for movement. He panted hard. *Thank you, Tengri, for the luck again.* He closed his eyes as the cold seeped through his fur and deel.

After several minutes, Bayan rolled to his knees and surveyed the surrounding rocks to be sure no one else approached. The Uyghur's mount had run off into the distance. He could not afford to chase it down. He needed to put as much space between himself and this body as possible before anyone came looking for it.

Bayan pushed himself to his feet and stumbled toward his sword, several feet away. He checked the Uyghur's belt for anything of use and found little more than a few coins. Limping, aching all over, Bayan retrieved Andayar and mounted. It was time to disappear. The Ming just might be his only chance, assuming he was correct and they wanted him alive. Bayan saw no other options. He could not live on the run forever.

CHAPTER THIRTY-ONE

Secrets and Desperation

Mandukhai's boots crunched as she shuffled toward Manduul's ger. The guards acknowledged her as they did every morning.

"I am told it was a quiet night," Boke said. His guard would have just begun. "He seems to have slept, though he had several fits of coughing in the night."

Ever since Bayan's betrayal, Boke had become overprotective of the Khan and Mandukhai, and much serious about his responsibilities. Boke demanded absolute discipline from every man under his command.

Mandukhai gave Boke her thanks as she ducked through the door.

The ger reeked of sweat and urine. The stench made Mandukhai gag as she entered. Manduul lay on the bed as he did every morning, but Mandukhai noticed the feverish sweat covering his body. Her heart leaped into her throat, and she ducked her head back outside. "Get me Lady Esige and Khosoichi immediately."

Boke frowned deeply, but he sensed her urgency and sent the other guard running with a clipped command. He peered past Mandukhai into the ger, but made no move to push his way in.

Manduul had wanted no one to know he was dying, even if everyone suspected as much by now. Mandukhai had not argued his point. Despite Manduul's urgent need for secrecy—a secret he did not well hide—Mandukhai understood she would need support as Manduul grew weaker. She had shared Manduul's fate with Boke weeks ago, only after he had given an oath of secrecy.

The Lords could suspect Manduul of being ill all they wanted. If they knew the truth, that would be something else completely. If Manduul confirmed his impending death, the Lords could turn against him. Mandukhai believed she could sway a few of them when the time came. Togochi. Alayitung, Unige. Those three, at least, respected her. The rest, she could not be certain of.

"Is he—?" Boke's voice cut off as he glanced suspiciously around them.

"Not yet." Mandukhai reached around the door and handed Boke a bucket. "I need clean snow."

Boke hesitated so long Mandukhai thought he would refuse. Finally, he took the bucket and ducked away to do as she ordered.

Mandukhai rushed to Manduul's unconscious body and pressed a hand against his chest. It still rose and fell, but his breathing was far shallower than it had ever been before. She wrinkled her nose as she realized the stench of urine came from his bed and clothes. Manduul had not gotten up to relieve himself.

Boke entered with the bucket, setting it on the stove to melt. The two of them set to work stripping Manduul down and removing the soiled linens, replacing everything with fresh cloth. By the time they had finished, the snow had fully melted. Mandukhai set the bucket on the floor to keep the water from getting hot, then she soaked a cloth in the still-cold water and pressed it to his neck and forehead. The fever made his skin burn to touch.

"Boke, be sure no one enters except Esige and Khosoichi," Mandukhai commanded. "If anyone asks, the Khan and I are ... busy."

Boke bowed and swiftly ducked out the door.

Esige passed him outside the door, casting a curious glance at him before entering. She frowned when she saw the state of her uncle, openly gagging on the stench inside. "Gross."

"He lives, Esige," Mandukhai said, "but he clings to life by a hair. We need to bring down his fever."

For a moment, Esige stood stiffly, scowling at Manduul. At last, she said, "This is the way of things. Let him pass."

"Fool!" Mandukhai hissed over her shoulder. "Do you not understand yet, Esige? If he dies before Unebolod returns with his men, Bigirsen could beat him to Karakorum. You will be given away. I will be forced into Bigirsen's bed or see his sword at my neck. We do not fight for his life. We fight for our own. Now help me!"

Esige paled, but the confession brought the girl to her senses. She rushed outside to collect more snow, which they used to pack around the sides of his body to help bring down the fever. *Don't die on me yet, you great bumbling elephant*, Mandukhai thought desperately.

By the time Khosoichi entered the ger, Manduul lay in bed, surrounded by packed snow. Mandukhai sat on a chair beside the bed, continuously pressing a cold cloth to his forehead to attempt reducing his temperature.

The shaman nudged his way past Esige—who had taken on the task of gathering all the clean cloth she could find in the ger. The wrinkles on Khosoichi's face creased as he frowned. He pressed an ear to Manduul's bare chest. The two women waited silently.

Khosoichi sighed as he stood. "The blood has entered his lungs."

"He cannot die, shaman," Mandukhai said with conviction. "So tell me, what can we do to remove the blood?"

He shook his head and stepped back. "Only a blood sacrifice will appease the gods."

Mandukhai stood and brushed the wrinkles from her deel, then wiped sweat from her forehead as she spoke. "Like he did for me. How many horses will it require?"

Khosoichi's shoulders drooped, and his gaze fell on Manduul. "You misunderstand, Lady Mandukhai. A thousand pure white mares would not save him. This kind of offering to the gods requires blood of the mother or bone of the father. He has neither of these, except ..." His gaze drifted to Esige.

The girl stiffened under the shaman's pointed gaze, and the implication was clear enough. Esige was the only living blood relative Manduul had left. With Bayan on the run and Borogchin dead already, Esige was all that remained. The very idea of sacrificing Esige to give Manduul a few more months to live made Mandukhai want to vomit. Mandukhai straightened and placed a reassuring hand on Esige's shoulder.

"That is not an option," Mandukhai said firmly. "He will still die soon enough, even with such a sacrifice. I will not trade her life for a few more moments of his."

Esige stared at Manduul, dazed. She would agree with Mandukhai. There was no way the girl would ever consider Manduul worthy of her own sacrifice. Esige bore very little genuine affection for Manduul any longer—not since he had given Borogchin to Bigirsen. She shared her private thoughts on her uncle with Mandukhai freely over the years. The way Esige's thin brows curled toward each other showed her distaste clearly to

Mandukhai. She could almost hear Esige's terse response to the suggestion in her own mind. Something along the lines of, "I would rather eat a rug." Or perhaps, "I would rather give birth to a yak."

Esige pressed her lips together in a thin line. The hate and anger she harbored toward Manduul these past five years were clearly on display. Then Esige pulled in a deep breath through her nose, releasing it just as slowly.

"He will not survive the day if we do not begin soon," Khosoichi said.

Esige pressed her trembling hands against her stomach. Her skin paled considerably.

"It's out of the question," Mandukhai snapped.

Esige's gaze became almost fevered. Her jaw clenched tight as every muscle in her body went rigid. Something in the girl changed at that moment. A stony resolve.

"No!" Mandukhai shouted. She recognized that look, having seen that precise determination on Unebolod's face a thousand times.

Esige raised her chin, her gaze drawn to something beyond Manduul. "I'll do it," she said, her voice devoid of emotion.

"Absolutely not!"

Esige turned slowly, as if her body moved through water, and she met Mandukhai's gaze with her own empty stare. "He is Great Khan. Offering such a sacrifice for a Khan is my duty."

Mandukhai slapped Esige. A red mark sprang to life on the girl's cheek.

Esige blinked in shock as tears welled in her eyes. She pressed her hand to her cheek and stared at Mandukhai with wide eyes.

Mandukhai seized Esige's shoulders. "You listen to me. You are my ward, and I will *not* give your life for an old man doomed to die no matter what we do. I forbid it!"

"You allowed Borogchin such a choice," Esige said flatly.

"Her fate was not set in stone! This is not a choice."

"My life could save not just his, but yours."

Mandukhai shook Esige's shoulders. "Listen to me, Esige. Doing this will save nothing. If anything, it will kill a piece of me. I need you after he dies. Who else can I trust?" She pulled Esige into a hug and held the girl close. "I can survive his death. I cannot survive yours. Do you understand me? His day has been coming for a long time. Sacrificing your life will not change that."

Esige remained stiff in her arms a moment longer, then her body sagged against Mandukhai. Esige pressed her face into Mandukhai's shoulder. Her entire body trembled with relief.

Khosoichi had tended to Manduul in a series of pointless tasks to give the two of them a bit of privacy. As they pulled apart, he rose and bowed his head to Mandukhai.

"Prepare yourself, my Ladies," he said. "I have a tonic that will wake him for a time, but when he sleeps again, he will not wake."

Mandukhai nodded. "Prepare your tonic. We will be ready."

Khosoichi removed several pouches from the layers of his robes and set to work mixing the contents.

As he toiled, Mandukhai called Boke into the ger. He gave commands to the two men outside the door with him and ducked in. Mandukhai closed the door behind him. Boke watched the shaman with a knowing look on his face.

"It is time, then," Boke said.

"Almost." Mandukhai moved to stand between Boke and Khosoichi, forcing the guard to meet her gaze. "The rest of this day will be critical, Boke, and I need your help to see us through. No one, not even Togochi, knows for certain what is happening to the Great Khan, even if everyone knows is ill."

Boke started, clearly alarmed that Mandukhai knew the entire capital knew of the Khan's illness.

"This news must stay quiet for as long as we can manage," Mandukhai continued. "But I cannot do this alone."

"How can I serve the house of my Khan?" Boke asked without a moment of hesitation.

Mandukhai released a shaky breath as a faint smile spread across her face. For the next few minutes, she gave her commands. The box. The Lord. The riders. The guards. Boke questioned nothing. When she finished, he moved with urgency to do as instructed, ducking out of the ger and barking orders at his men.

100 MILES NORTH OF HAMI – LATE WINTER 1470

Issama waited outside Bigirsen's ger for him to return from a hunting trip. Bayan's trail had led Issama's men to Bigirsen's camp, and Issama wished deep in his bones that Bigirsen had gone against Manduul's command to capture or kill the prince. If Bigirsen acted against the Khan, Issama could kill him without danger of repercussions. A few of Issama's men had casually searched Bigirsen's camps for the prince as Issama waited. They came up with nothing. If Bigirsen hid the prince somewhere, he did it well.

As he waited and the day wore on, Issama asked one of Bigirsen's wives about Borogchin, saying that he wanted to catch up with her. The woman simply paled and ducked her head as she politely made an excuse to leave. He found the response curious. No one would speak of Lady Borogchin.

Shortly before sunset, Bigirsen rode back into camp, straight to where Issama waited on a stack of saddles outside a ger. In their time apart, Bigirsen had visibly aged. His face was more weathered and revealed deep crow's feet; his hair had grayed along the temples with strands of silver in his braids like thick ribbons. Despite the superficial signs of aging, Bigirsen leaped from his saddle with an effortless grace that revealed his still-muscular form. Age had not diminished his ability to strike like a viper.

"I heard you were in the area, Issama," Bigirsen said as he handed his reins to a servant. "I assume you are here because of the prince?"

With the power of the Khan behind him, Issama recognized his opportunity to press Bigirsen. It sent a surge of excitement through Issama's body. "His trail led us here, yet we can find nothing else. Where is he, Bigirsen?"

As Bigirsen approached, his muscles tensed. His arms flexed in anger, straining the layers of fur. "In the desert, I assume. Hopefully dead by now."

"You allowed him to escape?"

Bigirsen's lips thinned as he scowled at Issama. "*Allowed*? He snuck into my camp when I was away, corrupted my wife's mind against me, and somehow sneaked back out of my camp with twenty spies watching the escape routes." Bigirsen stalked closer until he was nearly toe-to-toe with Issama. Fire of rage burning in his eyes nearly made Issama flinch away. "I wanted this boy dead, Issama, not on the run. You have failed me."

Though Bigirsen had spoken in a whisper, men and women all around watched them with apparent apprehension. They knew something he did not.

Issama lowered his own voice. "You asked me to drive a wedge between them. I did as you commanded."

"And it cost me a daughter, a wife, *and* a son." Bigirsen remained still a moment longer, challenging Issama to say or do anything against him. His cheek twitched into a half sneer as he stepped around Issama into his ger. "Get in here, Issama!"

A son? What happened to Borogchin and Nemeku?

Despite Issama's confidence, the fury that burned in Bigirsen's voice rattled him. He swallowed a lump that lodged in his throat and ducked into the ger.

"Everyone out!" Bigirsen snapped at the children and first wife.

She scowled at Bigirsen but ushered the children out the door without comment. Issama bowed politely to her as she passed. Then he took a seat on the bench.

"How did this cost you a wife and son?" Issama asked. Bigirsen didn't have to answer. Issama could surmise well enough what had happened. Bigirsen must have killed them for helping Bayan.

"That runt crept into my camp, into my own ger!" Bigirsen's face turned redder as he continued. "His mare was hobbled outside, and still she somehow hid him from me and lied right to my face. I knew he was here, hiding somewhere. So I left a trap for him before the wolf dawn. I took my men and said I was hunting. I left twenty men watching the camp. But he is slippery. Borogchin helped him creep right past my guards and my spies. Right out into the desert! Then—then!" Bigirsen paced as his anger picked up speed. "Then she sent my son—my *son*!—away with one of my own guards. I can guess where they went!"

Bigirsen's boots thumped against the rugs with surprising thunder. Issama had never seen Bigirsen in such a state. The pure fury rolled off Bigirsen's taut shoulders in suffocating waves. Issama did not dare speak until the rage passed. Experience had taught him to tread carefully when Bigirsen was in this sort of mood.

"Mandukhai." Bigirsen spit the name out like rotten meat. "That woman is like an infection under the skin that you just can't cut out. But I *will* cut her out if I have to dig down to the bone."

The confession sent a jolt through Issama. If Bigirsen attempted to kill the Khan's wife without just cause, he would start a war. Manduul might be dying, but that did not mean he was incapable of throwing all of his men at Bigirsen. *I have those men*, Issama realized. Manduul had given Issama all but the Khorlod *tumen* and a handful of Borjigin.

"Borogchin could have been such an obedient wife if it were not for Mandukhai," Bigirsen continued, oblivious to Issama's shock. "But that woman infected Borogchin's mind against me. Do you know what my wife said to me after she helped that runt escape my camp and sent away my son?" Bigirsen stopped pacing. The way he hunched bore so much hate and vehemence Issama recoiled before he could stop himself. "She asked me if *she* should show such jealousy toward *my* friendly relatives, as if that boy was guilty of nothing at all. She said she sent him home safely, an obvious lie right in my face again, and demanded to know why I wanted to harm her cousin when she had never harmed my family, as if he were nothing more than an innocent boy."

"So you killed her," Issama said, careful not to infuriate Bigirsen further with his tone.

Bigirsen quivered as he clenched his hands into fists. "Did you hear nothing? She helped him escape in open defiance of the Khan, of *me*! And as we bound her body to wrap in rugs for her execution, she stared straight at me in impudence." He paused, shuddering. "I will never forget what she said. The words are etched in my mind and my heart forever. She said, 'The mouse has become the elephant. The lion has become the sheep, and soon your fate will herd you toward your own demise at the hands of the dragon.'"

Bigirsen's nostrils flared. His neck became corded with tension. He reminded Issama of a barrel of gunpowder, ready to explode the moment the fuse ran too short. *He is destroying himself in this rage*, Issama thought. It filled him with some satisfaction, but he wanted to be nowhere nearby when Bigirsen finally exploded. He knew he had to defuse the situation before Bigirsen lost control.

Too bad I did not know Borogchin worked to undermine Bigirsen in his own camp, Issama thought. *She would have made a great ally.* He lamented the missed opportunity.

Issama offered a deep sigh and nodded, as if in complete sympathy. "The words of a mad and desperate woman," he said carefully. "She no doubt wanted to see you lose control like this, Bigirsen. If you are consumed with hate and rage, you cannot focus on the important tasks. Do not let her last words keep you from thinking clearly."

"You didn't see her face, Issama," Bigirsen growled. "It was not a ploy to unravel me. She meant every breath more surely than I have ever seen her mean anything before."

On a slim hope that Bigirsen would not lash out at him, Issama slowly drew himself up to his feet and edged closer. "At least now we know the truth. She was never loyal to you, Bigirsen. You mentioned that before she married you, she was to be married to Unebolod, and that she was friends with Mandukhai. Her loyalty was always with them. And while that does not lessen her betrayal toward you, she still gave you one essential tool."

Bigirsen's shoulders heaved with each breath, but he waited patiently for Issama to finish.

"Nemeku."

"Mandukhai will not give my son back without a fight," Bigirsen said.

"Let her keep him for now," Issama said. Bigirsen growled, but Issama pressed on quickly. "Focus on consolidating your power. Between the two of us, we control nearly two-thirds of the Mongol *tumens*. She cannot stand up against such numbers."

"Nemeku is of Borjigin flesh," Bigirsen said. "Mandukhai will corrupt his mind just as she did to Borogchin."

"We both know that a boy's loyalties will always fall to his father. Nemeku is *your* son. Do you truly think she can so easily manipulate him? Nemeku worships you."

All the tension building in Bigirsen slowly seeped out. Issama released a sigh of relief.

Bigirsen stared at him, and Issama could see the calculation working in the other man's gaze until, at last, he slapped a hand on Issama's shoulder and gave it a friendly squeeze.

"I have missed you," Bigirsen said, then he glanced toward the door. "Very well. Your men will join me in the south. We will gather our forces, consolidate our power, and crush Ming resistance. Then, we will turn our newfound power on Mongke Bulag while Manduul Khan is weak. Together."

Issama blinked. "What?" This had not been part of his plan.

"I need more men against the Ming, and you have brought thousands just when I needed them most."

"I am to hunt down the prince. If he somehow survives the Gobi, he could still ruin everything for us."

Bigirsen grimaced. "The Gobi is not such a large place that you need so many men to track one boy. Send out two thousand of your best trackers with supplies for the desert and orders to kill the prince on sight. The rest will come with me."

"But—"

Bigirsen clenched his fists and leaned closer. "You may have been given more power since leaving me three years ago, Issama, but you still serve *me*. I am still the Khan's Vice Regent, which makes me your overlord, and you know what I do to those who disobey my commands."

Issama dipped his head. What could he say to that? Bigirsen could have him killed before Issama took his men away from here. "At least let me send word to the families we left in Mongke Bulag," Issama said. "I would like my wives along. A campaign like this is long, and the nights are cold."

Despite all of his careful planning, Issama had no choice but to follow Bigirsen. That did not mean his plans had to be undone. However, he could not allow the Oirat to strike at Mongke Bulag without him. He would need to send word not only to the Uyghur families in Mongke Bulag, but also to Paisahan, the Oirat khan.

The patches of snow across the rocky desert offered water. Bayan's supply of meat and curd had run out the day before. Hunger gnawed at his gut like an animal attempting to escape. Without arrows, he could not hunt. Andayar needed to feed as well.

More than once, he and Andayar had been forced to flee deeper into the desert as the thunder of an oncoming army approached. But the sound seemed to come from every direction. The hammer of thousands of hooves would begin, accompanied by the calls of men with the thrill of the chase. But just as suddenly as the sound would rise, it would vanish without a trace, leaving Bayan in a panicked, cold sweat, as if some demon of the desert tortured him.

The grass was sparse, but Andayar used her hooves to dig it up—like any hardy Mongol horse. But the food was not always available, and he knew she had gone weak. Bayan had stopped nicking her for drinks of blood days ago when he worried about her own strength being depleted. He rode and walked in turns to give her rest, but it was not enough to fill her stomach.

If Andayar died, Bayan would die soon after. She was essential to his ability to make it safely through Ordos territory to the Ming border.

Even the days were bitterly cold. Bayan kept moving to keep his circulation going, but the nights when he rested brought the temperature to frigid. He huddled as close to Andayar as he could to use her body heat to help keep himself from freezing. The blanket beneath the saddle did little to stave off the chill, but he removed it each night to cover both of them as best he could.

Starting a fire grew more tempting with each day that passed, but Bayan knew that Issama's men would spot the smoke and close in on him as he slept. He would rather risk freezing. Bayan had not decided if he preferred the sweltering heat of summer or the freezing cold winter in the desert.

As he passed close to another dune, Bayan cried out in relief to see patches of grass peeking out of the unforgiving ground. A small oasis nestled between the dunes, offering a narrow strip of grass and a frozen stream. Bayan used his sword to chip away the top layer of ice and open a hole for them both to drink. By the time he completed the work, his hands ached from the cold until they grew numb. He dipped his hands into the water, lifting it to his mouth. As he took that first drink, Bayan choked.

Sputtering and spitting and coughing, he blinked at his hands. Fine grains of sand ran through the gaps between his fingers. A sob lodged in his throat as the brutal truth hit him. The frozen oasis was not real. He had dug a hole in the sand.

Defeated by the Gobi, Bayan pulled his furs tighter around his body and lay on the cold ground. Misery gripped him tight, grasping his heart and squeezing. He cried—a pitiful sound like a dying animal—but no tears would fall. *Lord Tengri, please, I beg you, save me. Share your fortune so I don't die here in the desert alone.*

As he lay in a ball on the ground, Bayan drifted off to sleep. Andayar's whinny startled him awake again. He squinted at the sky as the sun dipped toward the dunes to the west. Bayan moved slower than he would have liked to grab the reins before she ran off.

As he gazed west, she danced away, bobbing her head as if trying to yank the reins free. Again he squinted, this time searching the nearby horizon for any sign of attack or movement. And then he heard the hooves again. Thousands of them converging on him. His heart leaped into his throat and he surged into action.

Bayan climbed into the saddle. Andayar sidestepped, but he guided her slowly a few feet back. Unable to pinpoint the direction of the attack, he kicked her forward, yanking the reins to bring her straight east. She gave no protest as she lurched into action.

The moment Andayar's hooves hit the dune, her steps slowed. He guided her as quickly as he dared up the shifting mound. A slip could ruin her leg, and he would have no choice but to face down the men pursuing him.

Bayan's stomach turned to stone. Despite the cold, sweat beaded on his forehead and back. The muscles in his entire body tensed as if prepared for Andayar's eventual fall. Time seemed to move far too quickly as his heart pounded near the point of explosion in his chest. Andayar snorted from exertion, stumbling when the sand shifted beneath her hooves, but she did not fall.

In the distance, waving lines of shadowy movement drew his attention from the north. A dozen horsemen. Maybe more. And they closed in fast.

Bayan blinked sweat from his eyes, squeezing them shut momentarily. The sweat dripped into his eyes, stinging them with sand. He cursed and scrubbed his dirty sleeve across his face.

His breath caught as a rider raced dangerously toward him. Without thinking, he yanked the reins to avoid the collision. Andayar protested, squealing at him as she stumbled. Bayan drew his sword as the attacker's wavering sword pierced the sky. When he swung, the movement threw Andayar off her delicate balance and the two fell sideways. His sword sliced through air.

Bayan's back slammed into the ground. Andayar landed on the edge of his leg. Bayan cried out as the weight sent a surge of pain up his spine. *This is the end*, he thought as a desperate cry ripped out of him. *I will die here in the desert alone.*

Knowing his attacker had plenty of time to close in during his fall, Bayan sat upright, swinging his sword wildly to force the other man away. He breathed shallow breaths, scanning the horizon in all directions. Sweat made sand stick to his hands, neck, and face.

But no one was there.

Focusing on his breathing, Bayan listened for the thunder of approaching hooves he had heard before. The only sounds he heard came from his ragged breathing, shifting sand beneath Andayar's movements, and his own thundering heart.

Where did they go? he wondered, holding the sword upright, prepared for another attack. His arms quivered violently.

Between the panic increasing his heart rate, his hunger, and his thirst, Bayan grew dizzy. He gasped to calm himself, but it did no good. Movement drew his blurry vision to his side as Andayar rolled to her feet and began moving down the dune away from him. He closed his eyes and laid back on the sand.

What just happened?

He would rest here, just for a moment, to recover. *Was that my luck saving me, or a figment of my imagination?* he wondered.

Bayan had never felt so alone in the world.

Hot pain blazed in Bayan's leg, snapping him awake. He shielded his eyes from the blinding sun with his arm. Something moved over his leg, massaging it with hard movements. Bayan gasped, his breath catching in his throat as he tried shifting away.

"Calm down, you will live," a man said.

Bayan squinted to clear his blurry vision.

A young man roughly his own age crouched on the ground beside him. The cut of his clothes was simple. A herder, perhaps. Bayan had a hard time discerning the man's tribe. Uyghur, perhaps. Or Ordos.

"You clearly are lost, my friend," the man said.

Bayan gulped down air, swallowing a scream as the man massaged something into his leg. Bayan glanced at the man's side and saw the salve container sitting in a nest of bandages.

"Where are you headed?" the man asked.

Bayan licked his dry lips and noticed Andayar tied to this man's mount. "South."

"You were going the wrong way then," the man said, smirking.

Bayan grimaced at the joke, finding no amusement at this moment. For a moment, Bayan wondered if this man was real.

"You are in a dangerous place here," the man explained, focused on his task. "The Singings Sands claim the lives of men without mercy."

Is that where I am? Bayan had heard of this place. The most dangerous part of the desert. Men ran toward the sound of an army with hope of rescue or fled the sound of oncoming hooves in a panic, as he did, and would end up swallowed by the devil in of the desert. Never seen again.

Does he know who I am? Perhaps the man healed the scratches on Bayan's leg so he could collect a bounty on Bayan's head. How much would Manduul consider him to be worth alive over dead? The man didn't look at him as he continued rubbing in the salve.

I am so tired of being alone. I need help, and he clearly knows his way. Bayan licked his dry lips to add moisture, but it did little more than crack them open.

"I need a guide," Bayan said, hoping that this man didn't know who he was.

"Obviously."

"Just as far as the southern edge of the Gobi. I can pay." He pulled a pouch of silver coins from inside his deel. The last of his coins. "This is all yours if you can get me there."

"What's stopping me from killing you and just taking the coins?" He didn't look up from his focused work.

High Heavens let my luck hold out. Let me be right about him, at least for now. Bayan knew this could be his only chance. "If you wanted to kill me, you wouldn't waste your supplies fixing my leg."

The man snorted and began wrapping the bandage painfully tight around Bayan's leg. Once it was done, he stood and nodded. "Well then, if we are to be companions for a time, we should know each other by name. Mine is Dashai."

Bayan struggled to maintain a stony face. Dashai's name was like a herald. The name meant good fortune, and he certainly felt a strong share of it. If Dashai had not found him, Bayan probably would have died in the Singing Sands like so many others.

"Enkh," Bayan said, giving the name of his long-dead servant.

Dashai examined Bayan's dirty but fine silks and the golden belt at his waist. If he knew who Bayan was, he gave no indication. He also didn't question the obvious lie. "Well, Enkh, you carry a lot of coins for someone lost in the desert." Dashai untied Andayar's reins and offered them over. "I can take you south, but you need to rest that leg. And we need more supplies. We should start a fire for the night. It will freeze soon."

"No fires," Bayan said with so much intensity even he heard the panic in his tone.

"Why not? Without a fire we will freeze out here."

Bayan accepted his reins and limped urgently toward Dashai. "No fires. No others. Just you."

"Okay." Dashai frowned uncertainly. "But we still will need supplies, and they don't come from nowhere. We can burrow against a dune to block out the wind, at least, and rest for the night. Tomorrow morning, I will go get supplies. My family is close to here."

Bayan nodded in agreement.

"I don't know your business, nor do I care, but if you want my help, you will have to trust me. Hand over the coins, and I'll use them to get what we need."

Bayan chewed his lip. Refusing would leave him stranded in the desert to die. With a grimace and wince, he tossed the coin pouch to Dashai and waved toward the dunes. "Lead the way then, Dashai."

Bayan slid his sword into his belt. He would have to keep it close. Dashai could still choose to turn him in and collect a bounty.

As they set up camp for the night against the dune, Bayan kept a distance between the two of them, using the horses as a barrier. He hated not trusting the man who helped him. And he needed a friend in this horrible fate.

Perhaps, if Dashai didn't kill him in his sleep, if he helped Bayan survive the desert, as well as the men hunting him, Bayan would have a new brother to trust.

Lord Tengri, please don't make my faith misplaced. His luck had to hold out a little longer.

But he would still have to sleep with one eye open.

CHAPTER THIRTY-TWO

Fallen Wolf, Rising Dragon

Heat rolled off Manduul's body in waves as the shaman tipped the Khan's head back, pried open his mouth, and poured in the tonic. Mandukhai waited on a wooden chair beside Manduul. The next few hours would be critical to the transition, and if Mandukhai failed to align even one necessary piece on this board, all would fall apart.

Esige had wanted to remain with Mandukhai, but Mandukhai worried about Nemeku being left in other hands. Mandukhai did not know who would be loyal to Bigirsen during this transition of power, and she would not risk losing the boy. Even in Jaghan's care, Nemeku remained at risk. She needed Esige to stay with Nemeku—the girl knew how to fight, and no one would fight harder to protect Nemeku than Esige. She had not been pleased with being dismissed from the Khan's ger.

Mandukhai hadn't had the chance to tell Manduul about Nemeku's arrival. Now she never would.

Boke had organized men around Manduul's ger according to Mandukhai's orders—only those he trusted most—then left to collect Togochi. Mandukhai would need one of the Lords to bear witness to Manduul's last moments, besides just herself and Khosoichi. Soon, Togochi would arrive.

Mandukhai did not want to share this news with anyone else, but she would need support to smooth out the transition. Togochi was loyal to Manduul and highly ranked among the Mongol Lords. Between Boke's respected position among the warriors and Togochi's rank over most of the Lords, Mandukhai would gain the deference of the guards, warriors, and ruling class. Or so she hoped.

Khosoichi melted into the background of the ger once he administered the tonic to Manduul. He would be there to handle the unexpected crisis with Manduul's condition, and his spiritual position would be necessary once Manduul was dead.

Mandukhai reflected on her marriage to Manduul as she waited for the others to arrive—or for Manduul to wake. Their marriage to Manduul had been full of trials. His abuse and rape in the early days of their union had blackened her heart against him in ways that she had never forgiven or forgotten. It became a hard-fought struggle for control that transformed into mutual respect.

Yet despite the mutual respect, Mandukhai's heart had never belonged to him. It never could. She still loved Unebolod more than her words could ever express. Manduul's passing would deliver the opportunity for her finally to be with the man she had wanted for nearly six years. At long last, she and Unebolod could mourn the loss of their child together. Mandukhai closed her eyes as the pain from that loss scored her heart once more. It had branded her heart, and in dire, lonely moments, the wounds from that brand opened once more.

Manduul rasped out a word she could only guess was her name, drawing her back to the present. Mandukhai pressed a cold, damp cloth to his burning forehead. "I am here."

His eyes fluttered open with a great struggle. "It is a bad thing ..." Manduul rasped, then licked his dry lips. Mandukhai wet them with another moist cloth. "How I have lived ..."

Each word and breath that slipped past his lips rattled in a way that sounded painful. Mandukhai made a soothing sound as she pressed on the cloth.

"Esige," Manduul said.

"She is not here, husband," Mandukhai said in a soothing voice.

Each word he spoke pulled from him in a struggle to share his last regrets. "Tell her I am sorry. I made a grave error in judgment. Send for her sister. Bring her back."

Mandukhai hushed him. "Khans do not apologize. Borogchin's spirit is strong. She will be with us soon enough." In these last moments, she did not have the heart to share Borogchin's fate. Manduul had suffered enough, and he would meet Borogchin in the Eternal Blue Sky.

Mandukhai's chest tightened. She bit her lip, averting her gaze. Manduul noticed her reaction and mistook it for grief for him. He slid his trembling, clammy hand over hers.

"My dearest wife," Manduul said. Each word labored his struggling body and rasping lungs. "Your steady, firm hand has guided me with wisdom these years. And what did I give you? Pain. My deepest regret is how I hurt you."

Tears welled in Mandukhai's eyes. Did he truly mean that? Could she forgive him now, in death, for what he did to her? A lump swelled in her throat.

"I have failed you," Manduul said, then coughed, making Mandukhai worry he would not remain conscious much longer. The way Manduul's eyes grew distant only confirmed the truth. "I have left you with nothing but a mess of my own making." He blinked slowly. "Perhaps I should call him back."

Mandukhai did not need to ask who Manduul meant. Only Bayan had drawn such despair from him.

"You have not left me with nothing, my love," Mandukhai said gently. "You leave the Nation in my care until a new Great Khan is chosen, and I will honor you by guiding our Nation toward a brighter future. I give my word."

So much would fall into her hands soon, and Mandukhai doubted she could handle it. How could she, a woman, stand against the power of the Mongol Lords? They could crush her beneath their power. Only two other women had been given so much power in the entire history of their nation—and only one had ruled until her son became Great Khan. Mandukhai was uncertain she had power or influence like Ogedei Khan's wife, Toregene, who ruled the Mongol Lords for five years. Nor did she have the same intelligence as Kublai Khan's mother, Sorkhogtani. While she had prepared for Manduul's death since their marriage, Mandukhai trembled in fear for what was to come.

Manduul's head rolled to the side, and his gaze slid past her. "Bolkhu ..."

The way he spoke Bayan's given name made Mandukhai glance over her shoulder as if the prince stood behind her. She immediately felt foolish for even looking. Had delirium set in?

When she turned her attention back to Manduul, the tears that rolled down his temples surprised her. It made her heart ache for him.

Bayan had been the son Manduul had never had, and she knew the betrayal had broken what little strength remained in Manduul's already damaged body. Bargaining had followed the initial shock and denial of the truth, offering Bayan the opportunity to prove the accusations wrong. But the moment Togochi had returned and given his report to Manduul, that last lingering bit of hope burned away into anger that carried on for weeks, followed by intense waves of anger and depression. And in these last weeks, Manduul had simply given up.

"It's not ..." Manduul gasped for air. "Not too late. He is out there. Bring him home."

No. Mandukhai thought. She could not bring him home. If Bayan returned, he would take the khanship and her, and she would once again be denied her heart's deepest desire.

"You cannot undo this, Manduul," she said tenderly. "To cancel out an act of treason is to open the gates of destruction. The Nation will fall apart without order."

Manduul's lip quivered. He squeezed his eyes closed, which forced more tears to race down his temples. "I failed everyone. You. Esige. Borogchin. Unebolod. Bolkhu."

The door opened. Boke and Togochi stepped in and closed the door behind them. Both men froze in shock when they noticed Manduul's tears.

Togochi gaped at Manduul's frail condition, then edged closer to the bed as Boke took up a guard position near the door. When he reached the bedside, Togochi kneeled beside Mandukhai's chair.

"Brother," Togochi said, grief tightening his voice. His mouth moved as if he tried to work out other words. He slumped as he took Manduul's hand and pressed his own forehead against it. "How long?"

"He has been ill for some time," Mandukhai said, lowering her voice as if it would spare Manduul hearing of the fate he already knew had befallen him. "He feared what would happen if others learned he was dying. Only Issama and Unebolod knew, to my knowledge."

Togochi sobered, nodding stiffly with his head still bowed. "What did I do to lose your trust?" he asked, and the misery bled in each word. "I knew something was wrong and did nothing to help. I asked, yet you did not trust me, brother, to help you through this. I am sorry, brother." His voice cracked over the last words.

Manduul used his free hand to pat Togochi's forehead with a lethargy that only reinforced his impending death. "It is I who owe you an apology, Togochi. I should have shared the truth with you months ago. You have done nothing wrong. But I trust you now with the weight of the Nation."

Togochi raised his reddened eyes. "What do you need from me, brother? I will do anything you ask."

Manduul pulled his hand from Togochi. He trembled as he brushed Mandukhai's cheek. "Mandukhai the Wise. Our people, the Mongol Nation, will be better served with you as Queen Regent."

Togochi stared, glancing at Mandukhai from the corner of his eyes. Mandukhai had been prepared for this reaction and dared not show Togochi any of her satisfaction. Instead, she wore a mask of sorrow that bore some truth.

Boke shifted near the door, his armor creaking. "Is that your order, my Khan?" he asked. "Is Mandukhai to be Queen Regent?"

Manduul nodded slowly. His hand fell to the bed.

Togochi appeared stunned. The confirmation rendered him speechless.

"I will ensure your order is enforced," Boke said with a bow. "I give my loyalty to your house, my Khan, and will serve the Queen Regent as I have served you."

Boke's oath of loyalty was not formal, but Mandukhai could hold him accountable for it. She would need all the allies she could get in the weeks and months to come. Overwhelmed by his promise and relieved that Manduul had secured her position, silent tears rolled down Mandukhai's cheeks. Manduul blinked in a daze as he gazed at her.

"I have made many mistakes," Manduul said, and she could hear how he grew weaker by the moment. "I have undone the line of Genghis in my jealousy. I have destroyed the Yuan dynasty with my rage."

"Do not blame yourself for Bayan's mistakes," Mandukhai said, hoping that it offered him some solace.

"I deserve this broken-hearted fate," Manduul mumbled. His hand grew colder in her own. Manduul closed his eyes. "It is a bad thing ... how I lived." The last words trailed off as he took a few more rasping breaths.

Manduul slipped into his final sleep. His hand slackened in her own.

At that moment, Mandukhai realized he would never touch her again. It was a breath of relief. It was surreal. Her stomach suddenly became a tangle of knots, and a dullness ached in her chest as tears flowed unchecked down her cheeks. She did not love Manduul as a wife should love her husband. Yet as he slowly slipped away from this world, it alarmed Mandukhai to discover grief sinking through her limbs.

Togochi smothered a sob and firmed his jaw, but no matter how hard he clearly struggled with it, he could not keep his grief from creasing his forehead. The three of them remained in silence as Manduul took his final breaths.

One day. Dashai had told Bayan he would not be more than one day, at the most, before he returned with more supplies. He left Bayan nestled among the sand dunes with only a few strips of dried mutton to sustain him. Dashai promised to return with supplies from his family.

By afternoon on the second day, Bayan doubted Dashai's return. Dashai had taken the last of Bayan's coins when he left, as payment for the supplies. If he intended to leave Bayan to die, why didn't he just kill Bayan? It made no sense. Then Dashai could have taken Andayar, as well.

As the third day dawned, Bayan began doubting whether Dashai had been real at all, or just another hallucination brought on by the devil of the Singing Sands. He had to keep moving. Either Dashai had abandoned him, or he had never been real.

Bayan stumbled along through the desert for two more days, walking and riding Andayar in turns as he had done before. No snow had fallen in days, and what little snow had met the ground had melted immediately, leaving Bayan with no water. Numbness from the cold had spread throughout his body. More than once, Bayan had stumbled and fallen, nearly rolling down a dune. Sand dried his mouth, and he could no longer see clearly enough to spot the sun's movements. Was he headed south, or had he turned in the wrong direction?

The world became an endless blur of dunes and sand. *Lord Tengri, please. Don't let me die like this.* He had never prayed so hard for help. Nothing in his life had ever been easy, but this journey through the Gobi felt more and more hopeless with each passing breath.

As if in answer to his prayers, Bayan spotted a shimmering oasis in the distance. Hope bloomed in his chest. *It isn't real*, he admonished himself, *just like nothing else has been real out here.* But if his luck held out just a little longer, he could find food and water there.

Whether it was real, Bayan was in no position to risk passing it by. He practically tumbled down the dune toward the oasis, gripping Andayar's reins tightly to keep from losing his mount.

As he drew closer, Bayan was certain he had found a desert spring—and a small encampment of gers. Was this Dashai's family? Three gers faced south near the spring. They would easily spot him approaching. But thirst had taken over. He would die soon without water.

Only one person moved around the gers. By some stroke of luck, a young girl of maybe twelve or thirteen tended to camels. Bayan focused on walking with sure steps as he approached, holding up a hand to show no signs of threat as the other hand gripped Andayar's reins.

The girl froze, staring at him with wide eyes. For a moment, he feared she would flee. Bayan tried to speak, but nothing came from his dry mouth other than a cough.

Then his weakened limbs gave up. Bayan collapsed to the ground, slamming his face into the rocky earth.

Mandukhai and Togochi remained in Manduul's ger for a long time in silence. Khosoichi and Boke wordlessly excused themselves, leaving the two to mourn the Khan's passing. So much had changed in the past two days; so much had been lost.

Manduul and Borogchin were dead. Mandukhai controlled Borogchin's son, Nemeku. Mandukhai would do her best to protect Nemeku from the dangers of his own father.

When she had arrived in Mongke Bulag nearly six years ago to marry the Khan, Mandukhai had been young and spirited with her head stuffed full of fantasies about what she had wanted from her life. She had wanted to prove herself as strong as the legendary Khutulun, whose ability to beat men in wrestling and battle had been outmatched only by her own intellect. Mandukhai had desired a husband as unyielding as steel, who understood the ideas of compassion and steel as a balance. But instead of being strong like Khutulun, Mandukhai would need to be wise like Toregene and Sorkhogtani.

Togochi rose to his feet. The sudden motion drew Mandukhai's attention. He paced back and forth a few times, face screwed up in confusion. She held her breath, wondering what Togochi would do next.

Togochi strode toward her, then dropped to his knees and bowed his head before her seat. "Queen Regent," he said soberly. "I give you salt, ger, horses, and, when necessary, blood until a new Great Khan has been selected at *kurultai*."

A sudden lightness overcame her. Mandukhai pressed a hand to Togochi's shoulder, hoping he could not feel her trembling. An unexpected surge of strength rushed through her body. "Your loyalty will not be forgotten, Togochi."

He raised his gaze to meet hers. Despite the cold warrior's face, his eyes revealed the depth of his grief.

"We have much to do to prepare for the Khan's funeral," she said. "And *kurultai*. It will be a long road, Togochi."

He nodded. "If you want the Mongol Lords to carry out Manduul's last wishes, you will need an official order from the Khan. They will not easily follow a woman."

Mandukhai stood and moved to a drawer in one of Manduul's chests. From beneath her deel, she withdrew a chain holding a key. Manduul had given it to her a week ago. He must have known his death was close at hand.

In moments, she unlocked the drawer and pulled out a red lacquer box. "Manduul knew this day approached, and he prepared for it." She turned to Togochi, gripping the box in both hands and weighing Togochi's sincerity. "Everything we need will be here. He wrote it himself. The order to appoint me as Queen Regent. His will regarding his property and funeral. His wish regarding the next Great Khan."

Togochi stepped forward to take the box, and Mandukhai hesitated. Showing that she mistrusted his intentions would offend Togochi, and she *did* trust him. But her fate rested on those pages. Handing them over to anyone else went against her most basic instincts. Mandukhai knew she had to cover for her hesitation or risk insulting Togochi's oath. She placed it in his hands, brushing her hands over the smooth red lacquer.

"I understood why this box was necessary," she whispered. "But I can't believe we will be opening."

Togochi shifted the box to one hand and placed a hand on her shoulder. "Such a loss is never easy, but we both know the future of the Nation will soon enough be in capable hands."

For a moment, Mandukhai thought Togochi had complimented her, but then she realized what he had truly meant by 'soon enough'. Togochi did not refer to her, but insinuated someone else. Unebolod.

"Am I not capable?" Mandukhai asked.

Togochi's frown deepened. "That is not what I meant, and I'm sure you know it."

"I sent for Unebolod months ago, and he has not returned," Mandukhai said.

"This winter has been particularly harsh," Togochi said. "I'm sure Unebolod will return as soon as he can. He would not leave you alone for long."

Mandukhai's gaze snapped to Manduul before remembering he had died and no longer posed a threat. Still, she barely spoke above a whisper. "You knew."

Togochi's mouth twitched. "I know Unebolod better than he thinks. The two of you covered your tracks well enough, but his gaze strayed to you a few times too many." He glanced at Manduul and sighed. "Now you will both get everything you have wanted at last." Togochi tucked the red box close to his body. "I will see that Manduul's final orders are carried out, but we will need to send riders out to call the Lords back for *kurultai* to make Unebolod's installment official."

Mandukhai resented the assumption that it would, in fact, be Unebolod who became the next Great Khan. Yes, it was what she wanted and what he wanted, but Togochi had deftly cut her out of the decision with a few words.

"I will handle the riders and organizing the Lords for *kurultai*," Mandukhai said tersely.

Togochi's brows climbed his forehead. She knew he must have wondered why she would even consider any other to be Great Khan, and she did not even consider any of the other men worthy, but she would not be dismissed so easily.

"Your will, Queen Regent," Togochi said, grinning as he bowed. "You know, Unebolod once told me you were a dragon in women's clothing. I fear for any who dare challenge the rise of the dragon. I have no doubt you will burn them alive."

With that, Togochi turned and left with the box. Mandukhai watched him go, stunned and pleased. She was a daughter of the yellow dragon, and should any dare stand in her way, from this day forward, she would see them burn.

She had no other choice.

The girl pulled on Bayan's arm to sit him upright against the outside of the ger, then she pushed his legs out in front of him. He blinked at her in a daze as blood trickled from the corner of his mouth where he had hit the ground. The metallic tang was sharp and bitter on his tongue. She held up a skin of *airag* to his lips, helping him drink. After two gulps, his hands wrapped around the skin with greedy need. He guzzled it down. She pulled it away from his mouth, and though he tried to resist, she outmatched him in his weakened state.

"What is your name?" the girl asked. "You seem lost."

"Enkh," Bayan croaked, giving the same name he had given Dashai.

She looked over his fine—though filthy—clothing.

"Just a traveler," he said. "I won't be long."

"Well, Enkh Just a Traveler, you are not well prepared for the Gobi. Stay. I will get you food."

Bayan reached to stop her, but she easily pulled away and disappeared inside one of the gers. Bayan drank more of the *airag* as he watched Andayar graze on the sparse grass and drink from the small spring. *How was he still alive?* More than once, the desert had nearly claimed him, but then another Mongol would come to his rescue. Bayan was so exhausted he could not think straight. *Lord Tengri has answered my prayers and the High Heavens have shared fortune with me again*, he thought. There was no other explanation for his survival.

The girl returned with a small bag of dried meat and curd. Just the sight of it made Bayan's mouth water. Hunger seized his stomach. Bayan greedily chewed on the hard meat. It hurt his jaw, weakened as he was, but the flavor saturated his tastebuds like the touch of heaven. He closed his eyes as he sucked on the meat and chewed it in turns.

"Where is everyone else?" he asked through a mouthful of food, then added a bit more *airag* to the mix to soften the meat.

"Hunting. My brothers will be back before nightfall." She glanced at the sky.

Bayan followed her gaze but blinked at the blinding sunlight. "I can't stay," he said before tearing off another strip of meat with his teeth.

"You should rest, Enkh," she said, smiling innocently.

"Can't." Bayan pushed himself to his hands and knees, then used the ger for support as he stood. His legs shook. "Got to keep riding."

"Where are you headed?" she asked, standing with him and holding her hands out as if ready to break his inevitable fall.

"South."

She frowned. "Through the Singing Sands? It's a dangerous place to travel alone."

"Aren't all places?" he asked, shuffling toward Andayar. Hopefully, the mare had enough time to replenish herself. "How much farther?"

"About a day," she said uncertainly.

He gathered his reins. A day to the end of the Singing Sands. He could survive a day. They would reach the Flaming Cliffs. From there, it was only a matter of surviving the journey through Ordos territory.

"Wait." She held out a hand to him.

Bayan paused, which prompted her to rush back into the ger. A moment later, she emerged with supplies. "Take this with you. It should be enough food and water to get you to the next encampment about two days on the other side of the Flaming Cliffs."

Bayan accepted the pouch of food and skin of water, nodding at her with thanks. Then he climbed onto Andayar's back and bid the girl farewell before riding away.

A day through the Singing Sands. Soon, he would reach the Ming, gather their support, and turn around to clear his name and claim what was his. Whether he wanted to be Great Khan no longer mattered. It was the only way to ensure his survival. *Tengri will see me through.*

Unebolod sharpened his sword for the hundredth time as he sat in his ger and waited for Odgerel to finish preparing dinner. Having her to care for him had made the winter easier, but the quarters felt more confined, as if he had no space to move around without her nearby somewhere. More than once, Soke had teased him for ignoring such beauty. Unebolod had not failed to notice, but any time he considered taking her to bed, he would hear Mandukhai's voice or see her face. He had given his word, and his word was iron.

The Khorchin had moved camp closer to a forest near the Kherlen River valley, which offered better wood and game, but he was still too far from

Mongke Bulag. The brutality of this winter had slowed them down to a near standstill every time he thought they could move again. None but Soke even understood why he forced them to press on at every opportunity, and he would not explain himself.

Odgerel placed a tray of *buuz* on his small table and nodded toward it. "Eat, my Lord, and keep your strength up."

Unebolod grimaced and put his sword away. As he settled with the tray on the edge of his bed, the door opened and blew bitterly cold air through the ger. The Ongud shaman swiftly ducked in and closed the door tightly behind him.

"Getei," Unebolod said flatly. "I warned you about showing your face here."

Getei's back hunched as he wrung his hands together anxiously, glancing around the ger as if afraid danger would pop out of any shadow. "We must go, Lord Unebolod. Time has run out."

Unebolod rolled his eyes. As if he did not know how precious each wasted day was. "I hope you have more to say than that."

Getei met Unebolod's gaze, and the fear in his dark eyes sent a jolt of dread down Unebolod's spine. The food in his mouth tasted suddenly sour.

"The spirits have spoken to me, my Lord, the great spirit of the Khans."

Unebolod's heartbeat became sluggish, and he had difficulty swallowing the food in his mouth. Irritated with the meal, he set the tray aside. "And?"

Getei chewed his lip enough to make the cracked, dry skin break open and bleed. "They say the dragon rises, but a pack of rabid dogs closes in. If we do not reach Mongke Bulag soon, the dragon will fall."

The *buuz* rolled in Unebolod's stomach, threatening to rise back up. His heartbeat slowed, making it difficult to breathe. He did not need to ask who the dragon was. Unebolod knew Mandukhai had urged his return. If something happened to her before he could reach her, Unebolod would never forgive himself, and he would utterly destroy anyone who had dared turn against her. The nightmare about other men taking her as a wife rushed to the surface. *It cannot happen!*

"Odgerel, go fetch Soke immediately," Unebolod commanded. "Don't dawdle, girl, or you will regret it."

Though Odgerel did not understand what had just changed, she could sense the simmering anger and dread in Unebolod well enough to know when to jump.

As he waited for Soke's arrival, Unebolod paced the floor, running through plans in his head. He needed his warriors if the situation was so dire. Yet if he waited for the rest of the tribe, he could lose Mandukhai. The Khorchin counted on him to lead them. Mandukhai counted on him to save her. There was every chance that his people would resent him for abandoning them to run to a woman. But they would understand. They would have to. Their khan would become Khan of khans, but only if he acted quickly. *Please let them forgive me*, he thought.

The carts slowed them down. He would have to leave them behind to catch up when spring came. They had wasted too much time. He would ride out ahead of the rest of the tribe—alone if need be—to reach Mongke Bulag as swiftly as possible. He had no other choice any longer.

CHAPTER THIRTY-THREE

Threads of Gold and Silk

MONGKE BULAG – LATE WINTER 1470

Mandukhai knew she could not delay the announcement of the Khan's death beyond the next morning. Boke and Togochi insisted the men in the camp had grown suspicious amidst the activity of the previous day. Mandukhai had worked hard to keep Boke's movements minimal, but no secrets within Mongke Bulag would last long. People already suspected the Khan was ill. If she did not come out ahead of the news of his death with all her newfound power, the men would rip it away and disperse before she could bring them to heel. She could not allow it.

Mandukhai had Boke assist Khosoichi as he wrapped the Khan's body in white silk. When they finished, Boke confined the shaman under guard to keep him from speaking of the events. Mandukhai could not risk him slipping the news before her.

Togochi took Nemeku back to his ger when he left, where the boy stayed with Jaghan for the evening to give Mandukhai time and space to prepare for the morning. On Togochi's orders, and with Mandukhai's blessing, only one messenger left in the night, bearing the news of Manduul's death to deliver to Unebolod. The rider did not know what he carried, except that Togochi insisted he should ride the fastest mounts to death, if need be, to carry the news as swiftly as possible.

Esige had spent the evening creeping around Mongke Bulag with her ears open as she moved through the shadows. Thankfully, Esige only reported rumors of the Khan's absence all day. Some speculated the truth—that he had died or was on the brink of death. A few of the Mongol Lords in the camp had spoken over late-night *airag* of Unebolod's absence. No one dared utter Bayan's name. None even hinted at it. Mandukhai had prepared, though. Boke organized a group of warriors who would move in and smother any news of insurrection before it could ignite.

Mandukhai woke early the next morning, long before dawn. Tuya cleaned Mandukhai's skin, pinned up her hair, and layered on silk and fur. The way Mandukhai presented herself to the Lords and commanders mattered more than it had on the day she had been presented to Manduul. Then, she had only needed to captivate the attention of one man. Now, she would have to capture the respect of dozens.

As Tuya dressed her and readied her for the day, Mandukhai and Esige communicated in tandem to prepare the gathering tent for the proceedings. Esige took Mandukhai's orders to a handful of servants who worked there, returning to provide updates to the Queen Regent and seek further orders when necessary.

Togochi spent the morning sending word to the Lords and commanders, summoning them to the gathering tent "in the name of their Khan." He had reassured Mandukhai he would be careful to avoid questions and give no hint of the Khan's passing. They both feared the men would not come if they knew the truth ahead of time.

The chest of jewelry from Bigirsen comprised most of Mandukhai's collection. While she wore what was necessary daily to reflect her station, this would be no ordinary day. Tuya set the chest in front of her on the table, and Mandukhai flipped it open.

She could not adorn herself with so much jewelry alone. Mandukhai removed all the silver, coral, and filigree necklaces for Tuya to layer over her clothing. An amulet box of silver from which a round pendant of a lion hung below her breast. As Tuya placed the headdress on Mandukhai's head, shifting the red and blue coral beads to avoid them catching, Mandukhai thought she would collapse beneath the weight. Her earrings hung to her shoulders, matching the ornamentation of the necklace. Silver chains, bells, and a pair of silver dancing wolves connected the earrings to the pendant. They completed the ensemble with rings on nearly every finger and bracelets to hold her spirit within her limbs. Once the leather belt hook was connected on each hip, Mandukhai motioned for her father's knife, slipping it into her belt.

They placed the last piece on her head. Mandukhai ducked to make it easier for Tuya to put it on. They had worked through the night to create this new *boqta*; the smooth, nearly seamless silk perfectly matched her multi-colored clothing. Today, she would not bear the colors of one tribe but of all tribes, in threads of gold and silk. Making such a statement was bold, but if she could not be bold today, she never would be.

At last, as Tuya finished Mandukhai's ensemble. Mandukhai excused her servant to the gathering tent and took a moment to kneel before the altar. "Lord Tengri, Spirit of Genghis, High Heavens above, if this is your will, guide me with your strength and wisdom," she prayed. "I will do my duty according to your will."

Boke ducked into the ger, bowing deeply to the Queen Regent.

"The Lords, Ladies, and commanders await your arrival in the gathering tent," Boke said, keeping his body bent out of respect.

Mandukhai smiled. "Let's not keep them waiting any longer, then."

Boke stepped out first, and Mandukhai ducked low behind him to avoid bumping her *boqta* on the doorframe. As she straightened, Mandukhai squared her shoulders and stood as tall as she could, chin raised proudly. The guards closed in around her, escorting Mandukhai to the gathering tent.

Her passage caught the attention of the working men and women nearby, and they all paused to bow deeply to her. Perhaps they did not know what had changed, but they recognized her as their queen, and her attire made it clear to all that something important was about to transpire.

Mandukhai struggled to keep her face impassive as she crossed the snow-packed ground. Nerves coiled like an evil serpent in her gut, threatening to reveal her anxiety to all.

Patches of brown grass peeked through the snow, promising the coming of spring and rebirth—a good omen to bless this day. Assuming she could keep the Lords from coming undone.

FLAMING CLIFFS – GOBI DESERT – LATE WINTER 1470

Andayar began to fade. Bayan feared his mare would not escape the desert with him. She had slowed significantly, and the wear on her had become more apparent. They had reached the edge of the dunes. In the distance, the

Flaming Cliffs marked the end of his journey. Once he reached the other side of the cliffs, they would be fully in Ordos territory and closer to food and water. Though Andayar had grass to graze on here and there at the edge of the dunes, there had been no water yet.

Still, he breathed a sigh of relief to see the red cliffs in the distance.

Then the ground rumbled.

Bayan ignored it, recalling how that sound had haunted him in the depths of the Singing Sands. But it drew closer this time, and clearly approached from the direction he had come from.

Bayan glanced over his shoulder to see several men racing toward him, perhaps seven. He was too tired to count. He kicked Andayar to get her running, but she snorted in protest and stopped altogether. He cursed under his breath and knew his fortune had reached an end. No amount of prodding could force her to take more than a few lazy steps.

Please let them be a mirage, he thought desperately.

But the riders easily overtook him, forming a circle around Andayar. They were very real. *Or I have lost my mind at last.* Bayan straightened as much as he could, wondering if he had any chance with his training to kill them all before they could kill him. Perhaps at his peak, but he was too weak. If his luck held out, he might take three or four before the rest killed him.

One man guided his anxious camel with steady, expert hands. *I can't even take three of these men*, Bayan realized. His heart sank. *This one will kill me even if I strike at him first.* The man's calculating gaze swept over Bayan in his brocade squirrel fur-lined deel tied with the golden belt Manduul had given him and a finely made sword on his hip.

"What sort of man are you?" the man asked, clearly skeptical about why Bayan would be in the desert with such finery.

"A traveler." His only hope of escape now would be to keep his identity secret.

The circle closed ever so slightly. Andayar seemed indifferent to the danger. Bayan's hand rested on the hilt of his sword. Drawing it would be his final, feeble attempt at escape. The leader of this group noticed the subtle gesture, and his eyes narrowed.

"That's a fine mare you're riding through the desert, traveler," the leader said. "You are killing her."

Bayan glanced at the others, watching for any sudden movement. The Uyghur cut of their deels marked these men out as enemies. *Everyone is my enemy now.* Bayan's jaw tightened.

His insides twisted in a tight knot. Every muscle in his body ached as he tensed, knowing the only way to escape was to fight his way free. Andayar had made it clear she was in no mood to run. *Lord Tengri, I ask for another miracle*, he prayed.

The leader spit on the ground and sneered at him. "Too fine for a simple traveler. So is your belt."

Bayan tightened his grip on the sword. If he struck swiftly, maybe he could kill the leader first and the others would scatter long enough to give him time to escape.

"Give us your belt," another of the men demanded.

Bayan gaped at him. To take his belt constituted a grave insult. The belt, sword, and mare were all he had left in this world. The demand made it clear. He had no choice but to fight his way out. Bayan took a couple of shallow breaths as sweat beaded on his forehead despite the cold. He gripped the reins firmly and subtly, preparing to strike.

One man edged his camel closer. Bayan had but moments to act. He ripped out the sword from his hip, swinging it in a deadly arc toward the nearest attacker as he yanked the reins hard enough to make Andayar rear back on her hind legs. As his sword swept across the throat of the nearest man, Andayar's front legs kicked the leader's camel in the head, startling it away. The camel ran, and the leader shouted and struggled to get it back under control.

The remaining five closed in on him with deadly swift speed. Bayan had time to bring his sword around once more to take out another man. The hands of the other four grasped at him, ripping Bayan from Andayar's saddle. Panic surged through him. His heart hammered so hard he could feel it in his throat.

Desperate, Bayan brought his elbow back into his captor's face, which proved to be a mistake. The warrior released his grip, dropping Bayan to the ground beneath a mass of horse and camel hooves. He tried to spring back to his feet, but weakness in his limbs made him too slow. *High Heavens, I won't die like this!*

Two of the men slid from their camels, weapons drawn. One swiped out at his leg, slicing into Bayan's calf just as he got to his feet. As he stumbled forward, Bayan thrust his sword up into the gut of the second man in front of him. The sword caught in flesh and refused to slide back out, snared between the ribs.

The leader had recovered, standing over Bayan sneering as the man who had sliced his leg kicked Bayan's hand away from his sword.

"Issama sends his regards," the leader said. He raised his sword, preparing to plunge it into Bayan's chest.

Desperation pulsed through Bayan. Issama betrayed him. He had promised to help him and instead sent men to kill him.

No! Bayan kicked out, sweeping at the leader's legs as he raised his sword. But the impact was too weak. The blade of the sword pierced deep into Bayan's stomach. His breath kicked out of his lungs as he gasped. Adrenaline pulsed through Bayan's body, dulling the pain momentarily. He considered pulling his knife to drive it through the leader's eye. He reached a shaking hand to his belt.

"Long live Lord Issama," the man said, then twisted the sword with a brutal grin of satisfaction. As the leader yanked it out, the blade scrape across Bayan's ribs. He opened his mouth in a silent scream with no breath to give it life.

Blood poured from the gaping wound. Stunned and cold, Bayan placed his hands over the wound as slick blood flowed over his fingers uninhibited. Warmth poured out of him into the icy, hard ground, making him as cold as the stone beneath him. His fingers could not hold the wound closed. That final twist of the blade made certain of it.

The men around him spoke, but Bayan could not hear their words over the pulsing drum of his own fading heartbeat. They jerked at him, removing his blood-slick golden belt. Bayan struggled to pull in a breath, to speak, to beg. Nothing escaped his lips except a flow of blood. The weight of a mountain pressed down on his chest and he could not breathe to save his life. *Tengri ... please ... help me ...*

As his vision constricted, Bayan watched the leader gather Andayar's reins and tie them to his camel. Then they rode away.

Blood poured from Bayan's wound in a river. The boy whose mother and grandmother had defied Esen Khan to save his life, who had reigned beside a Khan who had promised him that he would conquer the world, lay stretched out on the Gobi rocks in threads of gold and silk.

Bayan's head rolled to the side. His vision darkened. In these last moments, his only companions were three dead men. Every part of his body numbed.

I die as I lived. Alone.

MONGE BULAG – LATE WINTER 1470

Lanterns along the support posts and copper pots of fire lit the gathering tent, reflecting light off the gemstones hanging from the silk as Mandukhai ducked inside. The Lords and Ladies of Mongke Bulag packed the gathering space on either side, as well as *tumen* generals and *mingghan* commanders.

All eyes turned to Mandukhai as she walked to the front of the gathering tent and climbed onto the dais. Some women leaned toward each other and whispered as their husbands observed with grim-faced wariness. Mandukhai held her chin high, avoiding their stares. A Khan did not subject himself to the skepticism of his Lords, nor would she. Still, that serpent of nerves writhed with horrible life in her stomach.

At the top of the dais, in front of Manduul's throne, Mandukhai turned to face the crowd with her clammy hands folded together inside the sleeves of her deel. A hush fell over the men and women gathered as they waited to hear why they were summoned so soon after dawn.

She cast a glance at Togochi and Jaghan, seated close to the dais. Togochi clutched the red lacquer box in his hands.

Mandukhai knew how she handled breaking the news of Manduul's death would induce a variety of immediate reactions. If she did not make her new appointment clear from the start, the most senior men would attempt to take control of the gathering. If she declared herself too quickly, they would lash out at her. She could not sit in Manduul's seat until Alayitung had officially declared her Queen Regent before the assembly.

Mandukhai waited for Boke and five of his most trusted men to take up positions across the back and sides of the dais. Her orders had been clear. Any man who might attempt to take her life would be killed as an example swiftly and without mercy in front of everyone. They could not see her as weak during this transition. In her deepest heart, Mandukhai prayed no one would act so foolishly, but men could be unpredictable.

"Noble Lords, Ladies, and celebrated warriors," Mandukhai said in a clear voice. Some men murmured their disapproval to each other. Having a woman speak first at such an assembly was unheard of. She pressed on despite the anxious lump in her throat. "I stand before you today in the deepest grief that only a wife could truly feel." The men once more fell into silence, as if knowing what she would say next and afraid they might miss her words. "Last night, my dear husband Manduul, your Great Khan, passed away."

Grumblings of succession and propriety began almost immediately, mingling in an assault of questions and commands. "What of the prince? Does he live?"

"We must find him!" a commander called.

"Where is Lord Unebolod?" Unige asked.

"Manduul Khan named the Khorchin Lords!" another commander shouted.

"We cannot have a Great Khan not of the bone of Genghis!" Alayitung insisted.

The demands and questions raised to a crescendo. Mandukhai nodded to Togochi, making the corals and bells chime, but the sound nearly drowned in the uproar. Men argued over succession. Women pressed to know the fate of their own tribes.

Togochi stood and approached the dais with the red lacquer box cradled delicately in his hands. His movement caught the attention of some of the Lords present, quieting them. Togochi bowed at the bottom step, holding the box up Alayitung, Manduul's Vice Chancellor.

Alayitung accepted the box, his brows drawn together as he opened the lid and pulled out the top parchment. As he scanned the page, the color drain from his face. She smothered a satisfied smile as he turned buggy eyes on her. His reaction drew silence from more of the gathering.

Mandukhai took a deep breath and raised her voice above those who continued to argue over ascension. They would either quiet themselves or risk missing what happened next.

"For months, my husband battled an illness that threatened to claim his life," Mandukhai said clearly. "An illness, he learned, which was brought on by the Golden Prince's deception. However, Manduul Khan knew his end would come. He prepared for this day. He has left his people without an heir, but he has not left you abandoned. Vice Chancellor Alayitung, please read the Great Khan's final commands to his people."

Alayitung shifted uncomfortably as all eyes fell on him. He licked his lips, cleared his throat, and lifted the parchment in front of him. "I, Manduul Khan, leave all rights, authority, wealth, and holdings to the head of my house, Mandukhai Khatun, hereby naming her Queen Regent of the Mongol Nation."

A wave of outbursts erupted from all the high-ranking noble Lords. They surged to their feet. Mandukhai's heart fell. She had hoped for a better reaction. Many of these men had known her for years. She thought she had earned their respect. Did *any* of them respect her at all?

"I will not follow a woman!" a Uyghur Lord shouted. Mandukhai struggled to pull back his name. Nahai? He was one of Issama's men.

This is it, she thought, praying they couldn't see how she trembled. Everything would fall apart. She clasped her arms inside the sleeves of her deel to control her shaking.

Alayitung glanced at Mandukhai. She gave a small nod, encouraging him to continue. He raised his voice as he read the rest of Manduul's command. "May Queen Mandukhai rule over the nation with the wisdom of the High Heavens until such a time that an heir of the great Genghis rises. Should no heirs remain, the Queen Regent shall rule until a worthy Lord has won her favor and become Great Khan at *kurultai*. So commands Manduul Khan."

The cacophony in the gathering tent exploded into outright rage as every Lord present shouted protests of blasphemy.

"Then who will you choose as a husband?" a Khorlod lord demanded.

"There is no bone of Genghis any longer, so what do we do?"

"He named Lord Unebolod!" Unige shouted. "We need to find him."

Mandukhai resented that these men immediately discounted her as a leader in favor of any other man—or that she should consider a new husband when her dead husband's body was not yet cold.

The Ladies present chattered in scandalized excitement upon hearing the news. A woman had not guided the nation since Samur—Bayan's great-grandmother—nor had a woman ruled since Ogedei Khan's wife, Toregene, and she died two hundred years ago. Like Toregene, Mandukhai's position was given by her late husband. This was not unheard of, but it certainly was not normal. It was a heavy burden Mandukhai did not know if she could bear. But she had no choice. Especially not when these men clearly thought her below this task. *I need to make my dedication clear to them right now*, she thought, *before they fall apart.*

"I accept this responsibility, given by my husband, with all the weight such a duty requires," Mandukhai said, uncertain if anyone even heard her. A few men and women looked in her direction. "I give you all my word that I will do what is best for the Mongol Nation, and everyone within it, least the spirits take my arms for overreaching my station. I will guide as Toregen Khatun did, in humble servitude, until a new Great Khan is selected." This drew more attention, but the commotion did not die down. Mandukhai braced herself, as if preparing for a great tide to wash her away. But as she spoke her final words, she raised her voice high above the din. "The High

Heavens have spoken. Only the motherland has the power to love, and I am the heart of the nation."

Again, the Lords and commanders burst into protests, despite her sacred oath. To remove limbs was to break the spirit. Few of the men seemed impressed by her pronouncement. *What more do they want from me? I offered them my very soul!*

A Uyghur commander burst out of the shadows of a nearby column, knife drawn. Women screamed in panic and shied away. Mandukhai hardly had time to blink before Togochi captured the Uyghur's wrist and wrenched it back, twisting the arm. The bone snapped. The Uyghur screamed. The knife clattered to the rug. Boke seized Mandukhai's shoulder, making her jump out of her skin as he yanked her back behind him. His sword was in his other hand, ready to kill.

Before any of the men followed the Uyghur's lead, Togochi shoved the offender to his knees.

"Bigirsen Kha—" The Uyghur's words cut out as Togochi sliced the man's own knife across his throat.

The rest of Boke's men closed in around Mandukhai. She could not breathe, stunned by this turn of events, staring at the blood as it poured out on the rug. *It should not surprise me they want to see me dead.* She just had not expected any of them to be so foolishly bold.

Togochi turned to the rest of the Lords and commanders, his arm coated in blood, knife clutched in his fist. Mandukhai could not see his face, but she knew him well enough to know he dared others to challenge her. Eerie silence penetrated the gathering tent, broken only by the sobs of a few of the Ladies. The Uyghur's final proclamation was clear enough. He wanted Bigirsen to be the next Great Khan. Mandukhai's gaze swept the crowd. Who else felt the same?

Satisfied that he had ended all protests, Togochi threw the knife down and turned to face Mandukhai. She eased her way out from behind her guards.

Togochi kneeled, bowed his head, and spoke clearly—though in the deep silence of the gathering tent everyone could have heard him. "By order of Manduul Khan, I give salt, ger, horses, and when necessary, blood, to Lady Mandukhai until a new Great Khan is selected at *kurultai*."

The impact of Togochi's oath only deepened the silence. He had given her the oath already, and she knew this was for show. Because until Unebolod returned from the east, Togochi was the highest-ranking Lord in Manduul's court. Everyone knew Togochi's position, and how deeply

Manduul had trusted him. Togochi commanded a *tumen* of Khorlod warriors. His allegiance to Mandukhai should sway several of the Mongol Lords.

Some men gaped openly at Togochi. The women covered their mouths in alarm. Everyone seemed to hold their breath.

"A man giving such an oath to a woman!" Mandukhai thought she heard one man say.

"I appreciate your loyalty and oath, Lord Togochi," Mandukhai said, nodding in gratitude.

She gazed at the nobles gathered—avoiding the dead body on the floor—and waited. But as Togochi rose and returned to his place beside Jaghan, no one else approached. Mandukhai's stomach dropped again. Even with Togochi's support, the Great Khan's final order, and the death of the Uyghur commander, they would not make the same oath. *I should not be surprised*. Mongol men could be stubborn when they set their minds to something. And the more power a man held, the more stubborn he could be.

Helpless, Mandukhai watched as, one by one, the men offered her little more than a bow of respect before leaving the gathering tent.

Only Alayitung offered Mandukhai his oath as well. "I respected all that Manduul Khan accomplished in the face of such resistance," he said. "So if he leaves this decision in your hands, I trust his judgement."

"Thank you, Lord Alayitung," Mandukhai said. "I will not forget who stood beside me in the months to come."

He bowed deeply, then left the gathering tent.

Only her guards and Togochi's family remained.

Mandukhai pressed her hands to her roiling stomach and heaved out a shaky sigh. The announcement was done, but this was far from over.

"No riders are to leave this camp without my permission," Mandukhai told Togochi. Her voice trembled, and she loathed the show of weakness. "See that the messenger lines are closed. I will send my own commands with news of Manduul's death to the other Mongol Lords."

"You cannot contain this for long, Mandukhai," Togochi said, watching the door as if expecting another attack. "These Lords will listen, but they will only give their oath to a Khan. Without a Khan, you hold no more power than Bigirsen. Perhaps less. And we now know that he has loyal men in your camp. If Bayan still lives, they might insist on electing him."

Mandukhai took a slow, deep breath and released it evenly. Bigirsen would kill her. She was certain of that now. Bayan, however, would be a far worse husband than Manduul had ever been. All she could do was grimace at Togochi's honesty. "We do not need long."

"And if Bayan lives?" Togochi asked.

"I don't know, Togochi!" Mandukhai snapped. She closed her eyes and centered herself before meeting his alarmed gaze. "I'm sorry. I don't have all the answers yet. But I will. Unebolod should return soon. Then the Lords will have what they want."

"Then Unebolod will finally become Great Khan," Togochi said.

"Do you have a more suitable Lord in mind?" Mandukhai asked, shooting a sharp glare at Togochi. "Do not assume to understand my mind. My husband gave me control of the Nation for a reason. This decision is mine to make and the men around me will not trample me over."

Togochi apologized and glanced at his wife, who smiled knowingly at Mandukhai. Only she truly understood the depth of Mandukhai's feelings for Unebolod, but Mandukhai had more than just a man to think about. She had a nation. A duty.

She had given an unbreakable oath, hoping it would garner more support. Now Mandukhai was trapped within her own promise. Until she knew the fate of Bayan's son, she could not name Unebolod.

CHAPTER THIRTY-FOUR

Fracture in the Heart of a Nation

Unebolod's spirits had lifted significantly since he'd ridden out ahead of the rest of his tribe. The carts had been a hindrance, but as the snow thawed, they would move more easily over the plains of the Mongol steppe. Eventually, his people would catch up to him, but Mandukhai's need had made it clear to him that he could no longer plod along with the burden of the families. He had left more than enough men with the Khorchin tribe to protect the women and children, and only brought along a *mingghan* of one thousand men. Soke could manage the tribe in his stead.

A week into the journey, Unebolod's men stopped a messenger and escorted the rider to him. The young man in the saddle appeared exhausted, but when he spotted Unebolod his shoulders rose and he sat straighter. The guards held the reins of the rider's mount as he eased himself to the ground and bowed to Unebolod.

"Urgent message from Mongke Bulag, my lord," the rider said, holding out a flattened parchment to him.

Fear and excitement warred within him as Unebolod accepted the message. Would it bear ill news of Mandukhai's fate, or good news? The moment his gaze fell on the dragon pressed into the seal, he released a breath of relief and slid his finger along it. The men watched and waited curiously.

Heaviness fell into Unebolod's limbs as he read the message. A feeling of emptiness settled in his stomach, and he was unsure if it was grief or relief.

This was it. Manduul had died at last. Everything Unebolod had waited so patiently for would finally be his—and he was so close to Mongke Bulag. Another week, perhaps two, depending on how hard his men could ride. He closed his eyes for a moment and let the sensation of relief wash over him. Finally, he could be with her and no one could stop him.

Unebolod's sense of relief and happiness drowned a moment later in guilt. The emptiness of his stomach became a twist of discomfort. Manduul had given him so much, and all Unebolod could think about at this moment was taking a dead man's wife. His dead brother. He pulled in a deep breath.

"The Khan is dead," he told his men, raising his chin and squaring his shoulders. "Mandukhai has been named Queen Regent until the next Great Khan is selected."

All of his men had been there when Manduul proclaimed Unebolod next in line after Bayan, and with the prince either dead or on the run, that only left him. The men with him understood this.

"You heard Manduul Khan yourself. Without an heir of Genghis, I will be your next Khan."

After a moment of silence for the Great Khan, the men smirked and nudged each other.

"But time is of the essence, men," Unebolod announced. "We must reach the Queen Regent before another man can try to steal her and the title from our tribe."

Unebolod turned his gaze on the rider. The boy appeared startled by the news, his face pale. He swiftly dipped his head in deference to Unebolod. "Ride until your mount collapses and take my response to the Queen Regent."

One of his men brought the messenger a fresh horse as Unebolod relayed his message.

Fifteen years of living in Manduul's shadow. Fifteen days until Mandukhai was in his arms.

Unebolod's patience had paid off.

MONGKE BULAG – SPRING 1470

The Khan's funeral pyre was not immense, but they had crafted its base with great care to stabilize it. Mandukhai had waited patiently for nearly two weeks for the men to gather enough wood to build something worthy of a Khan. Manduul's body had been packed in snow to preserve it as long as possible.

Beyond the pyre, Mandukhai noted how few gers remained in Mongke Bulag. Issama's messenger arrived four days ago with news of Bayan's death. The news had upset the tribes. While Mandukhai knew all of Issama's men hunted Bayan, some part of her thought for certain Bayan had found his own way. It would be no less than he had ever done. She did not mourn the loss of Bayan as much as she did the possibility that it could truly be the end of the bone of Genghis Khan. Unless, by some chance, his son still lived.

What had shocked her most was the news of where Bayan had died. In the desert, just as Genghis had shown her in the vision five years ago. Had his fate been sealed since then?

When Mandukhai had shared this news with the other Lords, it had been a sober night. Most of them stared at her in dumbfounded silence, understanding the weight of what this meant.

They would be at war if they did not agree on a new Great Khan. They would raise their black banners to fight for their chosen candidate. Mandukhai was all that stood between them and war.

Togochi had simply placed his hand on Mandukhai's arm and said, "You know what Manduul wanted us to do next."

She had only nodded, too stunned to realize the weight of what Togochi had implied. Too terrified to share the truth with him, that there could be another heir.

Issama also requested the remaining Uyghur join him and Bigirsen in the south, on the Vice Regent's command. Mandukhai had tried to stop them from leaving, but Uyghur made poor allies and she knew she could not tempt them away from their loyalty to Bigirsen. In the end, it was better for them to move as far from her as possible. Especially before Unebolod returned. He had no love for the Uyghur.

Siker had taken the news of Bayan's death well. She did not mourn him. "He was never truly my husband," she had said pointedly. How she could accept Issama as her husband, Mandukhai did not understand. But

Siker had seemed happy enough with the arrangement. What right did Mandukhai have to judge whom Siker could care for?

Only the Uyghur had left before Manduul's funeral. It had not been a festive event. Everyone had climbed the hill to the pyre, observed Khosoichi's ceremony, then returned home as Manduul burned. Several tribes had packed up that morning.

Manduul had left specific instructions on how to handle his funeral and what animals to kill or burn with him, as well as what to clothe him in. Mandukhai watched the pyre burn flames high into the sky, taking his body with it. Per his instructions, Manduul wore the white deel with golden threads Bayan had given him during their private ceremony. He had wanted to pay final respect to the young man who had given him hope and love, even if Bayan had also ripped it away with his selfishness.

Manduul had also left a letter for Mandukhai. Despite their rocky start, Mandukhai no longer doubted how absolutely he had loved her, even if she had not returned the feelings. She read the letter several times alone in her ger. She had even cried as he apologized and begged forgiveness for what he had done to her. Manduul had showered Bayan with so much affection Mandukhai had often wondered if he loved Bayan more than any other. Now she no longer doubted his true feelings for her.

Mandukhai didn't have the heart to keep the letter. Reading the words he wrote to her broke her heart. She did not want them looming in her ger to stir up misappropriated feelings in the days or years to come. Instead, she had placed the letter in the folds of Manduul's deel, over his heart, before the pyre was lit.

Mandukhai's blue fur-lined deel shifted as a breeze blew across the pyre. She raised her head and watched the smoke rise high into the sky, then fly away like a bird. The bells on her headdress and jewelry sang a sad song as if they, too, mourned Manduul's passing.

A rider had returned with a message from Unebolod the day before she received the news about Bayan. The words had been spoken, not written, and as the messenger relayed them, his face heated.

Unebolod's words still sang in her heart. "I return to you now, hindered only by nature herself, and when I do, I will light your fire for you." He had spoken those same words to her before he left. Just imagining those words in Unebolod's voice warmed Mandukhai's heart as surely as the pyre warmed her flesh.

Beside her, Esige stood in a brilliant jade deel and jewels of coral, silver, and jade to reflect her station. Nemeku clung to Esige's side, sucking on his thumb and huddled beneath her sheltering arm. Regardless of how Esige felt about dressing and acting like a princess, she wore it well. She stood tall and proud as tears rolled silently down her cheeks. Esige was every inch a princess, and quite a young woman as well. While Mandukhai knew the girl would have to marry soon, she loathed losing Esige to any man.

The wood released a sweet scent that masked the stench of Manduul's burning body. Mandukhai closed her eyes and breathed it in. This smell would forever remind her of freedom, she was certain.

Men and women slipped away without comment as the day wore on, and soon enough Mandukhai could see lines of carts, oxen, sheep, and mounted riders traveling away from Mongke Bulag, headed in all directions with the obvious intention of abandoning their Queen Regent in the Orkhon Valley—and she, powerless to stop them. How she wished she could have forced them to stay, but her job was to ensure a smooth transition, not to force stubborn, arrogant men to bend to her will. They were free to move around the steppe at their will, as long as they showed up for *kurultai* and did not oppose her as Queen Regent. It was the Mongol way to move across the empire as necessary.

Mandukhai swallowed hard as she worried over the future of the Nation.

The exodus of tribes was a brilliantly beautiful and brutal web she now found herself caught directly in the middle of. News of Manduul's death had been delayed, but she could not hold it at bay forever. Within a month, two at the most, every tribe would know their Nation was without a Khan, and she would have to keep them from falling apart or raising the black banner to claim the title which, for the first time, had no immediate heir from Genghis or his sons. *Except Batu.* Mandukhai chewed her lip. She still did not know if he lived.

"You should rest, Mandukhai," Esige said as she scooped Nemeku up in her arms to head back. "You cannot stop them from leaving any more than you can stop a river from flowing south."

Mandukhai watched Nemeku fiddle with one of Esige's coral chains. "No. But you can divert the flow in a direction that suits you. I did not seek this power, Esige, but Manduul saw fit to place the burden of a Nation on my shoulders. I must take it seriously. For all our sakes."

Nemeku perked up against Esige, his enormous eyes staring at Mandukhai in wonder. "Mom told me I have to have strength of spirit, and if I'm worthy, power will come to me. Does that mean you are worthy and have a strong spirit?"

Esige laughed and kissed Nemeku on the forehead. He stuck out his tongue in mock disgust and wiped the kiss away. "Nemeku, no one has a stronger spirit than the Queen Regent."

Mandukhai smiled at Esige, but the words made her heart break for Borogchin's fate all over again. "Go. I wish to remain a little longer."

Esige frowned, but she did not object. With Nemeku in her arms, bombarding her with endless questions, Esige glided down the hill toward the ger. Mandukhai's gaze slipped past them to Mongke Bulag, which had become a barren ghost of what it once had been. Only a few Borjigin and Khorlod remained, which left Mandukhai without a proper army.

Mandukhai remained on the crest of the hill beside the blazing pyre, watching as the nation divided, and she was utterly helpless to stop it. The burden of duty pressed down on her shoulders. She longed to unearth some way to bring the Lords together before they all raised the black banner.

"You could not wait for me?" Unebolod's familiar voice caused Mandukhai's heart to leap into her throat.

Doubting that he could truly be there, she spun around.

Unebolod's face was harder than she remembered, but he looked stronger. Clad in armor and fur, holding the reins of his mare in one hand, he was more handsome than she remembered him being. His long black hair hung loose beneath his fur-lined hat, with only two small tails framing his face and accenting his powerful jaw. A new style for him.

Mandukhai's cheeks heated with joy as happy tears welled in her eyes. Her stomach roiled with the wings of a thousand butterflies. Had he always been so handsome? The pure elation and freedom of this reunion surged throughout her body. More than anything else, she wanted to run into his arms, press her lips to his; yet some part of her felt the eyes of her guards on them. Though her heart wanted to leap into the moment, her mind reminded her that she was Queen Regent, not a love-struck girl. This contest for control of her next words and actions rendered Mandukhai mute and utterly still. Had he been faithful to her, as he had promised? What did he think of her, after more than a year away?

Unebolod did not smile, though his eyes shined in the firelight. "This is not the fire I meant," he said as he edged closer with the casual grace of a predator about to devour its prey.

Her chest rose and fell with quick breaths. How she wanted to be that prey!

He stopped so close to her that Mandukhai could not tell if it was the fire or his body that warmed her skin so completely. For a moment, they stood close, staring at the other. Mandukhai was certain he would kiss her. As Queen Regent, she would not make the first move, but the girl deep within hoped, pleaded for him to kiss her in front of the guards, leaving no question who she would give herself to, or who would be next to rule the Nation.

Instead of kissing her, Unebolod's hand brushed hers in a subtle gesture. Mandukhai's heart leaped. Her body came alive at that moment. She slid her fingers around his. He closed his grip on her hand with a firm tenderness that she had so long craved.

"It took you long enough," she said at last, certain that her words sounded as breathless as she felt. Like a giddy girl, Mandukhai could not hide her smile.

"It was snowing."

Mandukhai craned her neck toward him. Instead of kissing her, Unebolod gazed at their hands.

"The elephant may have died," Unebolod said, breaking the spell by reminding her of Manduul's burning body beside them. "But the lion still lurks around the dragon's den." He turned his attention south. "We must act swiftly."

Mandukhai nodded in agreement. But her heart ached at his delicate retreat. She could not allow her heart to impede duty. Unebolod would not.

Manduul and Bayan's deaths would leave a deeper fracture in the heart of the Mongol Nation, and all the Lords would raise the black banner to fight for their next Great Khan. They had no time for passionate reunions, or they risked more blood in the name of peace and unity.

Hand-in-hand, the two strolled down the hill toward Mongke Bulag.

At last, the future was theirs to take.

Curious to know how Bayan escaped Lord Bolunai? Scan the code to download the prequel, Prosperous Eternity.

Ready for the next book? Read on after the Glossary for a sneak peek at Chapter One of Mother of the Blue Wolf!

If you enjoyed the book, please leave a review! Reviews can help influence other potential readers' buying decisions, which is critical for indie authors like me.

Historical Notes

Before I launch into the historical facts in this book, I want to take a moment to explain the status of widows in the family structure. It was common for wives to pass on to the senior male of the family, sometimes the son or brother of the deceased. This happened in all families, no matter their social status.

When Manduul died, Mandukhai and Yeke would have become Bayan's responsibility. Since neither woman was related to Bayan, he could choose to take them as wives, a fairly common practice in these situations. However, with the death of both Manduul, Yeke, and Bayan, Mandukhai effectively became independent, cared for by the tribe.

The first major campaign Bayan undertook in his brief life was along the Ming border. Manduul sent him to reforge old alliances with the southern Mongols. Bayan used pride, ambition, and nostalgia to excite the southern tribes, who were happy to follow Ming rule until that point.

Some of the poor, disenfranchised Ming soldiers had, in fact, disguised themselves as Mongols to raid caravans of supplies. They also stole from the emperor and blamed it on the Mongols, according to *The Cambridge History of China*. By the time Bayan reached those southern districts, the local Mongols believed it was his fault.

A Ming force attempted to capture Bayan in 1468 but failed. It was nearly a year later, in 1469, when the emperor sent a much larger force to capture Bayan. Fortunately for Bayan, he escaped and fled into the Gobi desert with what remained of his men.

According to Arab writer Ahmad Ibn Arabshah, who traveled the Mongol world, it was not entirely uncommon for women to have a sexual relationship with other men in the husband's family. This further justified just why Bayan believed Manduul would forgive him for sleeping with Yeke, especially when Manduul clearly had no interest in her. Bayan also would have known that, to become Great Khan and further his legitimacy, he would need to marry at least one of Manduul's wives after his death. Yeke was a logical decision. Not only was she the senior wife, but her father still held a lot of power. While Mandukhai may have been the more appealing choice, she offered him no protection.

Though history is unclear about who provoked Bayan's servant to report Bayan's relationship with Yeke to Manduul, it is easy to surmise that Issama was the mastermind. However, Manduul adored Bayan. Bayan swiftly denied the charges, then accused the servant of slander. Manduul immediately ordered the torture and execution of the servant, as written in this book.

Bigirsen must have known his control over Manduul was slipping, because he sent Issama to Manduul to monitor and maintain influence over the court. It is then that sources state Unebolod "retired" from court and returned home. However, considering the position he was in should Manduul die, I believe Unebolod returned home to gather his own power once Manduul had given Issama command over the military.

The palace in Hulunbuir is now little more than ruins. The exact nature of what happened to the palace is unclear. It could be been destroyed by an explosion, by Ming forces, or disassembled. I felt an explosion would be much more dramatic and enhance Unebolod's loathing toward the gods. There was also no historical record of a plague, but the reason for Unebolod's delay in arriving in Mongke Bulag was undocumented. In fact, little was written about his movements at all.

Issama (also known as Ismayil) had his own ambitions, as his actions demonstrated. Once Unebolod was gone and Issama had control over the military, Bigirsen had far less power. To drive a wedge between Bigirsen and Manduul, as well as Manduul and Bayan, Issama implicated Yeke in a plot to overthrow Manduul ... with Bayan clearly on her side. According to *Erdeni-yin Tobci*, Issama informed Manduul that Yeke and Bayan met "in an isolated place" in a "conjugal embrace." He left Manduul to process the information. It played out a lot like it did in the book. Using Bayan's own weaknesses against him, Issama successfully drove a wedge between the Khan and the Prince.

According to *The Mongol Chronicles of Altan Tobci*, Manduul confessed he was not in good health to those near him. He grew despondent and sent a small envoy to ask Bayan just one question: *What reason do you have to be against me?* Bayan's response played out much as it did in the book. He panicked and fled. When Manduul heard what happened, he became enraged.

Bayan arrived in Bigirsen's camp, where he was welcomed and hidden by Borogchin. She warned him that her husband saw Manduul and Issama as underlings and would want Bayan's head. And again, as it played out in the book, Bayan hid as Bigirsen searched the camp, fueled by his anger. When Bigirsen came up with nothing, he pretended to go hunting to lure Bayan out. Unfortunately, no one saw Bayan leave the camp. He headed the only direction he thought he might find help ... toward the Ming.

Shortly after he disappeared from camp, Borogchin knew she would die and she sent her son away from Bigirsen to save him. Bigirsen confronted Borogchin. She defiantly called him out, according to *Altan Tobci*. Nothing more is written about her from the time she defies her husband, but it is safe to assume Bigirsen killed her, as she expected would happen.

Yeke's death is undocumented. She simply disappeared from records after Manduul condemned Bayan. It is safe to assume he killed her for her adultery and betrayal. Mongols believed that showing the blood of Nobles to the gods could incur their wrath, so they often came up with more creative ways to kill nobles. Rolling them in rugs and drowning or trampling them was a fairly common practice.

Issama seized control of Bayan's possessions and took Siker as his own wife. Bayan was lucky to have survived the desert as long as he did. While the path he follows in the book is a little different from the one he followed in real life, the results were much the same. His guide abandoned him. According to *Altan Tobci*, he ran out of food and water, stumbled across a girl who saved him, then eventually was found by Issama's men and killed just as he died in the book.

How Manduul died is *not* written. Even the exact year of his death is unclear in the histories, ranging from 1466-1480. It is safe to assume he died either before or around the same time as Bayan. This left Mandukhai alone with only Esige as her family. Though she was the queen of the Mongols, she was not actually named Queen Regent—or at least no record of it remains. But there is no doubt she acted as Queen Regent in the months that followed.

Acknowledgments

This story has been close to my heart for almost ten years now. Mandukhai is an amazing woman who lived in a time when men ruled the world. But she stood up against them to preserve Genghis Khan's vision and lineage. There is so much to love about this woman, and she deserves much more credit than she ever gets. She is an inspiration to all women who struggle against a male-dominated system.

As always, I owe a massive thank you to my friends and family for your endless support and encouragement. Some of you even listened to me cry when I had to kill a character or crush one of their souls. It means a lot to me that my friends and family let me release the emotions without judging me.

To my husband, Tazz, thank you for your patience and understanding when I needed space to just write. The freedom you give me to write makes all the difference, and none of this would happen without you.

Once more, I feel I need to extend my gratitude toward Jack Weatherford for unearthing Mandukhai's story and sharing the truth of her life with the world. Without your hard work, this series would not exist. I hope I have helped further her legacy.

As always, I owe a debt of gratitude to my fellow authors in the SPWG—Dennis, Mike I, Mike P, Gail, Jennifer, and Danielle. You continue to show incredible patience as I push these books through the group as quickly as possible.

To my Advanced Reader Team: Barbara, Carrie, Craig, Debbie, Emma, Heidi, Pat, Peter, Shaeyera, Sue, and Tangent. Your dedication to my books is nothing short of a miracle.

And of course, my readers. Without you, what would even be the point of writing? I sincerely hope you enjoy her story as much as I loved writing it. If you did, please show your love for this amazing woman by leaving an honest review on Goodreads and with the bookseller you purchased the book from. For indie authors, reviews are the fuel that keeps us going! Not only does it help spread the word about our books, but it helps validate our writing to other readers who may not have heard of us before. Thank you!

Mother of the Blue Wolf
Chapter One Heir of Genghis

Mandukhai paced the dais in the gathering tent, back and forth between copper fire pots, as she waited. News of Manduul Khan's death had spread swiftly beyond the heart of the Nation. Keeping such an event secret had only proven possible for so long before Mandukhai could no longer contain the truth. After the tribes surrounding Mongke Bulag had dispersed, word reached the east, south, and west. Now, the Oirat tribes were more active near the borders than ever before. She worried this meant war. Nearly three months had passed since Manduul's funeral and Unebolod's return to Mongke Bulag, which gave the Oirat time to prepare for invasion. They had coveted the title of Great Khan for centuries, and men like Esen had attempted stealing it. Mandukhai knew how that had ended. In revolt and death. Her father had led that revolt. She wanted a more peaceful transition.

Mandukhai had hoped for better support from the Lords regarding her new title of Queen Regent than she had received. Her grasp on the nation slipped little by little each day. Though the Mongol Lords respected her position as was proper, they had made themselves clear. She was not their leader, but a placeholder until *they* selected the next Great Khan. Many of them preferred Unebolod. *I prefer him as well*, she thought.

She and Unebolod had agreed that it was best for her to observe a period of mourning before she would officially accept any offers of marriage—a marriage which would give the man who wed her the strongest claim on the title of Great Khan. Mandukhai appreciated Unebolod's patience, but she knew it would only go so far. He didn't just want her. He wanted the title.

In her vision with Genghis five years ago, he cut Esen's hanging body from a tree and accused him of pretending to be a wolf. Some part of Mandukhai worried that the same fate awaited Unebolod if he took the title before she knew for certain what Batu's fate would be. There could be no doubt for Unebolod to be Great Khan. There could be no heir of Genghis remaining. Only then could Unebolod's path be clear.

Though they flirted with the idea of her officially proclaiming him, she had been careful to avoid the reality of this claim. He could assert himself and try taking the title, citing Manduul naming him next should there be no heirs of Genghis, yet he had not. Not yet.

And there was another heir. Mandukhai sent her Uyghur spy to hunt down the abandoned child months ago. Today, her spy returned to give the full report, but she was certain of one thing.

Batu lived.

The line of Genghis had not died with Manduul and Bayan. If Mandukhai handled this properly, no one would know who Batu was until he came of age.

Unebolod and I can marry, raise Batu, and when the time comes, and he is old enough, we can install him as the next Great Khan. Mandukhai rubbed her hands together, nodding to herself. It would work. It had to. Genghis had told her only he of his bone would have the strength to hold the fractured empire together. Surely that must have meant Batu. *I will tell Unebolod the truth once I am certain Batu will survive.*

She feared for the boy's life. For her plan to work, no one else could know who he truly was. Any man of ambition could kill Bayan's young son to eliminate the boy's rightful claim.

No one in Mongke Bulag doubted Unebolod's ambition. He had set up his ger where Manduul's had stood, a clear signal of his intention. Some nights, the proximity proved a true test of willpower. Mandukhai wanted to go to him.

She paused in her pacing and closed her eyes, hugging her arms against her chest. *I miss having his arms around me.* She wanted to give herself to him as she had years ago—so long ago! However, it would be improper for her to sleep with him until they made their marriage official, and she would not risk any breech of etiquette that might stir anyone's doubt. Unebolod agreed it would be best to wait, but she sensed his tension just as surely as her own whenever they were close to each other.

Today, Unebolod would spend the day with their meager army, training the men for a battle he was certain loomed on the horizon—and perhaps he even looked forward to. The Oirat tribes could attack any day. The tribes were much larger than the meager forces she held together with fish glue and prayers. If the Oirat attacked, they could easily win and steal the khanship. *Genghis, if this is part of your plan, please guide me!*

Genghis had not come to her in another vision. Were it not for her faith in the High Heavens, Mandukhai might have doubted the truth of the promise Genghis made her. That she would birth a pack of wolves to restore the fractured empire.

The door to the gathering tent groaned open. Mandukhai's eyes snapped open, and she turned, relaxing her features in what she hoped was a calm, collected manner. Seguse strode in, unarmed, and stopped in front of the dais. He bowed his head and waited patiently for Mandukhai to speak first.

"I hope you have good news to report, Seguse," Mandukhai said, settling back into her throne atop the dais.

Seguse stood and folded his hands behind his back. "That depends on how you define good, Queen Regent." His weathered face pinched tight. "The boy lives, but barely. He is in the care of one of my fellow Uyghur and his wife."

Mandukhai's stomach churned. She trusted Seguse, who had spied for Borogchin for years. But Uyghur often had prickly loyalties. "Can we trust him?"

Seguse fell silent as he considered this. "I trust him. He doesn't really know who the boy is. Khadag informed me he came across the boy just before Issama's men arrived with orders to capture or kill."

"Did Issama know the boy's parentage?" Mandukhai asked. Issama was now married to the boy's mother. That gave Issama a stronger claim on Batu's life.

"No. Batu lived with an old woman named Bachari, but he was horribly neglected, sickly, and crippled. Issama ordered the ger burned, the old woman killed, and the boy brought to him. It was little more than a means of acquiring her few animals to feed his men."

Mandukhai's nails bit into her palms. "But Issama had no idea?"

"No, Queen Regent. By some stroke of fortune, he did not know at all. Khadag took pity on the boy and smuggled Batu off to his wife, Saichai. She is a gifted healer."

Mandukhai uncurled her fingers and stretched her palm over the carved arms of the chair. Issama had nearly taken the boy. He still could if he ever learned the truth.

"Where is Batu now?" she asked.

"About a hundred miles north of Hami, near the Dragon's Spine of the Gobi," Seguse replied. "I saw Batu with my own eyes. He is not well, Queen Regent—far too ill to make the journey north before spring. He suffers from a sickness of the stomach and …" Seguse's nose curled ever so slightly in a clear disgust he tried to hide but failed miserably at. "And he has a hunchback-like growth. Saichai said he should have died long ago, and that he's been horribly neglected. She is doing everything she can to heal him. I did not tell them who Batu is, but I expressed your keen interest in his wellbeing. I presume it's safe to assume you will pay them handsomely for their time and financial burden."

Mandukhai nodded. She would pay them in bags of fine silver if it healed Batu and kept him safe.

"I told them as much and pressed the importance of keeping Batu a secret from others," Seguse said. "I reassure Saichai that you would reward her for his safety and healing, but only if he survived and arrived safely in your care this spring. As soon as he is well enough to travel, they will bring him to you."

"You have done well, Seguse," Mandukhai replied. "And as much as I wish I could send you back to ensure Batu's safety, I cannot."

"I am satisfied settling in Mongke Bulag for a time."

"If only. But it is time for you to leave Mongke Bulag."

He drew up to a stiff spine. "Queen Regent?"

"Lord Unebolod has no trust for any man of Uyghur blood," Mandukhai said calmly. "And you are one of the few remaining. However, I do not send you away without purpose. My scouts tell me that the Oirat are moving, possibly against our camp." She refused to call Mongke Bulag a capital any longer. It gave too much permanence to their position and soon they would move on to better pastures. "As a Uyghur, you can infiltrate their position and learn more of their intentions. I cannot have the Oirat kicking up a dust cloud before we have a new Great Khan." When Seguse did not respond, Mandukhai offered a kind smile. "I am promoting you, Seguse, to *jagan* officer. Gather a hundred men capable of carrying out this task with you—Uyghur men, if possible, and men who would be credible as defectors if not Uyghur—and ride west."

Seguse struggled with his smile, but it curled the corner of his lips all the same. "It will be as you command, Queen Regent."

"Do not attack the Oirat, Seguse," she warned. "Your job is to make them believe you have defected to their side. Join them. Serve me well in this, and you will be further rewarded."

Seguse formally thanked Mandukhai and waited for dismissal before leaving her alone once more. She sat back and smiled to herself. Soon, she would have information from deep in Oirat circles to advise her actions further.

Weary, Mandukhai rose and stretched her limbs, then rolled her shoulders. She needed fresh air to fuel her sluggish mind, and so she headed out of the gathering tent.

Mongke Bulag had become a ghost of its former self. Aside from the Borjigin, other tribes had drifted away, no longer tethered to a Great Khan. Only Togochi's Khorlod remained—numbering fewer than ten thousand—and Unebolod's Khorchin dominated the space. Unebolod's presence in Mongke Bulag dwarfed her own. Mandukhai knew that only his love and respect for her kept him from simply seizing control, and she adored him for it all the more.

As she approached her own ger, Mandukhai spotted Unebolod checking the saddle on his mare, tightening the girth strap, and adjusting the blanket. The mare bobbed her head and stomped as Mandukhai approached, which made the leather armor on the mount's chest creak.

Unebolod turned from his task. "I heard you did not rest well again last night," he said.

Mandukhai grimaced. Esige certainly had no trouble sharing anything that was not strictly a secret with him. The girl had so much respect for Unebolod—almost as a daughter would her father. "I am rested as well as I need to be. How is the training going with your men?"

She stopped close enough to feel the heat rolling off his body. As he gazed down at her, he subtly reached for her hand, brushing his fingers over her own and sending a jolt through her body. Such a simple touch. Such an intense response.

Mandukhai's guards lingered nearby, always watching, and she was certain they saw the way Unebolod touched her hand. Yet she did not care. Their job was to guard her, and Unebolod, as they well knew, was no threat. Boke had made a threatening move toward Unebolod shortly after his return to Mongke Bulag, but Mandukhai had dressed Boke down so swiftly and certainly that none of her guards had dared question Unebolod's presence around her again.

"Soke still has the men in the field," he said.

"All of them?"

Unebolod raised a brow at the question but did not answer directly. "Are you aware that Esige has been wrestling my men?"

Mandukhai smothered a smirk. "No. But I imagine she has done well."

Unebolod grimaced. "She has beaten all of them. My men are complaining. It's demoralizing."

"She learned from you," Mandukhai teased, her eyes shining up at him.

He inched closer. "No. I think she gets this stubborn will from you."

"Then I have taught her well."

The tension between the two of them hung in the air like a tangible thing. She wanted to kiss him, or for him to kiss her first. It didn't matter as long as his body pressed against her own. Mandukhai's heart raced. Her stomach tumbled.

Unebolod's throat bobbed, and he stepped back toward his mare. "I should get back out into the field with the men." His fingers reluctantly slid free of hers.

Mandukhai licked her lips. Had the air grown thicker? She watched, breathless, as he swung into the saddle and rode away.

Sensing someone watching her, Mandukhai glanced around.

Odgerel lingered in the doorway of Unebolod's ger. The young woman had arrived in Mongke Bulag with the Khorchin shortly after Unebolod returned. Though he insisted Odgerel only served as his cook, the young woman acted as if she were his wife in so many ways. Too many ways.

The moment Mandukhai met her gaze, Odgerel dropped her own to the ground and bowed only slightly as a show of respect. But the girl clearly did not respect her.

Odgerel was a pretty young woman, and Mandukhai often caught her staring at Unebolod with obvious admiration and desire in her eyes. She had wormed her way into his service during his time away from Mongke Bulag, and though she had not once spoken ill of the Queen Regent, Mandukhai often felt the woman staring at her with sharpened daggers for eyes. Today was no exception.

Mandukhai straightened her back and chin, then strolled back to her own ger. She would not give this girl the satisfaction of knowing how her presence unnerved her. When Mandukhai and Unebolod finally married, Mandukhai would be sure Odgerel knew her place—or she would be replaced. Mandukhai would not allow a moon-eyed girl to get between her and her future husband. *I need to learn more about this woman,* Mandukhai thought as she entered her home.

READY FOR MORE? SCAN THE CODE TO ORDER *MOTHER OF THE BLUE WOLF* TODAY!

FRACTURED EMPIRE SAGA

A MONGOLIAN HISTORICAL ROMANCE

A ROMANTIC HISTORICAL FICTION SERIES
BASED ON TRUE EVENTS AND FEATURING
EMOTIONALLY RICH CHARACTERS,
POLITICAL POWER PLAYS, BRUTAL WARFARE,
DYNAMIC RELATIONSHIPS, AND FORBIDDEN ROMANCE

WWW.STARRZDAVIES.COM/FRACTURED-EMPIRE-SAGA

BOOKS BY STARR Z. DAVIES

<u>Divica Stormborn Chronicles</u>
Stormvalor
Stormveil
Stormcrown
<u>Divica War of Two Crowns</u>
Volume 1: Darkness Falls
<u>Powers Series</u>
Ordinary
Unique
(extra)ordinary
Superior
<u>Powers Origins</u>
Miller: Origin
Enid: Origin
Celeste: Origin
<u>Powers Legacy</u>
Powers Legacy: The Prequel
Desolation
Infiltration
Insurrection
Invasion
<u>Fractured Empire Saga</u>
Daughter of the Yellow Dragon
Lords of the Black Banner
Mother of the Blue Wolf
Empress of the Jade Realm
Prosperous Eternity
<u>Stand-Alone Stories</u>
Stones: A Steampunk Short Story

About Starr Z. Davies

 STARR Z. DAVIES is an award-winning author of over 20 tales that span dystopian realms, epic fantasies, and echoes of forgotten histories. Dubbed the "Character Assassin," she weaves stories where heroes are tested by fire—both emotional and physical.

From her woodland home in northern Wisconsin, she crafts worlds while surrounded by her greatest allies: a supportive husband, two imaginative children, and a curious menagerie of robotic pets. When not conjuring new adventures, she dabbles in home enchantments, swims like a siren, battles through video game quests, and devours books like ancient tomes of power.

If you want to become friends with Starr, dark chocolate, Doctor Who, Parks & Rec, The Office, and the MCU are all fantastic ways into her heart. That or a love for fantasy books by indie authors.

Learn more about Starr and her books.

Keep up with Starr by signing up for her newsletter.

Want to be part of her community? Follow Starr on social media.

facebook.com/szdavies
instagram.com/s.z.davies
threads.com/s.z.davies
tiktok.com/starrzdavies

www.ingramcontent.com/pod-product-compliance
Lightning Source LLC
Chambersburg PA
CBHW051205190726
48288CB00006B/1827